Also by Judi Fennell

In Over Her Head

Wild Blue Under

Catch of a Lifetime

I Dream of Genies

I Dream of Genies

JUDI FENNELL

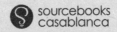

sourcebooks
casablanca

Published by Sourcebooks Casablanca, an imprint of
Sourcebooks, Inc.
P.O. Box 4410, Naperville, Illinois 60567-4410
(630) 961-3900
FAX: (630) 961-2168
www.sourcebooks.com

Printed and bound in Canada
WC 10 9 8 7 6 5 4 3 2 1

Once again, I dedicate this story to my husband:
my life with you is magical.

And to my children,
who were created by that magic.

Chapter 1

Scheherazade, the famed Arabian storyteller, had to come up with a thousand and one nights' worth of tales to save herself.

Eden should have it so easy.

But at least her life wasn't on the line like Scheherazade's, so that was a plus. Her mind, though, was another matter. There was only so much magic a genie could do to pass three thousand years of confinement and not go mad.

Unwilling to succumb to such madness, Eden flicked her wrists and snapped her fingers, her magic sending the butterflies, hummingbirds, and twirling glass balls she'd bewitched toward the ceiling of her bottle so she could have a better view through the hazy saffron glass. The rain of yet another Pacific Northwest storm streaked the storefront display window she'd inhabited for the last forty-five years, two months, and thirteen days. If the Arabian weaver of tales had used Eden's last half century as the basis of the stories that had saved her life, the poor woman would have been dead before her first sunrise.

"Mornin', babe." Obo, the cat she'd been cursed—or blessed, depending on one's viewpoint—to share this latest part of her penance with, leapt onto the shelf beside her bottle, licking his Egg McMuffin breakfast from his whiskers. The cat was a master forager. "Whatcha lookin' at?"

"Wilson." Eden nodded to the tree in front of the store. She'd watched it grow from a sapling to its current block-the-rest-of-the-world-from-view size for so long that she'd named it.

"Kind of pitiful that you named a tree after a volleyball."

"It worked for Tom Hanks."

"Yeah, but he was stranded on a deserted island. You've got the bustle of the city and hundreds of people right in front of you to keep you company."

Hundreds of people she couldn't interact with. She was on the outside looking in—well, actually, she was on the inside and wanting to *get* out. But the High Master had sealed her bottle with so much magic that nothing short of an explosion would set her free.

"And me, of course." The cat winked at her, his yellow eyes against his black fur making the motion noticeable. "You've always got me. I know I'm the bright spot in your day."

"In your dreams, Romeo."

"Speaking of lover-boy, has he been by yet?" Obo nudged the copper ashtray with the mermaid cigarette holder out of the way and curled his tail around her bottle before plunking himself onto his belly. Mr. Murphy, the store owner, hadn't shown up yet, so Obo could get away with hanging out here. Once the man did, however, all bets were off.

It was a sad state of affairs to look forward to these daily chats with Obo, who was high on her list of Least Favorite Beings ever since he'd let her take the fall for *his* necklace heist from Ramses II's tomb. It showed just how lonely and bored she was that she even deigned to talk to him, let alone looked forward to it. Other than her thoughts and her magic, she had only him to keep her company.

Oh, and "lover-boy" Matt Ewing. Couldn't forget him. And she didn't. He was pretty unforgettable, and heavens knew, she thought about him more than she should.

"No, he hasn't been by. I guess this weather's keeping him inside." Almost every morning, Matt jogged around the corner of the store in those tight, form-hugging running clothes. The perspiration slicking his face, that sexy curling hair, the controlled, even grace of his movements had fueled her fantasies ever since Mr. Murphy had moved her glass bottle to the front window.

"Or he could have had a hot date last night and it carried over."

Eden curled her legs under her, the curly toes of her slippers catching on the piping around the edge of the new sofa. She propped her elbow on the back cushion and plopped her chin onto her palm. "Thanks, Obo. That's helpful."

The cat licked his paw and swiped it over his ear. "Just callin' it like I see it."

Eden turned to look at him, brushing a wayward hummingbird out of the way, her gold shackle, er, bracelet flashing in the lone weak beam of sunlight that somehow fought its way through Wilson's leaves and the steady rain. "And how *do* you see it, Obo? You've been to his house. What's his world like?"

The cat shuddered and tucked his paws beneath his chest. "A damn sight wetter than yours. You should be thankful you're in this place. It's a monsoon out there."

The cat could be tight-lipped when he wanted to be. Which was often. All she asked for was news of the outside world and its people, descriptions of the smells and sounds, and the general feeling of being free to come and go as she pleased, but other than getting Matt's name out of Obo, the cat barely shared anything else. He had no idea how lucky he was to have the ability to go where and when he wanted.

She definitely didn't understand why he chose to be *here*. In this musty old shop, surrounded by things other people wanted to get rid of. How Mr. Murphy stayed in business was beyond her, because most of the stuff had been here as long as she had, and there certainly hadn't been any runs on antique plant stands or tarnished brass headboards.

Flicking her wrists again with the accompanying finger-snap that completed her Way of doing her magic, Eden arced a rainbow from one side of her bottle to the other, the purple ray disappearing into the shadow of the bottle's neck. The butterflies immediately began flying through it, and the hummingbirds raced along the ribbons of color that matched their wings.

She snapped her fingers again, and Humphrey *poof*ed onto her arm like a trained parrot. The dragonlet, a baby dragon about the size of her palm and her latest "foster child," reminded her of Bogart in his early movies, with a long face, high forehead, and large eyes, hence the name, though the dragon's eyes were blue to Bogart's brown.

In that, Humphrey reminded her of the High Master, but Adham was such a lofty name for such a tiny thing. And besides, like the Humphrey of those on-demand movies, this Humphrey was on loan, too—until he reached unmanageable proportions, which, with a dragon, was usually around the one month mark, meaning she had about five days left with this one before the hormones kicked in.

She stroked Humphrey's golden scales, then pointed to the rainbow. He gave her the tiniest nip on her palm—full blown dragon love could be really painful—then fluttered his little wings, his strength increasing daily. Today was probably the last day he could fly with the butterflies. The hummingbirds were fast enough to evade his beak-like jaws, but the butterflies wouldn't be a match; they'd more likely be lunch. But for today, he could play among the colors with them. Dragons loved rainbows.

She did, too, because of the happiness they innately engendered, especially on dreary days like today. But rainbows were infrequent manifestations for her because, while Mr. Murphy couldn't see in and most things couldn't pass through the magical barrier of her bottle walls without her okay, rainbows required an inordinate amount of light and, therefore, could be seen. Light shining from a dusty, and supposedly empty, old bottle would definitely be noticed.

"Uh, babe?" The gentle *whoosh* of Obo's fur thrummed softly along the ribbed lower portion of her bottle as he brushed his tail against the outside. "The rain might be murder on pedestrian traffic, but it's upped the vehicular kind. And the traffic light is red. A couple of interested kids, and your beacon there is going to get some notice."

Eden sighed, hating that he was right, but flicked her wrists anyway. The rainbow dissipated, leaving traces behind on the winged creatures. Humphrey sported a blue stripe down the ridge of his back and one of the iridescent Blue Morpho butterflies was going to have to change its name to Purple Morpho.

"Why are you here again, Obo? With the free run you have of this town, I'd think this has to be the most boring place you could be."

Obo's tail paused mid-flick and his ear twitched. "Ah, well, you know... I, uh, can't talk to mortals without freaking them out, and none of the animals in this country have been on the planet as long as me. Who else can I share the good ol' days with? You're the closest I get to normal, babe."

Which was sad because nothing in her life had been *normal* from the moment she'd gone to live with the High Master over two thousand years ago following her parents' death.

Eden sighed and gathered her magic to summon a pomegranate smoothie on the teak inlay table next to the lime green sectional she'd ordered last month. The persimmon-colored pillows weren't pulling the whole look together as she'd hoped. While she loved color, the backdrop of the saffron bottle made her art deco a little too avant-garde. Ah, well, she'd do some redecorating today to keep herself occupied. The satellite dish Faruq had given her for her birthday a few years ago came in handy.

Not that she'd ever admit it to Faruq. The High Master's vizier, charged with monitoring Genie Compliance, already had too much control of—and too much interest in—her life.

She sipped the smoothie. The dish, and the high-def TV that had replaced the antiquated electronics she'd accumulated over the years, were gods-sends. Much easier to shop, teach herself new languages, keep abreast of changing societies and customs, and learn all about new technology and the selling power of J.D. Power and Associates. Not to mention, how to make smoothies.

And with her bottle's magical ability to alter its interior without changing the dimensions on the outside, she could order up a swimming pool and Mr. Murphy would never know the difference.

Actually, maybe she'd do that. She'd like to hear Faruq's comment when he found out he was going to have to magick up a couple thousand gallons of water. And as for getting it through the magic channels to her, well, that ought to give him a few fits.

She took another sip of her smoothie. Such were the pleasures of her life.

"Hey, that looks good." Obo peered into her bottle, the tapered neck distorting his yellow irises until he looked like the Cyclops she'd seen off the coast of Crete that last summer she'd been on the outside. "Can you conjure one up for me?"

Eden set her treat down on the Egyptian brazier topped with a circular mosaic tile platter she called an end table. Nothing like combining Old World and New. "Sorry, Obo, but my magic won't leave the bottle for the mortal world while the stopper's in." Otherwise she would have zapped herself somewhere warm and sandy years ago.

"Well, could you calm the butterflies down then? Their flapping wings are driving me nuts. And the dragon…" He shuddered and dropped his head onto his paws. "I don't get *that* at all."

Humphrey did a loop-the-loop above her head and Eden held out her hand for him to land on as a reward. Baby dragons were so lovable and eager to please. Until they hit that unmanageable milestone—then their fiery heritage took over. It was a treat to be able to enjoy them at this stage, one far too rare for her liking.

As for her other cohabitants, they were the only living things Faruq approved to be in her bottle. She'd tried to talk him into a kitten after a few hundred years of solitude, but he'd refused. Said kittens would grow up to be cats, and cats were sneaky. That any cat he gave her might be able to figure a way out of the bottle.

It didn't speak well to the High Master's magic if his own vizier thought a cat could undo it, but Eden didn't buy Faruq's argument for one minute. Just one more thing he wanted to control about her.

So she'd volunteered to foster orphan dragonlets and hadn't complained when Obo had shown up. Not that the cat had any interest in helping her out of her bottle. Knowing where to find her so he could "share the good ol' days" was incentive enough, apparently, for him to make sure she stayed put. Probably worried what she'd do to him after he'd abandoned her during that necklace fiasco. A few hundred years ago, she might have done something, but nowadays, she was just thankful for the companionship. She'd told him so and had even tried bribing him into tipping the bottle off the shelf with promises of making all his wishes come true, but the cat had turned her down.

She hadn't held out any great hope of a fall breaking her bottle anyway. She'd been dropped many times over the years as her bottle had changed hands—sometimes on purpose—but nothing had budged that stopper.

She conjured up an acacia seedpod for Humphrey and his blue tongue flicked out to taste it. A bunch of cooing ensued, complete with little claw marks on her arm as he hunched into his "don't take my food" position over the pod. He happily munched away on the outer casing. Nothing like the throaty rumblings of a contented dragonlet. "What time is it, Obo?"

Obo didn't even look at the cuckoo clock hanging on the wall by the shop's door. "Matt's not coming, Eden. You wore your sexy little outfit for nothing." He opened one eye and the black slit of pupil thinned even more. "Thinking of auditioning for a TV show, are we?"

Eden shrugged. The costumes hadn't been purchased specifically with Matt in mind, but if the opportunity ever presented itself, well, hey. She had urges just as much as the next person. And after being cooped up so long with only Obo and Faruq to talk to, those urges were teetering on the brink of meltdown.

But she'd just *had* to buy the harem girl outfits, one in every color, after watching that genie on the television show. She didn't know who'd ratted out her race, but that Mr. Sidney Sheldon had gotten almost every detail right. Except the costume. No self-respecting genie would be caught dead in this little get-up while in The Service. But it was comfortable and it was colorful. And there was no one but her to see her in it.

"I wonder where Mr. Murphy is? He's usually here by now."

Obo sighed and rolled onto his side, his tail whispering along her bottle again. "Probably rowing his canoe in. I'm beginning to wonder if Noah's up to his old tricks."

Eden smiled. Crotchety and full of complaints—and a liar and a thief—Obo might be, but he was right; they didn't have anyone but each other to share the old times with. Unless she counted Faruq. And she wasn't about to.

But then the bells over the service door jingled, and Obo jumped to his paws so fast it was a wonder he *didn't* knock her bottle over. He ducked behind the black marble obelisk on the shelf next to her.

"If you're counting on the lack of sunlight to hide you, it's not working," she whispered, flicking the butterflies and hummingbirds onto the gardenia and honeysuckle bushes in her flower garden and Humphrey onto the mini acacia tree he used as a perch when she let him fly around. The twirling glass balls went into the padded box that prevented them from breaking whenever someone moved the bottle. "You better get out of here, Obo."

"Tell me something I don't know." The cat wiggled his butt trying to shrink into the shadows. "I have to go out the way he's coming in, so we'll need to distract him."

"Keep talking and that ought to do it," she whispered, using her magic to clean up a spot of yellow the rainbow had left behind.

Mr. Murphy walked into the room, but didn't flip over the OPEN sign like usual. Instead, he went behind a French Provincial sideboard beneath a Baroque mirror and brought out a large cardboard box—an empty one—that he soon started filling with every knickknack from the top of the sideboard. And from the bookcase next to that. And the top of the retro refrigerator next to that.

Eden ducked behind the big stone marker Hadrian had given her as thanks for the carpet ride all those years ago when he'd surveyed the land for his wall. True, Mr. Murphy wouldn't be able to see her spying on him, but years of habits weren't so easily forgotten, no matter how rarely utilized those habits were. "This doesn't look good."

"Gee, ya think?" Obo muttered, his back end tiptoeing toward the edge of the shelf. "I'm outta here, babe." With that, Obo executed the perfect stealthy leap cats were known for, hit the floor running, and was into the back room before Mr. Murphy heard anything.

Lucky Obo. Eden could only sit and worry.

—⁓—

Obo nudged his way out of the back of the shop. Skulking in the shadows again. Story of his life—and one he was heartily sick of.

For years, over two thousand of them, he'd been hiding. First from the assassins, then from tomb raiders, then from anyone who wanted a "pet kitty." He'd lived a life of luxury before being on the run, and while pâté and room service were heavenly, the plotting and backstabbing by usurpers was anything but. He'd been done with that life when his mistress had ended hers, and he hadn't looked back. Obo looked out for one thing and one thing only: his own life.

With the end of it approaching—nine magical lives could only take a cat so far—he had to look out for his *After*life now.

Walking along the back of the store, Obo tried to keep his paws out of the puddles. Futile, but worth a shot because nothing was worse than soggy paws. Well, except burning ones. He might complain about the weather here, but it definitely beat the hot sands of the desert. If he never saw a desert again, it'd be too soon.

Getting out of that part of the world had been an added bonus to Bastet's offer: keep an eye on Eden and balance the heavenly scales for a good number of his transgressions. He had a *lot* of transgressions to make up for, so this seemed to be a simple enough task.

All he'd had to do was pack up his meager belongings and get himself to this part of the world, then provide monthly reports via the mockingbird the goddess had sent to, well, *mock* him. A bird was her messenger? Seriously? Bastet was a cat goddess and she sent a *bird* to collect her reports? There was probably some sort of test in that, too: don't kill the messenger and knock off two extra bad deeds from his celestial tally.

However the goddess was keeping tabs, Obo was in.

A gutter groaned overhead, and its contents gushed down in front of him, a good portion splashing off the concrete and soaking his fur. He wouldn't mind being *in* right now, but any of his regulars—mortals who took in stray cats—lived far enough from Eden's store that he'd be just as soaked anyway.

Obo shook the rain water off and rounded the end of the building. Maybe Wilson would provide some cover. At least he could hang out in the branches to keep his paws somewhat dry.

He dragged himself into the crook of Wilson's lowest branch just as Mr. Murphy walked out of his store and dumped that cardboard box on top of a garbage can by the curb, then ran back inside and adjusted the CLOSED sign.

What was the mortal up to? Why was he tossing things he'd been trying to sell? Cardboard dissolved in this much rain. It didn't make any sense.

Then a trash truck turned the corner and it suddenly did.

Except—

Son-of-a-bichon! The top of Eden's bottle was sticking out of that box!

Chapter 2

MATT EWING WAS HAVING A SHITTY DAY IN A MONTH of shitty days—several months of them, actually—so when a half-naked harem girl knocked him onto the sidewalk and ended up facedown in his lap, Matt figured one of the shittier days of his life had just gotten better.

Especially when, raising himself up on his elbows, he got the best view of curvy female ass this side of a strip club: one covered in see-through pink gauze and sequins, with tassels caressing cheeks that were tight and firm and just the right size for his hands.

Matt's breath took a hiatus and, despite the rain, his mouth dried up like a desert.

Or was that *dessert*?

Matt shook his head. No, dessert was in the bakery behind him, not the woman lying across him. He sat up just as the trash truck by the curb pulled away with a groaning yawn, something metallic bouncing out and clipping his ankle.

"Son of a bitch." Well, at least his wind had come back. He kicked the thing away and got a good look at the woman sprawled with her face in his lap.

Now there was an image.

Okay, he was a sick bastard to even go there when she had yet to move.

"Hello?" He wiggled his legs, but she didn't budge.

A blue, no, purple butterfly flitted onto the slice of

midnight black ponytail that slid sideways from under a veil clipped to the crown of her head. The rest of her hair fanned an expanse of tan skin below the half-shirt plastered to her body.

He looked around. The storm left few people on the street, and those who were held their umbrellas so low they appeared to be dueling the weather. No one was paying any attention to the woman. Looked like it was up to him.

"Miss." He tried jiggling her shoulder. The butterfly moved, but she, sadly, didn't. Christ, he hoped she wasn't seriously injured, although it'd be just his luck if she was—mainly because *bad* was the only kind of luck he'd been having lately. The Riverview project was a no-go, Jerry hadn't called with an update on the Baker roof, and now, thanks to the weather, he'd have to reschedule a job that would've covered the cost of the damaged materials some moron had backed over and hadn't ponied up the cash for yet. Yeah, definitely a shitty day.

Matt eased out from under the woman and something slid off his thigh onto the sidewalk. Faceted yellow crystal, or maybe a hunk of glass, with enough weight to do some damage—an ornament or paperweight about the size of a walnut on steroids. That would explain why she was out cold.

He shoved the crystal into his pocket and turned her face to the side. Dark lashes swept tan cheeks. Her lips were pursed, and the rain was channeling into her mouth. Not good.

He put his hand on her back. She was breathing, but her outfit was hardly appropriate for the weather. The gauzy pants were soaked, plastering them to a pair of legs that showed her ass wasn't the only toned part of her and revealing those boy-cut shorts women were into these days. Why they thought guys liked clothing called *boy*-cuts on women he didn't get, but at least she had something on. Otherwise she'd be naked and wet in front of him.

He was definitely an ass for that thought.

He rolled her gently, then leaned over to block the rain. Couldn't have her drowning on the sidewalk. But he needed to get her someplace warm. And cover her, for God's sake. Who wore a getup like this without a coat? There wasn't even enough beading on the front to disguise the fact that she wasn't wearing a bra, and the butterfly landing on the tip of her breast wasn't helping matters.

"Miss?" He nudged her shoulder again. "Come on, Barbara Eden, wake up." Water rolled off the brim of his hat, plunking onto her gold bracelets, and the wind kicked up around them. Matt flipped up his jacket collar. He had to do something or she'd catch pneumonia.

Then a biker rode by and added half a puddle's worth of rain to the mess, a straight shot into the hole on the elbow of his sheepskin jacket, right through to his sweatshirt. Immediate sponge. Her clothing fared slightly better only because he was there to catch the brunt of the splash.

To add insult to injury, his stepbrother's black Navigator pulled up at the light. Matt pulled his hat low over his eyes and turned his head.

"Matt!"

Shit.

"Hey, Matt! Need a ride?"

The thing was, Hayden didn't try to be a dick, it just seemed that way. They'd been raised as if they were biological brothers, but the guy was golden, Midas, while Matt—thanks to the economy taking a nosedive for construction-related endeavors—was struggling to keep the Ewing name from being synonymous with failure. Hayden, lucky bastard, didn't even know the word.

"Matt, what happened?" The door to the SUV opened and Hayden's boys scooted to the far side of the bench seat. "Bring her over here! There's a pileup on the other side of town and you're not going to be able to get an ambulance."

More bad luck, which made Matt half-tempted to do what Hayden said, but the last thing he wanted to deal with was his brother's domestic bliss in the warmth of his new "toy" while *he* was worried about invoices, cash flow, and the employee he was going to have to lay off at the end of the month if he didn't get the most recent job he'd bid on. Not to mention the supplies he was going to be late picking up. And now the inanimate Jane Doe here on the sidewalk.

"No thanks, Hayden. My truck's not that far." Which was true. Except that it was on the other side of the park behind him. In his garage. He'd grab a cab instead.

Matt stood, keeping his back to Hayden, knowing he'd see his brother shaking his head. You'd think Hayden was older with the sadly knowing look he always managed when he didn't agree with Matt. Which was far too often for Matt's liking. But, dammit, she'd knocked *him* over; he was certainly capable of getting her medical attention.

Which he'd better do since she still hadn't opened her eyes. At least her breathing was even. Matt ripped off his jacket and laid it over her, brushing the butterfly away. Then he lifted her in his arms, glad to hear Hayden's farewell honk as the light changed.

She was a tiny thing. Barely a hundred pounds, even soaking wet. But then she sneezed and Matt realized just how exposed to the elements she was, even covered by his jacket.

He looked around, but there wasn't a cab in sight. Figured. Hell. Maybe he *should* have taken Hayden up on that offer of a ride to the hospital. Swallowed his pride. That, however, was something he'd never been able to do where Hayden was concerned.

Then she sneezed again, shivering this time, and Matt realized something was going to have to give and his pride was it.

He went to grab his phone to call Hayden back, but his groan mixed with the thunder that rolled across the sky. No cell. He'd left it on the dash of his truck—the one in his garage.

Shit. Eight blocks to the hospital wasn't normally a long distance to walk, but with this weather and her condition, his truck—and his house with warm clothes and blankets—were closer.

<hr />

Icy shards of glass pelted Eden's legs as she bounced against something hard. Her head ached. She was cold and her wrist hurt.

The next bounce shifted her slightly. Actually, her upper body wasn't exactly cold or uncomfortable, but her legs definitely were. She twitched her toes, trying to feel the floor, only… there wasn't one. She was floating?

Eden nibbled the inside of her cheek. She didn't remember floating today. Wait. What *did* she remember?

She searched her memory, but it was just flashes of light amid a blanket of nothingness. Eden sucked in a breath as a spasm of pain rippled across her temple and—

Wait. That was air. *Fresh* air.

She inhaled again. Fresh air, even rain-laden, meant she was out of her bottle. Fresh air meant she was free. After seventeen hundred ninety-seven years in her bottle, she was free.

Twelve hundred three years before the end of her sentence.

The bouncing slowed and Eden cracked one eye open. A raindrop sluiced along her lashes, the cold wind blowing it off. Thank the stars that she was still in the cold, wet, dreary part of the world she'd inhabited for the last century and not the arid desert of her homeland, because it meant that Faruq hadn't found her.

But someone had. A man. And not just any man, not this guy. He was no overweight retiree like Mr. Murphy, not with these arms. Toned muscles flexed beneath her as he adjusted his hold, and that chiseled jaw and fluid stride ruled out Faruq's eunuchs. No rounded features, no softness to this guy, even with the thick, ebony hair that curled at the ends just above his wet black sweatshirt, the creases at the corner of his eye, and the deep dimple in his left cheek—

Holy heavenly body—it was *him*!

Lightning sizzled the air and Eden almost squirmed in his arms, stopping herself at the last second when a butterfly landed on her nose. Maybe the sizzle *wasn't* lightning.

Matt Ewing. Here. Holding her. Every fantasy she'd had for the past five years coming to life in the cold, wet rain. And she was anything but cold.

Heavens, his arms around her felt just right. And the scent of him, coffee, cinnamon, *man*… Mmm, he smelled good. Very good. Like a desert oasis to a parched traveler. After her drought of human contact, that's exactly what she was.

The stars were truly aligned for her today. Freedom and *him*—she couldn't ask for more.

His cadence slowed and he jostled her in his arms, a few of his fingers sliding beneath whatever blanket he'd put over her and brushing the side of her breast.

Okay, so, yes, she *could* ask for more. After all, it'd been an incredibly long time since any man had touched her breast, let alone anything else.

When his fingers inadvertently stroked her again, Eden had to concentrate so she wouldn't turn into his touch and let him know she was awake. She didn't want this to end. And call her curious, she wanted to see what he'd do next.

The sound of jingling keys scraping against a door answered the question of *what*, but the question of *where* quickly followed.

A raindrop seeped between her lips and went down the wrong pipe. She swallowed the cough and wished he'd hurry up and open the door already.

"Damn. I must have forgotten to lock it." He cursed again as he half-fell inside, her slippers brushing the doorframe.

The warmth was a welcome change to the cold air freezing her lower limbs. The cushion he placed her on, however, was a far cry from the comfort of his arms.

"What am I going to do with you?" he muttered, brushing a strand of hair off her face.

Goose bumps prickled her skin at his touch and she had a good idea of what he could do with her. She knew what she'd like to do with him.

"I need to get you out of those clothes."

This was sounding better by the minute.

There was a little rustling, then she didn't hear anything—until a different voice said, "You're an awful actress, you know."

Eden opened one eye. "Obo? Where's Matt? And what are you doing here?"

The cat shook himself, water droplets spraying everywhere. "I'm doing the same thing you are, babe. Warming up. And Matt's in the other room. The *bed*room." He did a wink-wink/nudge-nudge toward some area behind the sofa.

She blew out a breath. Like she needed to be thinking like that now.

Okay, not that she hadn't already gone there, but follow him into the bedroom? She wasn't that desperate.

Or… maybe she was.

Eden shook her head. She had more pressing matters to worry about first. "What happened? How did I get here?"

"I'm not quite sure of the what, but the how was this. Mr. Murphy, for whatever reason mortals come up with for their stupidities, tossed your bottle in the trash with a bunch of other stuff. The garbage truck came along, the jaws came down, and the next thing we all know, you're facedown in Matt's lap." The cat smirked. "Talk about a wasted opportunity."

She waved her hand. The opportunity—wasted or not—was gone, and she was free. Tossed aside like yesterday's trash, but *free*. "What happened to my bottle?"

The cat raised an eyebrow. "More importantly, what happened to Humphrey?"

"Humphrey? Oh my stars, what happened to Humphrey?"

"Nothing, thanks to me. The lizard did make it out of your bottle, but I managed to take a flying leap out of Wilson and grab his tail before he followed the butterfly into Matt's line of sight. I gotta tell you, those claws of his might be tiny, but they're sharp." Obo rubbed his nose.

"Where is he now, Obo?"

Obo rolled his eyes. "I'm fine, thanks for asking. I could use some disinfectant, but I should live. Not sure about rabies, though. Has the little fire-breather had his shots?"

"Obo…"

Obo sighed. "He's investigating the inside of one of Matt's socks. Should take the little buzzard a long time to find his way out of that one."

"Where is he, Obo? This weather isn't good for dragonlets. They can't regulate their own temperatures yet."

"Yeah, that's what has me worried the most. Not the fact that you're out of your bottle—which is missing, by the way—or that Matt is gonna need some kind of explanation, or that Mr. Murphy was getting rid of you in the first place. Do you realize you could have spent the rest of your sentence mired in dump muck?"

There were a lot of things she realized, but the sound of footsteps in the hall meant there wasn't time to discuss any of them. She had to figure some way out of here, then get back to the store to search for her bottle. "Obo, you have to get out of here. Matt's going to come back and if he sees us talking, he's going ask questions. He doesn't need to know what I am."

Obo leapt onto the arm of the sofa and sat, his tail draping over the edge, the tip flicking gently. "Hey, chill. I have just as much right to be here as you do. More, actually. He feeds me and offers the warmth of his hearth on occasion, remember? It's how you know his name." Obo licked his paw, then brushed it over his whiskers. "Besides, he thinks I'm just an ordinary stray. But if you're really worried about him asking questions, I'd lose the butterflies. Those aren't exactly indigenous to the area, especially at this time of the year. Still, better them than Humphrey." He nodded to the pair of the butterflies that had landed on the coffee table.

"Oh. Good point." Eden flicked her wrists—ow! That left one hurt. She caught her breath and snapped her fingers—but the butterflies didn't disappear.

A third one, however, showed up.

"Uh, babe?" Obo's ears pricked forward.

Eden would have answered him—and would have summoned her magic again—if Matt hadn't walked back into the room.

Eden slammed her eyes closed and pretended to be asleep until she could come up with some sort of cover story or find a quick escape route.

"Hey, cat, you're back." Matt said, placing something

on the back of the sofa. "You better get down. She doesn't need you jumping on her chest."

She wouldn't mind Matt doing it, though.

Obo's meow was pure insolence as he leapt off, but Matt, poor guy, didn't realize it. Cats had perfected that attitude eons ago.

Eden bit the side of her tongue so she wouldn't laugh and hoped Obo took his baby-sitting duties seriously. Butterflies were one thing, but there was no way she'd be able to explain Humphrey.

When Matt started to unbutton the pearl buttons between her breasts, she had to bite her tongue for a totally different reason. Who would have guessed this hokey costume would have such perks? Matt's hands felt really good on her skin, and it'd been so long. And it was *him*.

Maybe she'd put off that escape route thing for a while.

"We'll go to the hospital once I get some dry clothes on you, but I hope to God you don't accuse me of rape when you wake up," he muttered, his knuckles brushing the swell of her breast. Which made her nipples tighten—and made Matt curse.

He'd probably noticed her body's reaction.

She glanced out of the corner of her eye—and saw *his* body's reaction.

Oh, yes, he'd definitely noticed.

So what was she doing just lying here? It'd been almost eighteen hundred years since she'd been out of that bottle and he was *him*. Mr. Hotstuff of the morning jog. McSteamy and McDreamy had nothing on this guy. She shouldn't let this chance go to waste.

She caught her breath and another rumble of thunder sounded as another button popped free.

Eden opened her eyes. Matt had no idea what he'd just unleashed.

But he was about to find out.

Chapter 3

MATT'S FINGERS FUMBLED WITH THE LAST BUTTON, but Eden didn't care. He was hot, she was on fire, and she was finally free.

She sat up, bumping his hand so that his palm stroked her breast, and planted a big ol' take-me-honey-I'm-yours kiss on his lips. Then she twined her fingers in his hair, slanted her head sideways, and the kiss turned hotter than a sandstorm in the Sahara.

Desire, pent up for far too many years, raced through her. She'd *known* he would taste as good as he looked. Every tedious day, he'd been the bright spot in her mundane existence—and the reality far exceeded her fantasy.

She nipped at his lower lip, then licked it, splaying her hands across his chest. She undid a few of his buttons, thanking the stars that he'd changed shirts. But it wasn't enough. She tugged and a button or two popped free. Her breath caught and she wished he'd just yank her against him and get on with it already.

And suddenly, that's what happened. She'd been in control of that kiss for all of about ten seconds before Matt captured her lips, speared his fingers through her hair, tore off the veil, and angled her face just right so fast it would've made her head spin if it weren't already.

Where she'd nipped at his lips, he devoured hers. Where she'd stroked his hair, he fisted hers and hung on tight. Where she'd merely touched him, he swept one of his hands between her shoulder blades and plastered her chest to his. He took as much as she wanted to give and gave as much as she wanted to take.

Which was a lot.

She was seriously considering—in the rare flashes of lucidity between kisses—how to get that last button of hers undone so she could brush her sensitized nipples across his chest, when Matt suddenly wrenched his mouth from hers and shoved her arm's length away, the butterflies dancing in figure-eights behind him. All five of them.

Five? Where'd the other two come from?

"What the hell was that?" Matt's hazel eyes, now a darker shade of green, widened as he sucked in a huge, shaky breath, and lightning flashed again outside the window.

He wasn't talking about butterflies. "Gorgeous, if you don't know, then you needed it more than I did." She traced the open vee of the shirt he'd changed into where she'd done a bit of her own unbuttoning. Toned and hard, with just a smattering of chest hair, he felt better than any of the silks in her bottle. "Which would lead me to believe you need something else as much as I do."

She buried her face against him, inhaling the masculine scent she'd been deprived of for far too long. Ah, yes, the stars must truly be aligned. The sweet tartness of apples, cool rain, and the sharpness of fresh air and the elements, *him*… Eden wanted to crawl all over him.

So she did. After all, she'd been confined for Eighteen. Hundred. Years.

Eden kissed along the column of his throat, wiggling

on the sofa to get closer. She'd take a good mattress any day over this narrow piece of furniture, but a sex-starved genie couldn't be picky—although she *had* picked one amazing guy to break her non-self-imposed fast with.

She ripped through a few more of his buttons, then slid her palms along his sides. He'd feel so good on top of her, all those tight, controlled muscles flexing and contracting.

Grasping his taut back, Eden pressed him against her, sighing beneath his ear when sculpted chest met aching breasts. It'd been *so* long.

Matt's hands swept up through her hair. He grasped the strands and tugged. "Lady."

Lady. Ha. That was something no one ever called a genie. If he only knew.

Ah, but he couldn't know. Mortals never believed she was a genie unless she did the cloud-of-smoke trick or some other magic—and that was the last thing she wanted to do. Magic left a spectral Glimmer in the spectrasphere and hyped up the transmission properties of her golden shackles, er, bracelets. Bad enough the bracelets pointed Faruq her way; if she used enough magic, he'd be able to pinpoint her exact location and whip her back into The Service faster than she could say, "Do me, baby."

Eden ignored the next tug on her hair and captured Matt's ear lobe between her teeth. Without her bottle, she was on borrowed time and she didn't want to waste any of it with explanations. If she kept him occupied he couldn't ask questions. Or worry about multiplying butterflies and baby dragons.

He inhaled when she sucked on his skin, but he wasn't

going to be deterred. He twisted sideways, moving away just enough that cold air snaked between them.

"Look, lady—"

"It's Eden."

"Whatever. Eden. I don't know what you think is going on here, but it's not my habit to pick up strange women and bring them home to make love to them."

"Why not?"

"So if you could—What? Why *not*? What kind of question is that?"

"A legitimate one. You carried me here, to your home I presume, and our bodies certainly enjoy each other. What's wrong with that?"

"What are you, some holdover from the sixties?"

Sixty *AD*, but she couldn't tell him that. "I would never have figured you for uptight."

"Look, lady—Eden. Free love and all that had its place, but these days, I'm not up for risking disease. And we're off the subject here. I brought you home to help you, not maul you. You hit your head, if you remember. Knocked yourself out somehow. Any of this ringing bells? Care to enlighten me about what happened?"

Great. The first guy she hooked up with after eighteen hundred years had a conscience diametrically opposed to her libido. She had the worst luck. McSteamy wouldn't be questioning her. No, he'd be jumping in with both hands. And lips. And a whole bunch of other good parts.

Matt sat back farther and gripped his knees, which had the added bad luck of bunching his navy blue button-down closed and hiding all that magnificent chest from her.

Her chest, however…

Eden leaned back against the pillow, cursing the fact that that stupid bottom button refused to pop off, so only the swells of her breasts were visible. Here's hoping he noticed.

Then lightning flashed and Matt gulped beneath a halo of seven—*seven*?—circling butterflies, his Adam's apple rising and falling the full length of his throat. He'd noticed something all right. And it wasn't the butterflies.

Eden hid a smile and leaned forward. She put her hands in her lap, knowing full well that by doing so her arms pushed her breasts together, giving her not-too-shabby cleavage some added *va-voom*. The man would have to be dead not to be interested. And she had firsthand experience of how not-dead he was. "Come on. It'll be fun."

Matt's Adam's apple bobbed again, but instead of taking what she so freely—and achingly—offered, he grabbed that soft gray something off the back of the sofa and tossed it at her. "Here." The thing hit her squarely in the chest she was trying to get him interested in.

Eden didn't bother hiding her sigh. It wasn't as if she had a lot of options, although, after eighteen hundred years, *anyone* would look good. But him, he looked fabulous. Still, she wasn't going to beg.

She also wasn't going to go down without a fight.

"Oh, all right," she muttered but brought her fingers to that last button on her shirt.

She ended up conceding defeat instead as her wrist protested—more painfully this time. "Ouch!"

"Are you okay?" Matt leaned forward and cradled her wrist in his hand. "This is starting to swell. You should take off your bracelet."

Eden snorted. Take off her bracelet. Yeah, right. "Good luck with that. There's nothing I'd like more, and if you've got any ideas to that end, I'm more than happy to hear them."

Only one genie had ever been able to remove the gold bands that trapped her kind in The Service to mortals, and Khaled had felt the wrath of the High Master at the same trial where she'd been sentenced to her bottle. Three thousand years' incarceration certainly beat the punishment poor Khaled had faced—all for wanting to be free. Too bad the only thing he'd been able to say to her before the High Master had bestowed the verdict was, "Diamonds."

As if she'd cared where he'd stored some treasure. Freedom was the real treasure and he'd guarded that secret as if his life depended on it. Maybe it had.

"Seriously, I don't care what sentimental value it's got." Matt's eyes didn't leave her wrist (and yet her breasts were only inches away!). "We have to get this off you. Your fingers are turning blue."

Yeah, they were. That, more than his inattention to her half-naked body, was starting to worry her. She'd try magic if it'd help, regardless of any spectral trail, but genie magic couldn't heal. It could conjure physical objects and transport mortals, but abstract ideals such as world peace and free love weren't within her capabilities, nor was returning the dead to life or curing illnesses. And unlike that TV star's blinking eyes and crossed arms, Eden needed to employ her Way to get her magic to work.

"What about ice?" She was running on limited options here—for more than just bed partners.

"I don't think so." Matt turned her wrist over. "How'd you get it on? Where's the clasp?"

He ran his fingers over the bracelet, then looked at the one on her good wrist and twisted it around. The bracelets had been specifically created to contour to her arm and not be confining—at least in theory. The truth was, she might not feel them, *per se*, but she knew they were there.

They were always there.

"Is there a hidden release somewhere? Geez, the guy who made these must have been a magician."

Something like that, but she couldn't exactly tell him the truth so she opted for silence. Couldn't get tripped up in a lie that way.

He looked up at her. "So—what? Was this some great idea you and a bunch of girlfriends came up with at someone's bachelorette party? Have gold bands soldered onto your wrists?"

That was a handy excuse.

She tried hard to put chagrin in her facial expression. "Um, yes. Something like that. Not such a good idea, was it?"

Matt sighed and set her hand in her lap. "You're lucky I have the right tools. Meet me in the kitchen."

He stood up and took a few steps—and, yes, she did watch the way his jeans hugged his backside. Eighteen hundred years was a long time without physical contact after all, and if all she could get was eye candy, she was going to partake.

"And why don't you change out of that wet shirt? We don't need you catching pneumonia."

It showed how worried she was that she didn't argue with him. Her hand was starting to throb. She'd have to get the ice on it soon because no tools Matt had would remove it. Many genies had tried through the centuries, some ending up losing their hands in the attempt, but short of amputating above the bracelet, there was no way to get rid of the damned things. If only Khaled had told her how.

"So are you going to tell him?" Obo jumped back onto the arm of the leather sofa and curled his tail around his legs as he sat. Another flash of lightning lit up the room for a few seconds.

"What are you doing? You need to watch Humphrey!"

"Chill, babe. Dragons aren't the brightest of creatures. Fierce, yes, but any brightness lies in their ability to light up a night sky with their breath, not brain power. He's still stuck in the toe. So, are you going to tell Matt?"

She grabbed the shirt Matt had tossed at her and bunched the shirt hem toward the neckline. "Are you crazy? I can't tell him what I am. As if he'd believe me anyway. And even if he did, a mortal's first reaction is always to wonder what I can do for him, which puts me right back in The Service. No thank you. I'm free, Obo, and I intend to stay that way." She pulled the neckline over her head. "Now if you wouldn't mind turning around?"

The cat smirked. "Oh puh-leaze. You were willing to get naked with him not thirty seconds ago. What made you turn into such a prude all of a sudden?"

Matt super-tuning her nerve endings to his special frequency, that's what. "Hey, I'm not giving you a show. For all I know, you could be some criminal or ne'er-do-well banished to feline form a few millennia ago." She snuck a peak over the top of the shirt. "Were you?"

Obo turned red. Which was interesting considering he A) couldn't do magic and B) had black fur. "Banished? *Banished*? I'll have you know that two thousand years ago I was the most royally treated feline in history. The palaces I've been in would put this place and any genie bottle to shame, as well as any beauty or luxury. Any type of beauty or luxury you can imagine, *including* beautiful babes. If you think there's something you've got that I haven't seen before, trust me, there isn't."

"So I'm supposed to be thankful some royal feline wants to see me naked? I don't think so, Obo." She circled her index finger. "Turn around."

Obo harrumphed, narrowed his eyes to slits, but finally did rotate a hundred and eighty degrees, his tail swishing along the inside of the sofa arm in the traditional staccato rhythm of an irate cat.

Eden ripped off her bodice's last button. She wouldn't be wearing this outfit again—free of her bottle, free of The Service, she was now going to be free of all the trappings, too.

If only she could get free of the bracelets.

Tossing her shirt behind the sofa, Eden then worked her arms into the sleeves of Matt's, maneuvering her injured one as delicately as possible. That sucker hurt.

"Two thousand years, Obo? Which of your nine lives are you on?"

"None of your business." The cat jumped off the sofa and headed toward the door Matt had gone through. "You might want to hurry it along. He ought to be back shortly. If there's one thing about Matt, he knows where every tool is. Keeps that workshop out back organized to the nth degree, like it's a museum or something."

Eden didn't bother mentioning that Matt could look forever and still not find any tool that would free her from the bracelets. She knew because she'd tried. Once Faruq had given her the satellite dish, she'd made good use of the delivery system captive genies employed for food and necessities while awaiting another mortal to "free" them from their bottle and place them back into The Service. The orders she'd placed were disguised as ambitious projects—it helped that she liked to watch all the home improvement shows and Faruq kept tabs on such useless information—but each project required an array of tools. She'd ended up with an interesting interior of her bottle, but sadly, the bracelets had stuck steadfastly. No way would Matt have better luck.

Still, she did need that ice. Eden stood on the burgundy carpet covering the hardwood floor and wiggled out of the rest of her soaked clothing. She smoothed Matt's gray sweatshirt down her legs almost to her knees, then followed Obo into the next room.

Glass-fronted cabinets hung on cream walls above stainless steel appliances. The dark oak cabinets and bead board below the hunter green chair rail and brick-red counter tops weren't exactly the bright, splashy colors she loved, but anything was better than the dusty glass window and Wilson's shadow.

Obo jumped onto the peninsula and skirted a wicker basket of apples before curling up in the recessed window above the sink. "So, what spin are you going to put on this, Eden? Amnesiac? Kidnap victim? Runaway? Any would work; Matt has a thing for helping out strays.

Present company included." He rolled onto his back and swiped at one of her butterflies.

Oh, *zift*! The butterflies.

Eden swatted at them, wishing she could get rid of them, but her injury wasn't allowing that to happen.

"Here we go—uh, Eden? You okay?" Matt walked in from outside while she was in mid-swipe and scared the camel spit out of her.

Catching her breath, Eden turned around, running a hand through her ponytail. "Um, yeah. I'm fine. Just, uh, stretching."

Obo sneezed.

Eden didn't dare look at him. If it wouldn't hurt the butterfly, she'd hope the cat would choke on it.

Speaking of which, Eden surreptitiously looked around the kitchen. Where had the butterflies gone now?

Matt placed his tools and a rolled-up bandage on the tile-topped wood table. He'd tucked the ends of his shirt in his jeans, closing the gap she'd worked so hard to make. *Zift!* What was with the guy? Men had always found her attractive—some inconveniently so—yet Matt had as much interest in her as if she were wearing an abaya. Of course, his shirt *did* cover her almost as much as one of the cloaks.

"We'll try the bolt cutters first, but if they don't do the trick, we'll go with the tile nippers. There's not much their diamond tips can't get through, but the bolt cutters might be quicker." He held out a chair. "Have a seat."

Short of telling him why he shouldn't bother, Eden had no option but to sit. She'd give him five minutes before frustration hit. And it would. She knew; she'd been there.

But wait—he'd said diamond tips.

Diamond.

Could it be possible?

"I think you should use the nippers." Could it be this easy?

"Nah." Matt removed a black leather jacket and hung it on a hook by the door. "Let's try the bolt cutters first. They've got more power behind them."

"But I think—"

"Eden, the bolt cutters will make short work of this, whereas the nippers will take longer. With the way that wrist is swelling, we don't have much time. Trust me. I know what I'm talking about."

That remained to be seen. And Eden wasn't betting on it.

She shrugged. "Whatever."

Matt sat next to her and she was struck by how big he was. She was used to being tiny, but without the full use of her magic she'd never been so aware of a man's strength and size. At least six feet tall, Matt dwarfed her with shoulders that were fit for a modern-day gladiator.

"Sorry to have to ruin your jewelry, but it has to come off to ease the swelling." He rolled her sleeve back.

She snorted. "Good riddance."

When he looked at her funny, she realized she'd better come up with a believable reason.

"Well, you know, drunken revelry, sheep mentality. That sort of thing. These have been a constant reminder. I'll be glad to get rid of them."

"Good. Just remember that when I've destroyed them beyond recognition."

Another flash of lightning streaked outside the

window while Matt wiggled one blade of the cutters beneath the bracelet. "Just a little more. Hang on."

He worked the tool into the barely-there space between her skin and the gold, and Eden's breath caught at the pain. If only the bracelet weren't so tight.

And, suddenly, the blade slid under as easy as could be, until the entire thing was in place. Matt closed the other blade and glanced at her. "Well, that was interesting. Ready?"

She nodded, then blinked back a few tears as the metal dug into her skin with the pressure. Enough already. She sucked in another breath and wished it was over with.

And then, just like their kiss—but with a screech of wooden chair legs against the limestone floor—her wish came true.

It *was* over.

And Matt and his chair were flying backward across the room.

Chapter 4

SHE WAS OUT. FREE.

Faruq gripped his scepter so hard the glass orb shook within its platinum casing, and he stared at the wall map where the one tiny star that had lain dormant now bobbed, mocking him. He'd watched Eden's marker sit quietly for years, content in knowing exactly where she was.

But now she was out. On the move. And, unfortunately, she still wore the antiquated bracelets, which emitted such a low frequency it'd be hours, if not days, before he could zero in on her location. Why hadn't he insisted she wear the newer ones? And that bottle stopper—

He was lost if she'd figured that out.

Faruq kicked the desk in front of him, sending his report notes skittering to the edge and startling the cobra in the basket beneath into a hiss. He waved his hand, putting the serpent back into a trance and the notes into a file folder on the blotter.

He was a fool. A pretty face, that sexy body, and his mind turned in one direction.

He'd switched her bottle stopper from glass to a canary diamond as a birthday gift before he'd learned about Khaled's escape. Before he'd known about diamonds' power over the bracelets. Gods, he never would have expected it to matter, but then, he hadn't expected

Eden, of all the genies under his management, to murder her master.

Oh, yes, Faruq knew all about what her master had wanted to do to his own children and why Eden couldn't have lived with herself if she'd permitted it, but even though she'd said it was an accident, she'd gone against The Code. He just hadn't expected her retrieval, trial, and judgment to happen so fast that he hadn't been able to switch the stoppers back without having to make explanations. The High Master, who loved Eden like a daughter, had been distraught enough. To admit his error—no, that hadn't been an option.

He lit the wick of the iron filigree lantern hanging from the hook by his inner sanctum, wincing at the flare of light against the darkening twilight. Lavender filled the air, doing absolutely nothing to calm him. He should have known his resistance to replacing her bracelets with the newer editions when he'd swapped them out on the other genies would come back to haunt him, but he'd wanted to give her the ones he'd designed especially for her at the perfect time and venue.

Sapphires, emeralds, rubies... Faruq knew how Eden liked jewels. How colors brought her to life. He'd wanted to use the lure of the gems when her sentence was completed. Offer her bracelets covered so thickly in jewels she couldn't see the metal bands. Present her with the rare crystal he'd selected to go with those bracelets for her and her alone. Show her the authority he had, the riches he could grant her, the power—*if* she agreed to be bound to him for eternity.

But now she was free and he'd lost any advantage he'd had. Lamplight flickered over the walls, intermittently illuminating the calligraphic designs there as if unnamed faces were accusing him.

Luckily, though, she hadn't yet discovered the stopper's ability to free her from her bracelets or he wouldn't have even this faint signal in her crystal, but he had no idea how she'd managed to break the seal on the bottle.

However she'd gotten out, she was now free in the world somewhere, centuries before her sentence was up, and the High Master was going to be more than annoyed. And an annoyed High Master was hard enough to deal with.

Faruq walked to the bank of glowing crystals, moonlight shimmering across them through the crescent window on the side wall. One thousand and one crystals—the irony wasn't lost on him at the number. One thousand and one genies under his control and only one thousand of them accounted for. One thousand radiant crystals, and the diamond one in the upper right quadrant that had, for the past seventeen hundred ninety-seven years, barely glowed, now sparked to life.

He'd be out of a job if he couldn't find her. Sentenced back into The Service—and praying that'd be the worst of it.

Faruq flipped his sleeves out of the way and gripped the edge of the marble altar of crystals, hanging his head. The High Master might treat her as a favored daughter— it'd helped in getting her death sentence commuted to confinement instead—but even a favored daughter had to obey The Code. And he, as the one who'd convinced the High Master to commute her sentence, he had his head on the chopping block as well. *He* was responsible for monitoring the genies. *He* was in charge of upgrading the bracelets as human technology had advanced and Khaled's discovery had come to light. *He* was the one to answer for Genie Compliance. And *he* was the one swayed by a pretty face.

You'd think he would have remembered Samson's lesson. Delilah had been an enchantress.

Just like Eden.

Faruq exhaled and shook his head, his turban only exacerbating his headache. The only thing worse than being a fool was being an old fool. He should have known better.

He had to get her back. Before the High Master found out, and before she figured out how to get the bracelets off.

If that happened, he might as well impale himself on the highest spire in Al-Jannah because, without the bracelets, Eden would be untraceable.

Chapter 5

EDEN BARELY HAD A CHANCE TO CATCH HER BREATH before two realizations hit.

One, the bolt cutters hadn't done squat with the bracelets, and two, somehow she'd done magic. *Without* snapping her fingers.

This could not be good.

"What the hell?" Matt twisted out of the smashed remnants of the chair and fell onto the floor, staring at his empty hands.

Great. Injuring the guy who was trying to help her. Eden jumped out of her chair and rushed over. "Are you okay?"

"I'm not sure." He pulled a chair leg out from under his left thigh, grimacing when it snagged on his jeans. "What was that?"

That was something he'd never believe. She barely believed it. She'd never heard of a genie being able to do magic just by thought. Everyone had a special Way. A certain pattern or movement or word, assigned by the High Master himself. Once you received your Way, it was yours forever.

Until now, apparently.

No. It had to be a coincidence. Had to be—and screwy magic was *not* what she needed right now.

She reached for a piece of the broken chair. "Um, maybe it was an electric shock?" That was believable, right? For both of them. "I told you to use the other tool."

Matt shook his head and got to his feet. "Metal on metal. I guess it's possible, although sending me across the room is a first." He looked around the kitchen again. "So where'd they go?"

"Where'd what go?" He wasn't just now noticing the butterflies, was he? Or the lack thereof?

The butterflies must have been victims of her Wayless magic. And Obo—was he, too? Oh, stars, what was going to happen to Humphrey? What if he got out of the prison Obo had made for him and Matt saw him?

"The cutters, Eden. Where are they?"

The tools were the least of her problems at the moment, but she was scared to find out where they'd gone. Usually when she did magic, she thought about what she wanted to have happen, did her little routine, then *shazam!* there it was. Not *shazam!* send-the-guy-racing-across-the-room. She hadn't consciously done anything with them; it was the unconscious possibility that was freaking her out.

"Um, the cutters aren't here." Master of the obvious, that was her.

"I know they're not here, but tools just don't vanish into thin air. They have to be around somewhere."

Somewhere being the operative word. Eden couldn't even begin to guess—didn't want to guess what had happened. If she was doing magic—screwy or otherwise—she was showering the area with magical Glimmer, and Faruq was going to be able to find her. What she really needed was her bottle. If she had that, she would be her own master. She would be free.

Matt checked the sink, but Eden wasn't holding her breath for that one. They would have heard the *clang*. Then he opened some of the cabinets and, again, she wasn't holding her breath. She hadn't thought anything about cabinets right before it happened. Besides, the wall cabinets went all the way to the ceiling; nothing could go *over* them, which was the only word she could remember that might mean something.

This had to be a coincidence. Had to be.

She looked around the room. The only thing cutters could have gone over was—"What about the refrigerator?"

The look Matt gave her epitomized what she was thinking, but she was desperate here. Maybe she was just imagining things. Maybe it really wasn't her magic doing this at all. Electric shock—it was possible. And the butterflies, they could have left on their own.

She wasn't quite sure how they multiplied so quickly, but it could happen.

Eden closed her eyes. Who was she kidding? If it looked like a duck...

Those butterflies were definitely duck-like. So were the tools. And with the way her luck had been going ever since that perverted last master of hers—

Eden blew out a breath and blinked back tears. She hadn't cried when the High Master had sentenced her and she wasn't going to cry now—no matter how blatantly lost tools and vanishing insects pointed to screwy magic and, therefore, scads of Glimmer and Faruq on her tail. "Matt, please. Try the refrigerator."

"How do you know my name?"

Oops. "Um, you must have mentioned it."

"I don't remember doing that."

"No, really. You must have. How else would I know it?" *The cat told me* wouldn't go over well. Especially since she couldn't tell him where the cat was. "Please. Can you check behind the refrigerator?"

Matt looked at her as if she was crazy. If only the explanation were that easy.

He shrugged. "What do I have to lose?"

Him, nothing. Her? Well, her grasp on sanity came to mind, followed closely thereafter by her newfound freedom.

Matt leaned into the appliance, the one and only high-light to this entire nightmare being the way his shoulders and arms and backside strained and flexed and bunched as he slid the fridge forward. But Eden couldn't even appreciate that because Matt whistled an *I'll be damned*, and her stomach felt like a dromedary sat on it.

Oh, sure, it was possible the tool could have flown out of his hands, angled just the right way to land in the one place where it couldn't be seen, without making a sound or banging into something along the way. It could happen.

Um, no. She was definitely doing magic.

Which explained not only Matt's little trip across the kitchen, but also, sadly, his bout of lust—and the subsequent dry-up of said emotion—out there in the living room.

"What are the odds?" Matt put her thought into words as he held the bolt cutters by one handle as if they were poison—which was exactly what they were to her.

How was she doing this? That was what she didn't know and what scared her the most—all the while leaving enough Glimmer in the spectrasphere that it might as well be in the shape of an arrow pointing directly at her.

Kind of like the tip of Humphrey's tail that flicked in the doorway.

Eden groped for one of the kitchen chairs and sat. How on earth was she doing it? And, more importantly, how could she control it? And what was she going to do about Humphrey?

"Eden? Are you okay? What's up with you?"

What was up was that there was a baby dragon about to fly in here and change Matt's perception of the world as he knew it, she was somehow transmitting her location like a big blinking beacon to the one being in the universe who'd be looking for it, her wrist was swelling up like a crystal ball, her magic had gone off half-cocked—maybe even fully—she was an AWOL prisoner who would soon have a control-freak, bounty-hunting vizier after her only to lock her up for the next millennium and a half—if that was the *worst* he'd do and there were no bets on that—she had no friends, no money, no clothing, no backup plan, no means of support, no bottle, no *cat*… nothing. Except a baby dragon who was about to become quite the handful in under a week. And she didn't have a clue how she was going to fix any of it.

Her breath hitched. It'd be so much easier if she could tell Matt what she was.

"I'm a djinni."

"You're a what?" Matt did a double take.

So did Eden. She had to be out of her mind to tell him that.

But, actually… Having him know what she was could be helpful. She wouldn't have to keep track of any lies, and since he couldn't summon her into The Service by virtue of her bottle being missing, there was no risk. And if he were going to believe her about magic, explaining Humphrey would be a piece of cake. Telling him could actually be a good thing. "You're more familiar with the term *genie*, I believe."

Matt snorted. That was flattering. "As in *I Dream of*?"

Eden nodded.

And waited.

Matt set the cutters on the table, then leaned on the back of the chair. "A genie. So, does that mean I get three wishes?"

And there it was. The quintessentially selfish question whose answer started with a *yes, master*, and ended with an *as you wish*.

Only not this time.

Eden sat back, her chin up, both literally and figuratively, and shook some hair off her face. He didn't believe her, but that would change. "There's a problem with the wishes."

"Why am I not surprised?"

She'd wipe that sarcasm right out of his mouth if she had fully functioning magic, yes she would. "There's a problem because my magic doesn't seem to be working correctly." She wasn't about to mention specifics like zapping that lust into him or bashing him against the wall, no matter how inadvertently. A girl did have her pride. And a sense of self-preservation.

"Your magic isn't working right." Matt pushed off the chair and walked to the counter, resting his backside and palms along the edge. He took his time crossing one ankle over the other. "Doesn't that make you a pretty pathetic genie?"

"You don't have to be insulting. I know you don't

believe me, but it's true. And we really don't have time for this." She held up her arms and cocked her wrists. The gold sparkled in the kitchen lighting. "These are a serious problem."

"Yeah, no kidding. I'm the one who went sailing across the floor."

"No, not that way. These are homing devices."

"Homing devices? Like a GPS?"

Ironically, yes. "I need to get them off or I'm going to have someone on my tail really quickly who I'd rather not have."

"Really? Who? Some big, bad blue genie who's going to come after you and whisk you off to the desert to do his evil bidding?"

Faruq wasn't blue. She let her wrists hit the tile table with a *clank*. "I'm not making this up, Matt. These bracelets transmit a signal that, if I can't get them off, is going to lead him right here, and, trust me, you don't want him coming anywhere near you. Me, he'd only want to capture. You? I don't even want to contemplate what he would do to you."

"So if you left, I wouldn't have to worry about what he'd do to me?"

Eden blinked. She hadn't seen that one coming.

Or maybe she had. She wouldn't grant his wishes, so why *would* he be interested in helping her?

But she did need his help. The no-money/no-friends thing. And his diamond-tipped tools. So she'd have to give in. Heavens knew, she had years of practice subjugating her wants for others' desires.

"Okay, Matt, here's the deal. My magic's a little hit-or-miss right now—which might have something to do with having gotten knocked out—and it's leaving a spectral fingerprint all over the place. The bracelets send a signal to his office, which gives him my general location, but combined with the Glimmer, they'll lead him right to your house, and then anything can happen. If you think that little trek across the kitchen was something, you're really not going to want to see what *he* can do."

She took a breath and swallowed the bad taste in her mouth, knowing what she was going to have to do and not all that thrilled about it. But she'd been around enough mortals to know how their minds worked. "So, Matt, if you'll try those diamond-tipped things, I will grant you one wish. If I can get my magic to work properly, that is."

Matt swiped a hand over his mouth. God, when would he learn? When you picked up strays—or damsels in distress—this is what you got. Lost causes and nut cases. Especially beautiful ones who could turn him on with one look.

Cara, his ex-girlfriend, was the perfect example. She'd strung him along after he'd rescued her from the abusive boyfriend, only to go back to the dickhead-with-meathooks, then end up in the hospital. And now he'd rescued a delusional supposed-genie with screwy magic. He'd sworn he wasn't going to do any more rescuing. *Sworn* it.

"Look, Eden, I'm sorry, but you need more help than I can give you. How about I take you to the hospital and they can work on the bracelets?" And give her something for the obvious concussion she was suffering from. Or check her in for a nice long rest.

"Matt, I'm not crazy."

"I never said you were."

She snorted. "Right. Look, I'll prove it."

This ought to be good. "Prove you're a genie. With magic that's not working? To quote you, 'Good luck with that.'"

Eden's blue eyes narrowed; she got that he didn't believe her. But, man, did he wish he could. Wouldn't it be great if she were what she said she was? That'd take care of all his financial troubles and he'd have the added bonus of having a sexy genie at his beck and call. Every man's fantasy.

"You know what?" She rose from the chair. "A little more Glimmer won't hurt with the rest floating around. I'll give it a shot and try for something small. You might want to stand back in case it misfires. I wouldn't want to injure you."

Matt stifled the impulse to roll his eyes. Misfire. Good God. She actually believed what she was telling him. He could really pick them. She needed a lot more rescuing than he was capable of.

But he could humor her, so he slid to the far end of the cabinets.

Eden shook out her arms and rotated her wrists. Well, one of them. She closed her eyes and snapped her fingers.

Nothing happened.

Big surprise.

She opened one eye and glanced around the kitchen. When her gaze met his, she quickly shut the eye again, readjusted her stance, shoved the sleeves up her arms, took a deep breath, rotated her wrists—wincing as she did so—and snapped.

Nothing.

This time when she looked around the kitchen, her shoulders sagged, and Matt half-wished something *had* appeared. "Eden, look, it's okay. Sometimes we get confused after an injury. It happens."

"I'm not crazy!" She spun around, searching for something. "Ah! There. Obo. Thank the stars you're okay! And you've got—oh, good."

The stray Matt had been feeding over the last few months sauntered into the kitchen with one of his socks hanging from the side of his mouth. "Oboe? Looks more like a cat to me than a musical instrument. Just how hard did you hit your head?"

Eden clenched her fists, her blue eyes flashing just like after he'd kissed her—

He didn't need to be reminded about that. The woman was injured.

"His *name* is Obo. And he asked me how you're taking all of this."

And obviously delusional. Just his luck. "He did what?"

She crossed her arms in front of her chest with a grin that would put the Cheshire cat to shame. "Obo asked if you believe me yet."

"The cat did." He needed to get her to a doctor. One named Doolittle, it seemed.

She nodded, looking very pleased with herself.

And he was very pleased looking at her, but no matter how gorgeous she was, no matter how much he'd enjoyed kissing her and wouldn't mind doing so again, the woman wasn't well. "And did you answer the cat, Eden?"

She jammed her fists to her hips, which had the extra

special feature of hiking his shirt up her thigh, letting him know that, yes, indeed, she was no longer wearing the boy-cuts.

Matt stifled a groan. He didn't need to be thinking about that either.

"Of course I didn't answer him." Eden crossed her arms, which pressed her breasts together, the swells outlined by his sweatshirt, reminding him, yet again, what they'd looked like beneath her opened top and—

Mind back on this *delusion, Ewing.*

"You didn't hear me say anything to Obo, did you?" she huffed.

"I also didn't hear the cat say anything, Eden."

"Of course you didn't."

Like that made any sense.

"Cats don't always speak English."

Now *that* made sense. Of *course* the cat wouldn't be speaking English. And of course the genie would be able to understand it.

The cat—Obo—sashayed across the kitchen, dropped the sock at her feet, and rubbed up against her legs. Matt would swear there was a smile on the feline's face. But then, that cat always did look like he was putting one over on him. Could this be why?

Matt shook his head. What was he thinking? The cat was just a cat. He couldn't talk. And Eden—the *genie*—couldn't understand him. She needed to get to a hospital pronto.

Matt reached for his coat.

"How do you think I learned your name, Matt?"

He stopped mid-grab. "What?"

"I asked how you thought I learned your name."

"I heard you the first time, Eden." Matt turned around. "You said I mentioned it."

Her grin mirrored the cat's. "I lied."

"You lied."

"Yep. I did. *You* didn't mention it. Obo did."

Definite brain injury. "The *cat* told you." Matt turned back for the coat. They needed to get to that hospital now.

"And he says you snore after four beers and that you're a Springsteen fan. When you're naked."

Matt forgot about the coat. He only sang in the shower. When he was alone.

He spun around to see the cat sitting at her feet with the tip of his tail nudging the sock, licking one paw as nonchalantly as ever.

"He says that if you sing 'Born to Run' one more time, he's going to organize a cat-howling party beneath your window every night until you stop."

"I—" How did someone respond to that?

Sitting down would be a good way.

Matt groped for one of the bar stools at the peninsula.

Eden, enjoying herself a bit too much at his expense, sat next to him. The cat jumped onto the counter and took a leisurely stroll over to the sink.

"Oh, and he also says you've got a hole in your black workout shorts and he'd really appreciate you not going commando in them anymore."

This was unbelievable. Unless she'd been spying on him—

Oh, yeah, Ewing. That's it. A heretofore unknown woman in a genie costume staked out the house long enough to know he sawed wood when he had too many, sang in the shower, and worked out with holey shorts, then she brained herself with a big crystal only to tell him she was a genie and wanted him to remove her bracelets because her magic didn't work.

He didn't think even two of those conditions could ever be strung together believably, let alone the whole lot.

"What else? What can the cat tell me that only it would know? That anyone wouldn't know from hanging around my house."

"You're accusing me of stalking you? Great. This was a waste of time." She crossed her arms with a huff and a tight set to her lips and for a moment—just a moment—he got a glimpse of that television Jeannie. All she needed was the blonde hair and costume, but her arm-crossing/head-nodding was almost perfect.

And she'd had the costume.

He couldn't believe he was even considering it, but the stuff about The Boss was right.

"If I'm going to believe you"—and he wasn't sure he was going to be able to, no matter how much proof the cat gave him—"then I need something else."

The cat stood up, picked up the sock, and hopped into the greenhouse window above the sink, circling once before lying down as if he weren't the object of discussion.

Matt wished he could be as nonchalant about the whole thing, but he either had a very badly injured woman here, or a cat that talked and a genie who claimed to do magic. Unpredictable magic, but magic nonetheless.

And he'd thought his shitty day had gotten *better* when she'd landed on him?

Eden blew out a breath. "Fine. Obo says you finally

threw out the pot pie your mother gave you because it was over a week old and that you'd only taken it because she'd guilted you into it, the baseball-shaped thing from the top shelf in the fridge that has Astroturf growing all over it is from the last guilt trip, you sing in the shower, you sometimes work out in the nude, and—" She looked at the cat. "You're kidding."

The cat licked its paw.

"What? What'd it say?" Did he ask that? Maybe *he* was the one with the head injury.

Eden snorted. "He said the fuzzy houndstooth handcuffs are under your bed between the leg and the wall." She cocked her head. "Houndstooth handcuffs? Are those for the *non*-strange women you bring home to make love to?"

Matt ignored his first thought. Mainly because the image of her in the cuffs and latched to his bed made his jeans uncomfortable. Scrubbing the image from his brain—and failing—he tried to form a coherent response. "They were a special order. For a coworker's bachelor party."

"And they disappeared before the party ever started."

Unless she was an employee of the catalog company he'd bought them from or the U.S. Postal Service, there was no way she could have known about those handcuffs. He'd bought them as a gag gift and hadn't told anyone. "How'd you know?"

She raised her eyebrows.

"Right. The cat." Matt was getting a headache. "Eden, really, I think a trip to the hospital is in order." For both of them.

She closed her eyes, caught her breath in a sigh more

frustrated than sad, then opened her gorgeous blue eyes again. "Matt, I'm *not* crazy."

"I realize you believe what you're saying, but it's just not possible. There are no such things as genies or talking cats or homing bracelets or magic spectral fingerprints—"

"Glimmer."

"I—what?"

"It's called Glimmer."

Matt shook his head. "Okay, glimmer. Whatever. But there's no such thing. Talking to cats doesn't prove anything. Magic just doesn't exist."

"Oh no?" She peered over his shoulder. "Then how do you explain *that*?"

Chapter 6

THE GROWING SMILE ON HER FACE WAS UTTERLY beautiful. *She* was utterly beautiful.

She was also utterly nutso.

"Seriously, Matt, turn around and explain that. I'd like to hear what you come up with."

Humor her. That's what you did with crazy people. So Matt turned around.

And started questioning his own sanity.

A donkey stood in his kitchen.

"Guess my magic isn't so screwy after all," Eden said, smiling all the more. "Looks like someone owes me an apology."

The donkey brayed and Eden laughed—and Matt realized what she'd said. Her magic wasn't screwy. Meaning she'd twitched up the donkey—the *ass*—specifically.

"How the hell did you do that?"

She held up her wrists and smirked. "Bracelet-wearing, bottle-living, navel-baring, cat-chatting, donkey-conjuring, card-carrying member of the djinn. At your service. Or actually"—her smirk turned back into a beautiful smile—"*not* at your service."

"But how…" She'd made a donkey appear in his kitchen. Words failed him.

The donkey, however, was having no such trouble. It brayed and began meandering around, knocking a chair over, its hooves clicking on the tile floor.

There was a *donkey* in his kitchen. "Does it talk, too?"

Eden shook her head. "Too stubborn to learn."

Why that should make him feel better, Matt didn't know. "Can you get rid of it, please?"

Eden sighed. Loudly. "Okay."

A couple of finger-snaps, some wrist twirls accompanied by a grimace or two, a few foreign words that sounded a lot like curses, but the donkey didn't go anywhere. Except over to the counter to take an apple out of the basket.

"It, ah, appears getting rid of him isn't an option at the moment."

"Eden, what am I going to do with a donkey?" *That* was his question?

"Obo says you could use him as a lawn mower in the yard."

The cat. He'd forgotten about the talking cat. He glared at the animal that was making its way back across the counter. "And does Obo have any other great words of wisdom?"

"Just that you can't touch him when it comes to sarcasm so he suggests you don't try."

Between the donkey's snorts and its apple-crunching, Matt could hear the low rumble of a purr as Obo nudged Eden's shoulder with its cheek, the sock never leaving its mouth. A cat with a sock fetish—that should be the weirdest thing in his day but, sadly, wasn't.

"No, Obo." Eden tapped the cat on the nose. "I'm not going to ask Matt to switch your food. I don't care what you know about him. He's already given you the self-filling food bowl. Beluga caviar is too expensive. And get...*that*—" she flicked the sock—"out of here."

The cat did that fluttery *chirrup* it did every so often, jumped off the counter, stuck its tail in the air, and headed out the door.

"Yeah, well, all that salt isn't good for you anyway," Eden called after him.

Matt tried to keep his mouth from hanging open but obviously wasn't successful because Eden pushed up on his chin until his teeth clacked. "Don't pay any attention to him, Matt. He was used to palace living in his first couple of lives. He's spoiled."

"*Couple* of lives?"

"Yeah, cats can—"

He held up his hands. "I don't want to know." And he didn't. He didn't think his brain could take it. Genies didn't exist. They *couldn't*.

Then the donkey knocked into the table, sending the tools sliding toward the edge, and Matt had to face the fact that they might.

He also had to make a grab for the tools before they smashed onto the tile floor. Today was already enough of a mess.

"Eden, let's get those bracelets off. Then your big blue friend won't show up, you can be on your way— with Francis here—and I'll even throw Obo in as a bonus." And he'd get his life back. Financial concerns, business worries, lack of a relationship aside, it was a good life. Not a hint of weird in it at all.

"Francis was a talking mule. This is a donkey. There's a difference."

Yeah, there was a difference all right. One was living in the annals of movie history, and the other was living in his kitchen. "Do you want the bracelets off or not?"

Eden held out her hands. "Yes. That's why I suggested the nippers in the first place."

Matt held out a chair for her at the table, took the one next to her, and picked up the tools. "Here goes nothing."

It definitely was *not* nothing. One snip was all it took to set Eden on the road to freedom. A few more snips and those little diamond-tipped miracle-workers sliced through the bond of her Servitude.

Diamonds. That's what Khaled had been trying to tell her. How easy the solution had been all along. No wonder Faruq had confiscated her collection of gems after her sentencing. She'd figured he'd wanted compensation for convincing the High Master to convert her death sentence to imprisonment, and she'd actually been grateful. That—that—that *ibn el-kalb*! Not a term she used often, but Faruq deserved it. He'd known, and he'd purposely taken her gems.

Matt's eyes met hers as he peeled the bracelet off her wrist. "One down."

"One to go," Eden whispered, so eager—or angry or both—that she was shaking. She closed her eyes as she felt the first slice go through the second bracelet. Faruq had wanted her for years. She wasn't delusional enough to think he was in love with her, but since the High Master treated her as a favored daughter, she knew her real attraction for Faruq—and why he wasn't about to let his ace-in-a-bottle escape.

She was now more determined than ever. Bad enough being used for what she could do for her master, but this? Faruq was playing with who she was as a person.

Matt finished cutting through the second bond. "How's the wrist feel? We should probably get it X-rayed."

She rotated it. Sore, but she didn't think it was broken. It felt much better now that the bracelet was no longer cutting off the circulation. "It's okay. I think it's just sprained. I'll wrap it and it'll be good to go." She reached for the bandage.

So did Matt.

And just like that, Faruq, her screwy magic, butterflies and dragons, even the donkey, faded into the background. Her skin started sizzling yet again where his fingers touched it and she couldn't move—because of that feeling *and* the realization that her magic hadn't created this.

Or had it?

Eden caught her breath. Transporting tools, conjuring donkeys, they were one thing, but she didn't want to *make* Matt want her. She wasn't that desperate.

Okay, yes she was. But she wasn't going to allow herself to be. Matt had to want her for her. Not because magic was involved.

Eden snuck a look at his profile as he wrapped her wrist, then closed her eyes and looked away so he wouldn't catch her staring. Only… she didn't want to stop looking at him. Did he feel this? What if he did? Her breath caught at the thought. What if he looked at her right now? What would she see in those hazel eyes of his?

She glanced back and wished he'd turn his head.

He turned his head.

Whoa. The look in his eyes held all the power of a storm, the blaze of lightning, and all its heat. She caught her breath again at the intensity, wishing he'd say something.

"Something."

It came out a whisper from such a perfect set of lips that had no business belonging on a man for any other reason than kissing. Which he wasn't. Kissing, that is.

His stare deepened, the green-brown irises going a deep, mossy color. Eden lost the ability to breathe—and even more so when he focused on her mouth. Magic or not, why didn't he just kiss her and get it over with?

He did.

Kissed her.

Pulled her close and drew her into his arms, sprawling her across him like a sack of grain. Close enough that her bones melted when he nibbled on her lips and his tongue traced the seam. Her eyes fluttered closed as she tried to catch her breath, only, his tongue slid inside. He tasted of... something. Warm and spicy and... She couldn't think.

Then his arms came around her, his hands clasping her shoulder blades, holding her to him as he angled his head, his tongue sweeping across her teeth, dipping to stroke hers and—

Oh my stars. Colors exploded behind her eyelids. Every shade of the rainbow and some she couldn't name, and she felt as if she were whirling in a sandstorm of jewels.

He cupped the back of her head, his fingers caressing her neck. Shivers danced down her spine. His fingers threaded through her hair, gripping the strands as she'd gripped the edges of her first flying carpet, and, just as exhilaratingly, Eden gave herself over to the flight.

And then she remembered exactly why they were doing this.

Magic.

Camel-spit! She'd *wished* him into wanting her.

"Matt." Eden wanted to cry. It wasn't fair. Not to her and most definitely not to him. When the magic wore off he'd hate her for taking advantage of him. And she'd hate herself because she knew exactly how it felt to have to do something against your will because of someone else's selfish desires. She didn't want him to hate her *or* to want her because of her magic.

So how do you want him to want you?

So many ways she didn't even want to contemplate. When was the last time a man had held her? Wanted her for who she was, not what she could do for him or what she'd done to him?

Too long to want to go there.

If ever.

Her breath caught. If only Matt could look at her and know he wanted her without any influence from her magic, *then* kiss her.

But, sadly, unless she regained control of her powers, she'd never be sure.

"Matt. Please." She struggled out of his embrace, and Matt let her go.

For all of about one second.

Then, slowly, he slid his palms up her arms. Cupped her face. Stared into her eyes.

"What, Eden?" he whispered. "What can I do to please you?"

He didn't wait for her answer. His kiss was different this time. Tender. Enticing. Tantalizing. He nipped at her lips. Drew his tongue along the bottom one, then licked the corner of her mouth as if savoring the taste of her. A kiss she'd fantasized about. For way too many nights.

Eden tilted her head when his lips slid along her neck to the spot below her ear, moist heat from his breath tickling her already sensitized nerve endings, and she had to close her eyes as the feelings rushed over her.

It'd been so incredibly long since she'd felt this. Felt *like* this. As if her breath was as fragile as a butterfly's wings, her skin as thin, desire buffeting everything inside of her as it emerged from a cocoon eighteen hundred years old.

Matt's fingers danced across her cheek, then trailed down her spine, every touch igniting a spark that only added to the storm gathering inside of her.

"And this, Eden." He kissed his way to her ear and swirled his tongue along the rim. "Does this please you?"

She shivered and clutched his arms.

"What about this?" He took her earlobe between his teeth with a tiny nip that sent aching need spiraling through her, to curl low in her belly.

Eden moaned, tightening her fingers on his biceps.

Matt scraped his teeth gently against her skin. "I want you, Eden."

"I want you, t—"

The words shocked reality into the situation. Of course he wanted her. She'd *wanted* him to want her.

Eden's eyes flew open. "Matt, it's magic."

"I'll say." He smiled against her throat.

"No, you don't understand." She pushed against his arms, but he didn't let go. "It's my magic that's making you want me." As sad as that was.

Matt kissed the hollow at the base of her throat. Thank the stars for big, gaping men's shirts so he could kiss her there. Even if this wasn't a good idea.

"So what's making you want me, Eden? Is that your magic, too?"

Even through the sweatshirt, she could still feel the luscious sensations of his fingers on her back and she trembled. "Of course not."

"Then I don't see the problem."

As he nibbled along her collarbone, she was finding it hard to remember what her argument was.

"I want you, Eden."

Oh yeah. That was it. "No you don't, Matt."

Matt reached for her hand and brought it to his lap, all the while kissing his way to her jaw. "Now tell me I don't."

It was a good argument. "But Matt, it's my magic." She removed her hand against her better judgment. Well, no, Judgment said it was a good idea to remove it; Libido was the one protesting.

"It certainly is." His lips found her earlobe again and Libido shouted for victory.

"No, you don't understand—"

"I understand that I want you and you want me, and God knows, I could use something good in my life about now." Matt cradled her face in his hands and ran his thumb over her bottom lip. "You were all over me in the living room, Eden. If I hadn't stopped you, we'd be naked and sweaty right now. So let's do it, Eden. You can, right? Genies can make love?"

She shook off his thumb because this conversation, these feelings coursing through her, they were too much.

Too intense. They could make her do something she really wanted to do but really couldn't. Not like this, not by compelling him with her magic.

She knew the aftermath of being compelled to do something and it'd never been her intention with Matt. "Of course I can make love, Matt, but—"

He put a finger to her lips. "Then there's no problem."

"But you're not yourself."

"No?" He ran his hands down her arms to entwine their fingers and kissed the corner of her mouth. "Then who am I?"

"Someone who's under my spell."

"I'll say."

His smile against her lips wove its own spell.

She shook her head, denying herself the kiss she so desperately wanted, trying to stick to her good intentions. "No, I mean *really* under my spell. Remember when I said my magic was acting screwy? I wasn't kidding."

That got his attention. He slid his fingers from hers and sat back, leaving her feeling bereft, an emotion she was all too familiar with.

"But you did the donkey thing, Eden. On purpose, as you so unflinchingly pointed out. That wasn't screwy."

"True, but I don't know how I did it, just that I did. I thought *jacka*— I mean, donkey, and there he was."

Matt reached up to run his thumb over her cheek and electricity sparked between them. "So you're saying that you *wanted* me to make love to you and that's how we got to this point?"

"That's not a news flash, Matt. I thought I made that perfectly clear out there." She flicked her head toward his living room.

Typical man; he smiled as if he'd won a prize. "Then what's the problem?"

"The problem is that you're not yourself, Matt. You don't really want me. You only think you do because I'm a genie." Everyone always wanted the genie part of her, not the woman inside. All her masters had wanted her for what she could give them, Faruq for the connection she could bring to the High Master, and the High Master himself because she was part of the woman he'd loved and lost. The same story over and over and over.

She pulled away from Matt, rocking her chair so hard it almost fell over. "Matt, you said you don't pick up strange women and bring them home to make love to them, remember? Can't get much stranger than a genie."

Matt sat back. Oh, hell. He *had* said that.

Because it was true. The one time he'd brought someone he barely knew home had been Cara when she'd been beat-up and scared. She'd had nowhere to go when he'd pulled her boyfriend off her and tossed him into the dumpster outside the bar that night. So he'd brought her home. Let her stay.

And then... and then the whole thing had blown up in his face. Taken his heart with it. And today—and Eden—gave a whole new meaning to the term *strange*.

Matt raked his hands through his hair. Thank God Eden had her wits about her. His seemed to have taken a vacation.

"You're right. It must be the magic. Potent stuff." Damned potent if the ache in his groin was anything to go by. "How long do the effects last?"

"I don't know. Longer than the Glimmer does, but I've never asked."

"You've done this before?" There went his ego.

But, even now, listening to her trying to explain it, he still wanted her. What did that say for his ego?

"No, I haven't done *this* before, but I have bewitched people, and everyone reacts differently."

"I don't feel like I've been bewitched." It was true. He didn't. Not by any magic.

Her, on the other hand—

Eden could claim what she'd done to him was magic, but with her hair mussed from his fingers, her lips pink and swollen from his kisses, the awareness in her eyes, her cheeks reddened where his stubble had scraped it, Matt wasn't so sure.

That first kiss had surprised him. But the Cara fiasco had happened six months ago and there hadn't been anyone since. He didn't pick women up at the drop of a hat, but he was as human as the next guy. When a gorgeous woman came on to him, well, hell. He wasn't dead.

Eden didn't need magic to bewitch him. But it was more than physical and that worried him. He wasn't winning any medals at keeping his business or Dad's dream alive, his relationship with his brother was strained at best, and his rescue techniques had been sorely lacking where Cara was concerned.

Add in the danger this guy who was after her posed to the attraction he felt for Eden, and Matt wasn't so sure he'd be able to do any better for her than he had for the other people he'd cared about.

Faruq stared at the canary diamond crystal. The canary

diamond crystal that had stopped blinking and gone completely opaque.

Kharah! She'd gotten the bracelets off, thereby shielding her location from him.

At least he knew the coordinates of the shop where she'd spent all those years, but it was on the western coast of the United States, halfway around the world in a populated area. Metropolitan. Techno-savvy inhabitants. Intelligent, for the most part, and practical-minded. Not a people who'd believe any of the wild stories he'd concocted in the past when he'd popped into another civilization. Where before he'd arrived in all his magical splendor, proclaiming the damnation of hell or whatever the worst had been in their belief system, the natives had fallen under his spell and in with his plan. But now? This modern age was extremely annoying, but he had no choice. He had to find her.

Back in his office, Faruq toed aside the cobra's basket to grab a large carpetbag, faded after centuries of use, that held his instruments and transferred them to a period-correct briefcase. He hated traveling among New World inhabitants but needed to blend in and use their resources to find Eden and bring her back to the fold. She was out of the magic spectral radar and, as such, invisible to his powers of detection. He was going to have to find her the mortal way. In their world.

And then figure out some way to slap on the new bracelets to return her to his.

Chapter 7

"TRUST ME, MATT," EDEN SAID, "WHAT YOU'RE FEELING is one hundred percent genie magic."

She tossed a swath of hair over her shoulder, the tips of which trailed across the back of his hand, and Matt had to stop himself from grasping it and tugging her into another kiss. It really hadn't felt like magic.

With the crap he'd been going through lately, was it any wonder he'd let his guard down and allowed himself to want her? Battling forces he had no control over, watching everything he'd worked and sacrificed for go belly up through no fault of his own, when she came on to him, he'd let it happen because it'd been so easy and because, let's face it, the woman was hot. And sexy. And gorgeous. He'd have to be a eunuch not to want her, and even that was doubtful.

If it was magic, so what? Wasn't he entitled to something going his way for once?

"And speaking of magic," she said, "let's deal with that wish I promised you. I'd rather keep trying now so that any Glimmer will fade before Faruq shows up. So, what's your heart's desire?"

You was the first thing that popped into his head, but Matt elected not to voice it. What a stupid waste of a wish. He'd never want anyone to want him because of magic—

Holy hell.

Matt sat back as the full import of what'd just happened hit him. She was a genie. A real-life, magic-carpet-flying *genie*. One he'd been busy kissing while a donkey roamed around his kitchen. And she'd bewitched him into doing that.

"Matt? Are you okay?"

"You really do magic?"

She sighed. "No. Francis is just a figment of your imagination. That dishtowel he's munching? It's totally in one piece and folded nicely in a drawer."

Matt swiped a hand over his jaw, barely able to believe he was having this conversation or to believe his eyes—and *her*. That kiss hadn't felt like magic, but did he really know what magic felt like? "Eden, this is a lot to take in. I mean, genies are myths. Legends. Stories—"

"TV characters and Robin Williams caricatures. I know. But we're also real and so is Faruq, so we don't have the luxury of time here, Matt."

"Faruq?"

Eden brushed her hair off her forehead and it cascaded over her shoulders—making it tough for Matt to concentrate on anything else. "Faruq's in charge of Genie Compliance. And by taking the bracelets off, I've just committed a huge sin. Faruq isn't going to like that."

Okay, that got his attention. "So why did you? Why put yourself at risk? Why not just keep them on?"

Eden leaned onto the back two legs of the chair. "Really? Keep them on? And be at his beck and call whenever the mood strikes him? Sit here like the proverbial duck so he can order me back into my bottle to serve the next master who sets me free?" The front legs of the chair hit the limestone floor with a thud. "You know, that TV show might have made it look all funny and lighthearted, but trust me, it's not. Masters with genies see themselves as invincible. Above the moral code at times. And I can do nothing to stop them. Not without facing the consequences. It's always, 'Yes, master; as you wish, master; what more shall you have, master; how high shall I jump, master?'" She took a deep breath and rubbed her bandaged wrist with her other hand. "After a few years, let alone a couple of hundred or more, you tend to get tired of being someone's slave."

Slave. Matt grimaced. "I never thought of it that way."

She rested her elbow on the table and plunked her chin in her palm, her blue eyes missing their earlier sparkle. "No one ever does. Everyone sees me as a giant lottery ticket that keeps on giving. A Get-Out-of-Poverty-Free card. Their own little toy to manipulate others who've wronged them. And most of them make disastrous wishes. So many go for material things, convinced that enough gold will make them happy. That enough minions will make them king of their world. But it never does. Happiness comes from within. *Stuff* only clutters up the place."

"You've seen a lot."

"More than I care to remember."

"A couple of hundred years?" She didn't look a day over thirty—er, twenty-nine.

Eden nodded. "Or more. Trust me, it's better if you don't know how many more. It freaks people out more than the magic."

A lot of stuff was freaking him out right now. "Eden, earlier. When you were unconscious. Where did you come from? How did that happen?"

Eden licked her lips. "I was in my bottle in the trash in front of the antiques store. Mr. Murphy was throwing a lot of stuff away. When the jaws of the truck clamped down, they created enough pressure on the bottle to break the magical seal the High Master put on it. And speaking of which"—she stood and pulled his shirt down around her legs—"thank you for your help, but I need to get going. If Faruq's not on his way, he will be soon, and my bottle is still out there somewhere. So, what's your wish?"

Common sense was telling him this wasn't possible. But his eyes and ears were proving it was.

Then she crossed her arms, his shirt hiked back up her legs, and his libido was telling him something else entirely.

Matt shook his head. *Focus, Ewing.* She was granting him a wish. One wish. What should it be? Unlimited bank account? A thriving business? Private island in the Caribbean? World peace? Ending global hunger? Eradicating disease? The choices were endless and the responsibility heavy.

"Oh, and it has to be something tangible. World peace is beyond my abilities. It has to directly affect you."

That put the kibosh on altruism.

"And you can't ask for more wishes either."

"I'm not five years old, Eden."

She laughed. Even if it was at his expense, Matt liked seeing the sparkle back in her eyes.

"You'd be surprised how often I get that one, Matt. But Gratitude Wishes have to be something tangible that I can do or get for you. And we need to hurry. I'd like to get a head start on Faruq."

Matt was having a tough time concentrating on a wish when he thought of *hundreds of years*. What amazing things she must have seen, who she must have known—

"Matt? Anything? Gold doubloons? A Ferrari? Box seats? Miss January? What?"

All good ideas, but this was his one wish. He had to make it count.

Matt pushed away from the table and began pacing. Money would be nice, but how much? Too much caused its own set of problems, and too little, well, it'd still be more than he had now.

But it'd also be charity.

He didn't do charity. Not anymore. A man had his pride.

But what about having her make his business thrive? Matt snorted, doubting that even Eden's magic could turn the construction business around any time soon. Besides, if she zapped it or twitched it or however she did it, it wouldn't be *his* doing. It'd be hers. What was the difference in taking a handout from her or one from Hayden? From anyone?

Bile churned in his gut. He'd been down that road before. It would be so easy to take Eden up on her offer, just as it would Hayden. Have them make all his troubles disappear. But there was a reason he hadn't done it before— which was the same reason he wouldn't do it now.

Matt shoved his hands into his pockets. "Eden, thank you for the offer, but I'm going to pass."

"Pass?" Her hands fell to her sides as her mouth fell open. "*Pass?* No one passes. Ever. This is a gimme, Matt. A gift. No strings. Whatever you want. The sky's the limit—although I could get you to the moon if you want."

Now there was a thought.

No. *He* took care of himself. *He* provided for himself.

His family hadn't lived extravagantly while growing up, and before Dad's illness they'd had enough to live on. But after, watching what the illness had done to Dad's independence and spirit, watching Mom accept handouts and charity and working too many hours to make ends meet, the ravages had gone deep, to both their bank account and their psyches. Matt had learned too young and too quickly the merits of making his own way in this world. Of depending on himself. He wasn't about to stop now.

"Really, Eden, I'm fine. I have everything I need. I helped you because you needed it, not because you could grant me a wish."

It was right then that Eden fell a little bit in love with Matt.

But she couldn't. Falling in love was genie suicide— and she didn't have far to look for proof. Her mother had fallen in love with her father, a Roman soldier, and once she did, there went her mom's magic. There went immortality. Eden didn't want to escape The Service only to die.

And besides, you didn't just fall in love with someone. Not like that. Love grew. It had to be fostered and tended to. Sacrificed for. Something that could be so monumentally life-changing didn't just happen.

Lust, on the other hand, was a whole different animal and one she was fully willing to cop to when it came to Matt.

Thankfully, the phone rang somewhere in the house, derailing that kind of thought. Okay, maybe not derailing it, just pushing it to the back burner for a while.

"Thanks, Eden, but like I said, I'll pass. Now if you'll excuse me, I need to take that call in my office." Matt squeezed her shoulder as he passed.

She couldn't believe he'd turned down a wish. Turned. It. Down. No one ever turned it down; she hadn't lied when she'd said that. No one ever did. Most people had a pages-long list, even if it was only in their head, and they could usually come up with a good two dozen before even taking a breath. To pass this up…

It was a good thing she wasn't in Service to him or she'd be a laughing stock of the genie world. Not helping her master. It was unthinkable. It was unnatural.

It was… absolutely wonderful. The first unselfish mortal she'd ever met.

Eden pulled Matt's shirt down over her thighs and followed him through the living room and into his office. She was going to help him. Somehow. All she had to do was listen and observe and something would come to her.

As for falling in love with him, well, that thought was a momentary aberration. She wasn't here to fall in love. This was her shot at freedom. She couldn't give it up for a mortal, no matter how wonderful and sexy and sweet and unselfish he was. A prison sentence was a better choice than mortality any day. But if she played her metaphorical cards right, she could avoid both, and that's what she had to remember.

No matter how much her skin tingled or her heart fluttered around him.

She reached the office a few steps behind Matt, just in time to hear the answering machine pick up the call.

"*Mis*ter Ewing," a woman said with all the snoot possible. "This is Henrietta Baker. You were supposed to finish the pool house roof today. By my clock, today has precisely fourteen minutes of reasonable business hours left. I appreciate that you do beautiful work. However, the party is tomorrow night and if the roof is not completed, we will deduct the appropriate amount from your bill until it is finished. Good evening."

"Shit." Matt hit the delete key on the machine and pinched the bridge of his nose.

"Problem?" Eden leaned against the door frame.

"Work."

"Oh, that's right. You're in construction."

"Is there *anything* that cat didn't tell you?"

"Um, well…" She scuffed her slipper on the hardwood floor.

"Never mind." Matt grabbed a stack of papers from the desk top and started riffling through them. "That was a customer. Jerry was supposed to have finished her roof hours ago."

Eden rested her palm against his desk. "Who's Jerry?"

"A guy who works for me." He picked up another stack and fanned through those. "I'm trying not to lay him off because he and his wife are having a baby and need both the money and the insurance, but if he can't finish the job on time, I'm going to have to." He tossed the papers onto the desk, then touched one of the keys on his laptop, and the screen brightened. "Profit margins are so tight these days that if that client shorts me on the bill, it's going to hurt. Big time."

"I could finish the roof for you if you want."

Matt's hand hovered over the keyboard. He was tempted; she could see that in his eyes.

But then he shook his head. "Thanks, but no, Eden. The woman watches us like a hawk when we're there. I can see me trying to explain that one."

When he picked up the phone and started punching in numbers, Eden glanced at the computer screen. The word *slate* jumped out at her. Slate roof; that shouldn't be hard. At least, it wouldn't be if her magic was working properly.

Matt put the handset to his ear with one hand and switched documents on the laptop with the other. "I'll just head over first thing in the morning and take care of it," he said, mostly to himself. "If I get up an hour or two early I should be able to finish and get to the Henderson project in a reasonable amount of time. Well, after I pick up the supplies I went out for today."

If *she* finished the roof, he'd *definitely* be able to get to the Henderson project, whatever that was, on time. And since those supplies were derailed because of her, obviously, she owed him.

Eden wiggled her fingers. Wow, what freedom. To do what she wanted for whom she wanted. All by virtue of being free. If there was ever a time for magic, this was it.

"Jerry, it's Matt. Call me when you get this. It's about the Baker—"

Eden left the room while Matt finished the call. He didn't need to know what she was doing. It'd be another offer he'd turned down.

And another reason to fall a little more in love with—

Oh no she wasn't. She was just surprised because no one had ever turned her down before. It was surprise, that's all. Not love. It couldn't be love. She wouldn't *let* it be.

Checking to make sure he couldn't see her, Eden rotated her wrists. Well, one. The unbandaged one.

Glancing back to see him still occupied, she unwrapped the other wrist. She flexed her fingers, the pain now barely a twinge. She rotated it once. Not too bad.

She rotated it again, this time snapping her fingers, and closed her eyes for an extra push of magic.

Her breath caught. This *had* to work.

I wish Mrs. Baker's roof to be finished just as she wants. Slate and all.

Eden opened her eyes. She wasn't certain, but she thought she felt the tingle of magic.

Or that tingle could be Humphrey's claws as he landed on her shoulder. *Zift!* How'd he get free? And what was she going to do with him?

She looked around and found the sock, scorched and full of holes. She whispered a very hoarse and very angry, "Obo!" but the cat either didn't hear her or chose not to. Either way, it wasn't helping her find a hiding spot for Humphrey.

"I left Jerry a message." Matt entered the living room with one hand massaging the back of his neck. "He's not answering his phone and—*what* is that?"

Eden grimaced. "Um, well, Matt, you know how I said genies exist—"

"It looks like a lizard. With wings." Matt took a step closer.

"It is."

"Lizards don't have wings, Eden." He took another step.

"Ah, true. But some, well, a particular kind—"

"What kind, Eden?" He was only inches away from her shoulder.

And from Humphrey.

Who let out his first puff of smoke.

The antagonistic action would mean far more when the dragon was full grown, but for now, it meant that those five days she thought she had with Humphrey had suddenly been cut in half. If she was lucky.

"What kind of lizard has wings and blows smoke, Eden?" Matt was staring intently at Humphrey.

The dragonlet swished his tail, the shield-shaped pointed end scraping across her throat. If he were to do that three days from now, she might not be around to finish this discussion.

"It's… he's… Humphrey's a… a dragon."

Matt just nodded. "A dragon."

"Well, technically, he's a dragonlet. When he hits maturity, he'll be a dragon."

"So, in addition to genies and talking cats and magic, dragons exist, too?"

She nodded.

Matt was silent for a second—or ten—then hunkered down to get a closer look. "And what are you doing with a dragon, Eden?"

Humphrey lunged at Matt who, luckily, had quick reflexes. Humphrey's bite wouldn't do much damage, but it would leave a mark. Several, in fact. All from his pointy, needle-sharp teeth.

"I… well, I guess you could call me his foster mom."

"Foster mom? What, do knights in shining armor exist, too, slaying enough adult dragons to create a foster care system?"

She wasn't going to let the sarcasm get to her. "He's an orphan, Matt, and I'm helping form his socialization patterns until he gets a little older." Which was sooner rather than later, but best not to ask too much of Matt yet. "Trust me, he's not supposed to be out of my bottle."

Matt rubbed a hand over his chin. "And you are?"

Good point. "Look, Matt, I have to find it. Once I do that, I'll be out of your hair and your life for good. And I'll take Humphrey with me."

She didn't know if he was in shock or denial, but Matt stared at Humphrey for a second or two longer, then shook his head and headed toward the chair where he'd dropped his jacket. "Sure, why *not* dragons? Mythology is alive and well and living in Seattle. What's next? Griffins? Leprechauns? Fairies?"

"Well, actually—"

"Don't tell me. Just please do not tell me. I think I've reached my quota of odd. For like, the next ten years." He kneaded the back of his neck. "Speaking of odd, I found this under you on the sidewalk. I'm assuming it's yours?" He pulled something from the jacket pocket and held it out to her.

Humphrey lunged again, his back claws digging into her shoulder. "Ow, Humphrey." She tapped the dragonlet on the tip of his elongated nose. "Thank you for protecting me, but Matt won't hurt me." Not physically, anyway.

She took the item. Oh, yes, it was definitely hers. And

a glaring reminder to get her mind off Matt and onto her pursuit of freedom. "This is the stopper to my bottle."

"Your bottle is yellow?"

"You were expecting pink?" She snorted. "That show didn't get everything right. Every genie has his or her own bottle or lantern color. Mine happens to be yellow." She wrapped her fingers around the crystal, remembering how pleased she'd been to get the new stopper—even if it'd come from Faruq. The previous one had gotten chipped and she'd nicked herself more times than she could count tumbling against it when someone moved her bottle. "You didn't happen to see the rest of the bottle when you found this, did you?"

"No. Sorry. I was more concerned with the unconscious woman on my lap."

What a waste of an opportunity. So true. And if she didn't have a conscience, it wouldn't be an issue. "Then I'll have to start searching back at the store."

"Why? Why not just grab a plane or bus and get lost somewhere? I thought the plan was for this Faruq guy *not* to find you. If you hang around and he shows up, chances are pretty good he'll find you."

She stroked Humphrey's ridged back and moved him to the other shoulder—away from Matt. Humphrey gave one last parting puff of smoke and a shake of his wings before settling himself in the crook of her neck and curling his tail as far around the back of her neck as it'd go. It was a cute, bonding move now, but in a few days? Death grip.

"Because, Matt, the bottle, along with that stopper and my bracelets, are all part of my being in The Service, and I'm not comfortable with any one of them floating around where they could fall into the wrong hands."

Especially Faruq's. But anyone, anywhere, could call her back to The Service if they found her bottle.

"I don't understand. We got the bracelets off."

Eden frowned. "The bracelets have been tracking my whereabouts, and you can rest assured Faruq's been paying attention via the crystal in his office—his ultimate control. But the bottle is what calls me to a master and the stopper locks me in place. Any of them makes me a genie. All of them make me compliant."

All of them made her a slave.

Matt tossed her the jacket. Humphrey uttered the beginnings of his first growl when she jerked to catch it. "Okay, then let's go find that bottle."

"Matt, thanks, but you don't need to. I've taken up enough of your time. You've done more than necessary." More than he'd ever realize.

"Do you think I want to let that trip across the kitchen on my ass go to waste? That's what'll happen if this guy finds your bottle. I've got a vested interest in making sure he doesn't. So I'll find something to put your dragon in, and then we'll get going."

She watched Matt head back through the kitchen. He was getting something to protect her pet. Her *mythical* pet as far as he'd been concerned before today. And he was doing that so he could help her recover the bottle to keep her freedom—not to enslave her.

Okay, so maybe she was falling headlong into *like*.

At least that wasn't as deadly as falling in love.

Obo was out of the house the moment he ran from the kitchen and shoved the open end of Humphrey's "cage" into Matt's shoe. The lizard couldn't find his way out of a paper bag—hence the sock being the perfect substitution. With the opening in the toe of the shoe, the dragon would never be able to get free. At least, for as long as it took Obo to retrieve what he needed. No way was he subverting years of preparation to baby-sit a lizard.

With all the Glimmer Eden was flinging around, Faruq would have no problem tracking her down, and the vizier wasn't what you'd call a fan of his. That worried Obo. A lot. About as much as forgetting his past worried him.

He slipped his head and one paw through the string on the leather bag he'd dug up from its hiding spot and slung it onto his back. He'd been carrying this clue to his lost years—and the key to the celestial paradise he was aiming for—for centuries and wasn't about to let a lovesick vizier with a god complex get hold of it. He knew Faruq. If that ladder-climbing control freak had any idea that Cleopatra's amulet was close by, Obo would be kissing it goodbye—something he had no intention of doing before returning it to Bastet for his Afterlife.

Chapter 8

"EDEN, GET THAT THING OFF MY SHOULDER."

"Shh, Matt. He's not a thing, he's a dragon. And he likes you."

"Great. A dragon likes me." Matt's truck swerved around the corner when Humphrey nipped his ear. "Eden, if you don't do something with him, we'll either have an accident or I'll end up looking like Van Gogh."

"But he doesn't like being cooped up in that cage." A sentiment she could heartily sympathize with.

She and Matt had scoured the area around the antiques shop for her bottle, coming up empty-handed except for the birdcage that had shared her display window. A bit mangled from where it'd fallen out of the garbage truck, it was better than the cardboard box Matt had brought with him. Humphrey had set that on fire twice before they'd found the cage. Then the poor baby had cried piteously until they'd gotten back in the truck and she'd let him out.

Humphrey climbed up Matt's ear and made a nest in his hair, rumble-purring softly. As long as the dragon didn't try to make fire again, Matt would be okay.

"Eden."

"Please, Matt. We're almost home. He'll be fine a bit longer."

"I'm going to have claw marks on my scalp. And blisters on my hands. I need my hands, Eden."

"But they'll heal and won't that be a small price to pay for dragon love? Do you know how rare that is?"

Matt glanced at her. "Actually, yeah, I do. About as rare as a donkey in my garage, pink stop signs, and a camel walking down the streets of Seattle."

The words, though true, stung. Eden choked back a sob. She felt like an idiot for it. She, head of her class at the Academy, couldn't manage her magic.

She tried again, this time wishing for something normal. A blue bird on that white picket fence across the street should be easy enough.

Sadly, though, what she got was a blue picket fence. With a white bird sitting on it.

A dodo bird.

Oh great.

"*What* is that?" Matt's truck swerved the other way, and Humphrey hiccupped a smoke ring.

"You don't want to know." She tried magicking the bird away.

It just blinked its beady little eyes at her with that goofy expression dodos had.

"Are you sure it's a good idea to keep doing magic, Eden? I thought you were worried about glitter."

"Glimmer, and there's nothing I *can* do about it, Matt. Except try to throw Faruq off the scent, as it were. If I leave enough of it lying around, he'll hopefully end up going in circles. At least it'll slow him down."

"If you say so." Matt turned another corner and pulled into his driveway. "Here we are. Home at last."

Home. The word had so much meaning, Eden wasn't sure she could speak. She'd had a home once. A real one. Before The Service. With parents and friends and

her own room. A window she could open any time she
wanted and smell the fresh air. They'd lived near the
sea where the roar of the surf and the tangy taste of
salt-laden breezes started each day. But then, in one fell
swoop, it was all gone.

She wanted it back. Wanted a home. People who
loved her, the freedom to walk along the beach or lounge
around reading a book or cook a meal. Where there were
no evil viziers waiting to take her into custody, no prison
sentences, no pink signs, and—she choked back another
sob—no displaced dodos.

"You okay?" Matt put his hand on her arm, and Eden
cleared her throat.

"Yes." A quick swipe with her right hand across her
eyes hid the lie.

Matt squeezed gently. "Let's head in. Things are
bound to look up—ow!"

Eden turned quickly to see Humphrey raking his
claws through Matt's hair like a cat scratching a post.

"Get this flying torch off me, Eden. The pony ride
is over."

She reached for Humphrey, but the dragonlet snapped
at her, and this time there was a tiny flame with his
smoke. "Uh, maybe you'd better let him ride on you until
we get inside, Matt. He doesn't seem to want to move."

"And we don't argue with dragons, right?" Matt
shook his head. "At least tell me he's house-trained."

"Um, yeah. Sure."

Eden followed Matt inside, trying to leave her down-
in-the-dumps mood at the door. Which reminded her—

"Are you *sure* the dump isn't open now?" She
hopped over the arm of the leather sofa and plopped

onto the cushions, crossing her feet on the coffee table—the feet covered in Matt's ex-girlfriend's slippers. Pitiful, really. No bottle, no magic, no clothes, no *cat*... Nothing. Aside from a pair of mangled bracelets, the bottle stopper, and the culturally inappropriate—and ruined—genie costume, she didn't have a single thing to her name. And with Humphrey hanging on Matt, not even her dragon, apparently.

So much for losing the mood; this was starting to sound an awful lot like a pity party. And she didn't do pity parties. Never had. She wouldn't give anyone the satisfaction. Especially Faruq.

"Why don't you just zap your bottle here? Then we wouldn't have to go mucking through the mire."

"If only it were that easy, but I can't. It doesn't listen to me."

"An inanimate object listens?" Matt shook his head as he hung up their coats in the front closet. "I guess I shouldn't be surprised by that since cats talk and dragons exist, but do you really want to try zapping us inside the dump? There's no telling where we'd end up."

"Thanks." Just what she needed; a reminder of her inadequacies.

"I'm only being realistic, which, with the way my day's been going, is a pretty amazing feat."

She couldn't help but smile at that. Matt was doing surprisingly well having his world turned upside down.

He sat on the coffee table and squeezed her calf. "So, we'll go digging through trash for your bottle tomorrow, okay? Now how do I get Humphrey off me?"

Humphrey was sprawled through Matt's hair and

snoring contentedly, little smoke rings puffing above his head like a sleepy coal engine easing into a train yard.

She leaned forward and managed to unlace each tiny claw from the grip Humphrey had on the strands, then settled him on the throw pillow beside her.

Humphrey burrowed in and started snoring louder. Eden hoped his smoke rings didn't ignite the fabric.

"So what time does the dump open?" she asked.

"I think six. We can grab something to eat along the way and—oh, shit."

"I don't need to eat if it's that big a deal."

"No. Not breakfast. Dinner. Tonight. I was supposed to go to my mom's house." He jumped up, looked at the clock, then pulled out his cell phone.

Eden walked over to the fireplace, trying not to listen in to his conversation, but it'd been so long since she'd spoken to her own mother—two thousand and twenty years to be exact. And, as usual, that stabbing pain that happened whenever she thought about her parents assailed her. She'd been fifteen when they'd died in the house fire.

She picked the stopper off the mantel, then sat on the hearth, rolling the crystal between her palms. It wasn't supposed to have been that way. Genies were either mortals Chosen to Serve, or born to genies whose magic allowed them to live forever. Unless, like her mother, they fell in love with a mortal and gave up their powers. Then they were able to die at the ridiculously young age of forty.

And *then*, in one of life's crappy ironies, Calliope and Antonio's daughter had been born with magical abilities that she'd had to keep hidden so she wouldn't be drafted into The Service. Another crappy irony was that she'd been staying with a friend the night of the fire.

Eden shook her head and crossed her legs beneath her. She'd been lucky, everyone said, when the High Master had taken her in. It'd been no secret that he'd loved her mother, and taking Eden in prevented her from becoming a rogue genie—a fate almost worse than death. He'd cared for her as if she were his own daughter and she loved him for that. For trying to give her some of what she'd lost.

But in the end, she'd had to fulfill her destiny as a genie. Life with her parents had protected her from The Service, but without them, she'd had no choice.

It was that lack of options that had spurred her when she'd seen what her last master was planning to do with his children. Sick. Just sick. And it made her realize that those kids had to have an option. She couldn't leave them at his mercy. Not if she wanted to be able to live with herself.

The thing was, she'd had as few options as the kids when it came to preventing what had been about to happen because genies couldn't harm their masters. She'd only wanted to threaten him, but things went awry, and suddenly, her life was on the line. But she'd gotten lucky—if you called three thousand years' imprisonment lucky—faced the consequences, and here she was.

Eden dropped the stopper onto the logs piled beside her. Her master's death had been an accident and, having lived the first fifteen years of her life out of The Service, she knew what freedom felt like. She wasn't going back.

So she would have to give up using her magic to

avoid detection—big deal. She hadn't used it when her parents had been alive. Magic wasn't all it was cracked up to be when performed under duress. Freedom was a powerful motivator. Wars had been fought over it, and, heavens knew, this was her own personal war. With Faruq as the enemy. She'd willingly give up her magic and risk rogue status to be free now. Nothing was more important to her than that.

Matt hung up the phone. "So, do genies eat like the rest of us?"

"No, actually, we shovel food into our ears with our feet. What kind of question is that?"

"Hey, I'm doing pretty good here for a guy who's been adopted by a dragon and had his idea of reality shifted a few degrees to the left. It's an honest question."

True. It wasn't his fault she had a chip on her shoulder about genie-hood. "Sorry. Yes, I eat the same way and same food that you do. Why?" She set her feet on the floor and started to stand.

"Good. Because my mother's invited you to dinner."

Only to have her legs give out. She fell back onto the hearth. "She *what*?" His mother. *A* mother. *Any* mother.

"I mentioned I was late because I was helping a friend and she told me to bring you along. I can always come up with an excuse if you're not up for it—"

"Oh no. I'm there. I mean, I'd love to go. Thank you. But what about my magic? What if something happens?"

"Don't wish for anything and we should be okay. Otherwise, we're going to have to make a quick exit."

Eden mulled that over. She'd wished him into wanting her, she'd wished the bracelets were off, she'd even wished for the donkey. Okay, so no wishing.

"All right, but I can't meet your mother looking like this." Maybe she'd do one last wish—for some clothes.

Matt swiped a hand over his face. "I, uh, think I have a few things of Cara's left over."

"Cara?"

"An old... friend. She was staying here for a while."

Eden might not have been out and about in the world, but she hadn't been completely out of touch. *Old friend* had several connotations, and with the way Matt wasn't meeting her eyes, she had a feeling she knew which one Cara fell under.

But it was the "old" part that registered. As in "previous." As long as Cara was "old," Eden could wear her clothes for the night.

"Okay, Matt. Point me to them and we'll be on our way."

"What about Humphrey? Do we just leave him here with Francis and Obo? Where is that cat anyway?"

She'd like to know the answer to that, too. He was supposed to be watching Humphrey, though since the dragonlet had developed his fire, she couldn't say she blamed Obo. Singed fur was not fun, and that meant leaving Humphrey in the garage with Francis was out.

The only other option would be to send him back to the nursery where he stayed when not in her bottle, and with the way her magic was acting up, who knew where in the spectrasphere she'd accidentally zap him to? And, heavens knew, she certainly wasn't about to try to conjure up a nursery full of dragonlets here. Talk about chaos.

"I'll come up with something." One more wish coming up—hopefully.

"Okay. Then let's get a move on. I don't want to

be any later than we already are. God knows, Hayden won't be."

"Hayden?"

"My brother." He turned away and muttered, "The perfect one."

Perfect? Eden eyed Matt. She might have become preoccupied with recovering her magic and her bottle over the past few hours or so, but she hadn't forgotten how perfect Matt had felt when he'd held her nor how perfectly he'd kissed her. If he considered his brother perfect, Eden had to meet the guy, because as far as her love-starved libido was concerned, Matt was pretty perfect himself.

Meeting Matt's idea of Adonis ought to be interesting.

Chapter 9

FARUQ WAITED UNTIL THE DOOR TO THE PUBLIC rest room closed before leaving the stall he'd materialized into. Talk about humiliating. He hated this mode of transport, but with the savvy populations of today's world, it was the only way he could assure he'd appear in an empty place. The hazard being, of course, the sights he'd inadvertently come across when checking out the stalls for a clear arrival.

But it couldn't be helped. Eden was somewhere in the vicinity and he had to find her quickly. He had his centennial meeting with the High Master at the end of the month. The last thing he needed to report was an MIA genie. Especially her.

Faruq checked his reflection. The business suit looked appropriate for this locale; he'd even had his hair styled properly after removing his turban. His goatee had needed some minor trimming to remove the Old World feel, but he looked the part, complete with black leather briefcase and a beige trench coat.

He opened the briefcase and withdrew all the necessities of American life: cash, an enchanted credit card, a driver's license, a cell phone, and the key to a local condo he'd purchased on eBay. The Internet was such a marvelous invention, the High Master must surely have had a hand in its creation, but whenever Faruq asked him, the High Master simply smiled.

The master djinni never shared the secrets of his power, which annoyed Faruq no end. But if Eden were on his side, if she belonged to him, the High Master would relent. He'd have to because Faruq would be his natural successor. Just as he'd planned.

Faruq tucked the phone and cash in the coat pocket, thankful, at least, that the Internet was available for djinn use. It made the accumulation of time-appropriate items so easy and authentic. He still cringed when he remembered the phoenix feather he'd produced for the signing of the Declaration of Independence. Damn that John Hancock for calling him on it.

Faruq navigated the revolving door of the office-building lobby and stepped into the cold dusk with its cloying dampness of promised rain. He already hated this place. Give him the dry breezes off the desert, the arid scent of sand, and the cool, warm fragrance of his inner courtyard oasis. Lush palms, fruit trees heavy with ripe dates, figs, and oranges, the myriad scents of freesia, jasmine, hyacinth, and bougainvillea blossoms.

He hailed a cab, its noxious black smoke causing him to cough. Even camel exhaust smelled better than this stench.

He smiled at his countryman who was driving and addressed him in their shared language. A small slice of home, but this place, this era, he could not abide.

It was time to bring Eden back to him. Where she belonged.

If only the High Master had permitted him to keep her bottle in his office, but no. She was to travel through the world on the whim of Fate as other genies did, so that when she completed her sentence, she would rejoin The Service with the first mortal to open her bottle.

One more problem he would have to deal with. A pittance compared to the one he was facing at the moment.

The cab passed this hemisphere's idea of a park with its manicured lawns and carefully culled trees, sterile benches placed haphazardly. Faruq shook his head. *Heathens.*

"You are certain you wish me to just drive through the city, sir?" The driver glanced in the mirror at him. The mirror. As if Faruq were just *any*body. If this peasant only knew who he was, the dog would be down on his knees, plastering his face to the asphalt in the most humble of bows. "The ride could become expensive."

"I'll decide what constitutes expensive. All you need do is drive. Carry on." Faruq dismissed the driver's concern with a nonchalant wave of his hand, which served the added purpose of flashing his Rolex, thereby assuring the man he could pay.

Tall buildings of brick, stone, glass, and concrete reflected the garish lighting, hiding the beauty of the approaching night. He could only imagine what it looked like in the dreary, rain-laden daylight and tried to picture Eden in this locale.

She would not last here. She needed light. Warmth. Colors. To see the sky in all its moods. She would be stifled here.

Faruq patted the briefcase on his lap. The new bracelets should remind her of her heritage. Their power would ensure she returned to it.

If he could only find her.

He leaned closer to the window and lowered it. The dank air had one benefit. The scent of Glimmer would linger longer than on a dry breeze. Now if only she would use her magic.

Ah, but he'd forgotten. Eden was clever. As her mother, Calliope, had been. With the blood of her mortal father, a Roman soldier who'd learned the art of war at the feet of a master, Eden would be a formidable opponent. She'd always hated The Service, unlike other genies who were content to serve mortals. She'd probably sung Fate's praises when she sat next to Khaled at trial. The fool must've told her how to remove the bracelets.

If only he'd anticipated that. One more mishap when it came to Eden. One more veil over his eyes when it came to her.

No more.

He would relish bringing her back into The Service again—only this time, it would be in Service to him.

She wouldn't come willingly. Eden had never been one to surrender. It was one of her greater attributes, and Faruq's blood quickened at the thought of taming her. Eden's spirit had always aroused him.

He'd admired it, and her, for centuries, but it was that face, so foreign with her blue eyes, and that body, designed, it seemed, solely for him, that had been the main attraction. Oh, her wit had always amused him, as it had all her masters, and her will, strong and unreserved, was sheer perfection. None of which he would ever allow her to know. She needed no encouragement to use it to her advantage.

She thought it was her connection to the High Master that attracted him and he allowed her to think so. But he didn't need her for access to the High Master; he was the vizier and no other genie outranked him for power or prestige. He'd ensured it. Eden would find no better match, mortal or djinn.

He needed to remind her of that fact.

The traffic, so noisy and foul, contributed its own odor to the air. Faruq sat back and closed his eyes, trying to sort out the various scents to find the one he was looking for. This would be so much easier in the capital city of Al-Jannah where genie Glimmer would visibly decorate the monuments and buildings, the plant life, and even its inhabitants, giving the city extra beauty— and pinpointing anyone who used unauthorized magic.

The cab rounded a corner, the driver barely missing a pack of young mortals. As much as Faruq would love to "suggest" the man take them down, it would anger the High Master for the bad karma and bring him to the attention of the mortal authorities. He did hate dealing with their silly laws.

Faruq settled back into the seat and closed his eyes again, inhaling the vile and officious air in this cold, dreary town teeming with mortals who would—

There! Was that the slightest trace of Glimmer?

Faruq leaned toward the driver. "Stop here."

"Sir?"

"I said, 'Stop here.'" Faruq slipped the modern currency through the slot in the divider between them, then opened the door when the man finally halted the vehicle. "I shall require your services further. There is enough there for you to attend me for several hours. Do not leave."

"But, sir, permit me to take you to the curb—"

"Do not question me, *walad*. You will remain here at my convenience." Faruq exited the vehicle—and was almost run down by another.

He raised his hand to send a bolt of pure destructive energy into the driver of the car, then remembered where he was. While not bound by the rules of those in The Service—he was above the rules, actually—he couldn't do magic here. Not when so many were watching. *Philistines*.

He turned to the driver. "Very well. Wait over there for my return." He turned up his coat collar and melted into the crowd, following that one tiny whiff that could lead him to Eden.

Obo ducked behind a trash can on the street across from a taxi cab that had discharged the last person in the world—or beyond—he wanted to see. Bulls' balls, Faruq had gotten here fast.

Dropping the leather bag beneath his front paws, Obo poked one set of whiskers out, twitching them, trying to catch Faruq's foul scent. It'd been years—close to a thousand, actually—since he'd gotten a glimpse of the Djinn's Gift to Djinn, as they'd all called Faruq behind his back. The vizier thought the obeisance given him was out of respect. Ha. The guy was delusional. Everyone knew what a trigger temper he had. No one wanted to be on the receiving end of that lightning bolt.

Obo risked peering out with one eye, just in time to see Faruq disappear through the door of a shop. *Murphy's Antiques*.

Son-of-a-bichon, the vizier was hot on her tail. It wouldn't take him long to trace her to Matt's, then who knew what would happen. Obo was going to have to warn them. And somehow he just knew this whole mess was going to wind up costing him the amulet.

He swept the bag beneath his belly as he sat there, contemplating how to minimize any losses with this latest development. He'd planned his End-of-Life for millennia and the amulet played a big part in that, so losing it wasn't high on his list of priorities.

A light flicked off inside the store and the flap of Faruq's coat reappeared in the doorway. Contemplating time was over.

And then Gigi or Fifi or PeePee—some silly little Paris Hilton–named, overstylized inkblot of a poodle— spotted him and started yapping. Fabulous. Now he had no choice. It was now or, well, now.

Obo picked the strings up in his mouth and raced across the street, wending through the pedestrians and the idiots on bikes, making it to the alley next to Coffman's Music in record time. He peeked back around the corner to make sure he hadn't been seen—

Only to find Faruq staring right at him.

Chapter 10

MATT THOUGHT HIS BROTHER WAS PERFECT? EDEN didn't see it.

Oh, Hayden was good-looking enough—they'd definitely hit the gene pool jackpot—but perfect? Big, blond, and handsome, but Eden wouldn't say he was anywhere near as perfect as his tall, dark, and sexy brother.

Eden smoothed a hand down her beige pants, adjusted the hem of Cara's sweater, and repositioned the handbag Matt had found at the back of his closet onto her shoulder while Matt's mother swept her son into her arms.

"Matt! Welcome home, honey." Then she reached for Eden's hand, smiling. "And welcome, Matt's friend. I'm Vicki Rogers. My, what a lovely pin."

Eden ran her fingers quickly over the "brooch" on her neckline, hoping Humphrey stayed put. Wishing Humphrey would be as good as gold when all else had failed, she'd been utterly desperate, panic choking her as they'd pulled in front of his parents' home. Apparently, desperation was the key. How that boded for this evening, they'd have to see. "Thank you, Mrs. Rogers. And for the invitation. I'm Eden."

"Please, call me Vicki. Mrs. Rogers is too formal for a friend of Matt's." She hooked her arm with Eden's and drew her around the foyer table with its pretty vase of red roses into the formal living room.

White wainscoting circled the bottom half of the walls, colonial-blue textured wallpaper on the upper half. Floral chintz covered the furniture, with heavy federal-style pieces gracing the perimeter. A fire warmed the brick hearth and two of the best-looking men—other than Matt—Eden had ever seen stood near it. One was the good-looking-but-not-quite-perfect brother who rose from his seat beside a petite blonde, and the other had to be Matt's stepfather. The men smiled and shook Matt's hand, though Matt responded with a reluctance Eden didn't understand.

Then the blond god turned his smile on Eden and she got the "perfect" reference. The guy could power a small nation with that wattage. But still, he didn't light her lantern the way Matt did.

"Hi. I'm Hayden, Matt's brother."

"This is Eden," Matt said, his arm snaking around her waist. Any closer and she'd be inside him—though she'd rather he be inside her.

Her knees turned to jelly with that utterly inappropriate thought. Good thing she hadn't wished it; talk about bad first impressions.

Eden worked a smile past suddenly dry lips to shake Hayden's hand. "Nice to meet you."

The blonde next to Hayden stood. "I'm Amanda, Hayden's wife."

"And I'm Paul. The dad." Mr. Rogers gestured to the wet bar in the corner. "Can I get you something to drink? Wine? Iced tea? A soft drink?"

Wine was out. Genies didn't drink alcohol. For good reason. It screwed with their chemistry and hyped up their magic. With the way her magic was going, that was the last thing she needed. And tea, she'd had her share of teas. Strong in the Far East, milky in England, sweet in Morocco, and julep-y during her stint in the South. But soda... She had yet to try the carbonated drink since Faruq considered it barbarian and had refused her repeated requests for it.

"Soda, please. Cola, if you've got it." Those television ads where people had joined hands, singing about "the real thing," had looked like a lot of fun. And to her lonely self, ideal.

"One cola coming up. Matt? What can I get for you?"

"Beer's good. Thanks."

"So, Matt," Paul said after drinks and appetizers had been served and everyone took a seat, "I heard Henrietta Baker's pool house is going to be a masterpiece."

Eden choked on the fizz in her drink while Matt, oblivious to what she'd done to the roof—or rather, *hoped* she'd done—popped a crab puff into his mouth. "That's the plan."

One minute; that's all she'd wanted to enjoy the new beverage and pretend that this was a normal conversation about a normal construction project with normal people and there wasn't a baby dragon masquerading as jewelry on her sweater who could start breathing fire any second, or that a donkey or camel or dodo bird could show up uninvited.

Eden snorted at the image of Matt explaining those. Then the soda bubbles went down the wrong pipe and she choked again. Which led to hiccups. Drat. She hated hiccups. She always got them around violets. And now, apparently, carbonated beverages.

She hiccupped again—

And a bud vase of violets *poofed* onto the table between her and Matt's knees.

———

That damned Obo! Faruq blasted the tree the filthy animal had run behind—and hopefully into—but when the smoke cleared no singed cat fur or charred furry body could be found. Obo had gotten away again.

Faruq had thought he'd seen the last of that *ibn el-kalb* the night he'd sent the asp to Cleopatra in the basket of figs. She'd thought the figs were a treat for their rendezvous. Ha. Pride goeth before the fall—and Cleo had fallen hard. He'd outsmarted one of the most cunning women of all time.

That made Faruq smile, if only for a second or two. She'd actually thought he'd help her after she'd used him? That still amazed him to this day. He'd given the Egyptian queen an amulet and one of his most prized djinni, Sarmad, so she could ensnare Caesar. It'd worked, but then she'd set her sights on Marc Antony. That pretender hadn't been part of the original plan to set her on the throne of the Roman Empire—with Faruq, himself, as master manipulator. Cleopatra had been delusional to think he'd choose her over the entire Roman Legion after that betrayal.

And Obo! Mortal then and the queen's boy toy, the little *walad* had recognized Faruq's fury and threatened to tell Cleo all he *thought* he knew unless Faruq gave him a djinni, too.

Luckily, Obo's greed had been his downfall. A jealous Antony—fueled by several "dreams" from Faruq—took care of the blackmailer by using Sarmad. Wishing

Obo into feline form with severe memory loss and presenting him to Cleopatra as a pet proved how brilliant Antony was—until he'd then killed Sarmad.

A mortal did not kill a djinni and live to tell the tale.

Knowing Cleopatra would have her prized pet with her as she awaited him that night to plan how to recoup the losses she and Antony had suffered at the battle of Actium, Faruq had seen a way to make them all pay.

Killing two problems with one serpent—it'd been the perfect solution. And the added bonus of Antony's suicide made it that much more perfect. No one would question a suicide pact.

Only… the cat hadn't stayed dead.

And Faruq hadn't known until just now.

He sent another jolt through the felled tree. First Eden, now Obo. Faruq didn't know which was worse. If the High Master found out—

No, he would not think like that. He'd held his position for three millennia; it would remain his for at least that many more. His name would be remembered forever, his brilliance extolled, his power feared. And Eden would be his.

Something scurried over by the tree line. Aha! The cat wasn't as fresh as he'd been two thousand years ago, whereas Faruq's magic was only stronger, his determination fiercer.

Faruq kicked at the dead limb snagging the hem of his coat. Greedy in human form and again in feline, Obo was not going to get the chance to ruin this for him.

Chapter 11

ONE SECOND MATT WAS NICE AND RELAXED, AND THE next, there were flowers beside his knee—flowers that hadn't been there when they'd sat down.

And Eden had a hand over her mouth as if she was going to be sick.

Matt could relate.

He leaned forward, sliding his beer in front of the tiny vase. Hopefully, no one noticed—

"Matthew Lawrence Ewing!" said his mother. "You did *not* have to bring me flowers. But thank you. They're lovely."

There went that wish.

Wish. Oh, hell. Eden was wishing again.

"Knock it off," he whispered to her before smiling at his mother and handing her the violets. "It's nothing, Mom. Eden thought you should have them."

Eden hiccupped and pinched his thigh.

Matt looked around for another donkey—just as his beer bottle toppled off the edge of the table.

Luckily, he caught it before it could do any damage. And, just as luckily, no one caught on that *he* hadn't knocked it off at all.

It was the hiccups. That's how she was doing her magic.

"I'll get you a glass of water, Eden," Amanda said, standing. "It usually helps get rid of hiccups."

Eden nodded but didn't answer. She didn't have

to—Matt had already seen a big glass vase—filled to the brim with water—pop into the foyer next to the one that was already there, and the previous roses were now violets.

Twins. Great.

"You know how Henrietta likes to talk, Matt." As if nothing out of the ordinary was happening, Hayden continued the conversation in that conciliatory tone he always used, whether he was giving a compliment or tearing apart an argument. It was a gift his step-brother had. One among many. "The entire Chamber of Commerce is on the guest list, so it'll be good word-of-mouth for you. The jobs should come rolling in."

Jobs rolling in weren't the problem at the moment; it was whatever Eden conjured up doing so that was.

Maybe he shouldn't have brought her. But it wasn't in him to leave her at his house. She was so disappointed that they hadn't found her bottle, and, while he might have put a moratorium on his damsel-rescuing activities, he couldn't leave her to face Faruq alone if the bastard showed up—not that Matt had a clue what *he* could do against a genie, but still...

"I heard the press is going to be there, too." Hayden stood to hold Amanda's chair when she returned after giving Eden the water. "I could call Henrietta and make sure she tosses your name around if you like."

Matt gritted his teeth. Hayden meant well—Hayden *always* meant well—but did he have to be so perfectly non-condescendingly condescending? Matt couldn't fault the guy for what he said; Hayden was just as perfectly nice as he was perfectly everything else, and the offer was genuine and done from the goodness of his heart.

But lately, Hayden's perfection rubbed Matt the

wrong way. From the initial offer of financial backing to the continual reminder that a job with Rogers and Son was always available, Matt hadn't wanted any of it. Paul had even offered to add an "*s*" to the end of "Son," as if that were some big incentive. It was nice, true, but every offer they came up with was another round of charity.

They didn't see it that way, of course. They'd always included him; Paul never differentiated between biological son and stepson. But Paul and Hayden never got it, never got where he was coming from.

Even before Dad had gotten sick, the dream of Ewing Custom Millwork was all there'd been. All his father had talked about. Dad had dabbled in part-time commissions while working his dead-end desk job, always dreaming of the day he could chuck it all and be his own boss, beholden to no one, doing something he loved. Make his mark on the world, the same way the craftsmen who'd come before him had.

He'd tried to teach Matt everything he knew about craftsmanship and business, but, at nine, Matt hadn't been able to grasp much more than the fact that this was Dad's dream. And, sadly, once Dad got sick, he had never had the chance to make it come true.

But Matt *did* have that chance. He'd taken the dream and his hard-earned money from as many jobs as he could manage while in school and run with them. Over the years, he'd adapted to the changing times, focused more on straight construction jobs to pay the bills. But every so often a project came along that would allow him to indulge his passion for recreating the historic works of master craftsmen and leave a little of himself—and Dad—behind.

Those jobs were too few and far between to make Ewing Custom Millwork its own viable entity, but Matt had held out the hope of growing Ewing Construction enough to be able to build his own Riverwalk-type projects, ones where he could showcase his skill and Dad's dream—and have a tangible reminder of his father.

So no matter how tough it got, no matter how rotten the economy, no matter what he had to do to survive in this business, he would do it. Except take hand-outs. Like Dad, he'd be beholden to no one, Hayden *or* a genie.

Matt glanced at Eden as she set her water on the coffee table and then folded her hands in her lap. The soft blue sweater brought out the blue of her eyes and set off the almost blue-black hair that hung straight down her back. He remembered how it'd felt running through his fingers, how she'd felt in his arms.

He hadn't planned to go caveman when Hayden had introduced himself; it just sort of happened. Which was ridiculous. Hayden and Amanda were happily married—yet another notch on the perfection belt—and Hayden had never put the moves on any of Matt's girlfriends.

Not that Eden was his to begin with—though she could've been if he'd taken her up on her offer. He was an ass for turning her down; she'd gotten that right. But then *she'd* turned *him* down. Because of magic.

Magic. Jesus. Matt glanced at her sweater. The dragon was still a block of gold, thank God, and Mom bought the bud vase, but how was he supposed to explain that extra vase in the foyer?

"So, what's next on the agenda, Matt?" Paul asked. "The Henderson project for the Historical Society?"

Matt pulled his mind back to the conversation, though

he didn't know why he bothered. It was the same thing time and again. *How's business; come work with us.* How many times did he have to say no?

"That's right, Paul. I'll be matching the millwork in the new wing to the original part of the building." Sadly, the Henderson project wasn't on the same scale as the Riverwalk deal, the brass ring of local projects. A lot of guys had been vying for it, but the first round of eliminations announced today had killed a lot of dreams. His included.

"Then that woodwork you tinkered with is coming in handy after all." His mom smiled, tapping him on the knee. "Just like your father."

Tinkered. Matt plastered a smile on his face and bit back a sigh at the same time. He loved his mom, he did, but once Dad had gotten sick, dreams took a backseat to harsh reality. He recognized what she'd gone through during Dad's illness: taking care of her ill husband, worrying about the bills, going back to work, raising him. It would be hell on anyone. If something hadn't earned money to keep them solvent, it didn't happen.

He and Dad had had to sneak out to the workshop after school when she'd been at work, with Matt pushing Dad's heavy wheelchair through the narrow doorways, then back again before she came home, cleaning everything up in the process. It was a lot of work, but the time they'd spent together had been worth it.

Then, later—after—it'd been a means of reconnecting. Of keeping the dream alive. Keeping Dad alive.

"Matt did more than tinker," Hayden said, championing him as he always did—not that Matt wanted him to. "It takes a lot of skill and patience to reproduce old millwork. Down to the same tools they used back then, isn't that right, Matt?"

"That's right, Hayden." It was all so familiar. And so pointless. Nothing ever got resolved, no one ever changed opinions, and after the day he'd had, he'd just as soon forget the whole thing.

Guilt poked Matt in the gut. Hayden was only trying to be helpful. Brotherly. Matt got it; he just didn't want it. Not unless he could give it back on an equal level. And right now, that wasn't possible.

"So, Mom, what's for dinner? You know how I love your cooking," Matt said in a concerted—and, thankfully, successful—bid to change the subject.

Mom rattled off the menu while everyone headed toward the dining room—with Matt running interference in the foyer by standing in front of the twin vases. He held Eden back so everyone else could go in first.

"It's the hiccups," he whispered. "That's what's doing your magic."

"I got that," Eden whispered back. "But that's *now*. I wasn't hiccupping before."

"We'll worry about before later. Just don't hiccup anymore."

"I'm trying, Matt. But what's worrying me is that my Way seems to be changing. What happens if blinking does it next? Or speaking? Something I can't control?"

Matt swiped a hand over his face. "Just don't wish anything."

"I wasn't *wishing* for violets. I thought about them."

"Then don't think."

She arched one eyebrow and cocked her hip. "Oh really? Care to share how *that's* possible?"

"Matt?" his mother called. "Is everything all right?"

"Yes." No. "We'll be right in." He pointed over his shoulder. "Can you hiccup this vase out of existence first?"

"I'll give it a shot."

One hiccup, one non-existent vase.

And one long dinner to get through.

Chapter 12

"SO, EDEN," AMANDA BEGAN AFTER EVERYONE HAD their share of roast beef and mashed potatoes, and the state of Rogers and Son was discussed ad nauseam. "How did you and Matt meet?"

Forget Rogers and Son; that question was enough to make Matt choke. He'd counted on Hayden's perfect manners to not have to discuss what'd happened earlier, but he hadn't thought about Amanda's. Her manners were just as perfect, and that was a perfectly reasonable question.

Now if only there were a perfectly reasonable answer.

"I, um—" Eden reached for the gravy boat.

Matt handed it to her. "We met by the park. She was injured and I helped her out."

"Injured?" Mom set her silverware down on her plate. "Are you okay? What happened?"

Eden ladled a spoonful of gravy onto what little was left of her potatoes, keeping her eyes firmly on her plate. "It was nothing, really. I wasn't looking where I was going, tripped on something, and fell." She put the ladle back and smiled at him. "Matt helped me."

And, for a moment, because of that smile, Matt forgot that he didn't want to play knight-in-shining-armor anymore. He forgot about the shitty economy and the lost Riverwalk bid and the jobs he still had left to do.

Forgot, even, that this family dinner coziness teetered on one misplaced hiccup.

But he didn't forget the magic. Definitely didn't forget that.

It was right to be sitting here with Eden at his mother's table. Right to have his family around them, as if this were an ordinary day and Eden an ordinary woman.

But she wasn't. And magic aside, there were so many things about her that Matt wouldn't consider ordinary.

But the magic couldn't be put aside.

"I'm glad to hear you're okay." Mom placed her napkin on the table. "What do you do for a living, Eden?"

Eden choked again and proved Matt right. Not only couldn't the magic be put aside, it couldn't even be controlled: the black marble obelisk on the sideboard behind the candelabra was new—about two-seconds new.

"She's, ah, into antiques," he answered, earning another choke from Eden, who covered her mouth with her napkin.

Matt didn't take his eyes off the sideboard.

And, yep. There. Behind Amanda, next to the coffee service, a copper dish popped in from nowhere.

"Oh, there's a wonderful shop down off Main," his mom continued. "Have you seen it?"

Eden couldn't answer. Because the hiccups had come back.

"Drink." Matt handed her a glass of water when, this time, a pair of brass castanets showed up.

Thankfully, they popped in on top of the napkins beside the coffee pot and not in the copper dish. No one would have been able to miss them with that noise, but miss them they did. Hayden and Amanda were finishing their meal with all the gusto good manners and Mom's exceptional cooking warranted, and Paul was helping himself to another glass of wine. Mom, as usual, wouldn't notice a white elephant if it charged into the room; she never did when Matt brought a girl home.

Oh, hell. What if Eden read minds and hiccupped a white elephant next?

"Murphy's Antiques, I believe it's called," said his mom, standing. "Would anyone like coffee?"

"I'll get it." Matt jumped out of his chair as if an elephant *had* charged into the room. No need to send Mom to the sideboard. At least, not until Eden hiccupped those items into oblivion.

Which she did at that moment. Thank God they were on the same page.

"Murphy's is where Eden and I met, actually," Matt answered, breathing easier—for the moment. "Mr. Murphy was throwing things out. That must have been what she tripped on."

"Oh, that's right." Amanda slid her cup to the edge of the table for Matt to fill with the coffee. "I hear he's closing the store."

"He and Kitty are moving to Florida," said Hayden while Matt filled his cup. "He tried to get the Raffertys to go with them."

Paul declined coffee, and Matt moved on to Eden.

"I can't believe he got Kitty to agree to go." Mom shook her head. "And I definitely can't imagine the Raffertys leaving their grandchildren."

When Eden hiccupped and a soft *meow* sounded from her bag, Matt could imagine all sorts of things. And not necessarily having to do with the Rafferty's grandkids.

Especially when Humphrey's tail twitched.

Matt did a double take. Please, God, let him be imagining things.

He wasn't. The dragon was *moving*. Taking a slow but definitive walk up her neckline.

He looked to see if anyone else noticed. Paul was finishing up his meal and Hayden was helping Amanda select which sugar substitute to put in her coffee. A little too much perfectionism there, but Matt wasn't going to look a gift horse in the mouth.

A golden dragon, on the other hand…

"Humphrey's awake," he muttered beneath his breath, filling Eden's coffee cup. "Make him stop."

Eden slammed a hand to her neckline, accidentally clipping the cup's handle and spilling the coffee on herself.

Everyone jumped, a chorus of "Oh my's" and "Are you okay?'s" filling the room. Matt grabbed a napkin and dabbed at the spill. "Does it hurt?"

She grimaced. "Only my pride."

"We should go."

The dragon's tail slithered out from under her hand. "Oh, but—"

"Now."

Matt grabbed her purring pocketbook, then helped her to her feet and put his arm around her shoulders, his fingers conveniently covering Humphrey.

The dragon didn't think so; it nipped his finger.

"Mom, I'm sorry. We should go and deal with this mess." It was a toss-up whether he meant Eden's ruined outfit or the two uninvited dinner guests they'd inadvertently brought along.

Eden chimed in with her own apologies while

Amanda and Hayden insisted they stay and his mother
wrung her hands.

Humphrey squirmed some more and so did the kitten
in the bag, and time suddenly became of the essence.
Spilled coffee, everyone would understand. A baby
dragon? Not happening.

"Dinner was wonderful, Mom. Thank you. I'm
sorry we have to leave like this." He shuffled Eden
out from behind the table toward the foyer. "No, really, don't get up. I can see us out. You guys enjoy
your coffee."

"Are you okay, Eden? The coffee's hot—"

Humphrey belched then, scorching Matt's palm.
Now *that* was hot. It was all Matt could do not to react,
but he did shuffle Eden faster. "She should take care of
it before it sets. Paul, Hayden, Amanda—a pleasure to
see you. Mom, I'll call you. We'll do it again." Without
the magic show and dragon fireworks.

Without Eden, too.

And, man, if that wasn't a bitch.

⌁⌁⌁

Eden held her breath as they hurried through the foyer.
No sense borrowing trouble with the violets—oh, *zift*.
Those should be roses.

She took a whiff—and hiccupped.

"Eden—"

"I had to change them back."

He didn't argue and they made it out of the house so
quickly it was as if by magic—and she could guarantee it wasn't. Thank the stars she'd figured out her new
Way; now if only she could control the hiccups.

They ran down the brick path amid the drizzle. "I feel bad about leaving like that," she said as Matt held the passenger side door to his truck open for her.

"Better like that than leaving with a fire-breathing dragon on your shoulder." He ran to his side and climbed in. "How is the little flamethrower?"

Eden looked down at Humphrey—who was snoring contentedly. "I'll never understand dragons."

"Does anyone ever understand dragons?" Matt muttered, starting the engine.

Eden laughed, the first free, non-hiccupped breath she'd taken since the violets had appeared. "You're taking all of this in stride, Matt."

"What else am I going to do? It's not as if I can control any of it."

She knew that feeling.

"You didn't have to invite me tonight, and I want you to know that I really appreciate it. It's been a long time since I've been to a family dinner."

Matt stretched his arm across the back of her seat as he checked for oncoming traffic. "Genies don't have families?"

Ah, the pain. Even after two thousand plus years, the pain was still raw.

"Most do. I... don't. Not anymore." She looked out her window. Didn't see anything for the rain and the darkness, but then, that wasn't the point, was it? "Yours is really nice, Matt. I liked them."

"Thanks." Matt fiddled with a gadget on his steering column and the wipers picked up speed. "So, the magic you did tonight—"

"I know, I'm sorry. I tried, but every time I choked on

something, I hiccupped. It was the violets. I'm allergic to them."

"I'm not mad, Eden, I'm just wondering why this magic was different."

"Different?"

"You know, that glitter stuff. Why it wasn't an issue."

Eden sucked in a breath. *Zift!* She hadn't even thought about that. She'd gotten so caught up in the idea of spending time with his family—his mom in particular—that she hadn't even thought about leaving a trail right to them.

Oh, stars. What was she going to do?

She felt like the lowest kind of low. Taking her personal wants and needs and putting them above the good of his family. This was why genies were given those shackles and instructed to obey their masters; doing magic for their own gain—doing *anything* for their own gain—put others at risk.

How could she have been so blind? So stupid? So... self-centered? If Faruq tracked her there—

"Oh Matt. I'm sorry. So, so sorry." The words came out a whisper, choked on the tears at the back of her throat. "It's no different. I shouldn't have come. I'll never forgive myself if something happens to them. Never."

And she wouldn't. She, more than anyone, knew how precious family was.

"*Zift!* I never wanted these powers in the first place, you know that? All I ever wanted was a normal life and family. To make my own decisions. I never wanted magic when I found out The Service came with it, but I didn't have a choice. Just like I don't have one with Faruq. He'll never let me go." She scrubbed at her eyes, blinking madly to keep the tears at bay. "And now he'll come after your family to get to me. Oh, stars, what have I done?"

"Eden, let's think rationally—"

"Rationally? You think I'm being irrational? You go ahead and think that, Matt, but Faruq? *He's* not rational."

"Sweetheart, calm down. Don't get hysterical."

"I'll get hysterical if I want to." She hiccupped once again and violets grew out of his dashboard like a psychedelic carpet. "See? Now *that's* hysterical."

She tried laughing, but it morphed to a sob so quickly that *that* was the joke. One tear drifted down her cheek and Humphrey crawled up to lick it away. Which started another one. When was the last time someone had shown her that kind of kindness?

Then Matt reached for her hand and the tears wouldn't be denied. "Eden, none of this is your fault."

"If only that were true," she said between sobs and hiccups. Stop signs were turning pink all over the place. Mailboxes, too. Someone's trellis. "It actually is, Matt. That's what you don't understand." She pulled her hand from his and put it in her lap, where it stayed for all of two seconds until the tears got to be too much and she had to wipe them away.

"I don't see how—"

"I killed my master. That's why I was in my bottle. Locked away as punishment. And if I hadn't done that, if I'd obeyed The Code, I wouldn't be here, and none of this would be happening."

Silence. Except for the rain. Even her hiccups had stopped. Oh lucky her.

"Why did you?"

It was to Matt's credit that he didn't run screaming from the cab, and bonus points for not doing the platitude thing.

But she had to make him understand—in a way the High Master never had.

"I didn't mean to. Well, I meant to scare him. Let him think I would because what he was going to do—" She licked her lips. "The children had no one else. No one to look out for them. Parents are supposed to love and protect their kids, not harm them or—" Her breath hitched, but nothing turned pink or popped into view. As if the fates knew better than to mock her now when the memory was still so fresh, the feeling of helplessness and unmitigated anger at what their father had been planning to do to them.

Eden cleared her throat. Sniffed back the tears. "Parents shouldn't do those things to their children. Shouldn't hurt or abandon them or put their wants above their children's well-being. Parents are supposed to love and support and be there for their kids."

Was she still talking about her last master? Eden didn't want to figure it out. Both events were inextricably intertwined in her mind. One led to the other and put her where she was today: AWOL and alone.

"That's why you don't want to go back. You don't want to have to work for men like him."

"Work for? That's a nice way of putting it. I have to do whatever they demand of me no matter how I feel about it. It's so demeaning. Humiliating. Lonely." Her breath caught. "I can't ever go back to that, Matt. I won't."

Matt stroked one last tear from her cheek. "Then

we'll just have to make sure we find your bottle before Faruq does."

Chapter 13

MATT PARKED THE CAR IN THE DRIVEWAY — BECAUSE HE had a donkey in his garage. Eden grimaced at that. She ought to do something with Francis.

"Are you sure you want me to come in, Matt? I can just take Francis and Humphrey and go. The Glimmer should be almost gone by now. Faruq doesn't have to know I've been here."

"What about Obo? Are you going to take him, too?"

"Well… okay. If you want."

Matt swiped a hand over his face. "What I want is to discuss this tomorrow. If you leave now, I'll never know what happens to you. If you made it okay." He got out of his side and ran around to hers as the rain picked up. "Let's not debate it. It's late, there's a storm kicking up, and you don't have your bottle. Tomorrow's another day. Let's go in and go to bed."

And with those words, any thought of arguing flew out of Eden's mind quicker than Humphrey's fluttering little wings as he woke up and flew onto Matt's head.

Matt wanted to go to bed? Well thank the cosmos and let the choirs sing.

He was right; tomorrow was another day and they had tonight. It might be the only night they ever had and she wasn't going to let this chance go to waste.

She made it two steps inside the front door before she dropped her purse, yanked off her coat, turned around, and plastered herself to him, all the crazy emotions from the day roiling through her. She just wanted him to make her forget. Take her to that plane where nothing but the two of them existed.

That's all she wanted. Hours of mindless passion with this man who was so much more than mere convenience.

But Matt pulled back from the kiss as Humphrey dove off his head, making a beeline for the finial on the end table lamp. "Eden, what are you doing?"

She locked her arms around his neck, settled her belly against the irrefutable proof that she shouldn't have to explain this to him, and kissed the base of his throat before she answered. "I told you earlier, Matt, if you have to ask, you need this more than I do." She kissed the dimple in his chin. It was a very sexy dimple.

"Eden." Matt slid his hands up her arms. "Wait. Remember no bringing strange women home and making love to them?"

She stood on her toes and trailed kisses up his cheek, reversing the path the raindrops had taken. "But I'm not a stranger, Matt. Not anymore. And you didn't bring me home, I came with you. There's a difference."

"Eden—" He captured her face in his hands. "Stop."

Lightning flashed outside, a poor cosmic punctuation to his words. The pounding rain helped drill it home.

Oh stars. He didn't want her. He'd actually meant *go to bed* in the literal sense.

Humiliation spiraled through her. *Zift!* What an idiot she was. As if talking about murder was a way to sweet-talk a guy into bed. Why *would* he want the emotional mess that was Eden, killer-genie-on-the-lam with haphazard magic?

Idiot. The tempo of the rain seemed to be saying it over and over. She was such an idiot. Pathetic.
Desperate. Which just made her more pathetic.

Choking back a sob, Eden steadied herself against
him, then walked away as dignified as she could—which
was really pushing the envelope.

And, yes, an envelope *poofed* onto the coffee table.

Eden wrapped her arms around her waist and stared
at the stone fireplace. Another flash of lightning brightened the room, reflecting her bleak face in the picture
hanging above the mantel and highlighting the kitten as
it scooted from her bag to disappear beneath Matt's sofa.

Was it too much to ask? Really? One night; that's all
she wanted.

But Matt didn't.

Humiliation, indignation, hurt... it seared through
her. And the *really* sucky thing in all this was that she
had no place to go. She still had nothing. Obo and her
bottle were MIA, so, too, was the kitten. Humphrey
made it perfectly clear he'd be more than happy to hang
with Matt, and even her clothes were ruined.

Eden closed her eyes against the wave of loneliness.
Maybe just this once she'd give in to the pity party.

Then Matt's hands landed on her shoulders, killing
that idea. And inspiring others.

Gods, she was wallowing.

"Eden, it's not that I don't want to."

She snorted and opened her eyes—and stared right
into the reflection of his. "Right."

"I mean it. How could I not? You're gorgeous."

"Yet you still managed to turn me down." She'd
given the guy plenty of openings. "Twice."

"I didn't want to take advantage of you."

That had her spinning around. "You're kidding, right?"

Matt took a step back. "What?"

"You don't want to *take advantage* of me? Um, hello? I have control of my magic, I'm not drunk, and I'm a big girl. And in case you hadn't noticed, here's a news flash: I was throwing myself at you. Which part of that means you're taking advantage of me, Matt?"

It was a toss-up which was louder: her question or a round of thunder. He was not going to turn her down for some misplaced idea of chivalry. One she didn't need and certainly didn't want. She wanted him. And, dammit, he wanted her. She'd *felt* that.

Matt didn't say anything.

Including *no.*

"Matt, do you want me?" She took a step toward him. Just one.

"I—" He swiped a hand over his jaw.

"Do. You. Want. Me?" She took another step and clenched her hands at her sides as the storm whipped up, rain pelting the windows and pounding the roof. This was the last time she'd ask. Yes, she wanted him, and eighteen hundred years had created a lot of pent-up frustration. After seeing the other men in his family tonight, though, she knew it was Matt she wanted, not just any man. But Matt had to be willing to risk something; it couldn't be all her. She was worth more than that.

Matt stared into her eyes, and she saw the moment he gave up the fight in a perfectly timed flash of lightning. "Want you? Jesus, Eden. I want you so much I can't think straight."

She took the last few steps into his arms and touched his cheek. "Then make love to me, Matt. For tonight. Here and now. Nothing else. No past history, no magic, nothing between us but what we create. Tomorrow—reality—will come soon enough."

Matt didn't even speak. He just wrapped his arms around her and lifted her, his lips finding hers in less time than it took to inhale.

Not that she thought she could.

Nor did she want to. She wanted to make sure her magic had nothing to do with any of this.

Electricity crackled in the air—the storm or them, she couldn't tell. Matt sank the fingers of one hand into her hair, cradling her head, angling it just the right way so his tongue could sweep between her lips, igniting a fire inside her that had been dormant far too long.

Eden sucked on his tongue, twirling her own around it, wanting to crawl inside his embrace. Wanting to feel every part of him against her. She slid her fingers beneath his collar, tracing the muscles of his neck and shoulders. Sleek and firm, they reacted at her slightest touch. By the heavens, he felt good. But she wanted—needed—more.

The wind swirled around outside, howling through the trees. Eden angled her head the other way and thrust her tongue inside his mouth, tangled with his, tasting the earthy remnants of his beer, the warm buttery flavor of the rolls, and the taste that was all Matt. The one that made her want more.

Her fingers found the buttons on the front of his shirt, fiddling with them, something she couldn't seem to stop doing around him—nor want to stop doing to him.

Then Matt plastered her against him and dragged his lips from hers to slide along her jaw into the hollow beneath her ear and Eden found it was all she could do to hold onto him to stay upright, let alone figure out how stupid little buttons fit through tiny little holes.

"Eden." His hot breath fanned the faint trail of wetness he'd left behind and made her shiver. "Tell me this has nothing to do with your magic." He nipped at her earlobe and she saw stars. Or maybe it was lightning.

"It doesn't." Her words were shaky. "I swear I didn't do anything."

"You did something." He sucked her lobe into his mouth, sending more shivers through her.

She didn't think she was capable of thought, much less magic at this point. "Matt, no, I really didn—"

He kissed her then, a long, drugging kiss, full of every intention he had, and Eden shivered yet again. "Yes you did. You popped into my life." He sucked her bottom lip between his, his tongue tracing along it, then released it with a little nip. "And knocked me on my ass. In every way imaginable."

As Matt's lips slipped back toward where her pulse pounded beneath her ear as strong as the wind pounded the trees outside, something warm and luscious ribboned around her heart, wending through her chest and into each limb, filling her with so much emotion she gasped.

And then she gasped again.

Emotion?

No. No emotion. Need, want, passion, yes. But no emotion.

She tugged on his hair and he looked at her, his eyes burning in twin flashes of light as they met hers, and Eden focused on that. On the desire. She took his mouth in a searing, all-encompassing kiss, wrapping her arms around his neck again and pressing her breasts against his chest. She needed to be swept away with the physicality of it, with the need and the drive to consummate this passion. She couldn't think of anything else, couldn't make it anything else. It was eighteen hundred years of pent-up need. Nothing. More.

Somewhere, lightning struck, the air supercharged with energy, but it couldn't compare to the burn she felt when Matt cupped her backside and hiked her higher, kneading each cheek, so close yet so far from where she wanted him to touch her. He walked through the living room, each stride creating an ache between her legs—more so when that swollen, aching part of her brushed his erection.

He sucked in a breath *and* her tongue then, repeating the same tongue-swirling thing she'd done to him. Eden groaned, shimmying against him, wanting him to take her now. Wanting him to make her wait until it was unbearable. Wanting so much that she thanked the stars he held her in his strong, capable arms because her legs couldn't have supported her if her life depended on it.

His strides quickened and Eden moved against him again.

Matt groaned and pulled his lips from hers, his breath heavy on her cheek. "I'm never going to make it if you keep doing that."

"Isn't that the point?" She rocked forward. Then back.

Matt groaned as loud as the next round of thunder. "I'd like to make it to the bed before that, Eden."

Ah, yes, the bed. Very good point. Eden tightened her

arms around his neck and lifted herself just enough that the man could get where he was going, but then—watch out. All bets were off.

Lightning strobed through the billowing trees outside and in through the blinds, giving her glimpses of a large bedroom with an equally large bed. He'd need a large one, as big as he was.

She shivered again and wasn't sure if it was because of his size or that one hand slid beneath her sweater, feathering along the side of her belly.

She wasn't going to think about magic. Not now.

Then he slid his hand higher, and any kind of thought became impossible.

Her nipple pearled against his palm, her breast aching with the exquisiteness of his touch, and Eden sighed, her head falling back. It was just so much effort to keep it upright.

And then he shoved the comforter aside, and laid her down, following her all the way so that she met the soft mattress and his firm, ripped body in one movement, the contrast doing funny things to her insides.

"Eden," he murmured against her jaw, both hands now making forays over her skin beneath her sweater, which did things that weren't so funny to her insides. "Tell me you're not having second thoughts."

Oh she was having second ones. And thirds. And fourths. But they all had to do with how many times the two of them could do this, not a single thought about not doing it.

"Matt, take off my shirt."

She felt his smile against her throat. "I love the way you think, lady."

She was no lady. There was nothing ladylike whatsoever in the thoughts running through her head.

One of which came true the moment she'd shimmied out of her sweater and Matt tugged one hard, aching nipple into the warmth of his mouth.

"Thank the stars," she sighed, then drew a long shuddering breath as she threaded her fingers through his damp hair.

When his hand found her other nipple, those stars popped behind her eyelids. It'd been so unbearably lonely—long. She meant long. It'd been unbearably long.

Lightning and thunder crashed outside, the trees whipping into a frenzy, rain pelting the house, but nothing compared to what she felt when Matt swirled his tongue around her nipple. She almost came right then, and shifted so that his leg fell between hers. She rocked onto him, needing the pressure at that most sensitive spot. She didn't know how much longer she could hold out, as the sensation continued to build with each flick of his tongue, each feathery touch.

And then her thigh stroked him and Matt groaned against her, grinding his hips just where she needed him to. Eden groaned right back.

Matt released her breast then, his eyes dark and focused in a one-two punch of lightning. "I want you."

She ran her fingers over his lips. "I want you too, Matt."

Matt raised himself onto his elbow and stared down at her, his breath coming fast and strong.

Then, as beams of lightning crisscrossed through the window, he trailed one finger from the dip in her collarbone down between her breasts, so slow it was torture, but so utterly sensual she wanted to writhe beneath it.

He continued down, softly now, just barely touching her skin, his eyes following the movement, to her navel. He dipped in slightly, then traced around the outside, the muscles in her stomach quivering. Back at the center again, he drew his finger down, tucking it beneath the waistband of her pants as far as he could.

"Take them off for me, Eden," Matt's voice, harsh and seductive, stirred her. "Bare yourself to me."

Her breath caught and she undid them with trembling fingers. She wiggled her pants and boy-cuts down to her knees where Matt then took over, sliding first one leg than the other out, each inch of exposed skin treated to the soft, seductive brush of his fingertips. Eden was on fire before she was even naked.

And then he was touching her. There. Where she wanted him. Where she needed him.

Eden closed her eyes against a flash of lightning—or maybe it was against the sheer ecstasy of what he was doing—and arched into his touch, the pulsing, burning need overtaking her. She gripped the sheets, fisting them, then wrapping them around her fists, digging her heels into the mattress, straining, yearning for something, just a little more…

Matt withdrew his finger and Eden's eyes surged open. "What—?"

He leaned forward and put that finger against her lips. "Shh. I'm not finished yet."

"Neither am I," she panted beneath a rumble of thunder.

"I know, trust me." His smile kicked back, winking that sexy dimple into existence, then he rolled onto his side to unbutton his shirt.

Eden didn't bother waiting. She grabbed hold of his

shirt and yanked the buttons apart so she could *finally* run her hands over the hard muscles she'd wanted to feel for what seemed like forever.

Then her fingers, industrious little things that they were, made short work of the buttons on his jeans. She needed his help to get them off, but within seconds he was just as naked as she was.

And, lit by what could only be a gods' gift flash of lightning, utterly gorgeous.

It'd been so long since she'd wanted a man as much as she wanted him—and she didn't mean just the physical release part of it. All her lovers had been casual; that was all a genie could hope for. One never knew when one's master would require obedience, so relationships never had a time to grow among the quick fumblings in some hidden corner where foreplay was as unheard of as simultaneous orgasms. Occasionally there was the opportunity for a longer affair, depending on the masters' generosity, but never the freedom to savor.

She was going to savor Matt.

Every single delicious inch of him.

Thunder rippled through the air in waves when she reached out to stroke his chest. All those planes and angles and tight, firm muscles, the sexy dusting of hair. She loved the differences between their bodies.

But Matt's breath caught, his stomach muscles quivered just like hers as she traced her finger down the long, lean length of his torso. Below his navel she followed the thin line of dark hair to stroke the base of him just enough that his breath caught again.

"Eden," he whispered.

She leaned in to him and kissed away the rest of what

he was going to say, then circled her fingers down to stroke his sac.

Matt reached for her—no, he practically lunged for her—spearing one hand through her hair, the other dragging her on top of him, her hand between them, but she wasn't planning to remove it. Her fingernails continued to stroke the velvet skin then slid up to grasp him.

He grabbed her arm. "You're killing me."

"We can't have that." She released him and dragged her palm up his length to the harsh rasp of his indrawn breath. She kept moving her hand up his stomach to first one pectoral, then the other, feathering each tight nipple, then swept across his shoulder and down his arm, to entwine her fingers with his.

Matt watched her the whole way.

He brought their joined hands to his mouth and kissed each of her fingers. His other hand splayed across her lower back and dipped down to stroke the cleft of her backside, sending shivers from that point toward her midsection. They were joined by the shivers generated by his lips, and they swirled together. Around her heart.

No.

No heart. No emotion. She wasn't going there. This was purely physical. She had to keep it that way. This was just one night.

Eden wiggled herself more fully atop him and guided their joined hands to her back. "I want you inside me, Matt." She punctuated the words with kisses to the corners of his mouth and one to each of his lips.

Matt gripped her hips. "Give me a minute to catch my breath." He kissed her breast. "Then I'll get a condom."

"No need." She smiled and turned slightly so he could kiss her other breast.

Matt obliged and Eden saw stars—lightning, whatever—again.

"Oh? Genies don't need protection?" he murmured between breath-stealing kisses.

When she finally found her breath, she answered him, though coherent thought was getting fuzzy. "No, actually we don't, Matt. Magic takes care of it. For both of us."

"Perfect."

"I'll take that as a compliment." Along with the attention he was lavishing on both her breasts now, playing particular attention to her nipples, Matt's fingertips were doing delicious things to the top of her butt and Eden couldn't suppress the tremors. Truth was, she didn't try very hard.

Then Matt trailed one finger along her hip bone and down, along the crease to her thigh, and Eden lost all capacity to think.

Thinking was highly overrated when feeling was so much better.

"Open for me," Matt whispered as his fingers found the very heart of her.

Eden heard and obeyed.

Bracing herself on his chest, Eden let her legs splay, and, oh, the minute she did, Matt was there, just the right amount of pressure, the perfect rhythm, the right length of his stroke. Eden closed her eyes and tossed her hair down her back, her inner muscles clenching as the ache grew.

Then Matt's other hand opened her more, and Eden

had to throw her hands behind her to his thighs to brace herself as she arched into his touch.

Colors exploded behind her eyelids as Matt's fingers delved and stroked, using her own wetness to drive her higher.

"That's it, Eden. Come for me, honey. Let me watch you."

She couldn't speak. Matt's finger slid down the length of her, stroking quickly at her opening, and Eden panted.

"Come for me, Eden," he whispered again, low and hoarse, yet so much louder than the thunder.

His erection behind her let her know he was as excited as she was.

"Matt." She wanted something. She knew what it was, it was just that she couldn't— "Matt."

"Come for me, honey."

Matt's finger changed angle and there—

That was—

Oh my stars!

Eden strained against him, her body moving in perfect rhythm with his, the hard, velvet length of him at her behind, sliding along the cleft, driving her crazy. God, she'd never been this turned on before, never this sensitized.

He rubbed her then, direct, full-on contact. Lightning lit the room, thunder crescendoing, and Eden felt the rush sweep over her stronger than any storm.

Pulsing, pounding, roaring through her, the sensation was more than she'd ever felt and Eden rode it, rocking into it, pulling back at the intensity, seeking it out once more, every muscle in her body clenching, contracting, throbbing.

And for a minute—or maybe a lifetime—Eden hung onto her sanity, her surroundings. Knew where she was for one last second before her body flew over the edge, and nothing mattered but the swirling tempest of color as her body shattered against him.

—⁓—

She was the most beautiful thing he'd ever seen.

Matt watched Eden's climax consume her, loving how her body flushed and her skin glistened, every muscle rigid and smooth and concentrated on the sensation between her legs, and he almost came himself just from watching.

He needed to be inside her. Now.

Matt's body, in opposition to the waning thunder, clamored for him to move, to lift her those precious inches and impale her on him, to take her over and over, sliding her along his length, touching every part of her, to feel her envelop him, contract against him, and take all he had to give.

He wanted to. Dear God, did he want to.

But then she shuddered, one continuous, sinuous movement from the top of her head to the most perfect, round, delectable ass that was sitting on him, and Matt didn't want to take her like that. He didn't want to lose himself in her, in the sheer feeling of it—no, he wanted to experience it *with* her.

It might kill him, but he was going to give it a try.

Another shudder wracked her body and, suddenly, there were butterflies everywhere. Circling the bed, in tandem with Eden's breath, they rose, then fell back as she exhaled, wings fluttering the scent of lovemaking all around them.

Matt didn't know how much more of this he could take. Yet, when Eden's head drifted to the side and her gorgeous, silky hair glided across his balls, he knew.

No more.

He slid his hands to her hips and guided her beside him onto the bed amid the tangled sheets. Her eyes fluttered open and she started to say something, but Matt kissed her. He had to. Some part of him had to be inside of her or he'd die with the wanting of it.

He kissed her again and moved on top of her, between her legs, and sank into her in one life-altering stroke.

Life-altering?

Matt paused. What did that mean, life-altering?

It couldn't mean—

Eden's hands grasped his butt, one finger tracing between, and he forgot what he was thinking about.

"Oh Matt," she growled, almost the same sound as the thunder that rolled off in the distance but so much better, "you feel so good."

Hell yes he did. And he knew just how to feel better.

Matt pulled out, smiling when she groaned and clutched at him. Then he thrust back in.

Oh, God, she felt so good, so unbelievably good. Matt pulled out again, then surged back in, unable to help himself. And then his body took over the rhythm, and he couldn't have stopped if he'd tried. He pounded into her, trying to get as close as humanly possible, every delicious slide of her skin next to his erotically unbearable.

"Matt," she whispered—gasped—his name and he had to taste her again. He kissed her, his body driven beyond thought, and he felt the rush start at the base of his cock. His balls tightened and he closed his eyes and thrust into her. Oh, God, the pleasure. It was intense. So unbelievably, amazingly intense that his breath caught and, for an instant, he felt as if he were floating, suspended in space, nothing before him or behind, teetering on the brink of something—

One more thrust and he took her with him over the edge. Soaring, as if they were flying, the blood pounded in his ears like wind rushing by, his body weightless as the sensations carried him, each contraction of her body fueling his response more. Up over a pinnacle, then down into the valley only to have her contract again, lifting him higher. Matt had never felt such a rush before.

And then he opened his eyes. "Holy hell."

Matt's curse had Eden's eyes fluttering open.

"We're… we're *flying*."

Chapter 14

THEY WERE SOARING IN THE NIGHT SKY ABOVE THE city, twinkling lights like a blanket beneath them, thousands of stars above, butterflies circling them, the sounds of the nearby bay a musical backdrop. A cool wind tugged at the sheet tucked around them and flapped the edges of the comforter beneath her, the rise and fall of the air currents as the storm blew out to sea carrying them as if they were a ship on that sea.

Eden looked at Matt. "You're okay with this?"

He was smiling. "Okay? Are you kidding? It's the most insane thing in my life, but if I took you so out of yourself that it sent us flying, who am I to argue?"

Eden rolled her eyes. "Oh, boy. You're never going to let me forget this, are you?"

"Can you? This is amazing. You're amazing. The butterflies are amazing." He dropped a kiss on her nose, grinning like a school boy. "It's like a whole new world from up here."

Oh, it was a new world all right. Never in all her two thousand plus years had this happened. Sex had been hurried encounters, no one staying around long enough to take an extended trip through the clouds—literally. She'd counted herself lucky if she'd had an orgasm.

But to have this—and the butterflies, beautiful and free—no one had ever made her feel like Matt had. As if *she* were beautiful. And free. As if anything were possible, not governed by The Code and a master's wishes or time constraints.

Oh, she'd had good sex in the past—although now she was going to have to come up with a new word because this had been so far beyond *good* that she didn't have a word to describe it. But no one had ever made her feel as if she were important. As if he cared.

Until now. Until Matt.

Eden closed her eyes. He couldn't care about her because she didn't dare return those feelings; the consequences were too great. This was just supposed to be about sex. About pleasure. Nothing more.

But to be up here, among the clouds, halfway to the stars, well, it had all the earmarks of something she could never have.

That seemed to be her destiny. To always want more. First, freedom, and now, when it was within her grasp, she wanted what she could have with Matt.

For a lot longer than tonight.

"So why a flying comforter and not a flying carpet?" His hair fell forward, all mussed and sexy, and Eden had to touch it.

"Whatever's handy. Besides, it's not as if I consciously thought about it."

He kissed her, brief but hot, and she groaned.

"Sorry, honey, but I've got to—" When he moved his hips against her, she groaned again. "Will this support my weight or are we stuck like this until you bring us in for a landing? Not that I'm complaining, mind you."

He'd given her the perfect excuse to keep him here, but she wasn't going to take it. At some point she had to put all of this in its proper perspective, and there was no time like the present. Before the situation—and her feelings—got any more complicated.

"You'll be fine, Matt. The comforter will support you all the way out to the edges. You can even dangle your legs over if you want."

"That, I have to try." He eased himself from her body but only to slide to her side, his palm resting on her belly. "But first I have to say that *that*—and you—were incredible, Eden. It was just… incredible."

She smiled. "Stuck on that word, are you?" But yeah, it had been incredible.

"Not a bad word to be stuck on." He kissed her and Eden's heart soared.

And so did the comforter. A good forty-five degree angle toward the moon.

"What the—" Matt pulled his lips from hers and stared at the ground. "Um, any chance you could get us horizontal again?"

"Oh. Sure." Eden took a few breaths trying to steady her heart rate and little by little, the comforter went back to horizontal.

"Incredible." She thought he meant her, but then he said, "Look, there's the Space Needle."

Eden rolled her head to the side. She'd been on many flying carpet rides—it was pretty much a standard request by new genie masters, but had never made love while doing so—

Had sex, Eden. Not love.

It was sex, pure and simple.

Well, maybe not so pure, and definitely not simple, but utterly incredible.

"Hey, I can see the stadium." Matt, hand on her

stomach, leaned to look over the edge on her side. "And Bainbridge Island. This is amazing."

He didn't know how amazing it truly was. To be so taken out of herself by the moment, to not only conjure the butterflies but send the two of them soaring among the stars during it. Unplanned. That had never happened before.

Had this been what her mother had felt like when she'd met her father? Was this why Calliope had been able to give up her magic and immortality? For this? This feeling of perfection and peace? Of everything being right in her world?

But everything wasn't right in her world. And it hadn't been since her mother had made the conscious choice to tell Antonio she loved him, the one action that would set the course for later events. Her mother could have, instead, accepted her father as her master and lived with him that way. She still could have borne his child and basked in their shared feelings. There were ways around speaking the words that removed her powers and put their child at risk.

Children needed their parents, and to lose them as Eden had, then be thrown into slavery—no, she'd never understand why her mother had done what she'd done, no matter how good Matt made her feel. Love wasn't worth surrendering her freedom.

"Thank you for this, Eden. For sharing it with me." Matt looked into her eyes. Maybe he did realize how amazing this was. But if he did, what did that mean? Could he feel something for her?

Did she want him to?

That ribbon of something started winding around her heart again, but she steeled herself against it. No. Why make it more difficult? Just enjoy the passion for what it was. "It was my pleasure, Matt."

His eyes twinkled in the starlight. "And mine, too, Eden. Matter of fact…"

And then his hands moved under the sheet and it was *both* their pleasure.

―――――

"I've got to go." The whispered words tickled her ear and Eden floated through the fog of sweet dreams as the bed beside her rustled.

"It's early. Get some more sleep. I'll be back to help you find your bottle." Matt's fingertips feathered her cheek. "The butterflies were a nice touch."

Eden snuggled down into the blankets, smiling when Matt kissed her forehead before he left.

Yes, last night certainly had been wonderful. She smiled when she remembered the butterflies that had followed them home on the comforter only to circle overhead as they'd made love yet again.

Eden stretched, feeling all the delicious aches in muscles that had lain dormant for far too many centuries. Heavens, what she'd been missing.

Something buzzed by her ear, the soft brush of wings against her cheek. Hummingbirds, too? Oh yeah, it'd been *that* good.

Eden opened her eyes. Humphrey, not a hummingbird. The little dragon was sitting on the pillow next to her, little smoke rings puffing through his nose, and reality rushed in.

Eden sat up, the sweet lethargy of lovemaking leaving in an instant.

Butterflies and flying comforters meant magic. Magic meant Glimmer. And all that Glimmer meant Faruq.

She had to find her bottle.

Now.

Chapter 15

"Yo, babe, we have to talk about the Glimmer you're leaving all over the place."

Obo shoved the bedroom door open and Eden spun around, pulling the sweater down. "Don't you knock?"

"Me seeing you naked is the least of your worries. And besides, compared to Cleopatra, sorry, but there's no comparison. Not that I'm in the market, you understand." The cat shook his head. "What am I saying? We've got worse things to worry about than your modesty. You might as well have left boulder-sized bread crumbs to this place. It was like the Halley's Comet of Glimmer last night. I mean, come on already! A cloud of butterflies? Why not eagles? An airplane, for Bastet's sake. I was choking on the stuff last night. Everywhere I turned it was like Glimmer was falling out of the sky."

It had been, actually. *Zift!* She should have thought about that—not that she'd really been thinking coherently last night. Plus, it wasn't as if she'd ever really thought about Glimmer before. It'd never mattered. Now… oh it mattered.

"Not to worry, Obo. I figured out how to control my magic, so I'll be out of here soon enough." Hopefully with bottle in hand. She wouldn't think about saying goodbye to Matt. "And what do you mean about Cleopatra? You really did know her? Those weren't just rumors?" The famous queen had died only a few years before Eden had been born, which put Obo at a minimum of two thousand years old.

"Forget Cleopatra." Obo hopped onto the bed. "We've got Faruq to worry about."

"True, but by the time he gets here, all the Glimmer should be gone, so I'll be able to mortal my way past him. He won't expect me to use their transportation."

"Whether he expects that or not is the least of your worries." The cat stretched out his front legs, claws poking holes in one of the feather pillows as he bared them. "He's here."

"He's *what*?"

"Here. As in nearby. In town. *Aqui. Ici. Edo. Honaa.* Get the picture? You need to get a move on if you plan on hiding from him. Oh, and you might want to take care of the donkey. The dragon, too. If the Glimmer doesn't lead Faruq here, the stench surely will. Or the torched house. Humphrey's been practicing his aim. Sad to say, it's off."

Zift. Faruq had gotten here quicker than she'd expected. He must have been watching the crystals that tracked genies in The Service like a hawk for him to notice so quickly. Thank the stars he hadn't shown up last night.

"I've got to get out of here." She held out her hand and called Humphrey, who dove down from the top of the door. Then she shoved her feet into Cara's pretty high-heeled boots she'd worn last night. Not the most practical, but she couldn't start zapping things now. Fresh Glimmer was easier to track.

"That's what I'm trying to tell you." Obo leapt off

the bed and followed her out the door. "And I'm going with you."

"Obo, that's not possible. I've got to hide. Stay out of sight. Bad enough I'm going to have to do something nonmagical with Humphrey, but having you along too will only complicate things."

"You want to talk complicated, babe? I just spent the last ten hours or so hiding from Faruq. Matter of fact, I've kept him following me, running all over town, to leave you free to do whatever"—he nodded back to the bedroom—"you felt the need to do. Then I risked my butt getting back here to warn you, not to mention having to give up my bed, kibble, and litter box to some random cat you dragged in. You owe me."

She hurried into the living room. "And I appreciate that, Obo, but what if Faruq shows up here? You've got to stay to warn Matt. You'll do more good here than if you come with me." She grabbed the shearling jacket off the sofa. She'd pay Matt back somehow for it, but she'd need a coat and this was the only one handy. She wasn't about to go flinging any more Glimmer around conjuring a new one.

"I've done my good deed. Now I want to save my tail. The rest of me, too. Best way to do that is to help you get your bottle so you can zap me as far from here as possible."

"But why did you come back in the first place? If Faruq has issues with you, you could have just run away. It's not as if you owe me anything."

Obo checked the claws on his front paw. "I, um..." He mumbled something.

"What?"

Obo set his paw down. "I, uh, owe Matt."

And didn't look happy about it. Which opened a very interesting can of worms, but Faruq was here and she didn't have time to go fishing. "Someday I'm going to want to hear why."

The cat zipped between her legs and ran for the front door. "Then let's make sure that day comes. Just be thankful Faruq's got a bone to pick with me, too, or he wouldn't have been chasing me around all night and could have followed your Glimmer back here."

"But that's all the more reason we shouldn't travel together, Obo. If he comes after me, you'll be safe here, and if he goes after you, same with me." She grabbed her pocketbook off the table by the door. "Thank you, by the way, for leading him on a wild peacock chase."

"It's goose and that's exactly what I feel like. Our best bet is to pool our resources and watch each other's back."

She put the bag down. There was nothing in it that she'd need, mainly because there was nothing in it. It'd just been for show last night.

Like Obo. He was all about the image—pretending to care that he owed Matt yet not following through. "What about Matt, Obo? Is this how you repay him for whatever it was he did for you? For giving you shelter? Food?"

Obo turned up his nose. "Kibble ain't no beluga caviar—"

"Obo."

"All right, all right. Rats, I hate it when you're right." He dropped onto his belly and crossed his front paws over each other. "But at least do something with the bracelets. Those things give me the willies."

The bracelets. Right. She didn't think they were

emitting anything traceable, but to be on the safe side, she ought to bury them. She certainly wasn't about to take them with her.

"Fine. But you keep an eye on Humphrey." She set the dragon down on the back of the sofa, wincing when she saw a few burn marks, then ran into the kitchen and dragged a chair over to the refrigerator where Matt had put the bracelets. She was about to climb up when Obo's hiss stopped her.

"Don't just grab them! Doesn't the touch of your skin set them off or something? Use a fork. Or a pair of tongs. A pencil. Something."

Zift! That was close. She didn't need them to magically encircle her wrists after Matt had worked so hard to get them off, and start transmitting again. That'd defeat the whole purpose of getting away from here.

Eden found a set of tongs in the drawer next to a pair of oven mitts and managed to triple-bag the mangled jewelry. Then she took an apple out of the basket and hurried into the garage to give Francis his breakfast, grabbed a shovel, and headed into the backyard toward the old oak between a large shed and the corner of the property, cat and dragon following—with dragon riding cat. What she wouldn't give for a picture of that.

The thick tree trunk hadn't yet been hollowed out by insects, making it too tough to chop down, and, therefore, the perfect landmark should she need to recover the bracelets one day.

Oh, not to wear. She'd never don the chains of Servitude again willingly. Those first fifteen years of her life when she'd been free had been wonderful, although she hadn't realized how wonderful at the time.

Back then she'd straddled two worlds—djinn and Roman. With her dark hair and skin, yet the blue eyes of her father, she'd been an anomaly. Someone for other children to make fun of and adults to steer clear of.

Eden dug a hole at the base of the tree. She'd hated being different. Hated not being able to use the magic she'd inherited from her mother and hated that her mother hadn't been able to teach her for fear of drawing the attention of the vizier and being placed into The Service.

The irony was, after the fire, the High Master had ordered her to Al-Jannah, the genie City of Paradise in the Sahara where her powers had to come to light—puberty was a bitch—and she'd had to enter formal training, an honor in their world.

Some honor. She'd been so thankful to have somewhere to go, to belong, only to be placed in The Service for her gratitude. Using her magic for others. A slave to her powers.

Eden dropped the bracelets in and refilled the hole. Not quite the six feet down they deserved, but enough to get them out of sight.

They'd never be out of mind, though.

"Okay, Obo, that should take care of that. Now you tell Matt and I'll—"

"You'll what?" Obo patted the dirt with all four of his paws while Humphrey grabbed the scruff of Obo's neck in his beak. "Meander around town, hoping to avoid Faruq while trying to find the bottle? You need more help than Matt does, babe."

"You're not going to let this go, are you?" She headed back into the garage.

"Bingo." Obo leapt onto a workbench that Francis had turned into a scratching post, and Humphrey levitated like a helicopter to land on the perch of an old birdhouse on a high shelf, smoke puffs emanating from his nose faster than she'd ever seen. Obo had a point about the stench; she really needed to let the donkey out.

She hated that he was right. "Bingo? What cat says bingo?"

"The ones who spend every Friday night at the back door of St. Stanislaus's waiting for a handout, that's who. You got a problem with that, pet?"

Pet. One of the most offensive and derogatory names anyone could call a genie. She couldn't believe he'd used it. The High Master had begun punishing those who'd used the term just before she'd been sent away, predating Torquemada by over a thousand years. Obo had to be really old to come up with that one. "So, Obo, you never did tell me which of your nine lives you're on."

"And I'm not gonna either. We've got more pressing things on our plate right now anyway. Nasty vizier ringing any bells?"

Eden rummaged around in an old chest of drawers at the back corner of the garage and found a length of nylon rope she could use as a bridle. "Right. So, do you know where the dump is? That's where we need to start looking for my bottle."

"Yeah, I know where, but we're not going to be able to walk it. Can you hot-wire a car?"

"Not without magic. And I'm not stealing one, so that's out."

"So we'll call a cab."

"And pay for it how?"

Obo smiled. "Ah, babe, that's where I come in. See? I told you you need me. Put the donkey out to pasture, then follow me."

Eden slipped the makeshift bridle on Francis, gave him plenty of rope to wander around Matt's backyard, then followed Obo back to Matt's bedroom, Humphrey hitching a ride on her shoulder.

"Have fun?" The cat smirked, nodding toward the bed.

"Where is it, Obo?"

"Sheesh, no sense of humor." The cat hopped onto Matt's dresser. "Second drawer, in the back. There's a green sock. Matt keeps a stash of bills there."

"I can't take his money."

"So you replace it once you have the bottle. It won't matter what you do then, will it? Faruq will be shooting the magical equivalent of blanks at that point."

It was the truth, but still, Eden didn't feel right taking Matt's money. Not when she knew how tight it was for him these days and the poor man he was going to have to lay off. "What's in this for you, Obo? Why not just get out and go in the opposite direction?"

Obo swatted at Humphrey who'd leaned close enough to scorch one of the cat's ears. "Knock it off, pea brain," he grumbled. "And stop asking questions, Eden. We're in a hurry. Besides, you scratch my back, I'll scratch yours."

"With those claws?" Eden shuddered. "I don't think so. What gives?"

"None of your business. I've got my own agenda. Which just happens to correspond with yours right now so you ought to thank your lucky stars. Grab that money so we can get the hell outta here, will ya?" He swatted at Humphrey again—and ended up swatting air. Humphrey's reflexes were improving exponentially.

"Agenda?" Interesting choice of words. Felines usually only had *agendas* when their End-Of-Lives were imminent. They could only pass into their Hereafter if they redeemed themselves for whatever transgressions they'd made in their nine lives. To linger for thousands of years, Obo must have a lot of atoning to do.

"Look, babe, you worry about your troubles and I'll worry about the rest. Unless you're planning to trade your, um"—Obo cocked his head toward the bed—"*expertise* for cab fare, I suggest you hurry."

"You're a pig." But she opened the drawer anyway.

"No, I'm a feline. I'm also a survivor. Let's not forget that in the scheme of things, shall we?"

Seeing the toe of the neon green sock—she loved color but didn't want to imagine what had prompted Matt to buy *that* color—Eden grabbed it, arguing with herself the entire time, only to yelp when her fingers closed around something cold, hard, and metallic beneath the sock. "What in the world?"

"Gun." The cat snickered. "Been locked in that bottle too long, haven't you? They didn't have these when last you were free."

"Keep it up, fuzzball. I can always have the cabbie stop by a vet's office before the dump."

Humphrey let out a short burst of fire. His aim was getting better, too.

"Big words from a magic-less genie," the cat said, but he did tuck his tail between his legs and *schlump* off the dresser. "Let's get moving."

"Are you sure you don't want to stay here? Warning Matt could save your immortal soul."

Obo slid through the door, then turned and stuck his head around the corner. "Don't you think I haven't thought of that? If only it were that easy. But it's nothing for you to get your slippers in a curl about. You have your cross to bear, I have mine. Now let's go get that bottle."

Matt shoved his truck into reverse and remembered at the last second not to peel out of the Baker driveway.

The pool house was finished. Apparently, long before he'd arrived on the scene.

And from the voice mail Jerry had left at two-thirty this morning—calling from Marybeth's hospital room where they'd been for the last forty-eight hours, almost losing the baby—Jerry definitely hadn't been the one to do it.

That left one person. If he could call her that.

How could she have done it? How? He'd asked her not to. *Told* her not to. Didn't she listen?

No. Of course not. Why should she? Why should anyone let him run his own business?

Matt pulled out onto the street, narrowly missing a squirrel. Great. He was mad enough to think about killing something, but didn't want to actually do it. Had Eden put some curse on him that whatever he wished for came true now?

Funny thing: most people wouldn't call that a curse. And, God knew, after the wish that had come true last night, he should be one of them.

But this, this wasn't what he wanted. One thing had

nothing to do with the other. Making love to Eden didn't mean he wanted her to fix things for him. It was his business, and it would sink or swim because of him. Not anyone else.

God, real slate. She'd used real slate on *half* the roof. The half that everyone at the party tonight would see.

He hadn't built the cost of half a roof's worth of slate into the budget, let alone the entire thing, and he also hadn't framed the pool house to hold the weight of real slate. The synthetic product was much lighter, so now he'd be dealing with a collapsing structure at some point, or he'd have to ask Eden to zap extra support into the walls and trusses. As for any profit after buying real slate to re-roof the rest of the pool house, he'd be eating that. Probably the only thing he *would* be eating.

Or he could come clean to Henrietta about how her pool house roof had gotten finished.

Yeah, and there would go any referrals. And his reputation. No one wanted a nut-job building anything for them. And it would *still* fall down because of the structure.

Shit. He hated this. The one thing he'd tried to have some control over, despite the economy, despite workers who didn't show up, he now had to have a genie fix for him.

This was what he got for his damned white-knight complex. Cara had been a mistake, the stray cat he'd taken in could speak, and now Eden.

Last night shouldn't have happened. He should have just dropped her at a hotel, or, better yet, the hospital. They took indigent cases. She was certainly one of those. But no. He had to go all Prince Charming—and had let Sleeping Beauty into his bed.

Matt's gut twinged. She was definitely beautiful.

He shook his head. Thinking with his dick again. That hadn't worked out so well in the past, remember?

Yeah, he did, and he was done with that when it came to women. The next woman in his life would be one who didn't cloud his judgment with a pretty face or sexy body. Or need rescuing. Someone who understood about his work and his desire to succeed on his own.

Thank God Henrietta had had some charity breakfast this morning and would never know he hadn't done the work. If not for that one blessing, this would have blown up in his face.

Unfortunately, it still would.

Matt stewed the rest of the ride home. The Henderson project would have to wait now. The pool house couldn't. Safety came before his pride in this issue. He'd help Eden find her bottle, get her to fix the place, then send her on her merry way. Out of his life where she didn't belong.

That's what he'd do. Matt convinced himself it was the right course of action the entire ride back to his house.

He bought it, too. All the way until he opened his front door and found someone in his living room who also didn't belong in his life.

Chapter 16

"WHO ARE YOU, AND WHAT ARE YOU DOING IN MY home?" Not that Matt really needed to ask. The guy sitting in the chair by the now-lit fireplace in his living room might be dressed like a successful businessman, but Matt knew exactly who he was.

Faruq looked up slowly at Matt's question, as if he didn't have a care in the world nor the good graces to admit he was in Matt's house illegally.

"Who I am isn't important. It's who I'm searching for that matters." Faruq flicked a hand and the newspaper he'd been reading disappeared in a cloud of confetti, littering the rug and coffee table. "That donkey out back. It's her calling card, so to speak. Don't tell me she's not here. I want her back."

Which meant she wasn't here and Faruq didn't know where she was. Matt hoped she found her bottle quickly.

"The donkey's mine and I don't know what you're talking about." Matt removed his coat and dropped it onto the back of the sofa, affecting a nonchalance he didn't feel. What he could feel was the raw power emanating from Faruq. The genie could kill him with one finger.

"Nice try, mortal, but there is Glimmer all over the beast. Where is she?"

Matt took off his hat and walked to the table beside the door. "The donkey? In the backyard. Just like you said."

"Don't toy with me or you'll be sorrier than you've ever imagined."

"Big words coming from a burglar." Matt put the hat down and picked up the telephone handset in one movement. "I suggest you leave."

Faruq uttered a harsh, foreign word and the phone disappeared.

Matt had expected that to happen. Still, he had to give Eden as much time as possible to find her bottle. If only she'd told him what she'd done with the roof, he could have gone with her and helped her find the bottle in half the time—

No he wouldn't have. He would have argued with her, demanded she return the roof to the way he'd built it, and he'd be there now finishing it, leaving her to face this guy alone when she returned.

"You're trying my patience, mortal."

Matt's fist clenched. "Welcome to the club. You're trying mine. Get out of my house."

Faruq waved his fingers to extinguish the fire, then stood. Tall and lean—and more imposing than Matt wanted to admit. Due, no doubt, to the fact that Faruq could do to Matt what he'd done to the newspaper, a disadvantage Matt definitely wasn't comfortable with. He had to find some way to even the playing field.

"You're not surprised by my magic," Faruq said, "which confirms my suspicion. Now where is she?"

"She's not here." He hoped.

Feigning disdain, Matt rounded the back of the sofa and headed toward his bedroom—and the sock drawer. Not that he expected the gun to do much if Faruq saw it, but maybe he could get off one shot. He'd have to make it count. The hours he'd spent at the shooting range with Cara would, hopefully, pay off now, because, sadly, they hadn't paid off for her.

Matt made it to his room before Faruq and had the satisfaction of hearing the genie *ooph* as the door smacked him in the face.

Matt ripped open the drawer and reached for the gun—

"Looking for this?"

Faruq appeared next to him, dangling the weapon that was now as mangled as Eden's bracelets.

Shit. The gun was useless. And shit, again, for the bracelets. He'd left them on top of the fridge. If Faruq had found the gun, he'd surely found those.

"Nice to see you made yourself at home." Matt was about to shut the drawer when he saw the green sock— the empty green sock. "What? You can't conjure enough gold and jewels, now you have to steal my money?" He held up the sock. "That's pathetic."

"I didn't steal your money. Though from the looks of those sheets"—Faruq nodded to the bed and his face darkened—"maybe Eden felt she was owed."

"You son of a bitch!" Matt hauled off and planted one on Faruq's jaw before either of them saw it coming.

To the genie's credit, he didn't kill him. Still, Matt found himself jacked up against the wall by his collar. At least he wasn't confetti, but being at someone else's mercy pissed him off no end.

"You're no match for me, mortal. You're alive only because I need information."

"Then don't expect any answers." Faruq was going to be sorry for a lot more than Eden's captivity.

"You think she's yours? That you have her? Ha. I'll

get her bottle from you, mortal, but until I do, I'll be your worst nightmare. I'll—"

"My worst nightmare? Who are you, Rambo? What decade are you in? Worst nightmare? Come on, put some originality into it. Threaten me like you mean it." If he weren't hanging off this guy's fist, fighting for breath, and in very real fear of the guy's powers, Matt would enjoy taking him on. He had a lot of frustration to take out on the prick.

The vizier lowered him to the floor, but didn't let go of his collar. "I should just kill you."

"Another original line." Matt grabbed Faruq's wrist. "Go ahead. Kill me. Then you really won't find out anything."

Faruq shook him. There was some muscle behind those chicken arms of his. "Tell me where she is!"

"You're the all-powerful being. You tell me."

"You're either very stupid or incredibly stupid. Do you know who I am?"

Matt rolled his eyes. Every second he could keep Faruq from going after Eden, the greater chance she had to escape.

Even if last night hadn't happened, and even though he was mad at her about interfering in his business, there was no way he was turning her over to this guy. Faruq made Cara's boyfriend look like the Easter Bunny.

"Yeah, I know who you are. You're the fucking blue djinn. Now get off me." Matt twisted one way, wrenched Faruq's arm the other, and made it through the bedroom door before Faruq had the chance to react.

Unfortunately, magic gave Matt only about one-tenth of a second head start.

Faruq materialized in the living room just as Matt reached the fireplace shovel—which the genie zapped out of his hand to embed in the ceiling.

"Don't anger me, mortal. Where have you hidden her?"

"So far from here, you'll never find her."

Faruq stroked his chin and Matt felt his flesh crawl—and hopefully not with anything nasty the genie had zapped onto him. But he wasn't about to check. He had to bluff his way out of this. But he'd feel a hell of a lot better if he had some sort of weapon.

Faruq tossed the flaps of his trench coat back and shoved his hands to his hips. "You don't know where she is."

"You go ahead and believe that." Anything to keep him talking while Matt scanned the room to see what he could possibly use against this guy.

"You don't know where she is. You're stalling. Why?"

Matt didn't answer him.

And then he saw something that made his blood run cold.

The bottle stopper. On top of the logs by the fireplace. She'd forgotten it.

Matt looked away, but Faruq had been watching him too closely. The genie's eyes narrowed. "What did you see?"

Matt lunged for the poker, but all Faruq had to do was turn it into a plastic fork—which he did—and the thing became ineffectual. But at least it got Faruq's attention off the fireplace.

"Ah, ah," Faruq wagged a finger at him. "I wasn't born yesterday, mortal. You will stay put while I investigate." A wave of Faruq's hand had Matt trussed up like a Thanksgiving turkey and lashed to a side chair. Complete with a gag.

This guy really didn't have his own repertoire, did he? Sadly for Matt, though, Faruq did know how to tie a damned knot.

"What was it?" Faruq walked over to the fireplace and fanned his fingers across the mantel.

Where was Obo when Matt wanted him? The cat could have followed this whole conversation and warned Eden before she unsuspectingly walked in. Or he could have hung outside the front door and warned Matt before *he* walked in. What the hell good was a talking cat if he wasn't around to eavesdrop?

Matt shook his head. His world had turned upside down and sideways in twenty-four hours and that wasn't including the comforter ride.

"Oh, this is so perfect." Faruq's chuckle sent shivers of dread up Matt's back. The genie turned around with the bottle stopper between his index finger and thumb, turning it as a jeweler would a priceless gem. "She isn't in her bottle. Tsk-tsk. I would have thought she'd pay better attention in her lessons, but the High Master's favor always gave her a false sense of security. Well, she'll have no security now." He walked over to Matt and waved the stopper beneath his nose. "Where is she, mortal? You can't protect her. Not from me. Not without this."

Matt glared at him above the gag.

Faruq bent down, his beady black eyes level with Matt's. "She is mine. Remember that. Whatever you think *that* was"—he nodded toward the bedroom— "she's mine. And I don't share."

The genie waved his hands and his modern-day clothes

were replaced with something right out of *Lawrence of Arabia*, long white shirt covered by a golden robe, a white turban, and a scimitar hanging from his waist.

Another wave of his hands and a small carpet floated beside him. Faruq sat on it, then curled his legs into the lotus position, revealing pointed, curly-toed slippers like Eden had worn. He laid the sword across his lap and held the stopper with both hands in front of him like a sacrificial offering. "She'll return for this. And when she does, I'll be waiting."

Eden and Obo were at the dump for less time than she'd expected. Faruq's reputation was no better with felines on this side of the Atlantic than the other. All she'd had to do was tell the cats at the dump what she was looking for and there'd been hundreds of interested participants. The can of albacore Obo suggested she bring as a prize helped, too. The manx who'd found her bottle had been enjoying the treat when they'd left with the bottle stashed securely in her coat pocket, a feeling as good as those from last night.

"You should have just zapped us back to Matt's house," Obo grumped for the fifteenth time. "You try riding on the floor of this hovel and see how you like it. Stupid dragon gets to ride in your pocket, but I'm stuck on the floor like a piece of trash."

"Ssh!" Eden reached down to muffle him. She didn't think the cab driver could hear the cat over the radio, but she didn't want to take the chance that he'd put them out on the side of the road here. Using magic would leave a trail right back to Matt's house and, after last night, she needed to know Matt would always be safe. She couldn't bear for him to face Faruq's wrath for being in the wrong place at the wrong time when she'd been freed from her bottle.

The cab pulled up behind Matt's truck, and Obo was out the door as soon as she opened it, streaking across the lawn for the cat entrance. Eden peeled some bills from the roll of Matt's money, then checked her pockets to make sure both the bottle and Humphrey were still in their respective pockets before heading up the brick walkway to Matt's door.

She looked at the house, the first place she'd been free since she was fifteen years old. For more reasons than just last night, this place would always hold fond memories for her. Especially after Matt's time on earth was over.

She couldn't think about that now. Seeing mortals pass was part of being a genie. Other than her parents' death, a mortal's had never bothered her before.

She straightened her shoulders. It wouldn't now. It couldn't because there was nothing she could do about it. She couldn't change his life span. So she'd go inside, get her stopper, and say goodbye, holding the memory of last night with her forever and leaving Matt safe and sound.

And then she opened the front door.

Chapter 17

"Ah, Eden, where have you been? Your charming mortal and I have been waiting."

Eden slid her hand out of the jacket pocket and didn't dare glance at Matt. "What do you want, Faruq?" Not that it mattered. But if she could keep him talking long enough to get the stopper, she had a chance of saving herself and Matt. If she didn't, well, that didn't bear contemplating.

"Come now, Eden, you were never the dense sort." The vizier slid off the floating carpet to rise to his full height—plus a few more inches she was certain he'd added just because he could. He was always over-compensating for something when he was around her. Promises of riches, displays of power, examples of the influence he could wield. He'd definitely take this opportunity to out-do Matt in the height department.

She'd love to tell him he couldn't even hope to compete with Matt, but she wanted him to forget about Matt and focus on her.

Faruq settled the scimitar at his waist, just in case she'd missed it. "I can't believe you were naive enough to think you could escape The Service, Eden. No one ever has, not without giving up their powers—or dying—though I am impressed that you finally figured out the diamond connection." He straightened his sleeves and walked over to her. "That was my mistake, but I'd already given you the stopper before we under-stood what Khaled had figured out. He told you at the trial, yes?"

Eden didn't answer. What did the stopper have to do with the bracelets?

Faruq took the last step separating them. "My mistake was putting you in the same room with him. I should have had the High Master deal with you privately, but then, who knows what he would have done, eh? The way he feels about you, he could have let you off with a wrist slap. That wouldn't have been ideal, not with you and your subversive tendencies. You needed to learn your lesson." Faruq ran the back of his fingertips along her cheek and Eden steeled herself against flinching. "To learn your place."

Eden looked away then, unsure if she was going to laugh or vomit. Faruq and his inflated ego.

But then she saw Matt. Tied up. Gagged. Glowering.

No, she wouldn't be laughing.

Matt looked angry enough to do major damage if he were free. Knowing what Faruq was capable of, how-ever, Eden was sort of glad Matt was in the position he was in. It'd keep him alive. Angry, but alive, and that was what was most important to her at the moment.

She looked back at Faruq. *Think, Eden, think.* She had to figure out some way to beat the vizier. She couldn't leave Matt at his mercy and she definitely didn't want to end up back in The Service.

A dash of black behind Faruq put Obo out of the equa-tion as far as help went—not that she blamed him. Cursed him? Yes. Blamed him? No. There was a reason the cat had been around for more than two thousand years.

Using Humphrey was out. Faruq would fry the dragon the moment Humphrey even attempted an attack. A full-grown dragon had a decent chance against a vizier; the dragonlet had none.

She was on her own.

Faruq leaned in closer to murmur in her ear. "If you come willingly, I'll let your mortal live. I see you've developed a certain… *tendre* for him. That will stop once you're under my command, however. Is that clear?"

Tendre? Is that what he thought? Well, it was better than him knowing the reality—

No. No emotions, remember?

Eden raised her chin. "I'm not going anywhere with you, Faruq."

Faruq smiled, a thin ribbon of motion not unlike that of the snakes he favored as pets. He billed himself as a charmer of both snakes and women, never knowing people snickered behind his back.

"You'll go with me, Eden, or I'll string your mortal up by his thumbs and peel off his flesh, one strip at a time. Or—" He stepped back and flicked one hand. A black cobra appeared on the rug in front of Matt's feet, coiled within striking distance. "I could let Ketu feast."

He'd do it, too. Faruq didn't have a squeamish bone in his body. She'd heard the stories of punishments to both mortals and genies alike.

Camel-dung. He'd won this round. But why'd it have to be a snake? She hated snakes.

Eden, eyes never leaving the serpent, wiped a hand across her forehead as if she were sweating, and shrugged out of Matt's jacket. She needed the jacket— and her bottle—to remain here. Without the bracelets or the bottle, Faruq could only blackmail her compliance, but she'd have a prayer of escaping. If he had her bottle, however, that'd never be possible.

Humphrey, on the other hand... well, the dragonlet wasn't safe no matter where he was, but she couldn't have one without the other, and Humphrey's best bet was for her to remain free.

"Fine, Faruq. I'll go with you. But only if you let Matt go. And get rid of the snake."

The cobra rose two feet off the floor, hood spread as it undulated in front of Matt.

Faruq smiled, looking all the more like his slithering friend. But he flicked his hand again, making Ketu disappear. He also turned the flying carpet into a Venetian gondola. "I knew you'd be reasonable. And as for that atrocious outfit—" One more flick and there she was, back in the garb of The Service. Red this time, with bells on the slippers. Ick. "Now gather your bottle and let's be going."

"I don't have it."

"*What?*"

She took a great deal of satisfaction in thwarting him. The only thing that'd be better was if she could tell him she was lying to him, but that'd defeat the purpose of doing so. Still, after being forced into this blasted outfit, she had half a mind to risk it. "I said, I don't have it."

"I don't find the joke amusing, Eden." He conjured another flying carpet the size of a bath mat to carry him to the gondola. More posturing.

"Fine, Faruq. Don't believe me, but I don't have it. Do you think I'd be standing here if I did? When I find that bottle I'm going to disappear and you'll never see me again." Eden held out her arms. "See? No bracelets. No way to hunt me down."

Faruq climbed into the gondola, swishing his robe around him with all the ceremony of a king, and settled against the back of the boat, a calligraphic star decorating the spot above his head. He should have been an actor instead of a vizier. "How in the cosmos did you manage to lose your bottle? A genie without a bottle is—"

"Rogue. Yes, I know. I also know that I'd rather be rogue than at anyone's beck and call ever again." She lifted her chin. "Especially yours."

———

Matt cursed behind the gag until his mouth was dry. Goddammit! He hadn't been able to protect her! Adrenaline coursed through him with impotent rage. Again. It was happening again. He was going to lose her.

At least Faruq hadn't found her bracelets so he couldn't have complete control over her, but Matt saw the way Eden had looked at him, tied here to this godforsaken hunk of chair. She was going to go with Faruq to save him. While he admired the nobility in that gesture—and appreciated it no end—he couldn't let her. She had to save herself. There had to be some other way out of this mess.

Options narrowed when Faruq drew Eden to him as if she were lassoed with an invisible thread and floated her off the floor and into the gondola with a slimy smile on his face—one Matt wanted to knock off. Along with all his teeth.

The vizier zapped a briefcase into being and floated it between them. "Oh, Eden. How you do underestimate me."

With a wave of his hand, the briefcase opened, and Faruq removed something from inside.

In the space of three seconds, he snapped a new set of bracelets on Eden's arms, and both genies disappeared in a puff of red smoke.

Chapter 18

MATT YANKED ON THE ROPES BINDING HIM TO THE chair. Son of a bitch, he had to get out of these and go after her!

He kicked his feet—or rather, tried to. The bastard knew what he was doing.

Matt tried wriggling beneath the binding, but the ropes were too tight. He strained and pulled, flexed his muscles, but nothing worked. The sweat pouring off him, however, made his skin slick enough that he could work his hands somewhat under the ropes, but it still wasn't enough.

This wasn't going to work. He'd never get free on his own. And with the phone gone, and his cell in his back pocket, he was shit out of luck.

Obo. The cat was somewhere in the house. He had to get his attention.

Matt rocked the chair, hoping that'd do it, but the damned area rug muffled the sound. He tried again, putting some muscle behind it, and shoved with the balls of his feet to move the chair backward. It didn't move the chair back, but it did move the carpet forward a little. Enough to give him a shred of hope.

He had to get out of here. Had to help her. She was alone, she'd said. No one in the world who cared about her. Forced to do the bidding of anyone who found her bottle, with no say-so. He knew what that felt like, having others determine your life, having no recourse, and he'd be damned if he'd let that happen to her again.

Matt wasn't sure how he was going to do that, but he couldn't just sit here while that bastard enslaved her again. Where the hell was Obo? The cat had to know something he could do.

Rocking the damned chair for what seemed like years, he finally inched the rug out from under it, then inched the chair away from the sofa so he wouldn't brain himself when it went over. He wasn't looking forward to taking a hit on the shoulder, but sitting here wasn't doing him or Eden any good, and hitting the floor would signal the cat.

If only he could reach his cell, but that option was out. Probably a good thing because he could only imagine how that phone call would go over. The truth would earn him a trip to a hospital with padded walls, not the cooperation of the police.

Hell. It was him and the cat.

Words he'd never have thought he'd utter—and it'd help if he *could* utter them.

He tried calling Obo again, but the gag muffled his voice.

And then the dragon crawled out of the coat on the chair, yawned and stretched his wings. Matt grunted. Hell, maybe *he* could do something.

Humphrey shook his head and Matt tried again. The little flamethrower seemed to like him. Matt was willing to risk more blisters to get out of his bindings.

He grunted again. This time, Humphrey got the message, his big blue eyes widening so much they took over his whole triangular face. Taking a running start off the back of the chair, the dragon worked his wings madly and soared into the kitchen.

Ten seconds later, Obo chased Humphrey into the living room, carrying a worn leather bag in his mouth. He dropped it on the arm of the sofa and did the oddest thing that, even though Matt knew he was capable of it, still freaked Matt out.

Obo spoke. "Look, you little fire hazard—" He broke off, cursing when he saw Matt. "Well, it could be worse."

Matt cocked an eyebrow.

"You could be dead."

True.

The cat sighed and shook his head. "Look, I'll try not to hurt you, but knots are a lot easier to tie than untie. Still, we should be thankful he didn't use chains—and that Humphrey's taken a shine to you. *And* that he didn't try to free you himself."

Obo leapt off the sofa, walked behind Matt and, with his paws on Matt's forearms, started working the ropes with his teeth. Humphrey sat on the coffee table, the tip of his tail swishing back and forth, his oversized eyes boring a hole through Matt.

Matt flinched whenever the cat's claws or teeth scored his skin, but anything was better than a cobra. Or Humphrey's fire.

"I warned her," Obo said, followed by a *pfft* that sounded a lot like spitting. "All that Glimmer. That's how he found her, you know. If you'd kept it in your pants, none of us would be in this situation."

Matt was in no position to argue with the cat. And besides, what situation was Obo in?

It was an education to hear the curses the cat chose

to use and how many times he got a rope ball stuck in his throat—and the fact that he actually excused himself when he hocked it out. Between the two of them—Matt working his hands and Obo working his teeth—they eventually got the rope off.

"Thanks." Matt's voice was scratchy and hoarse when he pulled the gag out of his mouth. He went to work on the ropes around his legs. Humphrey glided down and used his claws to work at the bindings. As long as Matt kept his fingers out of the way, the dragon was actually helpful.

"I'd say it was my pleasure, but really it wasn't. Faruq should never have been here at all. This isn't good."

"Where'd he take her?"

Obo could shrug. "My guess would be Al-Jannah, in which case you're screwed."

"Considering I've never heard of it and can't do magic, I'd say that was a foregone conclusion." Matt untied his feet and launched himself out of the chair. "So, where is this Al-Jannah? Baghdad?"

"If only. You're just lucky you're with me." The cat leapt onto the sofa arm and pawed the bag. "I can't believe I'm about to do this, but let's go."

Matt kicked the last of the rope off his leg. "I'll just grab my passport and meet you outside. The airport's not that far. You can clue me in on the way."

Obo did that infuriating half-smile. "Passport? Where we're going we don't need passports. But we do need to hurry."

Matt grabbed the jacket off the chair and tugged his keys out of his pants pocket. "I thought you said we're going to Al-Jannah."

"Yeah, well, it's not exactly the easiest place to find. Nor be found in once you're there. But let's worry about that when we get there." The cat picked up the leather bag and waited for Matt to open the front door.

A squawk stopped both of them.

Humphrey leaned off the edge of the table in the corner, a steady inch-long flame making his point for him.

Obo groaned. "Great. The little buzzard's incensed." He rolled his yellow eyes. "We have to bring him along."

"Are you serious? If anyone sees him, we're screwed."

"Look, Matt, we can stand here arguing as long as you like, but the longer we do, the more opportunities of ugliness Faruq has. Stick the lizard on your head, throw on a hat, and no one will be the wiser. You might be balder, but that's a choice you'll have to make. He certainly can't stay here."

Matt scooped up Humphrey, shoved the dragon and his wide-brimmed hat onto his head, then wrenched the door open and followed Obo to the truck. He shoved the key into the ignition, released the emergency brake, and pulled on his seat belt in one fluid motion that was surprising because inside he was shaking. Where were Faruq and Eden now? Had the bastard hurt her?

Would Matt ever find her?

He shook his head. He *had* to find her. Anything less was unacceptable—the reasons for which would stay unexplored at the moment, though. He could only take so much at one time and magical genies, flying carpets, talking cats, fire-breathing dragons, and making love with Eden only to lose her in less than twenty-four hours had him on overload.

"You might want to call someone to care for the don-key," Obo suggested. "We might be gone a while."

"This ought to be good," Matt muttered, feeling for his cell phone. Hayden would love this one.

He dialed his brother's number and Hayden, of course, picked up on the first ring.

"Matt?" Gotta love caller ID.

"Hey, Hay." Their inside joke from childhood that Matt hadn't used in longer than he could remember. Funny how it popped out now.

"Matt, how's Eden? Amanda and I were worried. Did the coffee burn her?"

If only Matt could come clean about how she really was. "She's okay, Hay, but there's been, uh, a family emergency. We have to go out of town. Can you do me a favor?"

"Of course, Matt. Anything."

It was always like that with Hayden. Whatever anyone needed. Offered freely and sincerely. Matt had never appreciated his brother's generosity more than right now—which was his problem in a nutshell.

Another thing that would remain unexplored for the moment.

"There's a donkey tied up in my backyard. Can you make sure he's got hay and water, and if the weather looks bad, put him in my garage?"

"A donkey? What are you doing with a donkey?"

"I don't have time for explanations, Hay. Can you do it?"

"Of course."

"Great. Thanks. I owe you." He hung up the phone before the words registered.

I owe you. Normally, those words would eat at his gut, but with the worry over Eden, they didn't bother him.

Something else for him to explore later.

"Can you go faster?" Obo stood up on the seat with his paws on the dashboard. "We have to get moving."

"I'm going as fast as I can, Obo. The last thing we need is to get pulled over. We're still at the mercy of the airlines, no matter how quickly we get there."

"That's where you're wrong, Matt."

"Wrong? What do you mean?"

"You really aren't getting this whole magic thing, are you?" The cat sighed and returned to the passenger seat. He swatted the leather bag over to Matt with his paw. "As much as it pains me, I'm giving this to you."

Matt, his attention alternating between traffic, his speedometer, the claws "massaging" his scalp, and the cat, reached for the bag. "What is it?"

He tugged on one of the strings and a gold coin, larger than a Kennedy half dollar, tumbled out onto his lap.

"Don't lose it!" Obo leapt onto Matt's lap, cat claws meeting the back of Matt's hand as they both searched for the coin.

"Do you mind, Obo? I don't need your claws in my groin." The ones in his head were doing enough damage.

He shoved the cat off him and felt around between his legs, shuddering to think what Obo's claws could have done there. Spiking through his jeans into his thigh was bad enough.

"Watch out!" Obo screeched.

Matt looked up in time to slam on his brakes to avoid rear-ending the truck in front of him. The forward momentum guided the coin into his hand and the few seconds before the traffic light turned green gave him time to study the thing.

Gold, with a raised edge and a profile with a feathered headdress on one side, an ankh on the back. If it weren't in such good shape, Matt would swear it was ancient. "What is this?"

The cat peeled himself off the floor and settled back in the passenger seat. "You wouldn't believe me if I told you."

"Right. Like something is going to be more unbelievable than genies and a talking cat."

Obo flicked his tail. "Good point. Okay, here's the deal. It belonged to Cleopatra and—"

"Hold on. Cleopatra? *The* Cleopatra? Julius Caesar's Cleopatra?"

"Well, technically, she was more Mark Antony's Cleopatra, but, yeah, that one. Although, why she kept aligning herself with men like them was beyond me. She'd always had a thing about autonomy before."

"How did you get Cleopatra's coin, Obo?"

The cat brushed a paw over his whiskers. "The how isn't important. Nor is the why. What *is* important is what that amulet can do."

"It can do something?" Matt wasn't even sure he wanted to know the answer to that question. "Is there *any*thing that can't do something? Milk carton, maybe? A tree? Stop sign? Oh, never mind. Those can change colors."

"Don't freak out on me now, Matt. The amulet's a big deal. You've got one shot to make it work. For all our sakes, don't screw it up. When we get in a less conspicuous area, I'll go over how to use it."

"Screw what up? Use it? What the hell are you talking about, Obo?"

Just then, a camel walked into traffic, and Matt was the only driver who didn't seem surprised to see it. Everyone else slammed on their brakes. Matt did, too, to avoid another accident, and the amulet went flying.

"Don't lose it!" Obo yelled and Matt fumbled to catch it, sending the car veering toward the sidewalk.

He caught the amulet and spun the wheel, throwing the truck onto two of its tires like the stunt driver he wasn't. The cat went tumbling off the passenger seat onto the floor. The truck wobbled but made the turn, fishtailing around a van. His hat flew off, depositing Humphrey onto the seat, and the amulet flew out of Matt's hand. It hit him in the chest and he smacked his hand there to trap it, all while turning the truck into the first opening he saw.

An alley.

A dead-end alley.

Matt grasped the amulet before slamming on his brakes. The truck kept skidding forward. Why couldn't he just find Eden and be done with the rest of this bullshit?

A flash of light burst ahead of him and Matt crossed his arms in front of his face, bracing for impact—

Chapter 19

EDEN YANKED HER ARMS OUT OF FARUQ'S GRASP, waved away the red smoke, and stumbled away from him, reaching for the chair where she'd dropped the coat—only the coat wasn't there anymore.

Neither was the chair. Nor was Matt's living room.

Now she stood in a tent big enough to house six families comfortably. A tent she'd never seen—nor wanted to because she knew what it was.

Faruq's harem's tent. Empty but for the two of them.

Somewhere amid the swirling sands that hid the genie capital city from the outside world, eclipsed in grandeur only by the High Master's citadel and the ancient buildings used for genie training, Faruq's palace was a beautiful bower that housed a scorpion.

But, oh, did he try to make this part of his lair appealing. A fine dusting of red Glimmer shimmered over everything. A harp with self-strumming strings. A fountain bubbling with champagne. Dozens of white doves cooing amid strands of twinkling lights laced through erotic acacia tree topiaries. A garden of sensuality that made Eden's skin crawl.

As did the lavish bed on the dais that looked as if it'd come straight out of the Playboy mansion, with brass ewers full of white and purple peacock irises flanking the corners. Draped in yards of red silk, a bottle of wine, two glasses, and a tray of fruit beside it, the whole setup reeked of tacky.

The marble bust of the High Master—could the loser be any more of a suck-up—was the crowning absurdity. Lack of imagination and finesse, that was Faruq. Unlike Matt—

She couldn't think about Matt. Not if she wanted to get out of here. If she started dwelling on Matt and last night and exactly all she was losing by losing him, she'd never be able to concentrate. Hell, she'd never be able to breathe.

"Welcome home, Eden." Faruq's smooth and smarmy voice grated across her nerves.

"You bastard."

"Actually, I'm not." Faruq removed his glass-orbed scepter from the silk ties that bound it to the bedpost and twirled it through his hands. "My parents were married. Not happily so, but then, who is these days? Happiness isn't exactly a requirement for marriage, is it?"

"You're not going to get away with this, Faruq." She rubbed her wrists where—*zift!*—he'd trapped her with new bracelets. Gaudy, showy—pretentious, just like him.

But he still didn't have her bottle. She had a chance. Miniscule, but better than none.

"And your mortal called my lines unoriginal." Faruq flicked his hand and a hundred flames appeared above a hundred candles, Glimmer falling in a shower of sparkles. "Please. Save me the histrionics. I will get away with it because I've done nothing wrong. I returned a rogue genie to the fold. But then, no one knows you went rogue. No one knows you went missing." He walked to the bed and looked over his shoulder. "Yet."

Eden swallowed the sick feeling that rose from her

stomach. She wouldn't give him the satisfaction—in fear or in bed. Bastard.

"Ah, smart girl. Learning to keep your mouth shut. I knew you had it in you, Eden. You were just misguided." He waved the scepter and the bedcovers slid back to reveal tacky red satin sheets, a comet trail of Glimmer following the movement. He removed his turban and set it on a blood red cushion atop an onyx pillar, then waved his fingers toward the walls surrounding the courtyard. "Do you know how many out there would change places with you in a heartbeat? How many would find it an honor? *Want* to be in The Service? Yet you, at the first opportun—"

"First? Are you kidding?" She stomped her foot, stupid bells on the toes of her slippers jingling. He thought he was so clever. As if bells would prevent her from hiding from him if she got the chance. "I've been in that bottle longer than I was out of it."

"Time has no meaning to us other than something to mark the passage of as we earn our Eternal Reward. Yet you would jeopardize that Reward for all of us by your actions. Do you really want this to become known? You may not enjoy being a genie, but I guarantee you'll enjoy being a pariah even less." Another wave of Faruq's scepter floated a stem of grapes above his head and he tongued two into his mouth, an action that'd be pitiful if it weren't so repulsive.

Genies would gain entrance to their Celestial Paradise on Judgment Day through Service to mortals in a One-For-All/All-For-One camaraderie. Screw it up and *pariah* would be a nice name to be called.

"So, let's discuss saving both your reputation and

your way of life. Or *someone's* life, anyhow." Faruq set the rest of the grapes down, then poured two glasses of wine—but didn't offer her one. Not that she cared. "The High Master may favor you, Eden, but he can't protect you from being charged as a rogue. That would threaten our very existence and we can't have that. Therefore, you will agree to be bound to me for eternity. In marriage." He raised his glass. "And your secret shall be safe."

"I'd rather die."

Faruq savored a sip of the wine, his obsidian eyes narrowing. "Yes, I was afraid you'd say something dramatic like that. And, again, unoriginal. I guess all those movies you wasted your time watching during your incarceration had to rub off, eh? Perhaps you would have been better served studying genie comportment and rogue punishment." He nodded at her wrists. "And the technological advances of new bracelets." His lips slid into that smarmy, know-it-all smirk she'd seen him do so many times it had to be second nature by now.

But he'd never dared look at her that way. The High Master's favor had protected her.

As it wouldn't any longer. Faruq was right. No matter how much she claimed that it wasn't her fault, that she was looking for her bottle, since she had neither the bottle in her possession nor a master, the High Master would consider her rogue. That, he'd never forgive.

Faruq laid his scepter across the pillows, picked up the other glass of wine, and took even, measured steps toward her as a panther might do to its hapless victim, an analogy that felt all too real. "So? What do you think? Are the bracelets perfect or what?"

Eden took the glass, meeting his eyes, an "or what" on her lips that she decided not to voice at the last second. Oh, she wasn't going to back down. There had to be a way to get the upper hand. Something she could blackmail him with or use for revenge. She just didn't want to clue him in to her plans.

Because, for as long as Faruq had been around and for as many people as he'd pissed off, there had to be *something*. She'd find it, and when she did, he was going to rue the day he'd ever threatened her.

Eden sipped the wine, letting it flow over her tongue like victory.

Until she realized that while finding blackmail material, she'd also have to figure out how to get rid of the new bracelets, recover the bottle stopper *and* her bottle, and keep Matt safe. And then there was Humphrey. And, oh yeah, some way to remain free.

She almost choked. *Remain*? She wasn't free. Hadn't been, not even for a minute. No matter how much she'd like to delude herself, from the second she'd left her bottle, she'd been on a race against the clock *and* Faruq, exchanging one prison for another.

Although Matt's arms hadn't felt like a prison.

She couldn't think about it—Matt—now. Not like that. Love between a mortal and a genie? Give up her powers and immortality? Her mother had done it—and who'd paid for it?

She had.

No, she had to concentrate on getting away from Faruq, and she needed her magic to do that. Without magic, she might as well just give in to him.

So she'd humor the bastard. Let him think he'd won.

Lull him into making a mistake. It wasn't the best plan, but until she could come up with another, it'd have to do.

She raised her glass. "Fine, Faruq. You win." For now.

Faruq clinked his glass with hers. "I knew you'd see it my way. This calls for a celebration. Who should we invite to announce our upcoming nuptials? Our family? Oh that's right, you have none. No one. Except of course, the High Master. Wouldn't want to lose him, would you, Eden?"

That was cruel and Faruq knew it. But she wouldn't let him see her pain. "Your point is taken, Faruq."

But it didn't mean she was going to accept it.

"Good. See that you remember it." He set his wine down and flourished his hands for a ridiculous, over-compensating gesture of darkening the sky as if it were night, Glimmer falling like stardust, the tent now lit only by candles and those twinkling lights—and even those Faruq dimmed. She hated that, in Al-Jannah, things were never as they seemed.

He waved his hands again and this time, Eden's clothing changed.

She'd thought nothing could be worse than that red harem outfit.

She'd thought wrong.

Diaphanous gold pants, cuffed at her ankles and ob-scenely transparent, and the gold thong beneath didn't cover as much as she'd like. On the matching bodice, held together between her breasts by the thinnest strand of gold chain, strategically-placed sequins hid her nip-ples, but she might as well not be wearing anything for all the coverage it gave her. The gold slippers were the only part of this outfit that actually concealed some of her body, and, luckily, they didn't have bells.

"Oh, come on. Really? You've got to be kidding me, Faruq."

"Actually, Eden, I'm not." He took the glass from her fingers, then curled his around them. "I've waited far too long for this."

He tugged her toward the bed. Eden was going to be sick. *Stars*, after last night with Matt, she couldn't allow him to touch her. Not like this. It would be an abomination and she couldn't do it. If only there were some way to outwit him.

A breeze ruffled the vase of peacock irises, giving her an idea. She was a genie. She knew how to do magic. And since Faruq didn't know her new Way, she could surprise him.

Sadly, she couldn't do anything directly *to* him. By virtue of his position and that damned scepter, Faruq could deflect magic against his person, but other things…

Eden pretended to stumble to mask the sound of her catching her breath, suffering Faruq's embrace as he caught her—and the quick, revolting feel he copped. Bastard.

He'd pay for this. She'd *make* him pay for humiliating her. For taking advantage of her disadvantage, a ploy Faruq was well known for.

"Can't wait to be in my arms now that the deal's done, Eden? A millennia and a half *is* a long time to go without, isn't it?" He grabbed her chin, forcing her to face him, so close she could smell what he had for lunch—which only turned her stomach more. "Ah, my mistake. You corrected that deficit last night, didn't you? With a mortal." He chuckled and it rankled. "The date doesn't fall far from the palm tree, does it, Eden? I would have thought you'd have learned from your mother's mistakes."

"Leave my mother out of this." No matter how much she wanted to, she couldn't keep the venom from her voice.

Faruq smiled his cold, calculating sneer. "Don't think you can best me, Eden. Those bracelets will remain on your wrists until I deem you trustworthy. We'll see how argumentative you want to be once you've given birth to a dozen of my children."

A *dozen*? The vizier had a high opinion of himself.

Luckily, the peacock she'd conjured poked its jeweled head into the tent just then or Eden would have lost the contents of her stomach all over Faruq's favorite *bisht*—not that that would have been such a loss.

The peacock shook Eden's pale yellow Glimmer from his feathers, any residual blending in with his normal iridescence. "Your Magnificence," he said, using the term that would make Faruq preen more than the bird, "your presence is required in the High Master's chambers immediately."

Faruq spun around, a self-satisfied smile on his face.

Thank the heavens for Faruq's social-climbing aspirations. The summons was the only thing that would get him off her.

For now.

Chapter 20

AT THE FLASH OF BLINDING LIGHT, MATT BRACED himself for the impact—

The one that never came.

Well, not unless he wanted to count the one where his chest hit the steering wheel after his brakes kicked in, but there was no accordion-type crunch to the front end of his truck.

That would be because there was no wall.

There also wasn't an alley. Or a road.

What there was, was sand. Miles of it. Everywhere he looked.

And sun. Hot, blistering, blazing sun.

And the cat.

And a dragon.

Humphrey rolled over, tugging the wing that was caught between the seats. Matt freed him as Obo crawled out from under the dash, his claws digging neat little holes into the leather seat. "Jesus J., Matt. Were you *trying* to kill us?"

Matt set Humphrey on the dash. "Jesus *J*.? I think you mean Jesus H."

"Oh really? Were you there? It's J. For Joachim. After Mary's father. But that's not important right now." Obo looked out the passenger window. "Well, at least you got us here. Talk about a friggin' miracle."

"Exactly where is *here*, Obo? I don't see a thing."

"That's the beauty of it." Obo turned around on the seat, then lifted his front paws. "Holy mother of the Maker." He did a four-footed version of a two-step with another round of expletives, followed by a leap back onto the floor. "You *had* to have leather seats, didn't you?"

Matt put his hat on his head, tilting it over his eyes so the sun's reflection off the sand wouldn't burn holes in his retinas. Humphrey spread his wings and flapped them slowly, his gaze riveted out the windshield. At what, Matt couldn't imagine. Nothing around them but sand. "Obo, what the hell's going on? We're in the middle of nowhere."

The cat licked one of his front paws. "We're not nowhere, Matt. We're right where we want to be."

"Oh? And where is that?"

"Paradise."

Matt swiped a hand across his mouth. Man, it was hot. "You have a warped sense of paradise, cat. I thought yours included beluga caviar, not scorpions and tumbleweeds."

The cat rolled his eyes. "Listen up, smart guy. We're waiting for the next sandstorm to appear. When it does, I want you to drive right into it, holding the amulet against your heart and wishing to see Eden. Then you'll find your paradise."

"Who drives into a sandstorm? You're trying to kill me."

"Trust me, I don't need to. You were doing a damned fine job of it yourself. What were you thinking, heading into an alley? I'm just thankful you got your priorities straight and wished us here."

Matt squinted out the window. "I still don't know where here is."

"Al-Jannah. The genie City of Paradise. Haven't you been listening to a word I've said?"

The problem was, the cat said too many things—and it was the very act of saying them that was still weirding Matt out. Now he had a missing genie—two, actually—and he was sitting in a desert waiting for a sandstorm, trying to come to grips with the fact that he now believed all of this alternate reality was real. But he drew the line at invisible cities. A guy had to have some standards.

"So do I have to be a genie to see this city? That's going to make finding it kind of hard, Obo."

The cat licked his other paw. "No, you don't have to be a genie. You can't see it because it's not here yet. It'll be in the sandstorm. That's what Genius here is waiting for." Obo nodded at Humphrey, whose tongue was running around the rim of his mouth as if he were salivating.

Or dehydrating.

Matt urged Humphrey onto his finger like a parakeet. "What sandstorm? I don't see any sandstorm." Nor did he see a city, a road, or a way back to civilization. This cat better know what he was talking about—and that alone worried the hell out of Matt.

"The next storm to come by."

Matt adjusted his leg on the seat and set Humphrey on his hat out of direct sunlight. "And you know this how? Why wouldn't it just be a regular old sandstorm?"

The cat went to work cleaning his belly fur. If he went any lower, Matt was going to kick him out of the truck. He wasn't going to be party to *that*.

"Because, Matt." Obo looked up, a fur ball hanging from the end of his tongue, which he then spat onto the floor. "The amulet's got a lock on it, like your GPS systems, and there are no such things as regular sand-storms here. It's always Al-Jannah. But no one knows it unless they know the way in."

"And you do. Next you're going to tell me the way in is to say 'open sesame.'"

"That would be a little obvious, don't you think?" The cat jumped onto Matt's lap and looked out the win-dow. "Ah ha. See? Sandstorm at two o'clock. Let's get moving. You got the amulet handy?"

Matt held it up and put the car in drive, turning to-ward the storm, questioning his sanity all the way.

"Okay, hold onto it and hit the gas."

He couldn't believe he was about to do this. "Won't I run into something when we enter the city?"

"It's a risk we'll have to take. I don't want to miss the storm or we'll have to find the next location, and who knows how long Eden has with that prick. Just make sure you're thinking of her when we hit the storm."

Eden. Matt's heart constricted as he remembered the look on her face when Faruq had slapped those bracelets on her. *Slave*. The word replayed in his head. No one should ever be under anyone's power like that.

Matt gripped the amulet tighter and pressed down on the gas, angling the car to intercept the swirling sand, holding his breath as thousands of grains pinged off his windows and visibility went no farther than the wind-shield while Humphrey crooned some odd purring noise atop his head.

The next thing Matt knew, visibility went to nothing, the truck was covered in yards of silk instead of sand, and someone was shouting his name.

Chapter 21

"MATT? OH, MY STARS! MATT!"

It took a second to register that they were out of the sandstorm, but when it did, Matt slammed on the brakes, threw the truck into park, and shoved the door open.

It opened a mere three inches before getting stuck on the fabric that stretched taut across the opening.

"Matt?"

"Eden? Is that you?"

"Of course it's her, you idiot. Who else knows your name here?" Obo clambered over his lap again. "Allow me."

Obo's front claws made short work of the fabric, slicing through it like a razor. His back claws were doing the same thing through Matt's jeans.

Matt shoved the door again, ripping more of the silk, and a swath billowed over his head like a deflating hot air balloon, but Matt fought his way free, knocking off his hat in the process. Humphrey, still atop it, breathed a trail of smoke all the way down.

Matt bent down to pick up both the hat and the dragon, stopping when he saw Eden.

Tied to a chair, her hands lashed to the arm rests, fingers bound by strips of cloth, no one had ever looked so good.

In two strides he was beside her. And kissing her a second later.

God, she felt so good. *Alive*. Warm and sexy and just as happy to see him as he was her.

Then she slid her tongue between his lips and Matt gave up thinking altogether.

"Oh, kiiiidddsss…" Something poked the back of Matt's leg.

Eden swirled her tongue around his and Matt couldn't have cared less about whatever was behind him—until four sharp razors jabbed through his jeans. That pain grabbed his attention really fast. He tore his lips from Eden's. "Son of a bitch!"

Obo leapt aside, avoiding the kick Matt leveled at him. *Instinctively* leveled at him, of course. What kind of guy would he be if he kicked a cat?

"Hey, look, you guys want to get all kissy-face sweaty, it's no fur off my back."

A smart-ass cat.

"However, I thought this whole rescue thing was to get you out of Faruq's clutches. Correct me if I'm wrong, but I hadn't realized you two were up for a three-some," continued Mr. Annoying. "You might want to check with Faruq on that one. Something tells me he's not one to share his toys."

"Point taken, Obo." Matt stepped away from Eden, but not too far. Damn, he was glad to see her.

Then he saw what was behind her beneath the part of the tent that was still standing.

A bed. On a dais. Flowers, wine, doves, soft lights. Who the *fuck* did Faruq think he was?

And then he saw what she was wearing.

He'd kill him.

He'd flat out kill Faruq for subjecting her to this, and

he wouldn't feel one ounce of remorse. Yet more sins to lay at the genie's stupid curly-toed slippers. "We need to get you something else to wear," he said, tearing at her bindings.

"Oh I don't know." She smiled and his blood went racing south. "You didn't seem to mind this sort of thing yesterday."

"That was yesterday." Before last night.

Eden's soft smile proved she understood the reference.

Obo, on the other hand, gagged. "Yeah, yeah, whatever. This is more important than some imagined fashion emergency, Matt. Pissed-off vizier ringing anyone's bells? Eden?"

It didn't take Matt long to get her free. "Come on. Let's get out of here."

"Oh, really? Going to drive down the center of town, are you?" Obo asked, shaking one back leg free of the silk. "Hold that thought while I paint a big ol' bull's eye in the flatbed."

"No. We'll leave the same way we got here. Amulet, remember?" Matt held it up.

"We can't." Eden lifted her wrists. "Thanks to these, Faruq can track us down in no time. Same as Glimmer. Worse, actually."

Yet more shit that Matt wanted to make Faruq pay for. "Great. So I've come to a magical city to rescue a genie who can't use her magic to escape a guy who can?"

"Pretty much." The cat, not surprisingly, snorted. He shook his other back leg, more silk caught on his claws.

Matt held up her jeweled wrist. "But aren't those diamonds? We'll pry one off and use it to get rid of the bracelets."

Obo snorted again. "Not to be Johnny Raincloud, but if Faruq gets back while you're playing jeweler, it's not gonna matter if the bracelets are off or not. What say we leave, and maybe, oh I don't know, hide, *then* try to get the bracelets off? All in favor?" Now his two front paws waved silk in the air and Humphrey burned a hole through the fabric covering him, clawing his way free.

Obo had a point. And he knew it, too, from the smart-ass smile on his face.

"Good call, Einstein." Matt grabbed Eden's hand. "So, how about zapping us home? We'll use the nippers, and you'll be free in no time."

Eden shook her head, a swath of her hair falling over her shoulder to offer some semblance of modesty, thank God.

For *his* sake.

"I can't zap us anywhere," she said. "Especially not there. It'll be the first place Faruq looks."

Matt didn't need the reminder. How, exactly, did one make a home magic-proof?

"Faruq found me once; he'll find me again. Remember that magic leaves Glimmer in the spectrasphere? In Al-Jannah, it literally hangs in the air like confetti and it's distinctive, just like the individual shades of bottles and lamps. Faruq can track me anywh—Hey!" Eden snapped her fingers. "That's it!"

"What's *it*?" Matt and Obo asked in unison.

"The Genie Placement System. It's a bank of crystals that tells Faruq where any of us is at all times. It's how he monitors the signals sent by the bracelets."

"Oh, sure." The cat snorted again and flopped onto his belly, spitting a wad of silk out of his mouth. Good to know someone was finding this a laughing matter. "Why not go for djinn's eggs while you're at it? You know, I think I'd be a much better human than you two."

Eden flicked Obo's ear. "Really, Obo, we could use some help here—" She pulled her hand back. "Actually, that's a good idea."

"What? Are you out of your veil-wearing mind? Djinn's eggs? You can't be serious."

"Yeah, I am."

"Oh, hell in a hand basket," the cat muttered. "How do I get myself involved in these things?"

"Yes, Obo, how *do* you get involved with them?" Eden nudged the cat with one of those ridiculous slippers. "I bet it'd make an interesting book someday. Or a case study. A defense, even."

"I'm not the one who's running from the bad guy, Eden." The cat swatted her slipper. "And you better do something about your dragon. He's going to be a liability real quick."

To prove the point, Humphrey lit the silk on fire and the flames licked their way toward Matt's truck.

Matt stomped on them before anything exploded, though his temper was nearing that point. "Would one of you care to tell me what you're talking about?"

"I'll let Madame Curie here tell you." Obo stuck his tail up and turned around.

Eden looked at him, and for the first time since Faruq had shown up, he saw her eyes sparkle.

"Djinn's eggs are a plant in the High Master's park. A tea made from the flowers can change a genie's Glimmer for a little while. I can use that to alter my Glimmer so Faruq won't be able to follow me by my magic. If we find the GPS and retrieve my crystal, it won't matter if I get the bracelets off or not. He won't know it was me."

"Okay, so we change your Glimmer, find the crystals, steal yours, then get out and go home. Did I miss anything?" Matt turned around and retrieved his hat.

"Yeah," Obo said, "the part where I find someone's nice comfy sofa to live out the rest of my life on."

This time, it was Eden who snorted. She flicked his back paw. "Good luck with that, Obo."

Obo jumped to his paws and his yellow eyes widened. "Uh, I think you mean, 'Good luck with *that.*'" Obo's fur bristled on his arched back.

The cat's tone had Matt spinning around. "Good luck with wh—? Oh shit!"

A horde of swordsmen swarmed down the stone steps behind an obscene pair of topiaries on the far side of the courtyard and Matt didn't need Obo's "Retreeeeeeat!" to grab Eden's hand and run.

The cat managed, despite slipping on the silk, to streak past them before Matt and Eden reached the truck.

"They'll be able to see where we're going in this," Eden protested.

"Better they see us going than we meet them coming!" Matt yelled, shoving that cute backside of hers into the cab two heartbeats after Obo. "We'll ditch the truck later. Right now we need to get out of here."

Silk covered the driver's-side window when Matt slammed the door shut, but he didn't need to see through that window to back up. Stomping on the gas, he fishtailed the back end of the truck, tires pealing, sending Faruq's clichéd love trappings flying, and tossing more silk across the windshield as another section of tent gave way. That was going to be a problem when they turned around, but Matt didn't have a choice.

"Hang on!" he yelled, spinning the steering wheel the opposite direction, executing a perfect one-eighty in the courtyard.

"Hang on? To what?" Obo half-yowled, half-screeched as he landed on the floor.

Eden, God love her, grabbed onto *him*. Talk about having priorities straight—

"Here they come!" Her warning cut into that thought.

Matt jerked the gearshift into drive, wrenching the wheel to the left to avoid the hot tub in front of him, and stomped on the gas again, spewing silk out from under his tires and dragging it off the driver's side window just in time to show the scimitar-brandishing warriors floundering beneath the spewing silk. Faruq's tent had come in handy for something—and thankfully not what Dickwad had planned.

"Where's Faruq?" Matt gunned the engine as an arrow shot over the cab roof. They sped beneath a flower-covered pergola.

"Away. But I don't know for how long." Eden looked out the back window. "Especially now."

"Now?" Matt jerked when a loud *whoosh* sounded behind them.

"Jesus J!" Obo leapt onto the dashboard. "Why not just send up fireworks, too, while you're at it?"

Matt glanced in the rearview mirror. "I didn't do that."

"That" was fire searing through what had once been Faruq's tent, the burning silk sinking onto that obscene platform Dickwad called a bed. Good. Saved Matt the trouble of destroying it.

"Hey, whaddya know? The little flamethrower came in handy after all!" Obo smacked the dash, then slid off backward when they bounced over something in their path.

"Humphrey!" Eden cried out, turning in her seat. "We have to go back for him."

"Are you out of your mind, Eden?" Obo grumbled. "Do you see what's back there? That's suicide. The lizard can take care of himself just fine. He'll probably head home anyway. Isn't there a field of dragon's blood trees around here somewhere? Unless he lit his nostrils on fire, he ought to be able to sniff that out, I'd think."

The cat hauled himself onto the seat. "Besides, do you really want to be skulking around corners with a novice dragon? No way would you be able to pull that off—son-of-a-bichon! Matt! Watch out!"

A lake appeared out of nowhere, with a boat moored to the dock he was heading straight for—a *swan* boat. Matt rolled his eyes as he spun the wheel again. Faruq needed a better M.O. "I'm on it, Obo."

"That's what I'm worried about! Do something!"

The turn tight, the truck clipped a marble pillar with a gigantic flower arrangement on it, giving Matt a great deal of satisfaction when the vase teetered then crunched beneath the tires—a satisfaction that was short-lived when a barrage of arrows, some flaming, *thunked* into the flatbed.

"Step on it, Matt!" Obo hollered.

"I know! The truck only goes so fast!"

"Tell that to the archers, will ya?" The cat dove onto the floor as an arrow destroyed the side mirror.

Matt zigzagged as another arrow pinged off the truck.

All they'd need would be one in a tire and this would be all over. The courtyard, surrounded by a high stone wall, seemed to grow larger the closer they drove toward the only exit he could see: a wide horseshoe-shaped arch in the center of the wall—where the swordsmen were also headed.

"Uh, Eden?" He nodded toward the congregating barbarians. "I think you're going to have to use your magic."

"But it'll lead Faruq to us."

"Just to get us on the other side of the wall. I'll do the rest."

"Heavens help us," the cat muttered from the floor, his paws clasped in—*prayer*?

Matt didn't take the time to do a double-take.

"Okay." Eden's grip tightened on his thigh. "Hang on to your hat."

"I don't have a hat," the cat grumbled just as Eden caught her breath and—

The next thing Matt knew, they were barreling down a narrow cobblestone street, a line—or six—of someone's laundry obscuring the windshield and flowing off the sides of the truck like streamers.

He slammed on the brakes, just missing the mule that wandered into their path.

"Your doing?" He glanced at Eden, trying not to notice the way her breasts rose and fell. Life and death situations were *not* the time to notice how sexy she looked in that outfit.

"Not funny." She let go of the death grip she'd had on his leg.

Pity.

"Of course the mule isn't mine. I wouldn't want to leave any more Glimmer around."

The cat *pfft*-ed something out of his mouth and climbed back onto the seat, dragging the amulet's bag with him. "Glad you two are finding our predicament funny, but I'm thinking this is, ya know, life or death. Anyone with me on this? Start planning what we're going to do next, or should we look for a comedy club? Whaddya say, oh great rescuer of damsels in distress?"

Matt would gladly strangle the cat right now. "We could kick you out of the truck."

"Considering we have to ditch it, that's not that big a threat."

"Chill, Obo. It's a normal reaction to stress." As was wanting to wrap his arms around Eden and not let go for a long, long time.

Yeah, keep telling yourself that, Ewing. Stress. That's the reason you're hyper-tuned to every move she makes. Uh-huh.

"You guys can crack each other up when this is all said and done." Obo leapt back onto the dashboard, standing on his haunches as he looked over the pile of clothing on the windshield. "We still have to get the crystal."

"And my bottle stopper."

Shit. Matt had forgotten about that. Could this get any worse? "Please tell me you know where it is."

She looked at him and together they said, "With Faruq."

Yeah, it could get worse.

Matt swiped a hand across his face. "So, say we get both of those items without managing to run into Faruq, then what? We can leave?"

This time the cat groaned. "Sure. If we find a way out of Al-Jannah."

"*Find* a way?"

The cat nodded. "You don't think you can just mosey on in and out of the most magical place on earth, do you? That's what the amulet's all about. Even though your average Joe Citizen can't use magic, there are all sorts of wards and spells and Glimmer all over this place. Keeps the locals in line and helps keep the riffraff out. Or *in*, as the case may be now."

"Wait. You brought me here, knowing we couldn't get out? What did I ever do to you? Is this about the beluga? Christ, I knew cats were finicky, but this is ridiculous, Obo."

"Get a grip, Matt. This has nothing to do with the caviar, though, now that you mention it, if we get out of this with our lives, I wouldn't mind—"

"Guys, you're losing focus here." Eden flicked Obo's ear.

Obo huffed. "Ow! Hey, he was off-topic, too."

Eden flicked the cat again.

"Fine." Obo sighed. "Look, Matt, it's not impossible. There are ways. We just have to find them."

"And what, exactly, do you know about it, Obo?" This time, when Eden went to flick his ear, the cat ducked.

"Let's just say that my checkered past is going to come in handy now." The cat turned around and poked a claw at them like an index finger. "But here's the deal. I need to make sure there are certain, um, events in order before we can find a way out of here, so you two are going to have to recover those items by yourselves. Trust me, you don't want me along anyway. I'm not exactly a favored son in many parts of this place. So I'll do my thing, you guys do yours, and we'll all try to not get ourselves killed. I suggest we rendezvous at the entrance to the Valley of Contentrum at sunrise. By then, you'll either have what you need or Faruq will have you, so it won't matter. Savvy?"

"Savvy?" Matt flicked him too—retaliation for the claws in his leg. "What? Were you a pirate in one of your nine lives?"

"How'd you know I was on number n— never mind. Don't you worry about my past. Savvy's a good word. Covers a broad spectrum. Kind of like the 'y'all' those Southerners use. Not the best grammar, but it does the trick. Now quit standing here yapping, and let's get moving. Sunrise, got it? And I'm going to need the amulet."

Matt was none too thrilled to give it to him, but when Eden agreed with the cat, Matt handed it over.

Handed over control of his life to someone else. Something he swore he wouldn't do again.

And to a *cat* at that.

Chapter 22

EDEN LED MATT THROUGH ALLEYWAY AFTER ALLEYWAY, the stupid curled toes on her slippers making running difficult. Who came up with these things? In her bottle they'd been whimsical; now they were just plain stupid. She needed new clothes, but she couldn't risk conjuring anything until she changed her Glimmer and wouldn't have to worry about the consequences.

Although, when it came to consequences, stumbling in slippers had some good ones: every time she stumbled, Matt was there for her.

She couldn't remember the last time someone had been there for her. Well, not since her parents had died, but she wasn't going to trip down that lane. She didn't do Pity Party.

Then she tripped in the alley instead, and Matt's strong hands gripped her arms.

"You okay?"

She nodded, not trusting herself to speak, trying to stave off both Pity Party *and* Screaming Hormones. Now was *not* the time.

Last night had only whetted her appetite. When this nightmare was over, she was going to whisk the two of them away for an uninterrupted, week-long flying-comforter ride. It'd be the least she could do for him since he'd come to save her—and the most she could do for herself. Eden turned down another alley but had to double back. A group of elders drinking *arak* and playing chess who had little chance of attaining the ranks of a genie in The Service weren't likely to be thrilled to help someone who had and didn't want it.

"This way!" She grabbed Matt's hand and ran through the back door of a salon.

A cloud of silvery-pink Glimmer hit her in the face so thickly as she entered that she choked on it.

"What the hell's this stuff?" Matt coughed.

"Glimmer," Eden answered.

"I thought you said no one was allowed to use magic?"

Matt waved his arms and the pink particles drifted onto him. Only real men could wear pink and still look sexy—not that now was the time to be thinking about things like that.

"The *Mawla* of Magic is always permitted to use magic," answered a woman shelving supplies in a cabinet by the back door. She turned around, smoothing her aquamarine sari in a controlled motion that had nothing to do with wrinkles and everything to do with sizing Matt up. And not in any way that made Eden jealous. More in a way that made her nervous.

The woman had pegged him for a tourist—the mortal kind. Attention they didn't need.

They also didn't need Matt asking any more questions, so Eden plastered a smile to her face and reached for his hand. "Place looks great. Aisha did a wonderful job."

She backed out of the room, dragging him with her, the woman's eyes on them all the way.

"The *Mawla* of Magic?" Matt asked in the corridor.

Eden peered around the corner. No one was watching for them. Yet.

"The *Mawla*—Aisha—reports to the High Master along with Faruq and a few others. She's the Master of Necessary Magic. Things like droppings-free birds, flying-carpet taxis, self-flaming street lanterns, that sort of thing. For the common good."

The front of the store had Aisha's Glimmer all over it. Fuchsia chiffon ribbons spiraled and twirled above patrons who sat on fluffy cloud cushions and bathed their feet in frothing mineral water baths scented with lemon blossoms. Not quite sure how this constituted common good, but then it wasn't Eden's place to question Aisha. She just wanted to get out of here without drawing any more attention.

Then Matt cursed, and, sadly, that wasn't going to happen.

Eden spun around as he was trying to prevent a metal basket of therapy stones from swiveling off a brazier. He couldn't, and the basket crashed onto the parquet floor, charred wood quickly adding its own scent to the Glimmer and lemon mixture. A fire would certainly get them more attention.

"This place is designed for pixies," he muttered, bending down to gather the stones.

"Not *for*. *By*." Eden kicked a stone that had burnt a tiny hole in her slipper, then nodded at a trio of the beings above the front window. Gossamer gold wings fluttered as the pixies serenaded the clientele with sweet, high-pitched melodies.

"Pixies? Real, live pixies?" Matt stood up, the basket forgotten at his feet.

"They're certainly not dead ones." Thank the cosmos she *hadn't* brought Humphrey; pixies were a dragon treat. She just hoped he found the dragon colony all right.

She picked up the basket and returned it to the brazier. "Come on. Let's go."

She avoided crashing into a salver of mint tea and scones that served itself to the clients, and dodged a broom dancing among the alabaster workstations as if auditioning for *Fantasia* but couldn't prevent the stupid curl of her slipper from catching a curtain of lavender silk and tugging it from the ceiling. It billowed behind her onto Matt. Poor guy didn't have luck with that fabric today.

The naked woman on the massage table behind the curtain, however, probably wouldn't complain that he got a face full of silk. After she stopped cursing, that was.

Then Matt joined in with the cursing, and so did the henna artist he accidentally tossed the fabric onto when he fought his way free.

A couple more mishaps had Eden wishing they had time to make amends, but their time was just about up. Someone was going to call the authorities about the disturbance, and in Al-Jannah, all Service Officers reported to Faruq.

Once Faruq learned she'd escaped, she could kiss any hope of freedom goodbye. She'd been ready to say to hell with the consequences of using her magic and wish herself free earlier in his courtyard, but then Matt's truck had plowed through the silk walls. For a moment, she'd thought he'd been a mirage brought on by lack of sleep and fear of what Faruq had planned for her. The lack of sleep she hadn't minded, given how that had come about, but the fear... She had Faruq to blame for the fear.

She *had* to outwit him. *Had* to get away. The only thing worse than being in The Service was being in The Service to *him*.

Matt caught up to her and dragged her out of the way of a pot of yucca plants that were laughing so hard the planter was in danger of toppling over, then out the door and into the street, just in time to almost be run over by a carriage that was being pulled by a—

"Is that what I think it is?" Matt leapt back and Eden went with him, ending up in his arms.

The day wasn't a total loss.

Eden shook her head. *Mind on the problem. Not on Matt.*

"If you're thinking unicorn, Matt, then, yes, it is." She looked back at the salon. The opening front door threatened to make the day that loss she was talking about. "Come on. We have to get out of here."

They crossed the street and ran into another alley. A woman shook out a *killim* on a second floor balcony. Other rugs draped over railings, and those apartments without balconies sported wrought-iron window boxes overflowing with flowers and ivy that trailed down the whitewashed walls.

"Are you sure we're not going in circles, Eden?" Matt whispered. "Everything looks the same."

"That's because we're still in the Old World part of the city, Matt. Everything is supposed to look the same. When we get to the French Quarter, it'll be different."

"There's a French Quarter?"

"Near the park where we're headed."

A Service Officer appeared at the end of the alley and Eden pulled Matt behind a mailbox—one that was *normally* pink—with her as she pretended to tie a non-existent shoelace. "*If* we don't get caught."

Matt squeezed her hand. "We won't."

He knew nothing about the city, about her world, but Eden let herself believe him—much easier to lean on him than worry.

But an APB couldn't have gone out already. Faruq should be waiting in the foyer of the High Master's audience chamber now; he couldn't know she'd escaped. His swordsmen couldn't tell him because they weren't permitted inside the High Master's citadel, so Faruq had no way of knowing she was gone yet. They still had the element of surprise on their side.

How much longer that element would last, Eden had no idea. Faruq was a smart guy; he was bound to figure it out sooner or later.

She was really, really hoping for later.

When the officer left, Eden led Matt around yet another corner and into yet another laundry-draped alley. Back alleys weren't the best way to see the city, but they were safer.

What would it be like to wander these streets, or those of the real Paris, at her leisure? In her own time? Her own clothes?

With Matt?

Eden shook her head. Fanciful thoughts had no place in the middle of a recovery mission.

Fanciful thoughts had no place in a genie's life at all.

The next alley ended in a small corner plaza. Horseshoe-shaped archways revealed mosaic-tiled inner courtyards, their entrances blocked by intricate wrought-iron gates. Empty balconies overhead were rendered useless by the long rattan blinds that covered both windows and railings to block out the sun, perfect for her and Matt's purposes. As was the plaza, vacant but for a couple of dodo birds that stuck their heads beneath arcing jets of water in the rectangular fountain at the plaza's center. Though no one knew which mortal had found his way both in and out of the city, local legend had it that the fountain had been the inspiration for the famous one in Granada's Generalife.

Eden wouldn't doubt that this entire city had been the inspiration for that famous mortal garden and its palace. The city was so beautiful, and the weather always perfect, with a vibrant blue sky that was either a trick of the sun shining through the magical dome created by the sands swirling around the city or Aisha's magic—Eden had never been sure—and just enough morning rainfall to keep everything green. Soft breezes served dual purposes of keeping temperatures constant and imbuing the air—and the laundry—with the sweet, heady scents of gardenias, lilies, orchids, hyacinths, and jasmine.

Eden had loved Al-Jannah when she'd first seen it. It was the most beautiful place on earth—until she'd learned her fate. Then it'd become a prison.

It felt like one again.

"Which way?" Matt kept a wide berth around the birds as they crossed the square.

"To the west. The park is near the Great Pyramid."

"There's a pyramid in the French Quarter?" His fingers tightened on hers.

"Near it. Al-Jannah has anything you can imagine, Matt. Pyramids, the Colossus of Rhodes, Stonehenge, the Coliseum." Dodos. "It's all here."

Matt stopped in the center of the plaza. "So none of those was our idea? We haven't come up with any of the great wonders of our own? It's always been genies? The alien theorists were right."

"We are *not* aliens, Matt. Some of those creations are mortals' and others are ours. But Al-Jannah is a mix of the best of both worlds." And with Matt now here, she'd say it was true.

"Thank God. I was beginning to feel useless."

"Hardly. You definitely weren't useless last night." She'd hate to think what a disaster dinner could have turned into if he hadn't gotten her out of his parents' home so quickly.

"Last night?" Matt smiled, long and slow, and Eden's insides turned to mush when she realized which *part* of last night he was thinking about.

Then his eyes turned that dark, lush green, and he tucked a strand of hair behind her ear, his fingers lingering over her jaw, and the moment turned hotter than the sandstorm he'd ridden in on. Eden allowed herself to revel in it for just a moment.

Sadly, a moment was all she had before a marching band struck up in the alley they'd just come from.

"What now?" Matt dropped his hand.

"Some kind of celebration. There's always one going on in Al-Jannah." Eden scanned the plaza as the music grew louder. Near the other entrance, the doors to the pub opened, spilling customers into the plaza, which sent the dodos scampering for cover in the building alcoves.

Flags and banners appeared around the corner behind them, blocking their escape from the advancing patrons, many of whom were staring at her. Short of blasting them with her magic, a virtual "Eden Was Here" advertisement, there was only one thing she could do.

Following the dodos' example, Eden pulled Matt into the closest alcove, and shoved him into the corner. Then, since everyone loved a lover—and Matt was quite the lover—Eden wrapped her arms around his neck and proceeded to kiss him—and herself—senseless.

Chapter 23

ONE MINUTE MATT WAS TRYING TO KEEP HIS MIND OFF the events of last night, and the next, he was sandwiched between a wall and Eden, and she was recreating them, kissing him as if it were their last day on earth.

If this kiss followed to the same conclusion, he wouldn't care if it *was* their last day.

Well, okay, yes he would. If only to be able to experience more of this. More of her.

But what *was* this? What was she doing? This wasn't what they needed to be doing right now.

Matt was about to tell her that when she shoved her tongue in his mouth. Who was he to stop a woman on a mission? That *he* was her mission only added to the argument.

The tempo of the music increased. The downbeat of the drums reverberated off the stone walls, the rhythm matching the beat of his heart. His blood thudded through his veins, coursing its way to one specific area, quickly negating his argument.

And when her breasts brushed his chest, those generous curves with the most perfect nipples he'd ever tasted, Matt got hard. Harder. Then an image of her last night in the moonlight seared his brain, and Matt was all for giving the parade-goers a show. He wanted her.

Pulling her tightly against him, he groaned when he made palm-to-skin contact. Smooth and silky, just like her hair when it had glided over his naked body, her waist was the perfect span for his hands.

He slid a hand lower. One cheek fit perfectly in his palm. He squeezed and she shuddered, her thighs clenching one of his, sending his blood roaring through his veins and his internal temperature soaring.

God, had it only been hours since they'd been naked on that comforter, floating beneath the stars? It felt like a lifetime ago and he wanted that life back.

Matt slid both hands under her butt, lifting so she'd have to wrap those legs around him, still kissing her, tasting her, drowning in her scent.

His legs trembled—from their position. That was the reason. Not that she shook him so badly that he couldn't stand for want of her.

Matt leaned against the wall just to be sure. And to take advantage of the shadows. No need to get arrested for public indecency.

She shifted in his hands. His fingers brushed between her legs, through the thin, practically non-existent fabric, and he felt her swollen flesh. Felt her heat. Her wetness.

And, suddenly, Matt didn't care about public indecency. All he wanted was to get naked with Eden and ease the aches plaguing them both.

He adjusted his hold, not wanting to let go, but he needed to take off his jacket, his shirt, something so he could feel her skin against his.

Eden tightened her legs and Matt had serious thoughts about how to get rid of his jeans, too. He was on fire. *She* was on fire.

The music grew louder, maybe all of two steps from the doorway, but Matt didn't give a damn. He was burning up and needed to do something or risk dying of heat stroke on his way to heaven.

Still kissing her, Matt managed to work his jacket down to his biceps. Eden slid her hands beneath the jacket and struggled with him to get it off—

Only to abruptly end the kiss.

But she didn't pull away. "Matt, please tell me that long, hard thing in your pocket is because you're happy to see me."

His mind went blank at *long* and *hard*, and this time he was perfectly willing to admit to wobbly knees.

Then she slid her hand along his side, pressing her tightened breasts against him, and Matt was perfectly willing to admit to anything she wanted him to.

But then she reached into the jacket pocket and pulled out—

Her bottle.

"What's that doing there?" Matt asked, the effect on his libido as instantaneous as if it were a bucket of ice water.

"You're wearing my jacket," she said, her feet reaching the ground, which removed her lips from kissing range.

"Correction. *My* jacket. You didn't have one on when we met, remember?"

She'd barely had *any*thing on—as if he needed the reminder.

A parade-goer's flag swung into the alcove, and Matt pulled Eden out of the way before it smacked her in the head, momentum throwing them against the wrought-iron gate. Good thing it was locked or they would have ended up plastered to the mosaic-tiled floor behind it.

Matt took the brunt of the hit and was rewarded by

the soft give of her body and that magical scent of hers that could have him forgetting things like public decency and his own name.

Eden, unfortunately, didn't see it the same way and shoved herself away from him. "Matt, stop. This is serious. You're wearing the jacket I had on when I found my bottle."

He was serious, too, but it certainly wasn't about a jacket. "What's the big deal, Eden? Seems like that'd be the right one with your bottle in it."

"The big deal, Matt, is that if the bottle were still at your house, far away from here, Faruq couldn't entrap me. But now, if he finds out we have it, if he finds me *with* it, with these bracelets, and he has the stopper—"

She didn't need to say it.

"And if he captures *you*…"

She also didn't need to elaborate. He knew what Faruq would do to him—the same thing he wanted to do to Faruq.

And the same thing he was going to do to the guy who, all of a sudden and with a loud, "*Yalla!*" thrust an arm into the alcove, hooked it around Eden, then carried her away.

Just like that, Matt lost her.

Chapter 24

"EDEN!" MATT YELLED, LEAPING FROM THE ALCOVE as if the hounds of Hell—or Faruq—were on his heels.

He got one last glimpse of her black hair before the crowd swallowed her.

Then he found himself swallowed as bodies surged around him and more music filled the air, an eclectic mix of marching music, Caribbean steel drums, Middle Eastern string instruments, and a bad rendition of "Bohemian Rhapsody." He could barely hear himself think, let alone what the guy next to him was trying to say.

Matt shook his head, pointed to his ear, and tried to swim upstream with the crowd. It was slow going.

Who'd taken her? Not Faruq, unless he'd OD'd on steroids. The vizier had some muscle in his chicken arms, but they were still chicken-like. That guy? Pure brawn. Could he be a bounty hunter? Did they have bounty hunter genies? Matt didn't know and it was pissing him off like nothing else. What was wrong with this place? A city full of magical beings and not one of them capable of zapping her back here.

Goddammit. How could he lose her? One minute she'd been in his arms, the next, *poof*! Gone with the djinn. He was sick to death of losing people in his life.

He shoved his way through harlequin clowns, medieval knights, a few Darth Vaders, and a legion of Roman soldiers, then hopped over a goat—no, make that a man. A satyr, of all things. Shouldn't surprise him. Not with flying carpets, unicorns, and the way the minarets were spinning above buildings along the route, roofs changing colors like a disco ball, or dragons doing loop-the-loops in and around them, or baby strollers with no wheels that hovered inches off the cobblestones. Nah, satyrs were par for the course.

The crowd grew bigger as more people joined the parade, buffeting him like a piece of flotsam in a sea of humanity, not one of them in any hurry. Hugging each other, linking arms, strolling along as if the parade were a walk in the park. A pair of old women even set up directors' chairs in the middle of the street to people-watch from inside the crowd.

This was bullshit. He *had* to find her. Had to save her. Story of his freaking life.

Matt shoved a hand into his pocket and wrapped his fingers around her bottle. Then, as he'd done with the amulet, he closed his eyes and wished it'd take him to her.

"*Marhaba.*"

Matt opened his eyes. A beautiful woman stood in front of him, as tall as he was, model-thin, and dressed as an Egyptian queen. Obo had mentioned one in particular; could this be—

"Cleopatra?"

"Hardly." Her laughter sounded like little bells, but no one seemed to notice.

No one noticed her either. Or they were so used to people in costume that they didn't pay attention.

But she was the most exotic-looking woman Matt ever seen. Black hair so shiny and thick it was almost viscous, moving like oil in a pool of water, with an ostrich feather in the front like a show girl's headdress. Her eyes reminded him of ancient hieroglyphs, almond-shaped and kohl-lined, but with a fire and intelligence behind them the stone drawings hadn't been able to convey. As if she saw and knew all. Given where he was and what had happened to reality since yesterday, Matt wasn't discounting anything.

"Come. Let us find a quieter place where we can talk."

Her voice was like the crystal clear water of a mountain stream, flowing over him to carry him with it.

Matt shook his head. *Crystal clear water of a mountain stream?* Since when did he even think like that? He'd watched too many beer commercials lately.

Then he looked around and found himself in an empty courtyard, behind another set of wrought-iron gates that were somehow no longer locked, and without a single recollection of moving. Maybe he'd *had* too many beers lately.

"Are you the *Malwa* of Magic?" It would explain how they'd gotten here. And prove once and for all that Eden hadn't bewitched him with her magic. This woman, however, definitely had. Or, if not him, then the amulet. Why hadn't that worked?

"Me? Aisha?" Again with the bell laughter. "I think not. Please. Sit."

A café table and a chair appeared out of nowhere, along with a beer, a basket of pita chips, and a bowl of hummus.

"Thanks, but I can't. I have to find someone."

"Sit." The woman spoke the word kindly, but she meant it.

Matt wasn't surprised to find himself doing it, nor that he had a chip halfway to his mouth before shaking off the complacency—and whatever spell she'd used—that had come over him. He stormed to his feet. "Look, lady, I appreciate you getting me out of that crowd, but I have to go."

Except his feet wouldn't move.

The woman folded her hands in front of her, calm and serene, while his insides felt as if he'd stuck his entire hand in a light socket. "Everything will happen in its own time, Matthew. Please, eat. You'll need your strength."

"Why don't I like the sound of that?"

"Because you are not a stupid man. You are brave. Resourceful. Strong." She waved her hand and a pizza appeared on the table.

"What's going on?"

"Eden is safe."

"Really? You know this like you know my name? Where is she? Who's got her? Bring her back."

"All will be well." The woman's voice was like a lullaby.

But he was in the midst of a nightmare.

"'All will be well?' That's all you have to say?" The hell with complacency. Matt concentrated on getting out of his chair, and actually did it. "Look, I appreciate your help and hospitality, but if you're not going to save her, I will."

"Matthew." And just like that, the woman's tone stopped him. Soothed him. Held him captive. Or, rather, her magic did. No wonder Eden wanted out from under anyone's thumb. This inability to control his own body, his own mind, was frustrating.

"Matthew, you cannot save everyone."

"Tell me something I don't know." Especially when he knew it in spades.

"That is not why you were put on this earth."

"Look, lady." He concentrated again and ended up freeing one of his legs from her spell. Or had she let him? "I don't know if you're speaking to this situation directly or in some cosmic, we-all-have-our-purpose kind of way, but Eden's out there with a kidnapper. Maybe it's not my so-called purpose, but I can't sit back and let her be taken against her will, so I'll have to take a rain check on a conversation about the merits of existentialism."

The woman brushed a nonexistent hair from her forehead. "You're a noble man, Matthew."

"Bully for me." So noble that he was the one ending up alone. The good guys were supposed to get the girl, yet that wasn't happening in his world, was it? His track record was oh-for-two: one who'd left him for a loser, the other taken by one. When he added in his dad and losing the business, he was oh-for-three. Or was that four?

Who the hell cared? He didn't have the time or the inclination to dwell on it. He had to move forward. That's what he did. Pushed through adversity to get to the other side.

"Honor, talent, drive, family. These are your strengths, Matthew. Focus not on what you've lost, but on what you have. So much more than you know."

But less than he wanted.

Not dwelling.

"Look, I don't know who you are or why you think you know what you know, but this is wasting time. I need to find Eden, not worry about some grand scheme, so if you wouldn't mind undoing this." He pointed to his leg that wouldn't move.

The woman nodded and waved her hands.

"Can I go?"

She pointed to the open gates. "Of course."

"Great. Thanks." Matt sprinted for the gate, a piece of pizza in his hand. Man could not live by hummus alone.

"I wish you to find what you seek, Matthew," the woman called after him.

So did he.

Matt ran to the edge of the parade, shoving her words from his mind. He couldn't focus on anything but finding Eden right now. His life would still be there when he got home.

If he got home.

The crowd hadn't thinned any and wading through it would be futile. Eden could be anywhere. He had to face that fact. And that he couldn't save her. Not in this. He had to trust that she could save herself.

He had problems with trust. Faith, too.

So he'd head to the French Quarter. That's where they'd been headed and if Eden could escape, hopefully she'd go there since she needed that crystal from Faruq's office. If she didn't, he could find the crystal himself, use it to find her, then go get her.

Since real men *could* ask directions, Matt stopped the next person to pass—an old guy on a Segway, the motorized vehicle surprising him more than any flying carpet or mind-reading parade-goer. Funny how he expected magic in Al-Jannah, but not technology.

"The French Quarter? Sure, I know where it is. Had some good times there, if you know what I mean." The old man winked. "Those can-can girls—ooh la la!"

"How far away is it?"

"Feisty, are ya?" asked the old man, his blue eyes twinkling. "Not to worry. It's not far. If you go to the end of the street, turn right at the statue of Mayat, then left at the one of the great hero, Rustam, down that street to Rick's Café. But I'd recommend La Magique. Those girls put on a show like you can't believe—and, in Al-Jannah, that's saying something. Have fun!" The guy leaned forward and the Segway headed off.

Matt ran down the street and was about to run past the statue when a glance at it had him coming to a screeching halt.

It was the woman he'd just spoken with. Same eyes, same dress, same feather in her hair.

Matt squinted to read the nameplate beneath the statue and the Arabic calligraphy shifted to English.

Mayat, Egyptian Goddess of Divine Wisdom.

He should probably take some comfort in the goddess' divine wisdom saying Eden was safe, but Matt wasn't going to be any kind of comfortable until Eden was back in his arms.

Where she belonged.

———

Eden spared one last look for the drunken "sheik" who'd snatched her out of that alcove, "You're pretty," being his excuse. Great. On the run for her life and she got a self-proclaimed Casanova.

That was why genies shouldn't drink alcohol. Ever.

She blew the hair out of her eyes as she looked around. It'd be a miracle if Matt had followed her, but with the way Mr. Party Animal had barreled through the throng of people with her tucked against his side, making forays down so many side streets for *arak* she couldn't keep track, she wasn't holding out much hope.

"Hey, babe!" A guy in a kilt skated by on a wheel-less hovering skateboard, making so many lewd gestures she was amazed he didn't fall off. "I got a wish you can make come true."

Her fingers twitched. She had a few of her own she wouldn't mind showing him, but until she was free from Faruq, she couldn't risk the Glimmer.

Except—

"Ooh, baby," said another creep, sucking air between his teeth while raising a toast. "I can rub you real good."

She'd actually had masters like these losers. And just as unoriginal, too.

She needed to get out of these clothes. For all that everyone in Al-Jannah aspired to The Service, none wore the outfit until they merited it, even in a parade full of costumes. For her to be doing so, well, people would remember her if Faruq came poking around, and she certainly didn't need to incite the natives. Nor did she need anyone remembering her when she headed to the High Master's park.

Ignoring more comments about her anatomy from the sexist pigs, Eden ducked into another alley, this time with the sole purpose of "borrowing" a set of clothes. The only ones she could reach without magic ended up with the pants being a size too big, and the shirt a size too small, but at least she could blend in with the crowd.

She stuffed the hated costume in a pile of old boxes behind one of the buildings and pulled her distinctive hair into a ponytail.

Now off to find Matt and the djinn eggs, and beat Faruq at his own game.

Chapter 25

FARUQ PACED OUTSIDE THE HIGH MASTER'S ANTECHAMBER, keeping careful watch on the gargoyles who were keeping an eye on him.

Ghastly things. They were what happened when he drank absinthe. The fact that he'd been drinking with a group of subversive artists with skewed senses of humor who'd ended up marketing the monstrosities to architects for rain gutters, of all things, was further proof of his impaired judgment. It'd been the last time he'd had the vile stuff.

Although, he wouldn't mind a quaff—or seven—now.

What did the High Master want with him? The djinn ruler couldn't know about Eden. No one knew about Eden. The GPS was his and his alone. The High Master had never ventured into his inner sanctum. *No one* entered his inner sanctum. Well, other than the one time he'd showed it to Eden to give her a little taste of what he could do.

So why the summons? He would have thought the High Master would be too busy preparing for the upcoming celebration to summon him, but then, he didn't presume to know what was in the High Master's mind.

What he wouldn't *give* to know, though…

He checked the blue-sand hourglass on the pedestal by the golden arches statue. The High Master had taken the world-centric feeling of Al-Jannah a little too much

to heart in Faruq's opinion. There was something to be
said for the old ways. The cleanness of the design, the
harmony of the symmetry, the simplicity of the decor.
Sparse yet beautiful. Practical.

Mortals' evolution—progress as they called it—left
a lot to be desired. Air pollution, global warming, trans
fats, the search for scientific answers to things they
didn't understand. The mystique of genies had devolved
from reverence to a beboppy television jingle and dumb-
blonde jokes. It was an abomination.

Could that be what this summons was about? Heavens
knew, Faruq had petitioned the High Master enough for
a return to basics, the beliefs of those earlier times. His
latest request was to be permitted to return mortal societies to a more subservient era. Remind them to be more
respectful of myth and legend. Of the Unknown.

Hmmm, maybe he ought to open the doors to The
Cave and give mortals the answers they'd sought for so
long. Then they'd know—and they'd fear.

No. Mortals could never have those answers. Never
learn the things the High Master and all who came before him had decided were too dangerous or too intricate
for mortals to know, the collection royal viziers had
guarded through the ages. Why give those lesser beings
the opportunity to ascend to the ranks of the Learned?
Knowledge was powerful—and so were a few of the
treasures in that cave.

It'd been a while since he'd visited The Cave—since
he'd fashioned Eden's bracelets, to be exact.

Faruq took another pass down the length of Persian
rug in front of the closed doors Xerxes the Great had
commissioned. Pity the guy never took delivery of

them—another fact Faruq would love to tell those know-it-all mortals but couldn't.

Kharah! Faruq pounded a fist on his thigh. He hated waiting. Waiting was frustrating.

Leaving Eden was frustrating.

Faruq closed his eyes, seeing her again in that glorious costume. He had to admit, he did like the embellishments mortals had added to the traditional garb. The exposed midriff was an improvement over the neck-to-belly covering, and the transparency they'd achieved with the fabric was sheer genius.

He'd imagined her in that costume when he'd sought out the gems for her bracelets. No ordinary sapphires and rubies would do for Eden. She had to have the very best. He'd visited the gem alcove in The Cave, selecting *star* rubies, sapphires, and emeralds for her. The most flawless amethysts, topaz, and aquamarines. And the perfect crystal to monitor her, just waiting for him to place it where it belonged.

Faruq smiled, the frustration of waiting warring with his pride. He'd chosen one of the rarest minerals on earth. Serendibite. Even if Eden figured it out, the chances of her coming across it on her own were almost nil—

Oh, *kharah!* eBay. He'd forgotten.

Faruq made a mental note to check the online garage-sale site. He wouldn't put it past some idiot mortal to be selling something he shouldn't even possess.

Faruq thrummed his fingers on his jaw. The waiting was becoming interminable. He had things to do—a person to do, if he dared be so crude.

Oh, he dared. He'd waited long enough. If not for this summons, he'd be *doing* her right now.

Chapter 26

MATT PEERED OUT FROM THE END OF THE ALLEY. Pedestrians, camels, donkeys, a few elephants—white ones—even a full grown dragon in the sky, but no Faruq. He released the breath he'd been holding and eased himself out of the shadows.

He garnered a few looks, but there were others in jeans, though no one in such a bulky jacket. Matt knew why, but he didn't dare remove it. The bottle was too precious.

He checked to make sure he still had it, pretending a nonchalance he didn't feel. What if he couldn't find her in the French Quarter? What if he couldn't find her, period? How long should he wait to see if she showed up? Did he even have a chance in hell of getting to that GPS without her?

Cursing Fate, Obo, the damn kidnapper, and, most especially, Faruq, Matt saw a bench across the street. When you were lost in the woods, you were supposed to sit in one spot for rescuers to find you; it seemed like good advice for a genie to find you, too.

He stepped into the street, dodging another unicorn-drawn surrey, and was about to cross when something caught his eye.

A long black ponytail disappearing around the corner of a building down the street.

Eden?

Matt ran after her, elbowing people and creatures out of the way. He turned the corner in time to see that ponytail disappear around another one, the clothing not familiar.

But her curves were.

Matt sprinted down the alley and rounded the turn, pulling back, his arms windmilling, when he saw the Chinese throwing star inches from his head.

And the gorgeous woman leaning off the window ledge holding it.

"Uh, Eden?"

"Matt!"

The weapon clanged on the ground, and Matt yanked her from that ledge into his arms. And kissed her.

He hadn't lost her.

Then she kissed him back and Matt's senses, already heightened from worry and adrenaline, switched to hyperspeed. He swung her around and pressed her back against the wall, his knee sliding between her legs, jacking her up to the perfect height, and palmed her cheek, his fingers tangling in her gorgeous hair. He tugged the binding, wanting to feel it trailing through his fingers as it had last night.

Matt nipped his way down her throat to nuzzle the soft hollow there, fanning her hair over her shoulders, across his lips, down over her breasts, and he cupped her.

"Matt—" She gasped in time with his thumbs flicking across her hardened nipples. "I—we—can't—" Her thighs clenched his leg and the slow burn in his veins blazed into full-on bonfire mode. "Faruq."

One word. So many consequences.

Matt dropped his forehead to her shoulder, his eyes squeezed shut. From the heights of passion to the depths of Hell with one word.

Shuddering as he tried to get his breathing under control, Matt set her on her feet and wrapped his arms around her, tucking her beneath his chin.

"I'm going to kill Faruq first chance I get," he growled against her hair.

"That won't be easy." Eden's fingers slid beneath his shirt, her nails scraping lightly against his back, and Matt wanted nothing more than for her to keep doing it.

Actually, he did want more. A *lot* more.

Damn Faruq. Another thing to kill the guy for.

Matt shuddered then pulled away from her. *Focus.*

He couldn't stop one finger from tracing her jaw, though. "Are you okay? Did that guy hurt you?"

She shook her head. "No. He was just a reveler. A non-issue. But Faruq—"

"You leave Faruq to me."

Matt said it with such calm and precision. Such determination. As if there was no doubt he could do it.

But Eden knew Faruq. Knew his power. Whatever Matt thought he could do to the vizier… he couldn't.

But she loved that he wanted to. Loved knowing that if the playing field were even, Matt would defend her. Loved that he'd have her back. Loved that—

She blinked back the tears that filled her eyes. She did *not* cry. And Matt's ill-advised altruism wasn't going to make her.

Just in case, she blinked again.

"Eden? Honey? Are you sure you're all right? Did that guy do something to you?"

She swallowed and dashed the side of her hand against one of her eyes. "I'm fine, Matt. Really. I'm, uh, just trying to plan. We need to get those djinn's eggs."

He studied her, his eyes a mossy green as he brushed a hand over her hair and dropped a kiss to her forehead. "Then point the way. The faster we're out of here, the better I'll like it."

"Me, too. But the plant only blooms for a half hour after sundown, so we have to wait a little longer." The wait was the least of their worries, but she wasn't going to tell him that now. Why should they both worry? She was doing enough for him, her, Obo, and half the citizens of Al-Jannah.

Yes, the djinn's eggs were her best bet, but she hadn't told Matt everything. The plants, also known as *Mandragora,* were part of the nightshade family. And were as deadly to genies as to mortals. Handling the flowers, let alone making a tea from them as she was going to, had to be done absolutely perfectly. There was a risk involved. A big one.

But it paled beside the thought of spending eternity married to Faruq. When it came to something *possibly* going wrong versus Faruq *ensuring* it, she was grabbing whatever straw she could.

"You don't have to come with me, you know, Matt. We'll find someplace for you to hide and I'll come back when I'm finished. There's no sense in both of us going."

"Are you crazy? You think I'm just going to sit here and wait? Not a chance. I didn't come after you and crash my truck into a tent in the middle of the Sahara Desert just to walk away. Let's do this."

There was that altruism thing again, and here came

her tears. She put a finger to her eye, pretending she had something in it. She'd known he'd say that, but she'd had to give him the out. She couldn't live with herself if she hadn't.

"All right." She took a deep breath, committing them to this. Gods help them—and she really hoped they did. "Let's go to the… park."

"Why don't I like how you said that word?"

"Because it's not exactly a place you want to hang around in." Nor be planning to steal something from, *Mandragora* especially. She took a step forward.

Matt grabbed her hand. "Why, Eden?"

"Because of what's inside it."

"What's inside it? What *is* inside it, Eden? It can't be worse than Faruq."

Oh yes it could—so much so that it terrified even Faruq.

And that's what scared her the most.

Chapter 27

OBO RAN THROUGH THE ALLEYS TOWARD THE EAST, the amulet banging against his chest. The goddess's temple was behind the moon-flowers, beyond the rain forest, through the strawberry fields to where the day, and the sun also, rose.

He hated being back here. But even more, he hated what he was going to have to do.

Being noble sucked.

"Hey, big boy." In front of a courtyard entrance halfway down the next alley, a svelte seal-point Siamese licked her whiskers, then stretched in the waning sun.

Obo stopped on a *dinar*.

"What's your hurry?" she asked, sauntering up the cobblestones toward him. "You're new around here, aren't you?"

A lot newer than her lines.

"Sorry, babe," he said, reaching for the leather strings that kept the amulet inside the bag and the bag where it should be. Last thing he needed was the bag to fall off and for her to see a disc of solid gold. "On a mission."

She undulated her tail, then circled twice in the center of the alley and settled herself there, her tail curling around her slim body, effectively blocking his exit. "Suit yourself. You tomcats usually do. But I can't believe"—she stretched a long, sinuously sensuous leg out behind her—"you're just going to walk on by."

Son-of-a-bichon, he wasn't going to fall for that old trick. How many kittens did he have to sire before he learned his lesson? No more, that's for sure. He was on his ninth life and leaving little "reminders" behind him was definitely not the way to make Atonement. He was just lucky none of the females had known he had the amulet or they would have been after him for kitten-support centuries ago.

Foregoing the pleasures of her company in his quest for his Eternal Reward, Obo dashed through the first gate he saw—only to find himself in an enclosed courtyard.

Bulls-balls, this wasn't what he wanted. Especially when a gypsy woman who was seated at a table, staring at a crystal ball, looked up and her blue eyes seared through him.

"Come here, Obo."

How'd she know who he was?

He hated this city. So many frustrated magic-users always kept him looking over his shoulder, as did the possibility of Faruq being around any corner. Plus, he'd pissed off enough genies through the centuries that he'd had to steer clear of Al-Jannah until the end of his last life, or his other lives would have ended a lot earlier than they had.

But now, with this gypsy knowing who he was, the length of his ninth was in jeopardy. All she had to do was sprinkle his name in a few of the less savory taverns and he'd have a price on his tail so high it'd make the High Master's minaret look like a toadstool.

Obo glanced around. Great. The gate to the street had shut and there wasn't another open door to be found. He really hated this city.

"Don't make me ask twice, cat."

Obo dropped his head an inch to relieve the ache from the weight of the amulet and took a few steps forward. Please, gods, let him live through this. Gypsies weren't any better than angry viziers.

"Closer."

Obo slunk over to the chair opposite the crone and leapt up, making sure to keep the strings of the amulet bag beneath the top of the table. Gypsies loved gold as much as any female he'd ever encountered—feline or human. Avian, too. Even that bearded dragon bitch who'd pulled out the original leather thong. He'd almost lost a few inches of his tail getting that back.

"You haven't been here in many lifetimes." The gypsy's voice deepened as she waved her hands above the crystal.

"And your point is?" All Obo could see in the crystal was swirling blue mist. The color matched the vest she wore over the light blue dress. What? Was blue required wear nowadays or was someone trying to gain favor with the High Master since it was his favorite color? Heavens save them from a High Master who favored red: red sky, red oceans... They'd all be walking around with twenty-four-hour headaches.

Well, at least the gypsy's clothing was feminine and appealing. The woman herself? Not so much. Her voice could earn her a spot in the bass section of a church choir, but her face was so far from angelic it'd have parishioners running for their lives. Tanned and lined to the point of leather, it looked like a wrinkled sock someone had left out in the mud. And the little Obo could see of her hair beneath the blue veil was more broom-like than a camel's tail.

As for her figure, well, he was no connoisseur of human anatomy, but having lived among them for more than a few centuries, he'd say this one wasn't a candidate for the bikini-wearing crowd.

"Your presence will be required at The Cave of Great Unknown at sunrise tomorrow."

Great. Sunrise tomorrow he planned to be dozing on Matt's hearth with a pinch of catnip and some tasty beluga caviar. "There might be a problem with that, Carnac."

The gypsy's lips twitched, then she scowled. "Your frivolity is neither wanted nor appreciated. This is no laughing matter. It is decreed that you will present yourself at The Cave of Great Unknown tomorrow morning, say the ma—"

"Please don't say 'magic words.'"

"—gic words, and you will enter The Cave. Or your mission will fail."

Obo banged his head on the table. *The mission will fail.* Great. Just friggin' great. "And these magic words are?"

"Do you really need to ask?"

"Are you kidding me? Seriously?"

"How do you think mortals learned them? Conjured them out of thin air? Why not 'Open Poppy' or 'Open Fennel'? No, sadly, a djinni shared 'Open Sesame' and the world hasn't been the same since. Remember that whole Free Will debate among the gods and nonhumans two millennia ago?"

Obo flicked his tail. Old news. Someone said something about something, and whatever. A volcano blew its top, thousands went into the Light, all while he'd been happily ensconced in a Greek palace, out of harm's way.

Where he wouldn't mind being right now.

But, nooooooo. *He'd* decided to be noble. "Okay, so what am I supposed to do?"

"Why else do felines go to The Cave? You will know when you see it."

Great. Clear as mud. Just what he didn't need. All-knowing beings who chose secrecy really ticked him off. At least it wasn't allegory. He hated those damned puzzles.

Of course, he also hated not knowing what he was getting into. But at least he had the amulet.

Obo ran a paw over the bag—you never knew what sleight-of-hand a gypsy could get up to—then hopped off the chair.

"Thanks for clarifying. I'll be at The Cave tomorrow at the appointed hour. Until then, I've got a goddess to see." The cat goddess would give him his final instructions. And if they clashed with the gypsy's, well, hey. He'd be out of here before the old hag knew he'd gone.

The gypsy stood up, the gold bangles on her wrists and ears clinking like church bells. Probably stolen from a church, too. "You're on your way to Bastet? Why didn't you say so?"

Obo looked over his shoulder. "I wasn't aware I had to clear my travel arrangements with you."

The gypsy clapped her hands—man-hands if Obo ever saw 'em. You'd think the woman would do something to make herself a little more attractive if she was capable of foreseeing the future, or whatever it was she claimed to be able to do, but apparently there was no accounting for taste—and vanity. Or the lack thereof. But at least she'd opened the gate.

"You think you're going to make it through that doorway, Obo?"

The gypsy was no better-looking when she smiled. The High Master was better-looking. Well, almost. Obo would even venture to say they could be twins. "Now that you opened the gate, I plan to."

"Might be tough with that huge rock on your shoulder."

Rock? What rock? Obo sped through the door, unwilling to give her the chance to close it on him again. He didn't have a rock on his shoulder. Besides, the saying was *chip* on the shoulder—

Hell. The gypsy really did know him.

Obo turned around, but she disappeared in a cloud of blue smoke before he could say anything. What was with all the blue?

Wait a minute. Could it—? Was she—?

Nah. It wasn't possible. Even with all the blue. The High Master never came among the people. Especially not to talk to a cat. And dressed like a woman? He'd never hear the end of it. While cross-dressing was earning acceptance, or at least tolerance, in the outside world, inside Al-Jannah, Obo couldn't see that one flying. Which said a lot, because pretty much anything flew in Al-Jannah. Carpets, footstools, pirate ships—but not cross-dressing High Master genies.

Right?

Chapter 28

MATT DIDN'T LIKE THE LOOKS OF THE PARK.

It wasn't that it was dark and dangerous, with trees too thick to see between or vegetation growing taller than a man's head. No, the only trees were the twisted, Whoville-ish cork trees that lined the northern horizon, and the rest was manicured and well cared for. Groves were strategically placed among perfectly landscaped gardens whose profusion of colors were definitely man—or, in this case, genie—made. Fountains, pergolas, and paths were tiled in the *Mudéjar* style. The place looked like the Garden of Eden.

That's what worried him. Paradise had harbored a serpent, and, from the way *his* Eden was acting, this place did, too. If the magical being they'd find here was enough to scare her, he wanted no part of it.

"So what's this thing called that we have to keep an eye out for?" He could have sworn the arched stone bridge moved as they crossed it. Expanded or something. A ridiculous idea in any other circumstances, but given that they were in the genie equivalent of Oz, who the hell knew.

Case in point: the river the bridge spanned was so blue it was almost purple. And the grass on the other side so green it was almost neon.

"The *Hadhayosh*." Eden stopped at the end of the bridge, her shoulder brushing his arm. "A terrible beast, like a bull, but bigger. It guards the forest from intruders and is capable of hunting us down before we find what we came for."

"Then why are we looking out for it? If we stand still, it'll find us."

"Now isn't the time for jokes, Matt. Concentrate. You'll feel it coming."

"Feel?"

She nodded—which he did feel since she was plastered to his side. Normally that wouldn't be something to complain about, but there was that fear thing.

Matt cleared his throat. Fear was not an option. Not if they wanted to get out of here with their lives. And the djinn's eggs—that name alone was enough to worry him since it sounded like a cloning experiment gone bad.

Hell, this whole thing worried him. Faruq, a deadly beast, not knowing what to expect. He hated that he wasn't the one calling the shots. Ever since his father died, he'd worked hard to be in control of his life. Yet here he was, having to rely on and trust someone else. Frustration was a mild term for what he felt.

"How long is that peacock going to be able to keep Faruq busy, Eden? We're going to need every break we can get."

"I'm counting on Faruq's aspirations to do that trick. He should wait around for the High Master for a long time."

The "I hope" she added at the end of that statement didn't make Matt feel better. The only thing that would, would be sitting in his living room with a beer in one hand, the remote in the other, a football game on the high-def, and this whole thing one big, nightmarish memory. Except for Eden, of course.

Matt took a deep breath. "Okay. So we go straight. Into the middle of the park."

She nodded.

"Where we'll find a small pyramid and, on top of it, the djinn's eggs."

"Yes."

"But this hottie thing—"

"*Hadhayosh*."

"Right. This *Hadhayosh* is going to try to prevent us from getting it."

"Right."

Matt patted his jacket pocket, checking on the bottle. "So how do we beat it at its own game? We don't have any weapons and neither of us is dressed for a marathon."

"We'll beat it, Matt. Trust me."

Trust her. The thing was…

He did. He trusted her to get them through this. He might even trust her with a bit more.

And if that wasn't a huge leap of faith for him, he didn't know what was.

Eden stepped off the bridge as the structure sighed again. She was surprised Matt hadn't commented on the way it arched up then returned to its original form, but then, this wasn't exactly a sightseeing trip.

Pity it wasn't. The park could be visited via guided tours, with both the *Hadhayosh* and the *Mandragora* under magical lock and key, of course. She'd been here on a class field trip and they'd studied the dangers before coming. The *Hadhayosh* liked riddles; answer them correctly, you live. Screw up, you die.

No pressure.

But she'd always been good with riddles—better than she'd be at outrunning Faruq on his home turf with her Glimmer leaving a trail of catch-me-if-you-can. Since she and Matt couldn't get to the crystals without the *Mandragora*, and they couldn't get the *Mandragora* without getting by the *Hadhayosh,* there wasn't much choice. Math hadn't been her strongest suit, but she could figure that one plus one plus one equaled the rest of her life.

The blue, green, and orange tiled path led into an orange grove flowering with yellow buds bordered by gardenias with an almost overpowering aroma. Too bad nothing could mask her and Matt's scent from the beast's powerful sense of smell—a trait that made it the perfect guardian for the *Mandragora.* No sense letting just anyone get to the plant; constantly changing Glimmer would wreak havoc in their world.

Exactly Eden's intention.

"I wouldn't have suggested it if I didn't think we had a shot, Matt. The *Hadhayosh* won't kill us without first giving us a chance to get by him."

"Nice guy."

The corners of her mouth inched up at the sarcasm. She loved that he was here with her. He didn't need to be, he certainly shouldn't be, but here he was.

But he won't always be, Eden. Remember that. Genies and mortals don't do *happily-ever-after. Especially the* ever *part.*

She knew that firsthand and it always came back to that. "Come on. Let's go."

The path wended through exquisite gardens of plants and flowers from all over the world. Pale peach English tea roses next to purple wisteria from Japan, the prim and proper observer counterbalanced by the untamed invader. Lemon-yellow Missouri primrose enveloping the exotic South Pacific orange-and-yellow bird-of-paradise spikes. Virginal bells of lily-of-the-valley dangling beneath the prominent blue trumpets of the lily-of-the-Nile. The profusion of colors and shapes, and the hummingbirds and butterflies darting between the gardens, were enough to make Eden want to forget about finding her freedom and live here among the beauty and tranquility for the rest of her life, where she'd be of Service to no one.

And where she'd *have* no one.

For now, though, she had Matt. And, for now, that would have to be enough.

When his arm snaked around her waist, Eden leaned into him and inhaled the scent that was solely his. His arm tightened, the muscles of his chest rippling against her back and the hand flexing on her hip doing delicious swirly things to her insides.

It'd been so long since she'd felt desire like this, and too long since someone had felt it for her. When his hand moved slightly, igniting another series of fires, her knees trembled.

"What was that?" Matt tensed and Eden realized her knees weren't trembling just because of him. She'd been so busy daydreaming, she hadn't recognized the first sign of the *Hadhayosh*.

With the feeling in her stomach no longer delicious, but definitely swirly—the sick and worried kind—Eden concentrated on the ground, studying the one small line of horizon that wasn't covered in pink creeping phlox, and tried to remember her Mythical Beasts course. The term was a misnomer because the beasts were as far from mythical as genies themselves.

Courage. Fortitude. Knowledge. Intuition. The four items necessary to defeat the *Hadhayosh*.

All of which were sorely tested when she felt another tremor.

But she had to defeat it, had to show no fear. So, as much as she hated doing so, she stepped out of Matt's embrace because, in his arms, she wasn't able to think straight.

The ground shuddered again, then split open at their feet. A giant rock rose from the gash as the *Hadhayosh* thundered into the clearing from a grove of crooked cork trees. Its head was as big as the front of Matt's truck, horns thick and curved. With a mahogany coat as smooth as a mink's and as long as a yak's, massive shoulders tapering to powerful hind quarters, sharp silver hooves on thick, sturdy legs, the animal's presence alone could strike fear into anyone's heart. But it was either face him or eternal Servitude to Faruq.

For Eden, there was no choice.

So when Matt shifted his weight, she elbowed him in the ribs. Civility was highly prized among mythological beasts, and she didn't want Matt doing anything stupid. Well, not stupid. Instinctual. Like run. But fight-or-flight wasn't an option, only outwitting the *Hadhayosh* was.

"Who goes there?" The air rattled with the beast's deep voice, the words, thankfully, in English. A somewhat upper-crust, polite, correct form of the language, but at least it wasn't Persian. Her Persian was a little rusty.

"No one goes here," she said, answering the first test correctly. That one was always an opponent-killer. The older girls in her dorm in Al-Jannah had liked to scare the new kids with *Hadhayosh* stories; she'd heard it enough times to remember the correct answer.

Too bad none of the survivors had known all the beast's riddles. Everyone's stories were different, so she and Matt were on their own.

The *Hadhayosh* shook its massive head. "Very good. You have answered correctly, but, to continue, you must answer the real question. Correct, you pass; incorrect, you die. Simple."

"Are you sure we can do this, Eden?" Matt whispered.

It was the *we* that got to her and filled her heart.

"Sssh," she whispered back, turning just enough to meet his gaze. Flecks of brown dotted his gray-green eyes, not the mossy green color she'd come to love. The heavens—and *Hadhayosh*—willing, she'd see that color again. "We don't have a choice, Matt. If we run, it'll kill us, and if we answer incorrectly, it'll kill us. So whatever you do, don't say anything except the answer, okay?"

Matt searched her eyes for a long, tense moment, then she felt his weight sink back onto his heels. "Okay. I trust that you know what you're doing."

One of them did, at least.

She faced the beast and squared her shoulders. "We're ready."

The creature lowered his lashes, snorted, then lifted them again. His eyes, which had been as brown as his hide before, now glowed orange. "What has a mouth but cannot chew?"

Matt squeezed her shoulder and bent down to whisper in her ear. "Don't answer that. Something's not right. The answer is a river, but it's too easy. It has to be a trick."

"Of course it is. Djinn's eggs are too important for it not to be."

"Then why—"

"I expected tricks, Matt. But we can do this. Trust me." She smiled when he squeezed her shoulder. Smiled even more when he whispered, "I do trust you, Eden."

Straightening her spine, she faced the beast. "A river."

The *Hadhayosh* snorted and waggled his head, the massive mound of muscle behind it swaying the opposite way in counterbalance. "You may pass."

With an earth-trembling groan, the massive rock slid back into the ground, the landscape behind it no longer a green meadow but a dense grove of willow trees.

Matt grabbed her hand and wasted no time running into the grove, not stopping until they could no longer see out the side they came in from. Or the *Hadhayosh.*

"So is that it? Or is he coming back?" Matt wiped some sweat off his forehead when they finally stopped running.

"He'll be back. We just can't tell when. Everyone who's done this"—and lived to tell the tale—"has a different story."

"Great. *That's* the trick part." He slicked his hair back. "This sucks."

"I know. We need to keep our eyes open." A white dove swooped over her head. She loved doves. Except when they were in Faruq's tent when *she* was in Faruq's tent.

Matt brushed something off her forehead. "I don't get why these djinn's eggs are here at all. Changing Glimmer sounds like trouble. Why does a way to do it even exist?"

Eden shrugged. "I don't claim to understand why the High Master does what he does. No one can. Not even Faruq, though he tries to. I'm just glad we have the opportunity."

"Speaking of the dic—of Faruq, we need to get those bracelets off you. Do you think he's figured out that you're gone yet?"

"I hope not. I can't see him giving up on the chance to curry the High Master's favor. Not until it's too obvious."

"Good. Then we've got some time." Matt raised her hand, and, and, heightened as her senses were, she felt his touch all the way to her curling-slipper-clad toes. And his eyes were mossy green.

Did they have time for something else?

His fingers slid over her palm and Eden wanted to make the time.

Matt cleared his throat and fiddled with the prongs around a yellow diamond the size of a canary's egg. "This is in too tightly. I'll need a knife or something to pry the stone out." He released her hand. "Damn. I hate leaving them on you."

"I think we'll be okay for a little longer. Faruq's too ambitious to give up if he thinks the High Master wants to see him."

"But what's to prevent this High Master from telling him he hadn't summoned him? Why wouldn't he have done that already?"

"The High Master's preparing for the blue moon,

Matt. It's a special event for genies, especially the High Master. He won't be interrupted for anything short of a full breach of Al-Jannah's walls. Faruq will wait because he'll think it's important."

Matt scrubbed a hand on his jaw. "I still don't like— Hey. What are the trees doing?"

Eden looked at the branches overhead. A drop of water plopped into her eye.

Ah. "They're crying, Matt. Well, weeping."

"Weeping?" Matt's mouth fell open. "The *trees* are weeping. Are they talking to you, too?"

She rolled her eyes. "Of course not. Not everything talks. Besides, they're weeping willows, hence the waterworks."

"Now I've seen everything."

Actually, he hadn't. And that was why they had to find the *Mandragora*.

"Come on, Matt. We need to keep moving."

They took two steps when the ground rumbled.

Matt grabbed her shoulder. "*Hadhayosh*?"

"I don't know. It could be." Great. She wasn't ready for this.

She also wasn't ready for the next rumble.

Nor the *whoosh* that followed it.

But Matt must have been because he picked her up, tossed her over his shoulder in a caveman move, and started running.

"Matt! What are you—?"

They heard the roar at the same time—

And recognized what it was.

"Flash flood!"

Chapter 29

WATER ROARED TOWARD THEM, THE SOUND WORSE than the tornado her bottle had been caught up in years ago—and that had been strong enough to whirl cows and houses around with her.

But at least then she'd been safe inside her bottle. Now, with the wall of willows weeping all around them, the only safe place was—"Up, Matt! We have to go up!"

Matt hoisted her into a big tree as the first wave surged beneath them, then he scrambled up after her. The willow's tears made the bark slick, but Eden flung herself across one of the thicker branches and managed to wrap both her arms and her legs around it.

Matt locked his arms around a limb just as his feet were swept out from under him. Luckily, he managed to work his feet over a branch to avoid going with the wave. He'd have a wet seat when the water crested, but at least he'd be alive.

Torrents of water swept beneath them, but with so few twigs and debris that Eden realized this was a common occurrence. That's why they'd been allowed to pass so easily. How many others had been so paralyzed by fear or caught unawares that they weren't able to climb to safety? *That* was the trick.

"You all right, Eden?"

Water plastered his hair to his head and ran down his clothing, and his legs kept slipping off the branch, yet he'd asked if *she* was all right. She could get used to having someone care about her.

She shouldn't, but she could. "I'm okay. How about you?"

It was a rhetorical question because there was nothing wrong with Matt in her opinion.

"I'm goo—oh, shit." One of Matt's arms slipped from the branch.

"Matt!" Eden tried to reach him, but they were too far apart, and with the water rushing as quickly as it was and forming whirlpools all over the place, she'd lose him before she could get to him.

Eden hitched her breath—consequences be damned. *I wish Matt would—*

He grabbed the branch.

Thank the stars! Eden stopped her wish. No sense spouting Glimmer if she didn't need to. "Are you okay?"

He tossed the hair out of his face. "I am now. I thought I'd lost the bottle."

She'd been too busy worrying about him to even think about her bottle. "And?"

"I've got it. We're good."

"*You* might be good. Me? I was scared to death." And with the way her heart was pounding... "Don't ever do that to me again, Matthew Ewing, do you hear me? I thought you were falling off."

"Hey, sweetheart, don't cry." He reached up for her hand, but she swatted it away.

"Hold on to the tree! And I'm not crying." The salty taste on her lips belied that statement, but he didn't have to know. "And don't call me sweetheart."

Because it sounded too damn good.

"Okay. Fine." He wrapped his arm around the tree. "See? I'm all right. Nothing's going to happen. We have the bottle and we'll get through this. Take it easy. Don't freak out on me."

"I'll freak out whenever I want, thankyouverymuch." Eden knew it was childish, but *zift*! He'd scared her. And he'd been worried about her bottle. For her. Not for him.

He'd come to Al-Jannah after her. *For* her. Not for him. How could that *not* freak her out?

Ten minutes later she still didn't have an answer, but at least the torrent had segued from surging to flowing quickly—enough to consider getting out of the tree.

"Feel like going for a swim?" Matt asked.

"I'm game if you are."

Matt smiled. "Sweetheart, I'm always game."

She didn't think they were talking about the same thing.

The current knocked them around a bit, but eventually the power lessened as the water level receded or the land angled up; she couldn't tell which and really didn't care. The trees thinned out, younger ones extending the boundary of the forest toward another green meadow. At the last row of saplings, their knees touched bottom.

"Thank God that's over with," Matt said, helping her stand.

But the minute she placed her hand in his, Eden knew *something* wasn't over. This. This incredible attraction between them, fueled now by the wild ride they'd just gone through.

And suddenly lips met lips, hands tangled in hair, body parts did all sorts of delicious things to the other's corresponding body parts, and Eden let the sensations wash over her.

Perhaps not the best word choice, but it felt so good to be kissed by Matt. Be wanted by him. Have his hands roam over her skin, his fingers dip beneath her low waistband, re-igniting the fire between them. There'd be no quenching this. If that flood hadn't done it, nothing could.

And ya know? She wasn't going to pass this chance by. Who knew if it'd be her last?

She slipped her hands beneath his shirt where a few buttons had popped off in their scramble up the tree. Good. Saved her the effort.

Stars, he felt good. Eden pressed against him, feeling the proof that he was as into the kiss as she was.

She trailed one hand down to stroke him. His wet jeans couldn't disguise how he responded to her touch. The groan he uttered against her cheek confirmed it.

"You're killing me, Eden," he growled against her lips.

"No I'm not. You're very much alive." She stroked him again to prove it.

Matt sucked in a breath. And then her earlobe, his tongue swirling over it, sending delicious waves of pleasure over her, so much better than the floodwaters. As powerful as those waves had been, so, too, was the longing to have him inside her again.

Oh, heavens, she couldn't. They couldn't. Much as she'd love to, the reality was, the *Hadhayosh* was still out there. So was the *Mandragora*. And so was Faruq.

Eden took her hand from his straining length. Not too far away, but enough that she wouldn't be tempted any more.

Well, no, that wasn't true. She was definitely tempted, and, judging by Matt's kisses, he was well beyond *tempted* and heavy into *engaged*.

And then the ground trembled.

Matt stilled. "Tell me that was because of what we're doing."

"I'd love to. Unfortunately, I don't think so."

"Shit." Matt stole one last kiss, then they looked around. They didn't have long to wait.

Hooves thundering, nostrils flaring, the *Hadhayosh* barreled down upon them and, once again, another massive rock jutted from the ground, swallowing the path.

"Who goes there?" the *Hadhayosh* asked.

"Didn't we just do this?" Matt muttered, placing one foot and half his body in front of her, his arm around her waist.

And, yes, she totally enjoyed being protected by him. Even if it was useless. No way could Matt stop the *Hadhayosh*. But it was sweet that he wanted to.

"No one goes here," Eden answered.

The *Hadhayosh* snorted and shook its massive head. "Very good. You have answered correctly, but, to continue, you must answer the real question. Correct, you pass; incorrect, you die. Simple."

Matt needed a weapon because if he had to listen to this bullshit one more time, he was going to go home with a freaking trophy to hang on his wall. Taxidermy had never been one of his pastimes, but that might be changing—especially when the beast asked his stupid, allegorical question.

"Food can help me survive, but water will kill me. What am I?"

Matt knew who he'd like to kill.

"Fire," Eden answered—and Matt wanted to kiss her. Oh, not because she'd answered the question correctly, although that was certainly a good reason, but general principle worked. That last kiss hadn't been nearly enough, and this stupid animal had interrupted it.

The ground rumbled again and the rock disappeared, the scar in the earth vanishing, too. The *Hadhayosh* sat on his haunches and cocked his head. "Well?"

Right. Leave.

But *fire* bugged Matt as an answer. The previous answer had been *river* and they'd almost been swept away. What would fire do?

They'd gone about a quarter of a mile when Matt got his answer.

Chapter 30

THE GARGOYLES WERE PLAYING CHARADES.

Faruq rolled his eyes. *Charades*. In the palace of the most powerful being on the planet. They couldn't come up with something else?

"George Clooney!" one shouted from his perch on the lintel.

The gargoyle next to the shouter flicked his stone ear. "Not Clooney, you idiot. That other one. What's his name? With all the kids?"

"Pitt! Brad Pitt!" another one hollered, hopping up and down on a corbel on the side wall until he almost fell off.

Did gargoyles shatter when they hit marble? Faruq wouldn't mind finding out.

"*Oceans Eleven*!" the hopper yelled before he did, indeed, fall off.

No, he didn't shatter. His hideous pug nose did become more squashed when he landed face-first on the floor twenty feet below, and one of the ridiculously small wings bent forty-five degrees more than it had moments before. There was also a two-inch depression in the marble. Heads were going to roll for that one; praise be, one of them wouldn't be his.

He hoped.

But the longer he waited, the more he worried.

Faruq thrummed his fingers against the armrest on the carved teak chair he sat in. What if the High Master found out she was in Al-Jannah? He'd told no one about her. Hadn't informed anyone he was headed to the North American continent. The GPS was locked in the inner sanctum beyond his office, and he'd whisked Eden into his tent so even his house staff hadn't seen her.

But what if somewhere, somehow, he'd missed something?

No. He was reading things into this summons. The High Master had summoned him regarding another matter. He was being paranoid for no reason.

Maybe the High Master wanted their centennial meeting early since preparations were going on for the blue moon, which happened on the same day as their meeting this year, October thirty-first, the mortal All Hallow's Eve, the night the dead walked the earth. It was a rare occurrence to have a blue moon on the same night.

Tradition had it that he and the High Master would convene their centennial meeting on the thirty-first, then fly up to Cloud Thirteen to watch the festivities, and, yes, partake. The High Master always had a good time that night, the most carefree Faruq ever saw him as he manipulated those souls who volunteered for the mission that kept the significance of the day front and center in mortals' minds. The holiday was hard to forget when dead Aunt Emily showed up in their parlor in all her transparent glory, or Grampa Joe materialized, whittling the piece of birch he'd started two hundred years ago.

Would a blue moon change their meeting dates? And if so, why wouldn't the High Master have warned him? His notes were in his office and, with everything that had happened with Eden, not as complete as Faruq would like.

He eyed the gargoyle who'd fallen off his perch. Perhaps he could convince the thing to retrieve his notes. It'd mean lifting the wards off the inner sanctum, but that wouldn't be a problem; no one would ever dare breach his security. He could instruct the creature to have his secretary buy all the serendibite off eBay, too.

At least he had a plan. Not optimal, but it allowed him to do something other than sit and stew.

Faruq waved the stone creature over, hiding his distaste at its nose that was not only smashed, but had shifted an inch farther to the right.

"You will retrieve a file and deliver a message to my secretary. Do that, and I will fix both your nose and the floor so no one will be the wiser."

The creature readily agreed, and Faruq murmured the spell that would allow the gargoyle to enter his offices for the notes that would aid him with the up-coming meeting.

It was almost too easy.

Chapter 31

RED-LEAFED BUSHES COVERED THE FIELD IN FRONT OF
Matt and Eden as far as they could see. Thickly trimmed
into large ovals, the bushes stood next to each other like
terra-cotta Chinese warriors on either side of the path,
an ocean of deep red beneath a lavender sky streaked
orange by the waning rays of the sun.

"I have a really bad feeling about this," Matt said as
they approached the first bush, a *Euonymus,* otherwise
known as a burning bush, hence the bad feeling.

"Me, too." Eden slipped her hand into his.

Matt took the comfort she was offering—or was
she searching for some from him? He didn't know and
he certainly didn't feel able to offer any. Swimming
through raging waters was one thing, but fire? He didn't
have any idea how they were going to avoid this one.

Well, their clothing was still wet. That helped.

"Hang on, Eden." Matt stopped her before she could
reach that first bush. He took off his jacket and held
it over their heads. "Cover your mouth with the top
of your shirt and breathe through it. Then wrap your
arms around my waist and hang on so we don't get
separated, okay?"

"Do you really think—" She took a deep breath. "Fire?"

"It'll be all right." He hoped. Good God, did he hope.

Matt buttoned his collar all the way up, ducked
his head to keep it over his nose, draped the jacket

over them, and wrapped one arm around Eden's shoulders. "Ready?"

"Would it matter if I said no?"

He kissed the top of her head through his shirt. "I love yo—er, that. About you. Your humor."

Jesus. What was he thinking? Love? No way. It was the adrenaline rush of this adventure. Life and death. In it together. White knight complex.

"You think I'm being humorous? If you say so." She tucked her hair down the back of her shirt and leaned into a lunge as if this were the starting block to a race.

Which, essentially, it was. For their lives. *Remember that, Ewing.*

Matt took a deep breath through the damp fabric. "On three. Ready? One. Two. Three!"

The minute they broke the plane between the two opposing bushes, the plants burst into flame with a loud *poof* and a blast of heat seared his back where the jacket no longer covered him.

"You okay?" he yelled as they passed the next pair of bushes, which also ignited.

Eden nodded.

Those damned slippers of hers made running difficult for both of them. Not that his boots were any better, but at least his legs were longer.

In front of the sixth pair of bushes, the tip of her slipper got caught under his boot and almost pulled both of them down, but Matt's reflexes kicked in, and he half-carried her with a hand beneath her armpit until she regained her balance somewhere around the ninth or tenth set.

By the thirteenth, Matt's back was singed enough that

he wondered if a spark had caught his shirt on fire, and by the seventeenth it was hard to breathe beneath the jacket and shirt.

By the twenty-fourth, the wind had shifted and the shirt over his mouth was no buffer against the thick smoke blowing over them, and Eden was coughing. But he also saw, among the tiny breaks in the smoke, what he thought was the end of the bushes.

"It's not much farther, Eden. You can do it!"

She nodded as another bout of coughing overtook her and she stumbled again.

The hell with that.

Matt dropped the jacket onto his head and swept her up into his arms, pleased that he hardly broke stride. Granted, his strides were slowing so that he wasn't sure he could continue to outrun the igniting bushes, but if they were going to die, they'd go down in a blaze of glory—

Hell. Not the best image right now.

Matt's boot hit a loose tile and he stumbled, the jacket now sliding down his back with Eden's bottle thumping his spine. Luckily, Eden grabbed the jacket before it hit the ground.

Another bush popped into flames beside them, the heat singeing the hair on his arms. Their clothes were dry by now—it was only a matter of time until they ignited, but at least Eden's hair was covered. Not much protection, but some. They only had a little more to go.

Calling on the last reserves of adrenaline in his body, Matt concentrated on the faint outline of what looked to be the last set of bushes.

Legs burning—from the inside out, which was much

better than from the outside in—Matt sprinted for that finish line.

Fire raced along the hedge of plants beside them, the *whoosh* of ignition now one continuous sound in his ears. Would they ever get free of this raging inferno? Dante's hell brought to life in all its pyrotechnic glory.

Eden worked the jacket over his head again, which gave him a modicum of protection against the flames. The bottle thumped by his right ear and Matt didn't care if he had a concussion when this was all said and done. As long as they were alive, he could deal with a bump on the head.

Then another bush exploded and Matt wasn't so sure coming out alive was possible. The fire was passing them and his lungs were burning. He couldn't keep up this pace.

When would it be over?

When the bush up ahead burst into flame and illuminated the area around it, he got his answer: soon. There weren't any more bushes.

Matt poured on the speed, sweat dripping off him, and sprinted through the invisible tape of the sweetest finish line he'd ever crossed. When the cool air touched him, Matt felt as if he'd won the biggest contest of his life—the Olympics, Super Bowl, and Tour de France all in one.

He took a few steps to slow down, then staggered to the side of the tiled path. Cradling Eden and coughing the smoke from his lungs, he fell to the sand, coarse grains of sand wedging through a hole in his jeans, to scrape his knee.

Eden climbed out of his arms and knelt in front of

him, her fingers going to his face. "Thank you, Matt. For getting us through that. For saving my life. Again."

He shook his head, unable to get enough breath to speak.

"Yes, you did. No one's ever put himself to that much trouble for me. Never cared—" Her voice broke and she closed her eyes. When she opened them again, a tear in each one threatened to spill over. "No one's ever cared enough. So thank you. I'll never forget it."

And then she kissed him. Softly, on the corner of his mouth, her lips tentative. Searching. As if she were afraid he wouldn't welcome her kiss.

Matt closed his eyes and allowed himself to enjoy the soft play of her fingertips against his cheek, the sweet warmth of her breath on his mouth, the floral scent of her skin still sweet beneath the acrid smoke, and the salty taste of those tears.

Her lips nibbled on his and Matt parted them, letting her in. For all her boldness last night, now she was almost hesitant. He'd let her control this kiss. Satisfy whatever it was inside her that needed satisfying.

She framed his face with her hands and angled her head. Matt kissed her back, softly. Simply. Their breath mingling, nerves stretched by danger. Relief in their escape.

"Beautiful," he whispered, meaning her.

"Yes," she whispered back, meaning, what? Him? The kiss? This?

Them?

Matt stilled. There was no *them*. There couldn't be. He had nothing to offer her. Aside from the business, what could he give a woman who literally had the world at her fingertips?

So this kiss—he hoped she found in it what she'd been seeking.

Eden rested her forehead against his and exhaled softly. "Thank you."

Matt didn't trust himself to speak. He ought to be thanking her.

And then the ground rumbled. Now what?

He and Eden climbed back to their feet and Matt slipped his arms into his jacket sleeves, then touched the pocket to ensure the bottle was still there.

And then the *Hadhayosh* thundered into sight.

"Who goes th—?"

"There. Yeah, we know." Matt raked his hands through his hair. How many more questions were they going to have to survive?

"No one goes here," Eden answered again.

The *Hadhayosh* snorted. Again. And shook his head. Again. Was there a script for this? If so, it was in desperate need of a rewrite.

"Very well," the beast said. "You have answered correctly, but, to continue, you must answer the question. Correct, you pass; incorrect, you die. Simple."

Yep, a script. Written and performed by a creature with a very limited vocabulary.

"What swallows that which is before it and that which is behind it, as well as anyone who watches?"

Limited vocabulary it might have, but this question stumped Matt. Eden, too, if that look on her face was anything to go by.

Before, *after*, and *anyone who watches*. There was something...

Matt closed his eyes, reaching back into his memory.

Something about that question. It resonated with him, but he couldn't quite grasp it.

"Matt?" Eden's whisper was shaky.

The heat from the fire was replaced by a chill so deep it was arctic. They were going to die because he couldn't remember.

Think, Ewing! Think!

He was trying to, dammit!

The beast pawed the ground. One strike. Two. Three.

It snorted and took a step forward, his massive hoof sinking an inch into the sand. "The allotted time has ended. You must answer or die."

Eden slipped beneath Matt's arm and wrapped her arms around his waist. Matt felt her spine straighten and her shoulders roll back. Fighting till the end of their time together. He loved that about her, too.

Wait.

The *Hadhayosh* pawed the ground. "Prepare to d—"

"Time!" Matt yelled, and time itself seemed to stand still.

Time was what swallowed those around it.

Matt waited, counting his heartbeats as he remembered that last conversation with his father. It'd been near the end; they'd all known it. Dad had beckoned him over. He'd patted Matt's cheek, a slight, weak movement, and looked him in the eye.

"Time marches on, son. Everyone is born and they die, but it's the memories they leave behind that define them and let them live on in others." Dad had brushed one finger over Matt's heart. "Keep me here with you."

Those had been the last words his father ever said to him.

And now, as the ground rumbled again, Matt realized they'd saved his life.

In more ways than one.

Chapter 32

THEY RAN AS FAST AND AS FAR AS THEY COULD ALONG the tiled path through the meadow before the stitch in Eden's side forced them to slow down.

"So, was that it? The last riddle?" Matt asked, pulling his hand from the pocket where he kept her bottle.

He was still looking after her. The blaze from the burning bushes didn't warm her as much as that knowledge did, and she'd carry the feeling with her when they eventually parted.

"I don't know, Matt. We're in uncharted territory." Both with the riddles and whatever was happening between them, but she'd enjoy the double entendre only in her mind because they still weren't in the clear. Only when she had the *Mandragora* would she relax. Well, after she survived it. "Thank the stars you knew the answer to that last question. How did you?"

Matt bent down to pick an orange peony from the side of the path. "It was something my dad said to me. The part about swallowing what's behind it? That's time passing. What's before it is time flying. Anyone who watches, time marching on."

"He sounds like a smart man."

"He was." Matt held out the flower to her. "I just hope that was the last test."

The ground rumbled, and Eden didn't have the

chance to take the flower because Matt's "Oh shit" put sentimentality on the back burner. It wasn't over.

Sure enough, the rock rose behind them and the *Hadhayosh* appeared, now wearing a blue fez and matching cape with gold tassels, and gold-hilted knives protruding from sashes around his front hooves.

"Who goes there?"

Enough already! Eden wanted to scream, but they hadn't come this far to blow it now. "No one goes here."

The *Hadhayosh* snorted. "Very well. You have answered correctly, and because you have done so three times, you must now ask *me* a question to which I do not know the answer. If you do, you may pass. If not, you die." He pawed the ground, his eyes glowing orange. "No one is smarter than the High Master, and since he has shared the secrets of the universe with me, his chosen guardian, I suggest you say your good-byes. No one should ever challenge the High Master's authority and expect to live."

"Who does this thing think it is?" Matt muttered. "The sphinx?"

"The sphinx's ancestor," she whispered back, trying to think. She didn't know any secret of the universe that the beast wouldn't.

Unless it was from a much smaller universe. Say, her own.

Matt wrapped his arms around her waist and turned her to face him. "If you distract him, I'll grab those knives and kill him."

She shook her head, not having the heart to tell him the knives were just for show. The *Hadhayosh* had as many powers as she did and could stop Matt before he moved another inch. "I can do this, Matt."

"Eden—"

"Matt, you have to trust me."

He searched her face, his mouth a straight line. A muscle ticked in his jaw.

"I *can*, Matt."

"Your time is up," the beast growled.

Matt took a deep breath. Then he nodded. "I do, Eden, but—"

She put a finger on his lips, then faced the *Hadhayosh*. "My question is, what's Matt's middle name?"

There was a moment of silence, then she felt Matt's lips curve against her finger. "I could kiss you right now," he said.

"Probably not the best time," she whispered back, her eyes never leaving the *Hadhayosh,* who was gaping at her. Hopefully it was because he was at a loss for words.

"What's *what*?" the beast roared. So much for no words. "I know the secrets of the universe and you ask me *this*?"

Eden tapped Matt's lips and bit back a smile. She was going to get the chance to take him up on that kiss offer after all. Her instinct had been right.

She stepped out of Matt's embrace and faced the *Hadhayosh* head-on. "Yes, what's Matt's middle name? You didn't specify any parameters, just a question to stump you. That's my question."

"Why, it's… I… That is…" The *Hadhayosh* stomped the ground and the fez tilted sideways, tassel spinning. Then with a disgruntled snort, it raised its thick lashes, the orange fire in its eyes gone. "I don't know."

"You are brilliant," Matt whispered behind her, his fingers circling on the small of her back, and Eden wasn't sure if her smile was because of that or the look of utter disgust on the beast's face. Both, probably.

"Matt's middle name is Lawrence," she said. "So? Do we get to pass?"

The *Hadhayosh* snorted and gouged ruts in the ground with his sharp hooves, knives flashing. For a few awful seconds, Eden wasn't sure he was going to let them go.

But then he knelt on one knee and lowered his head. "As you wish."

"Damn straight, I wish," Matt said, then spun Eden around and planted that kiss on her.

It was even better than promised.

"Mortal."

It took Eden a few seconds, and a second "mortal," to realize that the rock had receded back into the earth and the *Hadhayosh* was none too thrilled to see them standing there.

"Well?" the beast said.

Eden didn't have to be asked twice. She grabbed Matt's hand and turned to follow the path.

Only there was no path.

They were standing on the very end of it, and a meadow stretched out before them, dotted with a rainbow of butterflies and flowers beneath the pink and lavender sunset.

"Where's the pyramid?" Matt asked.

"I don't know."

Matt turned around, then cursed. "And where'd the animal go? This is insane. No pyramid, no path, and no answers. Now what?"

"We keep going."

"I don't like this, Eden."

"Me neither, but I don't think we have a choice, Matt." She was sick to death of not having choices.

Then something nailed Matt on the temple. "Now what?" He pulled the sticky ball out of his hair. "Son of a bitch! That burns!"

Another one hit him in the back and Eden thought she heard a sizzle.

The plants—the *pitcher* plants—were lobbing noxious spitballs at them.

She was right; they didn't have a choice.

Matt cursed again, wiped his fingers on his jacket, then grabbed Eden's hand. "Come on. Let's go."

With a trail of butterflies following them, they ran through the shin-high grass, dodging more spitballs, the occasional rubber tree that bounced through the field, and windmill palms whose madly spinning fronds buzzed the air. Those things could do some serious damage to anyone who got in their way, and she and Matt had to separate at one point to avoid losing a few arms.

Dodging the closest palm at a full run, Matt ran ahead of Eden when, all of a sudden, he pitched forward and started doing some windmilling of his own.

"Matt!" Eden raced up to him, grabbed the back of his jacket, and yanked.

It was either that or he would have taken a header over the cliff in front of them.

Chapter 33

MATT LANDED ON TOP OF EDEN — A GREAT REWARD FOR escaping the clutches of death not once but four times. Maybe more; he'd lost count.

But with her soft body beneath him, he couldn't think of better reward.

"*Oomph*! You want to get up, please?"

He was *up*.

Jesus, what was his problem? A life-and-death situation, and all he could think about was being inside her again? This adrenaline-filled, run-for-your-life thing was potent. Or maybe that was Eden. Either way, now was not the time.

Matt rolled off and helped her up, then they — carefully — walked to the edge of the cliff.

Below them, in a lush valley that looked more like the setting for *Jurassic Park* than something one would expect to find in the middle of the Sahara Desert, magical city or no, was what Eden had called a *small* pyramid.

There wasn't anything small about it.

While not quite on the scale of Chichén Itzá, it could give the Mayans a run for their gold. Unfortunately, this pyramid didn't have the convenient ninety-one steps up each side. No, this one was made of blue-veined white marble, as flat and slick as a sheet of ice.

"We have to climb that?"

Eden grabbed his arm and pointed at the top of the pyramid. "See that glow? Those are the djinn's eggs."

Glow? He was going after glowing plants?

Any moment the Mad Hatter was going to show up. Then the March Hare. Alice. Hell, why not the whole deck of cards, too, since he and Eden still had a freaking tea party to attend once they managed not to break their necks and the rest of their bodies on that monolith.

"Tell me you know how we're going to climb that without killing ourselves."

"Of course I do." She wiggled one curly-toed slipper. "These. They're perfect for walking up marble."

Such a normal sentence for her.

"Come on, Matt! Let's get down there before the sun disappears. We don't have much time."

"One problem, Eden. I didn't bring any rappelling equipment with me." Matt shook his head. Never in a million years would he have guessed he'd spend his weekend rappelling down a cliff, or pyramid-climbing with a gorgeous genie.

"Not a problem. Look over there." She pointed to a grove of eight-foot-wide redwoods. Really red redwoods. As in candy-apple and fire-engine.

A pair of donkeys stood there, munching away on a selection of bright yellow grass that smelled like lemon.

Donkeys.

It figured.

The donkeys carried them down the uneven terrain faster than any American donkey he'd ever seen, but then, he was in Al-Jannah. Which was why it didn't surprise him that the shrubbery the animals meandered off to munch beside a golden lake ringed in more of the cursed willows and burning bushes, with hundreds of butterflies frolicking among the leaves, was twisted red-and-white like candy canes.

"So, Eden, how did you know my middle name?" Matt asked as they set off on yet another path—a yellow brick one this time. Any minute Gene Wilder would pop out from behind some tree in a purple top hat and coat, singing about the Candy Man with a Munchkin and Oompa-Loompa chorus backing him.

"Your mom called you that during dinner."

Matt's steps faltered. He was surprised she remembered with everything that had happened during that dinner.

He wasn't delusional enough to think her remembering it meant anything special. He was, after all, the first guy she'd come across after being incarcerated for two thousand years. His ego winced at that observation, but Matt was nothing if not a realist.

Still, it did touch something inside him.

He watched her walk ahead of him—a metaphor for this whole journey. Eden hadn't taken a backseat to him or let him do all the work. She hadn't waited for him to make sure everything was safe. Hadn't looked to him for every answer. She was as much a part of their journey as he was, as instrumental in saving their asses as he was. Self-sufficient and reliant, the way she'd had to be to survive.

And while he'd stretched his knight-in-shining-armor muscles a few times, so had she, pulling him back from the brink on several occasions—sometimes literally. Eden could hold her own, and it was a novel experience. Though, surprisingly, not necessarily one he wanted to embrace. The first woman who hadn't wanted him to be her Prince Charming was the one he found himself wanting to be one for.

They followed the curve of the path around a giant baobab tree and reached the pyramid. A slick, solid slab of marble, four stories tall.

"Are you sure those slippers are going to be up to this?" Matt asked, seeing his opportunity. "I could find another way—"

Eden didn't say anything, but put one of those slippers flat against the pyramid. Her body went perpendicular to the marble and she walked up the side as easily as if it were the path behind them.

Ironic that part of the outfit Faruq insisted she wear was now instrumental in thwarting the dickhead.

"Would you mind ripping the lining out of your jacket, Matt?" she asked from fifteen feet up. "I can't touch the plants. Oh, and can you find some green tea leaves? And a few willow branches and burning bush berries."

Matt ripped out the lining and tossed it to her, making sure he didn't lose her bottle. "How do I know what the tea leaves look like?"

"You'll know when you see them."

Matt took her word for it.

Six minutes later, his faith was justified—although, after weeping willows and burning bushes, he shouldn't have asked.

Green tea leaves were green. And shaped like a *T*. They grew beside plants with leaves shaped like tiny alarm clocks that smelled like thyme, and a bush of yellow, snapping dragons with little orange flames puffing out of their snouts just like Humphrey.

Matt plucked six of the palm-sized *T*s, grabbed a walking-cane-shaped spike of sugar from a conveniently nearby grove in case Eden liked her tea sweet, gathered up the rest of the ingredients—dodging tiny flames on the burning bushes—then headed back to wait for her at the base of the pyramid.

She walked back down the pyramid as easily as she'd walked up, her hair flowing over one shoulder and down her back, brushing the smooth, delicious skin between the too-small shirt and the too-big pants that hung low on her hips. He'd kissed that area last night. Knew its flavor and texture. Felt it expand when she inhaled, contract when she exhaled. How it fluttered when she shuddered. How it felt against his palm. His chest. His cheek.

And when this was all over, when Faruq was no longer a threat, he'd take her away somewhere. Or he'd let her zap them somewhere, where they wouldn't be interrupted for days on end and he could explore her and this whatever-it-was between them.

"Oh, good. You found the T leaves," she said with a hop onto the ground in front of him.

He'd found something, all right. Matt shook his head and reached for the jacket lining she carried that held three glowing blue flowers the size of dinner plates.

But Eden shook her head. "The less we handle them the better. Djinn's eggs are a member of the nightshade family."

Matt dropped his hands. Nightshade? Nightshade was deadly. And if ingested, fatal.

So how the hell was she supposed to survive this?

———∿∿∿———

Faruq was certain smoke was billowing from his ears because his blood was boiling at being kept waiting by both the High Master and that rock-brained gargoyle.

The High Master had never kept him waiting this long, and the non-appearance of the gargoyle he'd sent for the notes—the *only copy* of his notes—had Faruq going beyond boiling, straight to steaming.

Gargoyles weren't the most intelligent of creatures, but surely a file sitting on his desk wasn't hard to find?

What if the simpleton *lost* the file?

The remaining gargoyles had moved on to I Spy. Considering the antechamber had little in the way of ornamentation, the game was pointless. As was all this waiting.

Faruq tossed his robes back and sat in the wicker fan chair in the far corner, half-tempted to flick one limb of the bonsai on the table next to him onto the floor. But that would only anger the High Master. The master djinni did like his harmony.

Faruq's was currently in the toilet, swimming among the muck this day had become.

Then that infernal peacock strutted in from the courtyard, poked at some fuzz on the rug, and asked the dumb-ass question: "What are you doing here?"

Peacocks were less known for their brains than even gargoyles.

"Waiting for my appointment with the High Master." Faruq strummed his fingertips on the rattan armrest with less than satisfying results. Finger-strumming was all about the noise it produced, thereby illustrating the strummer's ire. Faruq's ire was at Code Red levels, but the rattan mocked him with the puny little scratching noise. "The meeting *you* brought me to."

"I did?" The bird looked up, narrowed his eyes, his comb ruffling forward. "Oh, yeah. That's right. I did."

He went back to picking at rug fuzz.

Something wasn't right. The High Master was known for keeping people waiting, but usually not him. And definitely not this long.

"The High Master did send you for me, right, bird?"

The peacock lifted his head. Rug fringe hung from his beak. "It's *avian* to you, vizier."

"The name's Faruq."

"See how you like it?" The bird went back to scrounging for fluff.

"Fine. *Avian*. So—"

"Name's Peabody."

Peabody? The High Master's entourage counted a bird named *Peabody* among its ranks? Usually they bore regal names, such as Gilgamesh or Mahatma or Boleyn. Well, not Boleyn anymore. Not since that last one had tried to fly the coop and ended up losing his head.

There definitely was no peacock named Peabody in the High Master's entourage.

"All right, *Peabody*." Faruq tiptoed across the carpet toward the imposter. "Did the High Master ask you to summon me?"

"The High Master?" The bird pecked twice at something else, then ruffled his tail feathers, fanning them high over his back, giving Faruq the proverbial bird's-eye view of his lily white ass. "Not that I can recall."

Faruq bit back a curse because the gargoyles stopped their stupid game at the bird's display. The High Master didn't permit cursing within the hallowed and pristine

walls of his palace where everything was geared toward
Right, Positivity, Oneness, and Happiness.

Truthfully, all the glee and oneness made Faruq
ill. This wasn't some Utopia, though the High Master
could pretend all he wanted. Faruq was the one who
dealt with the nitty-gritty of reality, keeping the djinn
in line, balancing mortals and magic. He was the
one always walking a tightrope, and the one thing—
one!— he wanted as his reward was detained in his
harem tent, at his mercy, while he sat here on this wild
peacock chase.

"Who. Was. It?" Faruq asked the bird through
narrowed lips.

"Who was who?" The bird chose another spot to peck.

What in the cosmos was the bird finding to eat? The
High Master kept this place in pristine condition. More
oneness and positivity. *Blech*.

"Who summoned me here?" Faruq was two strides
from wringing the wretch's neck.

The bird scratched the back of his jeweled head with
one foot, then looked at Faruq, clueless to how close he
was to becoming dinner. "Beats me. All I know was that
I had to show up in that courtyard and lead you here.
I was hoping you could tell me. These are some fancy
digs. I wouldn't mind hanging around."

Oh the bird would be hanging all right. Off a roasting
spit as soon as Faruq found out who'd set him up so he'd
leave Eden alo—

Eden. Of course!

Faruq swore, not caring when one of the gargoyles
leapt off his perch and flew through the little door above
the arch into the High Master's chambers. Let the little

beast report him for profanity. Faruq didn't care. He'd underestimated Eden—again. When would he learn?

Right now was as good a time as any.

Just as it was the perfect time for *her* to learn who she was messing with.

Chapter 34

WHILE MATT FOLLOWED HER ORDERS AND RUBBED THE burning bush berries together to start a fire inside a ring of stones, Eden snuck up on a pitcher plant in the surrounding forest and managed to pluck it without becoming a victim of its foul spit balls. She poured out the liquid inside, wrung tears from willow branches into the empty pitcher, tossed in the crushed tea leaves, then set the pitcher atop the low flames.

While the tea brewed, she and Matt gathered a cushion-sized red mushroom cap for him and a purple one for her and sat on them, hovering, beside a babbling brook. She couldn't make out the language. Aramaic, maybe. Or Phoenician. It'd been a while since she'd spoken either.

"Since it's going to take a while for the tea to steep, let's take a look at that bracelet now, Eden." Matt lifted her hand and pried open the prongs around the canary diamond with a sliver of granite, but the jewel didn't make a cut in her bracelet. Or a dent. Not even a scratch.

She was afraid it wouldn't be that easy. Faruq didn't usually make empty threats. "It's no use, Matt. Faruq's too smart."

"Don't underestimate us, Eden. We got them off once and there are a lot more jewels to try."

Give up? No. Be realistic? Definitely. But Matt was determined, so she let him. She could always hope Faruq had screwed up.

An hour of Matt cursing, her wishing, and nothing happening destroyed that hope and left her with a pile of jewels and two denuded shackles still firmly attached to her wrists. Not only did Faruq not make empty threats, but he was a crafty *ibn el-kalb*. That's why she had to be at the top of her game and why she had to use the *Mandragora*.

"Matt, it's no use. We need the crystal." She peered into the pitcher plant. "This is going to take a while."

Matt set the granite sliver down with a sigh. "Are you sure this is the only way? Can't we petition this High Master of yours? Get some other genie to retrieve the crystal? Nightshade's deadly to humans, Eden. Isn't it to genies, too?"

Eden didn't want to answer that question. She was human, too, just an immortal one—but only in the sense that she, like all genies, could live forever. There were, however, things that could kill them. Poison being one.

"I can't go to the High Master, Matt. I'm rogue, and he'll never forgive me, let alone help me. I'd end up right back where I started. And finding a genie who's permitted to use magic in Al-Jannah is next to impossible. Namely because the only ones who are are those in training, and helping me would put a target on their back. I couldn't live with myself if we even could find someone who was willing. At least, with the tea, we have a chance. I'll be fine."

Her arguments were all true, if not completely truthful. If she used the tea properly, she'd be fine. If not, well, dying was better than what Faruq had planned for her. She was *not* going back to The Service. And especially not to *him*. Ever.

Eden eyed the pitcher plant. Twenty seconds. That's all she had to breathe in for the magic to take effect.

Or kill her.

She looked at Matt. Gorgeous, sexy Matt who knew how to treat a woman. Who'd come after her when she'd needed him to. Who'd turned down her offer of a wish.

There weren't many guys like him. She may have only been out and about in the world for three hundred years, but in that time she'd seen way too many mortals who were the complete opposite of him. Matt was different. Special.

And, for a little while longer, hers.

She looked at the pitcher plant. The tea had a long way to go until it was ready. She, on the other hand, was ready now.

"Matt." She held out her hand, her voice husky.

Passion darkened his eyes, and he took her hand, tugging her onto his lap so that she straddled him, desire shining in his eyes.

"I want you, Matt."

"Thank God." The corner of his mouth turned up, and he tucked some of her hair behind her ear. He liked playing with her hair, and she liked that he liked it. Then he cupped her cheek and drew her lips to his in a simple, gentle kiss—for all of about a second before the kiss exploded into something bigger.

Need and desire claiming her, Eden grasped the front of Matt's shirt and ripped. Buttons went flying. She was very good at that.

His tongue delved into her mouth, mimicking movements *he* was very good at, and Eden wanted more. More of the swirling, tumbling feeling in her belly—and lower—more of the hot rush of desire that threatened to overwhelm her, more of being wanted, needed, by Matt.

She slid her hands along his sides, then up over his pecs, her fingers combing through the hair there, her breasts tingling as she remembered what it'd felt like against her, brushing her nipples and igniting all sorts of fires under her skin.

She wanted more of this. More of him.

More... *more*.

Matt's fingers threaded through her hair, tugging her head back so his lips could trail over her throat, leaving more fire in their wake. Then his hand claimed her breast, his thumb unerringly finding her nipple, and Eden could only arch into the caress, gasping, the words she wanted to say muted without breath.

She'd died and gone to Paradise. An ever-after that couldn't last, but the memory of which would. Heat swirled through her with a sweet primal lethargy, and a growl worked its way from her throat.

"Matt." One word. That was all she could manage. But what it encompassed...

The bristle of his beard against her cheek only stoked the flames. So different, men and women. Sun and moon. Yin and Yang. Spark and fire.

Matt slid her top over her breasts. "I want to see you, Eden. Taste you."

She could imagine nothing more perfect. Eden wrenched her shirt over her head as Matt made good on his promise, dipping his head to draw first one aching mound into his mouth, then the other, his tongue swirling around the tips.

She squirmed against him and her head fell back,

eyes closed. It felt so good—*he* felt so good. *This* felt so good.

He gathered some of her hair and brushed it over the breast he'd just suckled, the new sensation increasing the urgency. She wanted him. Badly. Inside her. Taking her to the heights. Riding the current with her. Crashing all around her. The scents and the sights and the feelings she'd never get too much of.

His tongue flicked her nipple again and something else flicked her cheek. Eden opened her eyes. An iridescent green butterfly fluttered above her.

Then Matt trailed his fingers down her belly to slip beneath her waistband, his long fingers finding her quickly, and more butterflies appeared.

When he slipped his finger inside her, a rainbow of fluttering wings swarmed around them, cocooning her and Matt in their whispered music, their breeze fanning her heated skin.

"Matt," she cried, a wealth of questions and longing.

And Matt answered them all with his lips caressing the spot between her breasts where her heart pounded. "Come for me, Eden." His thumb found her and he slipped his finger out. Then in. Then out again. In, his thumb ever-moving.

Ah, yes. That was it. She rocked against him, matching the rhythm with her hips, feeling an answering tempo in his legs as his muscles flexed beneath her thighs, his breathing as shallow as hers, and Eden let herself—and the butterflies—soar as Matt took her to completion.

With butterflies swirling around her, her breasts firm and ripe, nipples rosy from his kisses, Eden looked utterly beautiful as she came, and Matt almost came himself.

With her legs splayed across his thighs and her hair trailing almost to the ground, she was everything he could ask for, and Matt shuddered with the desire he had to contain until he could find release inside her.

She was everything he could ask for. Strong, independent, yet so giving. So caring. A true partner, and oh, God, if the nightshade didn't work—or worse—

Matt thrust those thoughts away, the moment too beautiful to ruin with reality, and pressed another kiss to her heart, enjoying the powerful thudding his touch induced. Her hands gripped his shoulders, then ran through his hair, holding his head in that spot.

He kissed her again. "You're so beautiful." He inhaled the scent of Eden and gardenias—his new favorite flower. Butterflies were now his favorite animal.

"Matt." Her voice was throaty. "I want you inside me."

He didn't need to be asked twice.

He did, however, need to ask for some help, or he'd drop her when he tried to undo his jeans.

Her hands found his fly and tortured him—on purpose, he was sure—as she worked the buttons.

She laid the jeans open on his thighs and ran her fingertips over the boxers tented by his cock. She swirled her thumb across the head.

"Touch me, Eden." This was torture and, hell knew, they'd been through enough already.

Eden slipped him free of his boxers and grasped with both hands, covering his complete length. Her bottom hand squeezed gently while her other one—

God. She pumped his shaft, her fingers brushing the underside of the head, and Matt felt his orgasm churn in his balls.

"Sweetheart," he said through gritted teeth. "Get. On." He shuddered. "Me."

This time it was Eden who needed no further invitation. Half-standing, her breasts so close he could taste them—so he did—Eden worked her pants off and strad-dled him again, sinking onto him in what was probably only a few seconds but seemed like a lifetime.

And then she lifted herself off, only to plunge back down, and Matt could well imagine a lifetime of this.

The butterflies swarmed together then, a coalescent body swirling clockwise around them, whipping the air into a frenzy to match the rush of blood through his body.

Matt gripped her hips and lifted her, then drove him-self upward as he pulled her back down.

Her thighs clenched his. "That's it, Matt. Just like that. Perfect."

It was perfect. It'd never been more perfect. No one had ever been more perfect. Strong, driven, resourceful, capable... no one was as perfect for him as Eden, and their bodies fit together in a way that confirmed it.

He couldn't imagine a life without her in it.

Matt angled his hips again, earning a half-moan, half-sigh from Eden and another ball-emptying jerk of his cock.

"Eden—" Jesus, he could barely breathe, let alone speak. "Can't. Wait."

"Come, Matt." She leaned against him and swirled her tongue in his ear.

Matt tried to stop it. Tried to hold out for her, but when she kissed him, sucking his lobe into her mouth, all bets were off.

Gripping her hips, pushing her down onto him,

spearing himself into her, Matt came. And came. He came until there was nothing left inside and the sweat poured off his body. Until his balls ached with the contractions and his cock was so sensitive it twitched inside her with every breath she took.

Until there was the very real possibility that he was falling in love with her.

Chapter 35

TWO HOURS OF SWEET, HOT LOVEMAKING LATER, MATT lost his breath all over again, but this time it wasn't because he was watching Eden come.

This time it was because she was inhaling the tea vapors, and his eyes never left hers.

He counted out twenty seconds for her, time never seeming so long. Or so important. If he lost her—

There was no *if*. He *was* going to lose her. The tea could do her in, or they'd fail to recover the rest of the items and Faruq would recapture her, or they'd recover the items only for Eden to disappear. Another fucking no-win situation for him, and that's why, no matter what he thought, no matter what he wanted, no matter what he might be feeling, he couldn't fall in love with her. He couldn't allow himself to be that vulnerable again—although, really, there was no *again* about it. What he'd felt for Cara was so far removed from this as to be laughable. Pity he wasn't capable of laughter.

"Well, that's that." Eden set the pitcher plant down. "And?"

She nibbled one of the lips he'd nibbled not ten minutes ago. "I can't tell until I do magic, and I can't do magic until we're away from here. But it didn't kill me, so that's good. You know the saying, whatever doesn't kill us makes us stronger."

"Don't even joke about it, Eden." Because he'd never be able to laugh about this.

"I know, Matt." She cupped his cheek and her blue eyes softened. "Let's go. We don't have time to hang out. The effects won't last forever."

Other effects, however, did.

―⁓―

The trip back through the park was much easier—in terms of physical danger. Emotional danger?

Whole other story.

The pitcher plants were in the seventh inning stretch, the *Hadhayosh* bowed when they walked out of the field of flowers but made no move to detain them, the burning bushes were mere embers, and the river the weeping willows had cried was no more than a puddle.

The flowers on the orange trees had blossomed, and a flock of hummingbirds was happily drinking from the gardenias, filling the air with a winged lullaby as he and Eden crossed back over the stone bridge that... *sighed?* when they hit the ground on the other side.

Yeah, it was a sigh and Matt could totally relate.

But he kept his thoughts to himself. He'd deal with them and his emotions after they were free. He'd have a lot of time then.

They ran through the streets to Faruq's offices with the almost-full moon illuminating their way and providing enough shadows along the streets full of Al-Jannah nightlife that they could make it back undetected.

Their sides heaving, they stood beneath the towering red stone walls of a castle, the crenellations on top barely visible from this angle. This wasn't an office building; it was a fortress modeled after Spain's Alhambra, a beautiful example of Moorish architecture he'd studied in college, but, unfortunately, not with the intent of sneaking inside.

"You ready for some magic?" Eden whispered.

None could ever match the magic of what'd they'd shared by the pyramid, but Matt was a realist. "Give it your best shot, Eden."

"First, a test." Eden hitched her breath and Humphrey appeared in her hand, a double smoke ring puffing from his nostrils.

"Hey there, buddy." Matt was happy to see the little guy. Humphrey seemed to be, too, nipping at Eden's palm, then Matt's outstretched finger.

"Ow." Matt shook his hand, laughing.

Eden smiled. "I was hoping he made it out of Faruq's compound okay." She stroked a finger along the crest on the dragon's back. "Time to send you back to your nursery, Humphrey."

Another breath, and the dragon disappeared in a tiny sprinkle of green glitter. Eden's eyes were just as sparkly when she looked at him. "The tea worked. Ready?"

"Hell yes. Let's do this."

"Okay, hang onto me."

As if that was a hardship. Matt wrapped his arms around her, and, with another hitch of her breath, the world in front of him turned a hazy green. Tingles jackhammered into him, and he had the strange sensation of his body dissolving into mist.

But as quick as it took him to realize it, the mist coalesced back into his body, and when it dissipated, they stood inside an ornately decorated antechamber full of

Persian rugs, intricately carved furniture, mosaic-inlaid tables, a mother-of-pearl-topped sideboard, brass lanterns, painted vases, a hookah—

But no bank of crystals.

"Now what?"

Eden tapped her lip. She knew Faruq. Knew how he thought. He wanted her for what she could do for him in his career. Wanted her because he had the need to control. To dominate.

That bank of crystals was the ultimate control. His ego would demand he have it close by and while he'd love to show it off, he enjoyed the power it gave him too much to risk anyone tampering with it. He'd keep it close but secure.

"We have to find his private office. The crystals will be somewhere nearby." She'd been to his private office once. When she'd first killed that bastard who'd called himself her master, Faruq had transported her to his inner sanctum, as he'd called it. Offered to save her life if she'd marry him.

Some life that would have been. She'd turned him down without a second thought.

"Any idea where that is?" Matt asked.

Faruq's office had boasted every luxury: sumptuous furniture, magnificent paintings, sculptures of ivory, alabaster, and gold, bottles of ambrosia from the gods, and a massive desk that had probably been an altar from a deity's temple. A lesser deity because a higher one wouldn't have let Faruq get away with stealing it.

The door behind that desk didn't have a knob. She'd commented on it in an effort to get Faruq's mind off the ridiculous idea of her marrying him.

At the mention, he'd straightened his shoulders and thrust out his chest. "Marry me and you'll see how powerful I truly am. How much I can give you."

She'd laughed at him.

And she was laughing again. Because he'd let her in. He'd told her where she'd find what she'd need to escape him. And he'd showed her how to find it.

"Matt, look for a door that has a window carved with the Vitruvian Man."

"Da Vinci's study on the proportion of man?"

"Is that what it is? Faruq said it illustrated how mankind is confined by mortality. That square that goes outside the box? The djinn. According to Faruq, it represents how we can move within and beyond mortal boundaries, showing how much better we are than mortals."

"Unless Faruq drew it and gave it to Da Vinci, not quite." Matt raked his hands through his hair. "He didn't draw it and give it to Da Vinci, right?"

Poor Matt. Eden smiled. Faruq hated that mortals could produce such works of art. He liked to claim everything beautiful in the world as djinn-made. "No, Matt. Faruq didn't give it to Da Vinci. Your artwork masterpieces are all your own creation. Genies had nothing to do with that."

Other than inspiration in some cases, like double rainbows or the aurora borealis, but why go there?

"Score one for us."

"Let's score another and find that door. That's where the crystals are."

Thanks to Faruq's need to feel superior, it didn't take them long.

Da Vinci's drawing was etched in octopus ink in the middle of a dried giant squid mantle stretched across the door's window frame. Light could pass through the semi-transparent "canvas," but its composition prevented anyone from being able to see in. Not knowing what security measures Faruq had installed to protect the room, Eden grabbed Matt's wrist when he reached for the knob.

"Wait. There might be magic protecting it." Or Faruq's damned snake.

"Good catch, Eden. How do we find out?"

"I'll throw some magic at the door. We don't want to be in the way if it bounces back, so stand aside." She rolled her shoulders, then shook out her hands. "Ready?"

"Have at it, sweetheart."

Sweetheart. She could get used to that.

Eden shook her head to clear it. If she wanted even a chance to consider that possibility, she'd better focus. Faruq wasn't stupid; he was going to figure out the peacock was a decoy.

So she took a deep breath, shook her hands out once more, raised her fingers, and hitched her breath.

Green flames shot out of her fingers.

Chapter 36

MATT WAS HOPING FARUQ'S EGO WOULD MAKE THIS EASY.

When Eden's magic came under no counterattack, he let himself believe it might be.

And when the door behind the desk opened with another blast of magic and Matt saw what was behind it, he realized Faruq's ego was bigger than Matt had given him credit for.

The vizier was entirely too complacent. Thank God, because complacency bred mistakes, and Faruq had just made a big one.

Moonlight shone through a half-moon window high on the side wall onto hundreds of crystal obelisks. Right there, as accessible as you please, they rested in orderly lines across a span of pure white marble, each one glowing a different color, some more brightly than the others, the pulse inside them like a heartbeat.

All but one.

On a wooden shelf beneath a map of the world where correspondingly colored stars blinked, a yellow crystal, the same shade as Eden's bottle, lay. "Yours?" he asked her.

She nodded. "Yes. Faruq's ultimate control. Every genie in The Service has one. Blinking means we're out of our bottle in Service to our master. Steadily lit ones mean the genie is in his or her bottle, awaiting a new master. The ones with no light—" She reached for hers.

"Careful."

"It'll be okay, Matt. There aren't any wards or spells in here, or my magic wouldn't have worked."

"I'm not worried about the magic. I'm worried about you. Have you ever touched your crystal before? What if it does something weird since it's connected to you?"

Her hand stopped inches from the crystal. "I hadn't thought of that."

He had. Every possible scenario of losing her had run through his mind the minute they'd walked into the room—hell, from the moment he'd first seen her, if he was going to be honest with himself. "I'll get it."

Eden's hand wavered, and so did she.

And Matt had a feeling he knew why. It hurt, but he understood.

If he had her crystal and her bottle—which he did— he was a good portion of the way to being her master. That word, *slave*, replayed in his mind. The way she'd said it, the way she'd looked.

He would have hoped, after all they'd been through, that she'd trust him enough to know he wouldn't do that to her.

"I won't use it against you, Eden."

She pulled her hand back and bit her lip. "Of course you won't, Matt. I know that."

Strong, independent, driven, focused, caring, compassionate, and she put up a brave front, too. Why was the one woman he could see being a part of his life the one who couldn't be?

Matt took a step toward the crystal, and—

Something hissed.

Faruq's snake. It rose in front of him, weaving from side to side, unblinking eyes devoid of emotion as it stared at him, the forked tongue flickering. Anticipating a taste?

Matt didn't breathe.

But Eden did.

And, in less than a second, the snake dropped to the floor, coiling backward into a basket there, the only sound a sibilant snore.

Matt spun around to see Eden brushing her hands. "How—?"

"I hate snakes."

A smile tweaked the corners of Matt's mouth. She hated snakes. Another reason Faruq wasn't getting her.

Matt picked up the crystal. Six inches tall and heavier than it looked, the base was perfectly square, the angles perfectly carved, the surface perfectly smooth. Perfectly beautiful. But not to Matt because of what it represented.

He slid it into his pocket where it *clinked* next to her bottle. Two down, one to go. Then they could get the hell out of Dodge. "Let's go."

"Matt?" She was staring at the crystals. "I want to get rid of all of them."

"Eden, we don't have time."

She ran her fingers along the edge of the marble. "There's no guarantee, Matt. No guarantee that we'll get away with this. That Faruq won't win. If I can ruin this for him, it'll give others a chance I never had. A chance to choose."

He couldn't refuse her. Not when he knew her horror at being someone's puppet. She'd never forgive herself for not doing something. And he'd never forgive himself for not helping her.

"All right, what do we do with them?"

"Pile them up and I'll blast them to different parts of the world. It'll take him years to find them, if he even does, and in that time, who knows? The whole system could change."

"Fine." Matt started plucking the crystals from their homes. Green, red, blue, purple, a diamond—"Eden?"

She looked up.

He held out a green crystal. "Is this an emerald?"

She shook her head and pointed to a darker green one in the bottom left quadrant. "That one's an emerald. The one you're holding is demantoid. It's rare."

He held out the purple. "And this? Amethyst?"

"Tanzanite."

A deep red one.

"Garnet."

He arched an eyebrow. There was a wealth of jewels here and he didn't mean of a monetary nature. A gemstone had set her free once, maybe it would again.

"Give me your bracelet."

For the space of a heartbeat she looked confused, then she put her arm in his. "I hope you're right, Matt."

So did he.

———

Obo crawled out from under the aqueduct's lowest arch and into the shadows surrounding the goddess's temple. The moon reflected off the water in the fountain before the portico, bathing Bastet's statue in jade from the stones that surrounded the pool.

Coast clear, Obo raced across the plaza and hid beneath the lip of the stones. A pair of dodos pecked near a pomegranate tree on the opposite side, but he wasn't worried about them. If they even saw him. There was a reason the name had crossed over into everyday English.

A cloud passed in front of the moon, casting enough of a shadow for Obo to run across the plaza and up the steps of the temple without the birds seeing him, and he zipped behind Bastet's statue before the cloud drifted away.

His paws made no sound on the lapis lazuli mosaics that led into the worship chamber within the temple. Pyrite, carved into tiny statues of every breed of feline, dotted the tiles in a haphazard pathway. When the moonlight hit them, the gold flecks in the mineral gave off soft, twinkling light like the strands mortals put on trees for the winter solstice. It was a nice ceremonial touch, and tonight, goddess knew, was all about ceremony.

At the altar, Obo stopped. For all his talk, this meeting was nothing for him to be flippant or sarcastic about. It would determine his Eternity.

He removed the bag's cord from around his neck, slipped Cleopatra's amulet from it, and placed it on the floor. The Egyptian queen had been a favorite of Bastet's, and vice versa. Whichever way the favor went, Obo would take all the help he could get.

"Oh mighty Bastet," he said, bowing before the marble statue of the goddess, a human with a cat's head seated on a throne.

He felt her essence enter the temple. Saw the statue shimmer as she inhabited it.

"Ah, Obo." The goddess tsked—never a good thing. "You cannot hope to gain your Eternal Reward by bribery."

"But goddess, the amulet is what you said would earn me Celestial Paradise."

"That is true, Obo. But not to *buy* my favor. That works for corrupt politicians, not gods of the realm you seek to enter. What were you thinking?"

Obviously not what she was.

Son-of-a-bichon! He'd carried this thing around with him for over two thousand years. Protected it. Almost lost part of his tail over it. *Had* lost one of his lives because of it. All for tonight. For the chance to give the goddess the sacrifice she required and learn the secrets of his past.

"I don't understand?" The question sounded more like confusion than anger—which wasn't a bad thing. He'd already strayed over the line by bribery; he didn't want to compound it by disrespecting her as well. Then he'd never earn his Eternal Reward.

"And that is the problem, Obo." The statue's hand moved with a harsh slide of stone as it separated from the throne's armrest. "Go. You have not yet learned what it takes to enter our realm. Follow the gypsy's order, then come back to me, and I will decide your fate. As of now, you are not worthy."

The statue went still and her presence circled once around him before drifting away.

Not worthy. What did she want? Blood?

Obo sighed and shoved the amulet back into the bag. He slipped the cord over his neck and went out the way he'd entered.

Not worthy. Each word fell on a footfall. He *wanted* to be worthy. He was *trying* to be worthy.

Who was this random gypsy to decide his worth?

Chapter 37

IT TURNED OUT MATT WASN'T RIGHT ABOUT THE CRYSTALS. Not a single one made even a scratch on her bracelets.

But the exercise was by no means a loss. Not only had they found her crystal, she'd screwed up Faruq's dictatorship and had given her fellow genies a chance at freedom, taking great satisfaction in the burn marks and scorched papyrus that blasting the crystals to all corners of the world had left on his desk.

She'd also enjoyed what it felt like to have Matt care for her. With every gem he'd tried, every look, every touch, Matt couldn't have been clearer that he cared for her than if he'd said it.

He hadn't needed to. That he cared wasn't in doubt; what good could come of it was. She didn't want to hurt him, but she wasn't going to put him in danger by hanging around after she escaped Faruq. Because, no matter that she'd be free, Matt would always be her weak spot, and if Faruq thought she really cared, Matt would never be safe. She'd have to leave him for his own good.

For these last few hours, however, she wasn't going to deny herself the pleasure of him and what-if.

She took the notion to heart, and, once the damage was done to Faruq's control center, she zapped them on a whirlwind tour of Al-Jannah, spreading enough Glimmer everywhere to keep Faruq busy while they searched his palace for her stopper. She'd made sure the last stop on their tour had been the observation deck of the genie version of the Eiffel Tower where the kiss they'd share there probably turned the Glimmer into fireworks, but Eden hadn't cared. When the green Glimmer eventually changed back to her yellow, she wanted Faruq to have no doubt who'd destroyed his GPS.

She returned them to the street outside Faruq's offices and conjured buttons for Matt's shirt. The vizier would come here to check the crystal when he learned she was gone, so that's where the magic needed to end.

"We're hoofing it back to Faruq's palace, I take it?" Matt asked as they stepped out from the palm she'd materialized them behind.

"We have to. If I zap us there, the Glimmer will follow us. I can't conjure another donkey for the same reason. It'll trail Glimmer after us. And I don't want any unicorn driver to remember seeing us."

He kissed her cheek. "I was joking. We outran burning bushes, we can certainly make it to Faruq's no problem. Let's go."

Her cheek was still tingling when they rounded a corner and almost ran over a gargoyle.

"What the hell is that?" Matt asked as they ducked behind a saguaro cactus coat rack outside a tavern.

Eden peeked out. Yep, there it was, walking right down the middle of the street, as nonchalant as you please. "It's a gargoyle."

"A gargoyle. Let me guess—it talks, too."

Eden nodded, absently. What was a gargoyle doing *walking* down the street of Al-Jannah? With a—skunk? And both of them drunk as a—well, it was no secret where the expression came from.

But gargoyles were rarely seen in the streets. They lived in their lofty heights, and when they did come down among the common folk, they certainly never walked because their density damaged every surface they stood on unless it was denser than they were. Not many things qualified.

The only good to ever come out of a gargoyle walking anywhere was the invention of mosaic tiling. More out of necessity than anything else since there'd been piles of broken tiles all over the place. Everyone, from the tile makers to the artists, to the architects and homeowners, had been relieved when the High Master had given the creatures wings. The bent one this guy sported explained why he was walking. It also explained the chunks missing from a few doorways he'd passed. But it didn't explain what he was doing here.

"So I said to Faruq." The gargoyle weaved sideways and almost stepped on the skunk's tail. "I said, 'I'm not your servant. Go get your own file.' 'Course he was none too happy, but, whaddya think? The nose adds character, right?" He turned his profile sideways.

That had to hurt—and Eden definitely wasn't surprised to hear Faruq's name in connection with it.

The skunk twitched her tail.

"Yeah, that's what I think, too. An' it was a good thing my buddy Hannibal warned me Faruq left the High Master's palace before I accidentally ran into him. He wanted me to go to his office for that file, you know. On his desk. And tell his secretary to buy some stuff called serendipity, serenity…" The stone creature shook his head with a shivers-up-the-spine screech. "What was it called? Serenade?"

The skunk twitched her tail, and the stone on the gargoyle's face stretched into a grotesque smile. "Yeah, that's it. Serendibite. I dunno why he wants more. Everyone knows he's got a stash in that cave of his. Greedy S.O.B."

The two of them stumbled around the next corner.

"Now I've seen everything," Matt said.

"Actually, you haven't." But that gargoyle had given her an idea. And when Matt saw what she was about to show him, he would, pretty much, have seen *everything*.

"Follow me."

Faruq aimed a kick at one of the filthy doves that paraded around town as he headed back to his palace and Eden. Sure, white doves were the symbol of romance, but they still did what every other bird did—shit all over everything.

Kind of how his life was going.

The gargoyle had yet to return, and he'd fallen for that stupid peacock trick, wasting precious time—hours—on the bird's machinations. If he'd been thinking straight instead of being half-consumed by fear—and half by lust—he never would have fallen for it. And he sure as hell wouldn't have sent a damned stone imbecile to get the most important file he possessed.

That's what his desire for Eden had done to him. The genie he'd never been able to have. Well, he would now. To hell with seduction and romance; Eden was his and he'd make damned sure she knew it.

He waved a hand to unlock the gates of his palace, the ebony doors slamming open in a shower of angry red Glimmer, the action jarring a boar's head off the wall. Another wave of his hand had the head floating back into place. He'd make a spot next to it for that gargoyle's when he found him.

His servants bowed before him, their foreheads so low to the floor he could crush their skulls into it without much effort. And if he weren't so hell-bent on getting back to Eden, he'd do just that. Inept, all of them. What fool had let that bird in? He would have him beheaded at sunrise.

And then Faruq strode into his courtyard.

What was left of his courtyard.

He'd have them *all* beheaded at sunrise. His guards especially, their bodies posted on spires ringing the palace walls as examples of what happened to fools who didn't know how to serve their master.

Then he saw the tire marks.

Actually, no, he wouldn't behead all of the guards. That *honor* he'd reserve for the captain—as well as the infernal, interfering mortal Eden had chosen over him in her bed.

And he'd make her watch.

Chapter 38

EDEN LED MATT DOWN MORE ALLEYS, ACROSS MORE streets, behind more buildings, and through two more deserted squares—in the opposite direction of Faruq's palace.

"I thought we were going after the bottle stopper, Eden?" Matt whispered when she shoved him into the shadows so the griffin coasting above the alleyway wouldn't see them.

She didn't think it was one of Faruq's spies, but anything was possible. "We have no guarantee we'll find it, but I know how to get rid of the bracelets. Let's do that first."

They crept in the shadows toward the cross street. "Sweetheart, we already tried. Every jewel. It was a waste of time."

"It wasn't, Matt, because it put us in that alley with the gargoyle at the right moment. I know how to get them off, and that's where we're headed." Except they had to make a detour when a crew of pirates surged out of the pub on the corner. Liquored-up pirates could be just as dangerous as the *Hadhayosh,* and she and Matt had filled their quota of danger today. The year, even.

"I'm missing something," Matt said. "What does a gargoyle have to do with your bracelet?"

She held up her hand and peered around another

corner, waving him on when the coast was clear. "We're going to the cave where Faruq has a stash of serendibite."

Matt caught her hand and turned her around, pressing her back against the building, and, inappropriate and ill-timed as it was, the swirly feeling started again. She would have thought they'd quenched that thirst for at least a little while, but apparently an eighteen-hundred-year deficit took longer to slake.

She was about to kiss him when sanity prevailed—sanity helped by Matt's question.

"Faruq's stash of *what*?"

Eden took a deep breath and metaphorically tucked her hormones away. If only she could do so physically, but she was asking enough of the universe with this latest twist. "Serendibite, Matt. It's a gem. An extremely rare one."

"It doesn't surprise me that Faruq has it, but what makes you think it'll work?"

"We tried every crystal in the GPS and every jewel in my bracelet, but none were serendibite. If Faruq wants his secretary to buy it up, I'm betting it's the key."

Matt tilted her chin back, the admiration in his eyes ratcheting up that feeling in her tummy. "Pretty clever, Eden. If I have to be on the run from some crazy, magic-wielding genie, there's no one I'd rather be with than you."

He actually kissed her after that statement. Her. The one who'd put him in danger in the first place.

She didn't deserve Matt—and more importantly, he didn't deserve to be in the danger he was in. All because of her.

She should have left him the minute she figured out her new Way. She could have dribbled enough Glimmer all around the city so that her stop by Matt's would have been merely one among many. Faruq wouldn't have figured Matt to be anyone special to her and would have focused instead on following her trail.

But she'd been selfish. She'd wanted Matt. After hundreds of years of kowtowing to others' wants and desires, she'd decided to fulfill her own.

So she'd stayed in his life, put him in danger, all because he had a sexy body, killer green eyes, and could scratch an eighteen-hundred-year-old itch like nobody's business.

Talk about using someone for what they could do for you. She was just as guilty as all her masters.

Faruq stood in his office, having materialized directly into it, and felt the anger surge through him. At Eden. And himself.

He'd let her in. He'd actually lowered his guard—and the security wards—and hadn't seen this coming. He was getting soft. Losing focus. All over a half-mortal harem girl.

She wasn't going to get away with this.

Faruq took two steps toward his desk before the shock had him fumbling for the back of one of the chairs there.

Scorch marks streaked his desk. Charred flecks of papyrus, a gash where something sharp had gouged the beautiful desk he'd claimed his first day on the job—it was ruined.

Bracing himself on his palms, Faruq circled the desk, eyeing the pitiful few remaining objects still on it. An old issue of *National Geographic* magazine had a gaping hole through the middle as if a cricket ball shot straight through, and the enameled in-bin he'd bought at the souk last week was smashed to smithereens. He'd haggled over that price for a good half hour, wearing the merchant down in the end.

And the file—

The file was in tatters, not a single word legible.

All his work. A century's worth of notes. Reports. Observances. Rumors and secrets. All of it gone.

Faruq groped for the chair behind him. Sank into it. He'd start with the mortal. Torture him one body part at a time. The sick feeling in his gut subsided as he imagined how Eden would plead with him for her lover. And how he'd demand everything of her.

He placed his palms on the desk and stood. Destroy his career, would she? Make him look like an ill-prepared incompetent at the meeting with the High Master? Deny him his destiny?

Oh no she wouldn't. But he'd deny Eden hers.

Tiny particles grated beneath his palm. Faruq looked down.

Glimmer.

As if he needed proof. Only—

This wasn't Eden's Glimmer. Hers was saffron yellow, which was why he'd originally chosen the canary diamond. But this green, whose was it? Who had she recruited to help her?

Faruq spun. The crystals. He had to check the crystals. They would tell him. A surge of magic sent the door behind him flinging open as he strode through—

And slammed to a stop.

Gone. Every last one.

Who'd done this? *Who*? Faruq tore his gaze off the empty marble altar and scanned the shelf above it.

Her crystal was gone as well.

Shock held his body still, but his mind never stopped moving. He was done for. Every genie out there was now unaccounted for. His most important role, the thing that brought him his power and glory—it was gone.

When the High Master found out, it'd be over. His reign finished. All he'd strived for. All he'd planned, connived, and manipulated for. Bartered and brokered and bribed for. Doing whatever had needed to be done to work his way into this position, one step below the highest power in their world. In *any* world.

And now it was all gone.

Anger welled up in him so deep and so thick it threatened to choke him. But he wasn't going down without a fight. Oh no. Some slip of a half-mortal girl wasn't going to best him, and that mortal sure as hell wasn't going to get away with it.

They were peons. Nothings. Yet they dared this—this—

Faruq raked the turban off his head and scrubbed his temples. How? Where had he gone wrong?

He looked at the mess of what had once been his desk. The barrenness of his GPS.

He knew where he'd gone wrong. He'd underestimated Eden. That'd been his first mistake. The second had been allowing her mortal to live.

Faruq straightened his back. No more mistakes. He'd follow the Glimmer and find whoever it was who'd help her. He'd learn her plan and punish the traitor.

And then he'd give Eden the surprise of her life.

Chapter 39

"WHAT IS THIS PLACE?" MATT STOOD BEFORE A TOWERING mound of rock, half a football field in width, double that in length, with the back end sloping into the ground. Several larger, circular stones created a face on the façade, the largest one as the mouth as if Picasso had set out to create a Halloween masterpiece.

He'd certainly succeeded. Out of all the beauty Matt had seen in Al-Jannah, this mountain, backlit by moonlight, was easily the ugliest thing going. Well, next to Faruq.

"It's The Cave of Great Unknown," Eden said.

Of course it was. It couldn't be called The Cave of the Way Out, or The Cave of the Missing Crystal, now could it? No. Great Unknown was what he got.

"Okay, so how do we get in? Open Sesame?"

With that, the stone "mouth" rolled to the right.

"You're kidding me. *Open Sesame*? Why not *abracadabra*? *Hocus pocus*? *Alakazam*?"

"Come on, Matt." Eden tugged on his jacket until his feet moved. The moment they were inside, she uttered the words he should have seen coming. "Close Sesame" rolled the stone back into place.

Black as pitch didn't come close to describing the darkness. And with the absence of sound, he wouldn't be surprised if they'd entered a new dimension. Pissed, but not surprised.

"Eden?"

"Hold on," she said, off to his right. "I know it's around here somewhere."

A couple of *clinks*, a *clank* or two, definitely a *thump,* and an *ooph*, then suddenly the place was lit up like a stadium on game night.

Matt blinked against the sudden glare. "Magic?"

Eden chuckled. "In a manner of speaking." She nodded to a switch over her shoulder. "Edison's. The whole place is wired."

Matt blinked a few more times to let his eyes adjust.

Then he had to blink a few more times to let his *mind* adjust.

Treasure.

Everywhere.

He was standing in a grand foyer, big enough for half the National Football League to practice in. Alcove after alcove angled back off long corridors stretching deep into the cave, red-banded arches decorating the entrance to each.

Beyond the doorways were countless priceless artifacts and treasure. Scrolls. Amphora. Steamer trunks. Piles of gold objects gleamed in the first alcove so brightly Matt couldn't make out individual pieces.

He shielded his eyes and turned toward the next alcove. Silver. Gleaming and untarnished, as if it'd been recently polished. Suits of armor and shields. Pots and more. Copper in the next alcove, iron the next. To his right were rooms of diamonds and sapphires and emeralds. Rubies so big they looked like apples. Amethysts the size of baseballs. Aquamarines like robins' eggs that'd fallen from their nests.

"What is this place?"

"The Cave of Great Unknown."

"If it's so unknown, how did you know about it?"

"Oh, not unknown to us but to mortals. This is knowledge we have that mortals don't. You would call it King Suleiman's Mine."

"Suleiman? As in Solomon? King Solomon? That Solomon? That treasure?" He had to be dreaming. That was it. He hadn't gotten much sleep last night, had been on the run all day with nothing to eat but a breakfast sandwich and that slice of pizza Mayat had fed him—he was so tired he had to have fallen asleep somewhere and his mind was projecting all of this because it could not possibly be true. Genies, flying carpets, magical talking beasts, King Solomon's treasure—

And then Eden slipped her fingers between his, and heat raced along every nerve ending in his body, and Matt knew there was no way he'd sleep through *that*. No way he'd imagined what had happened between them at the pyramid. No way he'd imagined what he felt for her.

"Are you okay with this, Matt? I know it's tough to take in, but—"

Matt shook his head. The cave was nothing. Its treasures were nothing—not when compared to Eden.

Here, in this cave, with all these treasures that'd been hidden for centuries, Matt realized that the only treasure he needed was Eden.

He wasn't *falling* in love with her; he'd already fallen. For all the good it'd do him.

Matt slid his arm around her waist and dropped a kiss to the top of her head. "You're right, it is a lot to take in, but I'm fine, Eden. Let's go find this jewel and set you free."

—⁓—

Obo reached the back of The Cave of Great Unknown, checking the scrub grass around him. Nothing moved behind its sparse cover.

Why'd the cave have to be all the way out here? Desolate, abandoned. Even the moon, shining on it from the back, didn't want anything to do with it. He hated this place.

Hated it more now that he was going to do what he had to do. "Why else do felines go to The Cave?" the gypsy had asked. There was only one reason, and it made him sick just thinking about it.

He'd counted on the amulet smoothing the way for him with the goddess, but she'd told him to follow the gypsy's order. Now he knew how Eden felt, having to do what someone else commanded.

The amulet was the key to his past; he knew that, since that's when his memories began. And he was going to throw it away.

Obo sighed, checked that the bag's string was tight, then flared his claws. Rock climbing wasn't exactly a cat's forte, but better to have all systems go so he wouldn't slide off. He stretched out first one leg, then another. A third.

Stalling, cat.

Yeah, yeah. Obo took one last look around, then wiggled his butt and leapt onto the first semi-level stone he found. One down, a zillion to go.

A dragonfly buzzed over the top of the next rock.

What was the stupid insect doing awake at this time of night? What was *he* doing awake at this time of night? He ought to be asleep on the hearth by Matt's fire, dreaming of fields of catnip and walls of sandpaper to scratch up against, not bloodying up the soft pads of his feet on a monolith of jagged rocks.

Muttering a curse as a back leg slipped out from under him, Obo scrambled to climb onto the next rock, this one higher and narrower than the last. Where the hell was that crevasse?

Obo swished his tail behind him and found one. Funny thing about these crevasses—mortals and genies would find them inconsequential. Natural fissures created by rainwater.

Only cats knew they were more than that. Obo contracted his pupil until it was as narrow as the next crevasse he found and peered in. Copper gleamed below, the composition of the rock making every angle within act as an upward-reflecting mirror, giving him the perfect window into the room but preventing rainwater and light from getting in. Bastet's followers had been delivering things to these rooms since The Time of Mists and Chaos and knew how to use the crevasses.

Unfortunately, this room wasn't the one he wanted.

He leapt onto another rock, the amulet bag banging against it, the *twang* reverberating up through his neck muscles. He found another opening but, again, it was the wrong one. Those wax dummies in the room below gave him the creeps.

The next rock was larger. Smoother, thank the gods. He leapt onto that, but his left front paw slipped into the next hole, and his chin hit the slab with a *thunk*, giving him a headache.

Cursing in Old Persian, he worked his paw out, then looked down. Stone tablets with writing on them. A weathered chalice of some sort. An ornate stone box lined with gold—

Definitely not that chamber. He'd never been inside The Cave but knew enough about the storage system to know that Egyptian amulets and Christian relics didn't share space.

After too-many-to-count curse-filled minutes of searching every crevasse he could find, from the Forty Thieves' cache to American Revolutionary and presidential history, to the secrets of the Far East, Obo felt as if he'd taken a whirlwind world tour through time.

Finally, he found the room with a statue of Bastet in the center. The goddess was into herself, wasn't she?

Obo ducked and searched the sky. Now was not the time to diss the goddess who would decide his Eternity.

But dammit, he didn't want to get rid of the amulet. Besides being the key to his past, it'd been his safety net for all these years. What was he supposed to do without it? What if he couldn't make it back to the temple safely? That amulet had protected him for over two thousand years. No matter how many times he'd crossed a street at rush hour, he'd arrived on the other side without a clump of hair missing, singed, or crushed. Yet the moment he'd stepped a paw here, on this rock—the end of the amulet's journey—he ended up bloody and sore.

Looked like she *did* want blood. His.

Obo glanced around. Behind him were the buildings of the capital. Moonlight streamed through the windows of the minaret in the High Master's palace, illuminating the park and the giant walls of the city beyond.

Before him, hidden within the swirling sands that were visible only to the outside world, stretched the vast expanse of the Al-Jannah desert. Different than the Sahara, this desert held land mines so deadly he still shuddered from the stories.

This was it. What his life had come down to. He either did as the gypsy and the goddess bid, or he risked the danger of that desert because, if he didn't, he could kiss Atonement goodbye.

Obo shook the amulet from the bag. Cleopatra had been a nice lady by all accounts. A bit bloodthirsty and power hungry, but for some reason, she'd helped him escape Faruq's "Asp Surprise" by giving him this amulet instead of using it to save her own life. She'd been distraught when word had reached her of Antony's death. Not a sentiment Obo understood, but one for which he was grateful.

Obo nudged the amulet close to the crevasse. Tilting it on its side, he slipped it effortlessly through the opening that stretched and molded to its shape. Followed by the leather bag, the amulet pinged off the interior shaft like a pinball. Dozens of feet it fell, landing atop a green altar in a plate of gold coins, knocking several off and leaving others teetering on the edge.

Story of his life.

Obo sighed. It was done.

And so was he.

Chapter 40

MATT TOOK THE ALCOVES ON THE RIGHT, EDEN, THE ones on the left, to search for the serendibite. So far he'd come up empty for that gem, but the gems he *had* found...

Japanese, Macedonian, and Mayan artifacts. Greek, Roman, and Minoan columns. Olmec monuments. Atlantean and Etruscan carvings. Persian textiles. Pottery, scrolls, masterly crafted furniture—his father would have loved those.

The loss hit Matt again, a straight shot to the gut, just like always. One thought and it was as if it were yesterday. Dad had died too young. Too soon. Matt had loved spending time with him, learning how to use a chisel or hold a rasp. Turning the lathe. Listening to him bring the history of the pieces he was working on to life. They'd had some of their best times in Dad's workshop. But not enough. And here he stood, staring at a treasure trove he could never share with his father.

It wasn't fair. It hadn't been fair when he was nine, and it wasn't fair now. Even though he was an adult who understood the nature of terminal illness, he'd lost more than his father back then. Treatments had cost money and his mom worked nonstop to pay it off, always too busy and too tired. Up early to get him off to school, then work, with cooking, shopping, cleaning, and laundry in there somewhere, only to fall into bed exhausted at night.

He'd helped as best he could, but Mom had worked so hard to hold their family together that she hadn't had the time to hold him. At nine, he'd needed to be held.

Then she'd found Paul and life had gotten easier. But it hadn't gotten better, not for him. Hayden had had both of his parents. Divorced, yes, but he could still see his mom. Matt hadn't had that luxury.

But he didn't hold it against any of them. It was what it was. Mom had done what she'd needed to do to survive, and Paul and Hayden had welcomed him into the family. But it had sucked. Through no one's fault, and that's what sucked the most. He'd had no one but Dad's illness to blame, and how could he rail at that?

"Matt?" Eden walked into the room. "Did you find anything?"

Matt cleared his throat. The past was the past. He couldn't change it. But the future? That was still up for grabs. And if they succeeded in doing what they'd come here to do, there was a chance Eden could be part of his. That was his focus now. He couldn't lose the present by hanging in the past.

He turned around. "No serendibite in here."

"*Zift.*" She raked her hair off her forehead. "This is going to take a while."

"You thought we'd just walk in and find it?"

"Hey, Faruq left the crystals unattended. Anything's possible."

"True." The guy's ego was as big as this cave. "So, I guess we head to the next corrid—" He heard something. "What was that?"

"What was what?"

He put a finger to his lips and whispered, "That noise."

"What noise?" she whispered back, hurrying over to him.

Matt pressed her against the wall, tucking himself between her and the pillar that supported the doorway arch. "You didn't hear it?"

"Obviously not if I asked you what noise."

Good point. "I heard something clink. Like metal on metal."

"Maybe something fell over?" She peered around him into the corridor.

He didn't believe it any more than she did. He leaned over her to see what she saw. "Too much of a coincidence. Have we found anything else that's been toppled in any room? This place is too well cared for."

"You think it's Faruq?" Her voice wavered.

"Unless this is a hot spot for tourists." Assured that the coast was clear, Matt pulled her with him through the corridor and behind the archway to the next alcove, a room full of wooden artifacts and Bronze Age tools. Norse, from the looks of the boat along one wall. And that spear hanging above it—Odin's? Matt wouldn't be surprised. The hammer below it was probably Thor's.

Matt didn't care whose they were. He grabbed both and gave her the spear, which was light enough for her to swing, even if it was almost as tall as she was. That could work perfectly to keep her beyond Faruq's reach—provided they surprised the vizier before he had the chance to use his magic. A big *if*, but better than being sitting ducks.

They crossed the corridor and plastered themselves on both sides of the pillars at the entrance to another alcove.

Matt looked inside. Egyptian antiquities that put the

Tutankhamen exhibit to shame and made the boy king look like a pauper. Rows of marble obelisks ringed the room like a spire-topped fence, preventing anyone from getting near the ostentation on the walls. The tables behind them were covered in more obelisks. Ankhs and other symbols of Egyptian gods and royalty decorated the room, gold and gemstones glittering in the light.

A rug hung on the far wall, and Matt could think of only one so famous in history—and from this country—that it had to be the one Cleopatra had used to deliver herself to Caesar.

At the center of the room stood a tall altar made of green basalt, with a stone bust of some god in the center and overflowing with gold. Drinking vessels, jewelry, coins—

Coins that had fallen onto the marble floor beneath.

"There's our noise." Matt headed over and began picking up the fallen gold when Eden's shout had him spinning around.

"Matt! Look! It's here!"

Above her, amid a row of gem-colored obelisks, was a light blue one. Unlike the other obelisks, however, this one's color was pulsing. Like a heartbeat. Like the crystals in the GPS.

"That's got to be it." She caught her breath, and the obelisk floated off the shelf and down toward her outstretched hand.

Matt reached out to grab it before it touched her. "Careful. We still don't know what'll happen if you touch it, and with the way it's started pulsing even faster, I don't want to take any chances."

Eden held out her arm, and Matt wasted no time.

Neither did the bracelet. One stroke of the serendibite

across it and the metal opened. The bracelets were off in under ten seconds.

Thank God Faruq *was* that overconfident. Now they could get the hell out of here and Eden could zap them to Faruq's courtyard to search for the stopper. Then, hopefully, they'd be home free.

And then he'd have a chat with her about what their future held.

He shoved the obelisk inside his jacket pocket and held out his hand. "Two down, one to go. Let's go find your bottle stopper."

Eden linked fingers with Matt, caught her breath, and wished them outside The Cave.

But their bodies didn't dissolve into mist.

There was no rushing sensation, no feeling of lightness, of floating, and she still felt the solid floor beneath her thin slippers.

"Whenever you're ready, Eden." Matt's words, so calm and trusting, threw her off-balance.

When she was *ready*? They should be outside by now.

She re-gripped his hand and shifted closer. Took a deeper breath. Wished harder.

Eden opened one eye. Still in The Cave.

She let go of his hand, shook out her fingers, then grabbed his hand again. Maybe there was something about the density of the rock that affected her magic.

She tried again.

And, again, her magic didn't work.

"Eden?"

She felt him turn beside her and, this time, when her breath caught it had nothing to do with magic.

"Eden?" Matt's tone was as worried as she was. "Are you all right?"

She exhaled and looked at him. *Zift.* "No, Matt. It appears I'm not." She wrapped her arms around her waist. "I can't do it."

"Can't do what?"

"I can't get us out of here."

Matt swore. And swore again. A third time. "Let's put the bracelets back on. Maybe it only works with them on."

Putting those shackles back on was the last thing she wanted to do. "There has to be another way, Matt."

"I'm grasping at straws here, Eden. Maybe there's something about The Cave sealing your magic inside unless you have bracelets on. Kind of like Lo-Jack for the treasures, easily traceable if a genie wants to help himself. It's worth a shot. Unless you want to be stuck in here forever—or until Faruq finds us."

Actually, she wouldn't mind spending eternity in here if it meant she'd be with him—

Except that her eternity and his were vastly different. Exactly her reasoning for not falling for him.

At some point her heart would start listening to her common sense.

"Come on, Eden. We have the crystal. I'll take the bracelets off once we're out of here."

Apparently now was that moment.

Eden held out her wrists.

Matt put one of the shackles back on. In less than a second it sealed itself along the cut he'd made, and Eden felt as if a door had closed in front of her. As if her world, with all the possibilities it'd held, was now cut off. She'd never realized how much of a prison those bracelets truly were until she'd lived without them again, even for these few precious seconds.

"Go ahead. Now try," Matt said after putting the second one on, his tone soft, as if he knew what she was going through.

But then, he did, didn't he? His freedom was tied to these bracelets as much as hers was.

Heart pounding, Eden tried again. She double-hitched her breath and pictured the spot right outside The Cave, not wanting to tax her system by wishing them across a few continents and an ocean. Baby steps, that's what would work.

Only… it didn't.

Her magic didn't take them anywhere.

Eden tried again.

Matt exhaled, and she could feel the tension coiled inside him. Felt the same in her gut.

"Okay, let's think this through. You levitated the obelisk off the shelf, so obviously you can do magic. It's getting out that's giving us trouble, right?"

She hitched her breath and wished one of the gold and turquoise falcon statues off the wall. It soared overhead like a real bird with an intermittent flap of its wings. "My magic's working fine."

"Then it's something to do with the door. Maybe we should try opening it the same way we did before."

They raced back to the entrance, both shouting "Open Sesame!" the entire length of the main corridor.

The stone didn't move.

Matt tried prying it open, but the door was too big. And magically sealed.

Eden tapped her lip and tried to think. No need to panic. Panic never helped anyone. What had she heard about this cave? What lore did she know?

She'd never heard anything about magic not working— but then, she'd never spoken to anyone who'd actually been inside The Cave without an escort. Oh, everyone knew where it was, field trips were a given in school, but, funny, no one laid claim to having taken something from it.

Which meant that anyone who'd ever tried must have encountered Faruq—and had never been heard from again.

Obo felt every mile he'd run tonight in the aches and pains in his haunches. He was getting too old for this. Which was why he had to get back to the goddess for his Eternal Reward.

He'd made Atonement, did what everyone wanted him to, fulfilled his part of the bargain; it was time she fulfilled hers.

He retraced his steps across the temple plaza, avoiding the dodos who'd moved all of two feet since he'd last been there, and tried not to watch the path the moon took across the sky. It'd be morning in a few hours, so he had to either have a successful meeting with the goddess or meet up with Matt and Eden for the trip back.

If it was the latter, he hoped Eden had managed to keep herself free of Faruq or the trip back was in serious jeopardy, especially without the amulet.

Ah, well. Faruq couldn't track him, so he'd find another way to disappear.

Obo ran through the lapis lazuli corridor, past the

pyrite figurines, and into the goddess's worship room to bow before the altar.

He had to hand it to her; she swirled into that room and that statue the moment his head hit the floor as if she'd been waiting for him. That had to mean he'd earned his reward, right?

"You really are a piece of work, Obo, do you know that?"

Not exactly the words he wanted to hear. "Goddess?"

"You left the amulet."

"That's what you told me to do."

"I told you to follow the gypsy's order. I said nothing about leaving the amulet."

Obo shook his head and flopped his whole body onto the floor. "I give up."

"Yes, that's your problem." The statue heaved a sigh. "Look, Obo. When will you realize that it's not all about you? You've lived over two thousand years as a cat. I would have thought at some point during that rather long-lived party you call a life you would have figured out that selfishness is not what it's all about. It's what got you turned into one in the first place. And how many kittens did you leave behind? Any *one* of their mothers getting help from you?"

He'd *known* that would come back to haunt him. But what did she mean about being turned into a cat? He'd always been a cat.

Hadn't he?

"What about all the mortals you mooched off until something better came along? That little girl outside of Rome was heartbroken when you left. Do you even care?"

Lucrezia. Obo didn't know how much she'd missed

him—she'd certainly found other intrigues to keep herself occupied. Mistress of poison, was that girl. But, speaking of intrigues, he wanted to focus on this *turned into a cat* thing—

"The list goes on and on, Obo. We've kept tabs on you. Depositing the amulet with the other treasures doesn't begin to make amends. Now, go back and see what you can do to fix this."

With that, the goddess flew out of the statue in a breath of hot air—and, no, he wasn't making any analogies. He just wished he knew what the hell she meant. Fix what?

Taking his own deep breath, Obo shook out the aches in his legs.

If the goddess didn't kill him, he swore that her puzzles were going to.

Chapter 41

"NOW WHAT?" MATT POUNDED HIS FISTS AGAINST THE rock one last time, then rested his back against it, his eyes bleak. "Is there another entrance to this place? Another way out?"

Eden shook her head. "One way in, one way out." Or maybe it was just one way in. "We'll have to wait. Maybe Obo will figure it out when we don't show up. He'll find us."

Matt shook his head. "I'm not leaving my fate in the hands of a cat. Not again." He raked a hand through his hair. "If we can't get out, we better make sure we're prepared in case it's not Obo who opens the cave. Once Faruq figures out your Glimmer trick, he's going to come after that crystal."

"I need to get these bracelets off, too. I can't be caught in them. Not again."

Matt pulled the serendibite from his pocket, and once again the bracelets fell off. "We need to come up with a plan. Prepare a defense." He snapped his fingers. "I know. Zap some of the Greek statues in here, and we'll throw costumes from the Aladdin's Cave room on them so Faruq thinks they're us. Can you do anything about making them seem as if they're alive?"

"Sure. That's easy. Animatronics one-oh-one." She zapped a statue—Hera—into the main entryway and changed the white marble skin, eyes, and hair color to match her own, tossed on a hated harem outfit, and imbued the statue with more animatronics than any mortal had ever seen, flourishing her hand before her doppelgänger like those game show hostesses she'd watched on the television in her bottle. "Voilà!"

Matt smiled. "Feeling godlike, are we?"

"That's god-*dess*. And I might as well go for the top goddess." She brushed her hands. "All right. Now it's your turn. Who do you want to play your part?"

"It doesn't matter. As long as Faruq thinks it's me."

Eden knew exactly who she'd pick, and, despite the seriousness of their situation, she was having fun. "One distraction coming up."

When the green smoke disappeared, the Wax Figures room was soon missing one hat-wearing, whip-carrying celebrity.

"Harrison Ford?" Matt laughed. "I'm flattered."

The actor was the one who should be flattered.

"You need to get him out of those clothes, Eden."

As soon as the words were out, Matt's gaze met hers, and Eden realized his mind had gone where hers had. It wasn't Matt's double she'd love to get out of his clothes.

"We, uh—" Matt's words broke the spell. "We need to get all of this set up, Eden. So, if you wouldn't mind—"

She wouldn't mind.

Then he waved his hand toward "Indy."

Ah, yes. The setup.

She whisked clothing similar to Matt's from various rooms within The Cave, thankful that Faruq liked to catalog history. The first pair of jeans, a button-down, even a similar coat—this one with the lining still intact. Then she zapped animatronics into the figure and stepped back to admire.

Definitely good-looking, but the guy was no Matt Ewing. No man would ever be Matt Ewing. Still, it could fool Faruq.

"Now for the weapons," Matt said, putting the hat from his double's head onto his own, and he headed to an alcove they'd searched earlier.

"Weapons will be useless against him, Matt."

"As a distraction, Eden. We'll need something to get his attention so we can escape. He'll notice knives aimed at him."

"All he'll do is deflect them."

"What if they're coming from everywhere at once? We only need a few seconds. I'll take any advantage we can get."

Together, with his ideas and her magic, they booby-trapped the entrance of The Cave, amassing artillery that would make Genghis Khan jealous. Matter of fact, some of those artifacts *were* Genghis's.

Knives, spears, crossbows, a row of cannons, and more animatronicked statues: Brunhilde; Ares; his Etruscan and Greek compadres, Laran and Mars. Diana, goddess of the hunt. Cupid with his arrow cocked, leading his similarly armed militia of cherubs. Genghis and El Cid. King Arthur and William of Orange. Robert the Bruce and Edward I. Teddy Roosevelt and George Washington. Whoever they'd come across with a weapon in their hands, Eden had transported to the foyer to make up their army.

Surveying the preparations, Eden had to admit the setup should buy them a few seconds, which, if she choreographed it right, should be enough.

They'd have to be enough. The alternative was unthinkable.

But she had to think about it. Faruq had no mercy, especially after what she'd done to him. Not only had he lost her and his other one thousand genies, but he'd also lost face. He was going to be more than angry—did she really want to spend an eternity paying for it?

And if not, what was the alternative?

There was only one.

Which meant that they *had* to win. The stakes had risen so far above simply her freedom that they had to escape Faruq because that other option wasn't an option at all. Especially not for Matt; poor guy hadn't signed up for any of this when he'd helped an unconscious woman on the sidewalk half a world away. None of this was his fault.

"I think we're ready." Matt took the hat off his head, swiped his forearm across his brow, and was settling it back on when Eden stopped him.

Actually, something *was* his fault. And she couldn't blame or condemn him for it at all.

Eden took his hat from him and stepped closer. "I definitely think we're ready, Matt. And I don't mean to just sit and wait." She ran her fingertips up his arm.

"You don't." It wasn't a question. And when his eyes turned that mossy green again she knew the answer.

"No." She cupped his cheek. "I don't."

The corner of his mouth ticked up. "So what *do* you think we should do, Eden?"

"There are lots of things we could do." She flung the hat to the side like a Frisbee. It landed on Cupid's arrow, twirling around the tip.

"Looks like you've got something specific in mind." He settled his hands on her waist, his fingers slipping beneath the waistband and finding her skin in one smooth move.

"You could say that."

"What would *you* say?" The teasing left Matt's eyes and, just like that, the moment got serious.

"I'd say that I want you, Matt."

Matt swept his fingertips from her temple to her jaw, feathering the barest of touches along it to her chin, then his thumb brushed her bottom lip, his eyes now so green they were almost black, and she felt his heart quicken beneath her palm. "This is becoming a habit, Eden."

"Are you complaining?"

"Hell no. I want you, too. So much."

He half-groaned something else as his lips claimed hers. Eden stood on her tiptoes to reach him, twining her arms around his neck, pressing herself against the rise in his jeans, his abs contracting as her breasts brushed them, and she couldn't wait. But the closest bed was at least a five minutes' walk away. They'd never make it. Good thing she was a genie. They didn't have to walk.

They also didn't need something as ordinary as a bed.

When Matt's lips left hers for the hollow beneath her ear, Eden made her wish, having no trouble whatsoever doing the breath-catching thing because she already was.

One more hard-to-catch breath and they were floating.

"What the—?" Matt removed his lips and tongue from her neck and looked around him, his body going rigid.

Well, *more* rigid.

And then he relaxed—though, thankfully, not *all* of him. "A carpet this time, eh?"

Eden smiled, standing on the step she'd created in the carpet to be eye-level with him. "I thought you deserved something special."

Matt cupped her cheek. "I already have something special." His eyes searched hers, so intense they seemed to see into her soul.

Eden shivered, half in arousal, but the other half…

She closed her eyes, a quick blink, but enough to break the spell. She cared; heavens knew, she cared. But it couldn't be more. If she fell in love with him, if she told him, she'd give up her powers and Faruq could claim her the moment he stepped foot inside this cave. There'd be nothing she could do about it. Nothing she could do to protect Matt. No matter what she felt, that was the most important outcome of all.

"Make love to me, Matt. Now. Right here."

Without a word, Matt knelt before her and held out his hand.

Every time they'd been together, it'd been as if it would be their last, and, now, when that was a very real possibility, Matt made it seem as if it were the first.

She took his hand and allowed him to draw her down onto Cleopatra's rug. What could be more perfect than being with Matt on the carpet that had brought two people together to find love and make history? If she couldn't let herself love Matt, this was the closest thing to it.

"You look so beautiful, Eden," Matt whispered, his body following hers as the carpet cradled them together in the air. "You take my breath away."

She brushed his hair out of his eyes, those beautiful green eyes were now so many shades she couldn't count. "You make me feel beautiful, Matt." In a way that had nothing to do with what she saw in a mirror.

Matt ran the backs of his fingers over her cheek, her throat, her shoulder, then threaded them through her hair, fanning it out around her. "I want you, Eden. I—"

He shook his head and buried his face in the crook of her neck, inhaling as if he couldn't get enough of her and Eden had never felt such heaviness in her heart. This wasn't simply about satisfying an urge. He made her *want*, and not just physically.

He made her want for everything she'd never have, for nights spent in his arms, days spent laughing with him. The possibility of bearing his children and growing old with him. But she was a genie; such things held grave consequences. With Faruq after her, such things were impossible.

Matt slid his fingers beneath the neckline of her shirt, stroking the swell of her breasts, his breath hot against her cheek, the nuzzle of his lips sending fire coursing through her. She might not have him forever, but she'd have the memories.

And, by damn, she was going to have some great ones to keep loneliness at bay for eternity.

She rolled onto her side and framed Matt's face in her hands, shivering when his hands skimmed her waist. "Matt." She kissed the dimple in his cheek. "*You* are beautiful. You didn't have to help me, yet you did. You risked your freedom, your life for me. You invited me to share your family, to know them and you, and I'll never be able to thank you for that gift. It is so rare for a genie to receive a thank-you, much less such a gift, and all without asking for a thing from me. Without taking what I offered. I'll always treasure our time together. I'll treasure knowing you, Matt. Forever."

"And I'll love you forever, Eden."

Eden's hands fell away. "Wha— What did you say?"

"Something I should have said the moment I realized it. I'm in love with you. I know we don't have forever—well, *I* don't—and we may not have much longer, but now, here, I had to tell you. I love you."

"Oh, Matt," she whispered, her eyes misting. "You can't."

"Look, I know we can't have a future together. Faruq will always be after you and he'll try to use me to get to you. I get that. But we can block out the rest of the world for now and I can love you, Eden. If only for a little while." He put a finger against her lips. "And I'm going to show you how much."

Eden cried. She couldn't help it. Big dollops of tears slid from the corners of her eyes, tracking down behind her ears, along her hairline, dampening the carpet beneath her.

He loved her.

As she lov—

Eden wrapped her arms around his neck and pulled him down to her, regret cascading with her tears as they soaked his collar.

Never had her magic been more of a curse than it was at this moment.

This was what her mother had felt when she'd met her father—it was clear now. Eden was willing to give up immortality, willing to give up magic, for the chance to live with this man for the rest of a suddenly shortened life, the consequences be damned. She wanted his children, created by their love, and if any of them were magical, she'd hide their powers. Keep them free from The Service so they could be a family.

As her parents had done.

She saw it all now. Why her mother had given up her magic, why she'd elected to have a child. Why she'd taught Eden not to use her powers.

All for love.

And it was for that very same love that Eden would say nothing to Matt because she'd need her powers to save him from Faruq.

"Sweetheart, I'm sorry. I didn't mean to make you cry. It was selfish—"

She put a finger to his lips and shook her head. It was the most generous thing any mortal, any *man,* had ever done for her and she couldn't let him think otherwise. And if she couldn't tell him how she felt, she'd show him.

Magically, Eden flipped them so that Matt was under her and she was floating just a hair's breadth above him. With a quick catch of her breath, she dispensed with their clothing. Another breath dimmed the lights, and she charmed a harp in a distant room to play for them. A flutter of her fingertips drifted gardenias around them, their scent filling the air. Two petals stroked her cheeks to wipe away her tears, then fell onto Matt's lips.

She kissed him then, softly. A touch as soft and tender as the petals.

Matt threaded his fingers through her hair, trapping some of the petals against her cheek with his thumb, and his tongue stroked the seam of her lips. "Let me in, Eden."

He already was.

Eden opened her mouth, praying the words wouldn't

spill out. No good could come of it. Well, no permanent good. And that's what she had to think of. Matt didn't deserve to die because of her, and unless she kept her magic, he would.

Matt's tongue played with hers, his hands slipping from under her hair to stroke down her back, exerting the slightest pressure for her to settle herself on top of him.

Eden's lips curved, and she lowered herself ever so slightly—to where one particular part of her met one very particular part of him.

Matt groaned in her ear as her pubic hair brushed against the head of his erection. "No fair. Get down here."

"I will. Give me a moment." She wiggled her hips, eliciting another groan from him.

"Eden, I don't think I have a moment." He sealed his lips to hers, his hands clutching her backside, his chest expanding as he tried to pull her on top of him or himself up to her.

Something. Matt wanted something.

And she had a pretty good idea what it was, because she wanted the same thing: forever. But since they couldn't have forever, they'd have now.

Eden straddled Matt and released her magic so that they were touching, skin to skin, chest hair to breasts, pelvis to pelvis, and all parts in between.

His hands slid down her thighs to her knees, pulling them up toward his waist. "I want you so badly, Eden, I'm shaking."

She felt the tremors wrack him, felt the perspiration seep from his skin, the hot, hard muscles clenching as she slid against him. "I want you inside me, Matt." The memory was all she'd have to keep her company in the coming years.

She wouldn't think like that now. Now was all about this. Here, them, now. The sensation of him filling her that traveled from her womb, up through her heart, and wrapped itself through every cell, every nerve, every part of her that had ever hoped and wished for something—someone—as wonderful as this.

She might not be able to say the words he wanted to hear—the words she wanted to say—but she'd show him and allow herself to feel his love. To know it. To revel in it.

Matt's hands slid to her hipbones, his long, strong fingers clasping her as if he'd never let her go, his thumbs almost meeting where they were joined as he drew her down onto him. "Ah, Eden, that's it. You feel so good. Right there."

She slid against him then, loving the feel of his chest hair brushing her breasts, a hundred different sensations at once. Loved feeling his pecs flex against her in a different yet amazing caress.

He lifted his thighs beneath her, changing the angle, giving him more control over the rhythm. His hands caressed her thighs, long, powerful strokes over supple muscle, thrusting himself into her, tilting her hips so perfectly.

"Kiss me, Eden," he whispered hoarsely.

She grabbed the carpet beneath him, moving it with her magic to cradle his head and bend him toward her so she could reach his lips without dislodging herself. Magic had purposes beside lifesaving ones, and if she was going to sacrifice what she felt for Matt, by the stars, she was going to get some use out of it.

Her hair fell over their arms, stroking along skin so

sensitized that it was like tiny brushstrokes, silken and soft and utterly arousing.

Matt claimed her lips with an intensity that would surprise her if she weren't feeling the same thing. His hands, which had been so gentle yet insistent on her hips, now pressed her down on him as purposefully as his tongue plunged into her mouth. He swirled his hips and his tongue, both doing crazy things to her insides, and Eden felt herself swell and open for him, felt the sweet rush of moisture that signaled that final moment, felt her blood race, her skin tingle.

"Work me, Eden," Matt whispered. "Hard, baby. Come against me hard."

Eden tilted her hips, her tongue doing its own foraying inside that wonderfully warm and sexy mouth of his, her fingers stealing down to run across one nipple, turning so slightly to give herself access—

Only to have Matt take that very same liberty. He brushed her nipple and she gasped into his mouth.

"I want to see you come," he said against her mouth, his eyes open and intent, a deep, dark hunter green, his pupils dilated as they fixed on her. "Come for me, Eden."

Her breath caught and Eden wished—

She closed down her mind. She couldn't say what she wished or it'd be all over for them.

Instead, she closed her eyes and rocked back, feeling as if she were soaring up to the heavens, the air dancing over her sensitized skin, Matt's fingers directing her movements against him.

Up and down, then up again, each movement sending him surging inside her, his thighs contracting beneath her, his fingers tightening with every surge, splaying as he pushed her down onto him, tension and passion etched onto his face as he gritted his teeth and closed his eyes, the muscles in his neck straining. "Yes, that's it, Eden. Again, baby. Again."

She braced herself on her palms by his neck, her breasts welcoming every caress of his chest as they surged together, the rhythm quickening, the moment of release just there, just before them.

Matt's neck arched as he came and she felt her own release rise within her like a leaf on the first wind of a storm, rising and swelling, dipping slightly but reaching ever higher, until—at last—the air currents met, whipping that leaf into a frenzy, spinning, swirling, tumbling, turning, churning as it—they—fell together into the fury of the storm.

—⁓—

"We're flying again, aren't we?" Matt whispered a few moments, hours, lifetimes later.

Eden peeled open one eye. They were doing lazy circles below the domed ceiling, gardenia petals and butterflies twirling around them like music box ballerinas.

"Yes, Matt, we're flying."

On the wings of—

Something she couldn't say.

Chapter 42

FARUQ WAS SERIOUSLY CLOSE TO KILLING THE NEXT living thing that crossed his path and if it was the last dodo bird in Al-Jannah, so be it.

He landed on the top of the Eiffel Tower where the latest trace of Glimmer had led him. He'd been bouncing from north to south, left to right, up and down then up again, through every quadrant of the damned city. Twice sometimes.

He'd had it with this fucking traitor, whoever he was. And without the crystals he had no way of finding out.

The crystals—

Of course! The crystals!

Kharah! Faruq almost hurled himself over the railing when he realized the time he'd been wasting. What did it matter who was helping Eden when she was the one he wanted and he had the means to find her?

Exhaustion was catching up to him. He should have seen it immediately, but he'd let his anger blind him. He'd let Eden blind him. He'd always been blinded by her. Adam and Eve, Samson and Delilah, Arthur and Guinevere—men were constantly blinded, then betrayed, by women.

No more.

Faruq flicked the trace of Glimmer off the railing and watched it flutter toward the ground, the green turning yellow in the fading moonlight.

...Yellow?

Faruq conjured his scepter and a silver platter from the dining room in his palace and jumped aboard. Sleeker, smaller, more aerodynamic than those antiquated carpets, the flying platter zoomed down the side of the Tower so fast it overtook the particles before they dissipated.

The *yellow* particles. *Saffron* yellow.

Faruq caught the Glimmer and closed his fist around it, cursing in every language he knew. Eden had found the *Mandragora*. And survived it.

She was the one who'd destroyed the crystals, his desk, his file, and his career.

She'd led him on a merry Glimmer chase. Made him look like a fool.

Even worse—a lovesick fool.

He was going to enjoy making her pay.

Faruq let the Glimmer filter through his fingers. He didn't need to follow it to find her. She would lead him to a dead end; he should have seen that from the outset.

But he knew how to track her. Her new crystal had survived the desecration the others had suffered because it hadn't been in his office, and without it, she'd never get the bracelets off. All he had to do was place the new crystal on the GPS and he'd know exactly where she was.

Faruq changed his stance on the platter, and it veered north. She thought she was so smart. That she could hope to outwit him. Ha! A little girl playing in a man's world. He was older, more powerful, and far wiser than she could ever hope to be. Did she think he'd just let her have her way? Pull one over on him? Did she think he'd make it easy for her?

Did she really think he was that stupid?

She'd underestimated him and that would be her downfall.

The morning rays were just starting to brighten the horizon. The dawn of a new day—and a new life for Eden. With him.

And the end of one for her mortal.

Chapter 43

SOMETHING WOKE MATT.

For a few seconds he didn't know what it was. Then he opened his eyes—and didn't know where he was.

And then it came rushing back. Eden, the magic, the cave. The lovemaking.

At some point after discovering the delights of waterfall-powered Roman baths and before the sumptuous buffet she'd conjured for them, the carpet had drifted into this medieval room, the great canopy bed there beckoning them, and they'd made love enclosed in the privacy of the curtains that draped each side.

And it had been love for him.

Matt took a deep breath and turned his head. Eden's face, upturned and soft in sleep, rested against his bicep. Her lips still swollen from his kisses, long lashes sweeping her cheeks, soft breath flaring her nostrils slightly, she snuggled against him, one slim, muscled arm draped across his abs, one toned thigh resting on his, and Matt had to resist the urge to wrap his arm tighter around her to keep her next to him. To keep her safe.

They still weren't home free. But one more item and she would be. He, on the other hand…

Well, if all went according to plan, he'd be back home, still facing the same problems, and this would be nothing but a memory. One he'd treasure for the rest of his life. As he wanted to treasure her.

Then something pinged off the canopy again, and Matt remembered they still had to get out of here if he wanted to *have* a life so he *could* treasure it.

He put his fingers over Eden's lips, fighting the tug in his gut when she reflexively kissed them. "Eden."

"Mmm," she murmured, running her leg along his.

There was nothing in this world he'd rather do than return the gesture—except live long enough to have another opportunity.

Something pinged again, this time on the silver dish on the bedside table.

It was a gray rock about the size of piece of popcorn. One that hadn't been there last night.

Gravel rained down next, a tinny ring against the platter. Matt slid to the side of the bed, cautiously peered out beneath the canopy, and looked up.

The hammer beam ceiling, with its ornate coffers and detailed spandrels, was intact. Probably in better shape than its twin in England's Hampton Court. What Matt wouldn't give to be able to explore the thousands of years' worth of architectural history in this cave.

But first things first, and with the arrival of more gravel, architecture took a back seat to survival.

So did waking Eden gently.

Matt sighed, but shook her. "Eden," he whispered, more urgently this time. "Eden, wake up. We need to get moving. Something's happening."

Those incredible eyes of hers opened, pure and innocent. Well, maybe not so innocent after what the two of them had done during the night, but she looked calm. Serene. Without a care in the world.

He hated to be the one to take that away from her.

"Something's going on." He told her about the gravel, showed her the rock.

She slid silently onto Cleopatra's rug, which lay on the floor next to the bed, and without him even being aware of it happening, zapped their clothes back on. Then, keeping an eye on the ceiling, she rounded the bed and reached out a hand to him. "Do you think it's Faruq?"

"It's someone. Or something." Matt tucked her against him and kissed her hair, inhaling the scent of gardenias and her. "Looks like we're about to find out."

~~~

Obo shook his back paw, grumbling anew. When he'd last been here, he'd had the amulet and *still* he'd gotten cut from the rocks. Now, without it, his paws were turning into a fleshy pulp. There'd better be a decent spa in the Afterlife. Hell, he'd better have *earned* a decent Afterlife.

More gravel loosened beneath his paws as he scrambled up to the next level. This was ridiculous. Why did the goddess want him to stay with the amulet? For how long? He was going to miss the rendezvous and then where would he be?

Stuck in this gods-forsaken desert. He hated the desert. The sun had yet to rise above the horizon, but its heat was already making itself felt. For some reason, the High Master hadn't deemed it worthy to climate-control this part of Al-Jannah as he had the rest of the city. He'd created snow on the genie version of the Matterhorn; he couldn't share a *little* of that cold air with The Cave?

Screw this. The rock was starting to burn the pads of his already raw paws. He certainly wasn't going to wait up here to fry for some vulture's breakfast.

Obo turned back the way he came. It was a freaking long way down. The things he did for the goddess…

Cursing the entire way back—knowing ancient languages came in handy because some of them had very inventive swear words—Obo hit the equally hot sand at the base of The Cave where the sun had shown as much mercy to it as Bastet had to him. Damn damn damn! He jumped around like a kangaroo. This was bullshit.

Demanding more than his aching legs had left in them to give, Obo raced around to the entrance of The Cave where the sand hadn't yet burned to a crisp. That was coming, he knew. The giant gaseous orb had the rotten habit of traveling across the desert and burning everything in its path. The ancients he'd lived with had revered it; he found it annoying.

Obo huddled in the pitiful shade offered by an overhanging rock. Surely the goddess didn't want him to just sit out here and burn to death? Singed fur was nasty.

But— Hold the phone. She'd said he wasn't supposed to have left the amulet. And the amulet was *inside* The Cave. Where it was cool.

Yeah, so he was rationalizing, but it was hot out here. And The Cave was full of treasure. He rubbed his paws together. He'd go in and hang out, and the goddess couldn't complain that he hadn't followed orders.

Obo shook his fur and twitched his tail. He'd heard lots of stories about this place. The gold, the treasure, the Roman baths. Hanging out in the lap of luxury wasn't going to be such a hardship.

Planting himself in front of The Cave, Obo said the magic words that would reveal this paradise to him. "Open Sesame!"

—⁓—

Eden and Matt had just made it to the foyer when the rock started to slide.

"Quick! Over here!" Matt grabbed his hat off the arrow and led her to the hiding spot they'd constructed, where they could, hopefully, slip out before Faruq figured out what they'd done.

"You ready?" he whispered as the pale morning light slid through the opening.

Eden nodded. She was definitely ready. To get away from Faruq, Al-Jannah, and The Service. But not Matt.

"Get set."

She leaned back against him and hitched her breath.

"Just a little more."

Her magic started moving the statues. Cupid and his army pulled back on their bows, the diamond-tipped arrows quivering the tiniest bit, and the crossbow archers cocked their bolts in readiness.

The stone rolled open a little more.

The knights readied their swords and lances.

The opening widened and Eden, eyes now accustomed to the light, searched for Faruq's silhouette. Only—

The little black ball in the center of the opening wasn't Faruq.

"Obo?"

"Holy doomsday!" Obo jumped straight up in the air, his fur shooting out in all directions. As did his legs, tail, and ears.

"Freeze!" Eden aimed one hand at Obo, stopping him midair, and the other at the militia about to make a pincushion of the cat.

Matt cursed while Obo blinked at her. She recognized the moment the cat realized his last life wasn't up yet.

She lowered her hand and Obo accompanied it. The minute his paws touched the sand, she released him from the spell.

"Jesus J. Christ." The cat shook his fur, his paws twitching as he stepped into The Cave. "Would you look at this place? Who were you expecting? Lucifer?"

Eden was just about to answer when someone else did.

Sadly, it wasn't Matt.

"Actually, cat, I believe they were expecting me."

Chapter 44

FARUQ, BACKLIT BY THE SUN IN THE CAVE'S ENTRANCE — red mist swirling around his feet and up his body, circling his scepter, and radiating out to fill the room — raised his hands, warding off the attack Eden put in motion as soon as she recovered from the shock.

He was too fast. A wave of his fingers threw up an invisible force field, and her magic sizzled as it hit it.

Matt cursed. Eden grabbed his hand and wished them outside as fast as she could catch her breath.

But she was too late. Faruq's magic had blocked the only way out.

The vizier sauntered forward, kicking the red mist and Obo out of his way. The cat *yeowl*ed and ran through the knights' legs.

"What could be more perfect? The two of you at my mercy. So, which will it be? Surrender or suicide? Hmmm?" Faruq flicked his gaze over Matt. "You, we won't miss. Well, perhaps Eden will, but then, that plays into my scenario, doesn't it?"

With a movement so insignificant she almost missed it, Faruq ripped Matt out of her grasp and jacked him up to hang him from Cupid's arrow, the statue now frozen in a position perfect for keeping Matt dangling. All the cherubs, which, moments before, had been on *their* side, now fluttered their wings maniacally, their arrows within stabbing distance of Matt's legs. One wrong move—

Eden didn't even want to contemplate it. With his scepter, Faruq was almost invincible.

"What do you want, Faruq?"

He waved his hands and the mist dissipated toward the ceiling. "Come now, Eden, must you ask? You've been a bad girl. It wasn't enough to destroy my palace, you had to do the same to my office? The crystals? Where are they, by the way?"

She raised her chin, hating that she was so small more than she ever had. "You'll never find them."

"So true. I have better things to do than follow your pathetic attempts at a scavenger hunt. You, however, *will* find them. Or your mortal will die. Slowly. Painfully. You will do *everything* I say, or he'll die." Faruq twirled the staff of his scepter between his palms. "See how this works? You keep me happy and I keep him alive. Anger me, and, well, let's just say, it won't be pleasant. But it will be long. Drawn-out. Exquisitely painful. *Faahem*?"

She understood all right.

Matt wriggled on the end of the arrow. "Look, you son of a bitch—"

"Matt, don't." Trying to get out of his jacket? What did he think he could do? Faruq would kill him before he took two steps. If the cherubs didn't get to him first. This was not the time to be a hero.

But Matt kept wriggling anyway, heavens help him. "Let her go, you bas—"

Faruq made a "closed" motion with one hand and Matt's mouth clamped shut. "Honestly. Just. Shut. Up. You don't know who you're messing with and I've grown incredibly weary of you. If you weren't a means to gaining Eden's compliance, I'd end my suffering right now. *Kharah!* If I'd realized what a hindrance you'd be, you wouldn't have made it out your front door."

He waved the scepter and Matt's jacket zipped up the front like a straightjacket. Then Faruq turned to face her so smoothly she had a feeling he was hovering a few inches off the ground. Overcompensating yet again.

"So, Eden, which will it be? Marriage, or do I turn your mortal into griffin food?"

She couldn't distinguish what Matt was saying, but from his tone she could definitely guess. "What guarantee do I have that you'll let him live?"

"None. You're going to have to trust me."

"I'd rather trust a cobra."

"That can be arranged. Matter of fact—" He traced a figure eight in the air with his scepter and Ketu appeared in a niche on the wall, then slithered across the floor to coil beneath Matt, the serpent's unblinking stare making fear writhe up Eden's spine.

She really hated snakes.

"There. Now that he's properly restrained *and* threatened, we should discuss the location of the honeymoon. Paris? The South Pacific? Cloud Nine?"

"Go to hell, Faruq."

"Ah, my dear, where I go, you go, thanks to those brace—" He stared at her wrists. "Where are they? How did you get them off?"

As if she'd tell him.

"The serendibite! You found it. Do you know how long it took me to find that compound? To devise the perfect bracelet? Yours were one of a kind, Eden."

She didn't care if they were from Andromeda—the galaxy *or* the princess. "You're not as smart as you think, Faruq." She just wished she were smarter. Her brain had been working at warp speed, trying to come up with some way to set Matt free and get out of here, but with the force field in place and that scepter, there *was* no way.

She was going to have to bargain with the bastard and hope for some miracle later on to earn her freedom.

She should have just gotten back in her bottle when she found it. Even though it was an accident, The Code didn't allow for accidents. She should have accepted both her destiny and her punishment and finished out the sentence. If she had, she wouldn't be in this predicament. Matt's life wouldn't be on the line. She wouldn't have to choose among disappointing the High Master, spending the rest of eternity as Faruq's slave, and Matt's life.

In the end, there was no choice to be made.

"Fine, Faruq. You win. Set Matt free and I'll marry you."

Matt didn't need to be conversant for her to understand what he was saying, but he managed to kick an arrow out of one of the cherubs' bows to emphasize his point.

"Matt, please. It's the only way." She'd rather have this conversation in private, but no way would Faruq permit that.

Matt shook his head so hard his hat fell off, knocking two more arrows out of the little bows, which then fell between the knights' legs, who then started hopping around, which caused Ketu to attack. The clang of the snake's fangs against Longshanks' armor reverberated through the room, and Eden got great satisfaction watching the cobra's head vibrate before it fell back, unconscious. One opponent down.

Reacting to the strike, other knights jostled one another, which resulted in several annoyed—and weaponless—cherubim as their arrows became lost beneath the knight's feet.

"Yes, 'please, Matt,'" Faruq mimicked. "Do it for Eden." The vizier spat and removed something from the folds of his *bisht*. "You two make me ill. I've had enough." He waggled something yellow in front of him.

Her bottle stopper!

"Hand over your bottle, Eden. We'll do this the official way and worry about the wedding later."

Matt's eyes widened, and Eden turned from him before either of them gave anything away.

"See, Faruq? I told you you weren't as smart as you think you are. My bottle was destroyed. By a mortal garbage truck." She crossed her arms and added a smirk for good measure, gloating as if every word were true. "Looks like you're going to have to come up with a crush-proof type of glass in addition to a new set of bracelets."

Faruq looked like he wanted to spit toads. And since her magic was useless against him with him holding that damned scepter, she hoped he would. The poisonous kind. Then she could bewitch the amphibians so they'd spit their poison at him and she'd grab the stopper while he was otherwise occupied.

She had to get that stopper. It might save them yet.

—⁂—

Obo tucked his tail between his legs as he slunk through the maze of armaments Matt and Eden had lined up for their attack. Good thing they hadn't unleashed their firepower right away, but it was too bad he'd jumped the gun for them by showing up before Faruq.

If only he hadn't misunderstood the goddess and had kept the amulet in the first place. Then there would have been no early arrival on his part, and Faruq would have walked in at the perfect moment. One skewered vizier and all their troubles would have been over.

What had the goddess been thinking, telling him to follow the gypsy's orders? She'd *had* to know what he'd do with the amulet.

Or—was this what he was supposed to do anyway? Had she known? Was he supposed to save everyone?

He coughed on a hair ball but managed to gag it back down with only a tiny snort. Him. Save everyone. That'd be the day. Right now he was more concerned about his own tail than Matt's and Eden's—

Shit. No he wasn't.

Obo paused as he wended through the legs of some horse who'd done something for someone in history.

When the hell had he started caring? About anyone other than himself, that was. When had he changed?

Shaking his head, Obo dashed down the corridor. He was getting to be a softie in his old age. He'd heard that happened. That cats liked to curl up in the sunshine and ended up not caring who petted them. He'd sworn it wouldn't happen to him.

Ah, the best laid plans of mice and Obo…

He reached the first alcove, the one with all the gold. All that beautiful, shiny fortune just waiting for his sticky paws—

But that wasn't where the amulet was.

Obo sucked up his greed and tip-pawed down the

corridor as fast as his scarred pads would take him. This room was much easier to find from the outside. When he wasn't burning the skin off his paws, that was.

He ducked past a few more alcoves before finding the Egyptian treasure room. Now where was that thing?

Practically crying as he passed over jewels and gold that could go a long way to greasing someone's paw— though obviously not Bastet's if she didn't want the amulet—Obo found the altar where he'd dropped the priceless relic and braved another round of possible broken bones clambering up on it, what with all the loose change—*gold* change!—hampering him. He could have lived like a maharaja for all nine of his lives with only a tenth of this gold—

Forget about it.

Obo wasn't sure if that was his thought or one the goddess put there, but now wasn't the time to figure it out. He had people to save.

He found the leather bag and worked the amulet into it, trying to come up with a way to take some coins with him. Short of dumping them into the bag with the amulet—and he'd be an idiot if he thought he'd get away with that—he was going to have to take a pass.

This had better be worth it. If he were doing this only to have some new challenge thrown at him when all was said and done, well, maybe his Eternal Reward wasn't worth the effort.

Oh who was he kidding? Eternal Reward not worth the effort? If he bitched about climbing hot rocks for twenty minutes, no way was he going to be able to handle an eternity doing so.

Obo traced his steps back down the corridor and into

the entryway, ducking behind a trebuchet Eden had zapped there, and skirted behind the Tin Man's army. Seriously, who thought being covered in plate armor was a good idea?

Then he tucked himself in the perfect position to see all three players in this drama. Poor Matt. Guy could really use a break.

Oh, hell.

Obo removed the bag from his neck and slid the amulet out.

He could give Matt that break.

He sighed. Loudly. Which garnered him the attention of one of the little winged abominations. There was something seriously wrong about a baby wielding a bow and arrow.

Obo shook his head. No time to think about that now. Baby Einstein had just seen him and was playing whisper-down-the-cherubim-lane. It wouldn't be long before Faruq found out where he was.

Which meant he had to act now.

Obo bent over and kissed his amulet goodbye.

Chapter 45

THE ONLY OTHER TIME MATT HAD FELT THIS HOPELESS was when he'd watched his father die. Watching Eden throw her life away brought all the despair back again.

He had to do something. She had forever to look forward to; she couldn't sacrifice her freedom, the rest of her life, for him.

But he needed time to figure out what.

Well, as Dad had said, time swallowed those who watched it pass them by, so he'd better figure it out quickly.

Matt swung his legs, knocking one of the cherub's arrows into its leg with a *chunk*. There had to be something sacrilegious about that, but at the moment, he was more concerned about getting off this damned hook so he could get them out of here.

The cherub he'd kicked bent down to rub his pudgy marble leg and that gave Matt an idea. If a scrawny little arrow could get the statue's attention, just think what the heels of his boots could do to Cupid, who was within striking distance.

"Your bottle has been destroyed?" Faruq's incredulity was almost worth being stuck here, giving him a bird's-eye view as the vizier's turban wobbled along with his voice. First time he'd seen the jackass at a loss. Ah, what must he have felt when he'd discovered the mess in his tent and then his office?

Score one for Eden. Making those crystals disappear

had been a brilliant move. Now if Matt could somehow keep Faruq from finding out about all the things in his pockets, that'd be another coup.

Thinking of those things, Matt realized he'd better do something quick. When Faruq had enclosed him in the jacket, it'd tightened across his body. The bottle's shape was going to give itself away if Faruq bothered to look in his direction. And unzipping the jacket would cause Faruq to do just that.

His eyes had met Eden's when Faruq had waved the stopper. They had to get it away from him.

"Yes, Faruq, my bottle was destroyed." Eden put her hands on those hips Matt had held onto last night—and wanted the opportunity to hold again. Along with the rest of her. "So you're going to have to trust *my* word. Let Matt go and I'll do what you want."

Over Matt's dead bod—no. Scratch that. Over *Faruq's* dead body.

But how?

Matt looked at the army he'd assembled. Every one of them had their eyes trained on him, thanks to Faruq's magic. Big difference from real soldiers with minds of their own. A difference he hoped would work to his advantage.

Behind Robert the Bruce, Matt caught a flicker of a black, furry tail.

He glanced at Faruq. The vizier was too intent on Eden to notice—a sentiment Matt would appreciate if he weren't swinging for his life.

What was Obo up to? He'd fully expected the cat to go into hiding until Faruq's smoke cleared.

"I'm going to need something a little more concrete than your word, Eden. You owe me. I'm the one holding all the cards here. And—" Faruq's arm shot out. "I'll hold on to you, too."

Dickwad yanked Eden against him, trapped her arms at her sides, and plastered his foul mouth against hers.

Matt kicked then. For all he was worth. Every curse he knew sputtered behind the damned spell Faruq had placed on his mouth.

Then, somehow, Eden was whirling free of Faruq and doing that wrist-twirling thing she'd tried before, only Matt saw her catch her breath, too.

"Matt, talk!" she yelled just before Faruq caught her from behind, once more pinning her arms at her sides— arms she didn't need to use to work her magic.

Pity Faruq didn't know that.

Yeah, right.

Matt smiled—and found that he could. Somehow Eden's magic had freed his mouth. And somehow he had to free her from that bastard.

Matt yanked the jacket zipper down, raised his arms and slid to the floor in one fluid movement, then grabbed one of the confused knights' weapons and retrieved his jacket before Cupid realized what had happened. Matt swung the jacket around him and put his arms into the sleeves so quickly he half-thought it was magic, then checked the pockets to make sure everything was still there.

He was about to step over a cherub to help Eden fight Faruq when Obo leapt toward him, chucking a small, round, gold Frisbee at him.

The amulet!

"Catch!" the cat screeched as he landed four-pawed— and twenty-clawed—on Matt's shoulder.

"Use it!" Obo hissed, struggling to keep hold.

"Use it?" Matt whispered back, rushing toward Eden, stuffing the amulet in his pocket. "For what?"

"To get us out of here!" Obo yelled as Matt came within arm's-reach of Eden.

Get out of there? Was the cat crazy? He wasn't leaving without Eden.

Too bad Faruq caught a glimpse of him right before Matt could grab hold of her. The dickhead whipped her behind him, his lips still moist from that abomination that passed for a kiss.

"Get away from her, you piece of shit." Matt lunged toward Faruq, flinging Obo off in the process. Right onto Faruq's robes. The cat was good for something.

Faruq stumbled back and raised his scepter.

Too late Matt saw Faruq's long, bony index finger aiming at his heart.

"No!" Eden launched herself onto Faruq's back, knocking the scepter from his grasp. A blast of red energy sank into the marble floor as the glass orb shattered, and a *boom* shook the foundation. They all struggled to remain upright while gravel rained down the walls and a hunk of ceiling plaster bounced off the back of El Cid's warhorse.

"Retreat!" Obo howled as he climbed up Matt's back, using a jacket pocket for leverage.

Luckily, the cat threw Matt off-balance enough that he stumbled backward—mere inches beyond the upward thrust of the twisted platinum that had once housed the scepter's orb.

"You are more trouble than you're worth, mortal. I'll kill you now and be done with you." Faruq circled his hands, palms flat, as if he were gathering the air into a ball, a red haze beginning to circle in front of him.

Matt ducked behind George Washington, hating the fact that he was forced into hiding. He should be out there fighting, but his fists were no match for magic. "Nice, Faruq. Scared to fight like a man?"

Faruq, damn him, didn't take the bait. "A mortal man, you mean. Neanderthals, all of you. Your kind never really evolved." He circled that ball of red faster, and Matt could hear a faint whirring like a power saw coming to life. "The world would be a better place without you. All of you."

"Faruq, what are you saying?" Eden grabbed one of Faruq's sleeves. Matt saw through the ploy to destroy that gaseous ball and Faruq, damn him, didn't stop forming it. "Weren't you always the one saying genies exist to serve mortals?"

"As if you believe that, Eden." Faruq shook her off. "Rhetoric designed to control the masses of magical beings and keep the High Masters and viziers in power. Why, without mortals, we'd have the run of this beautiful world. We'd never have to hide our powers. We wouldn't have to subjugate ourselves to them. We djinn are so much more powerful, so much more advanced, so much better equipped to rule this world, we should never be in Service to them. That's why I *will* become the next High Master. With you by my side, the High Master can choose no other." The vibrating ball of air continued to rotate even though his fingers stilled.

Faruq cocked an eyebrow at Eden. "You, of all djinn, should understand, Eden. You killed a mortal. Without an ounce of remorse."

"That's not true! I didn't want to kill him, but it was an accident."

Faruq began circling his hands again. "It doesn't matter. You don't leave me a choice, Eden. I can't permit this mortal of yours to live. He'll always come between us, and I've waited too long for you. Have had to share you with too many others. It's time for me to take my rightful place. And you, too. You're mine, Eden." The circling air was now flame-orange. "And I intend to ensure it."

Eden had about half a second to convince Faruq she meant what she said, or he'd kill Matt, no matter how much she begged or promised. "Faruq, if you kill Matt, I'll kill myself."

Thank the stars, that got his attention. Faruq lowered his arms, and the fireball hovered in front of him, no longer spinning. She needed to buy time and if she could keep his attention diverted for a few more seconds, the flames would go out and Matt could use the amulet she'd seen Obo give him.

She had no hope of beating the vizier with her magic. This threat was her only weapon.

"You wouldn't dare kill yourself." Faruq's gaze never left her face.

"Oh? Do you really want to take that chance? What do I have to live for if you kill him? A return to prison or marriage to you. Sorry, but neither of those is preferable to death. The only way you can have me, Faruq, is to let Matt go free."

"Eden—" Matt began, but she shook her head. She had something Faruq wanted; only she could fix this.

"Let him go, Faruq. I'll do whatever you want. For

as long as Matt's alive." It wasn't an empty promise. If she couldn't get free, spending Matt's remaining fifty or sixty years with Faruq was a lot better than forever.

And once Matt's life ended naturally, well, what would she have to live for? She certainly wasn't going to spend eternity kowtowing to this imbecile. But she'd let him believe she would to protect Matt.

And it was in that instant that Eden realized she had the perfect weapon to save Matt *and* gain her freedom in one fell swoop.

Now all she had to do was drop that bomb at just the right moment.

Chapter 46

FARUQ STROKED HIS GOATEE, HIS BLACK EYES narrowed. "Very well. I'll allow the mortal to live out his natural life—"

"Without any interference from you whatsoever. And you'll leave him alone once he returns home." Faruq was looking for a loophole; it's what he did, but Eden wasn't going to let him win this one. It was too important.

Faruq nodded—slightly. "But of course, Eden. I am, at the very least, a man of my word."

Only when it worked to his favor.

Eden hitched her breath to conjure the one thing that would ensure Faruq's compliance, then remembered to flick her wrists in her Way that Faruq was familiar with.

Suddenly, a shimmering waterfall flowed from the ceiling, a veil of iridescent white, the soft gurgle sounding like church bells more than a rush of water as it dissipated into a reddish mist before it could hit the floor.

"Faruq?" She inclined her head. She hadn't been an ace student for nothing.

Faruq's eyebrows formed a vee in the center of his forehead. She'd gotten him. Good. Bastard had been planning to renege on his promise. Big surprise.

"Very well," the vizier growled and shoved his hand into the water.

The flow parted around him, forming an arc over his

hand, not a drop reaching his skin. Beneath his palm, a reddish stone floated directly in the center of the waterfall.

"On pain of mortality, I vow to allow your mortal to live out his natural life without any interference from me once he returns home."

Redder than any of the rubies or garnets in Faruq's GPS, harder than any diamond, and radiating with an intensity just short of blinding, the Stone of Jabir granted eternal life to magical beings. To swear on the stone, as Faruq had just done, was to put one's immortality in jeopardy. It'd been created during The Time of Mists and Chaos, with no one certain how or why or by whom, but every genie knew that breaking an oath placed above the stone meant death.

"And you, Eden," Faruq said. "I want your promise."

"Eden, don't!" Matt took a step forward, but Eden shook her head, allowing the love she felt to shine through.

She had to make it look good so Faruq wouldn't guess what she was up to, but at the same time, she wanted Matt to see how she felt, in the event this all went wrong—or right, depending on how she looked at it. Whichever interpretation she put on it, it would mean the end of her and Matt. Better that than the end of Matt.

"Matt, please. It's the only way. I'll never survive if he hurts you. Do this for me. If you feel anything at all for me, do this. So that I can at least know you're alive and living the life you would have if I'd never entered it. Use the amulet, Matt. Do it for me. Please. Use the amulet."

"Chick's got a point," Obo said from his perch on Matt's shoulder.

"Blah, blah, blah, whatever." Faruq waved the scepter

around. It didn't matter that the orb was broken; the real power was in that platinum.

She had to time this right, so Matt would be beyond Faruq's reach when she unleashed her ace in the hole.

Funny how this would have twisted her insides last week if she'd ever thought to do it.

Funny how she was planning to do it when she'd vowed she never would.

Funny how none of that mattered.

"Please, Matt? For me? We'll always have our memories. Let them be good ones, not final ones."

"She's mine, mortal. She always has been. Keep your paltry life if it's so important to her but know this: use the amulet to return to that foul place you call home or be locked away forever within my castle where you'll see me with her for the rest of your life and know you can never have her. Take the offer. You'll not get a better one." Faruq twirled the end of his goatee between his slimy fingers and Eden wanted to retch.

"Eden, I won't—"

"Matt, please. He'll do it—and worse. And I'll be stuck with him forever. Please, just go. For me, Matt. For me."

"I love you, Eden."

She felt his pain, and it made what she was about to do so much harder.

"Go." Faruq banged the staff of the scepter on the floor and more plaster rained down.

Matt didn't move.

Matt didn't, but Obo did.

"Oh, for gods' sakes!" the cat hissed. "You'll thank me for this someday." He climbed down Matt's jacket, stuck his head in the pocket, and grabbed the amulet. Then he smacked it against Matt's chest and yelled, "Home, Jeeves!"

As Matt's image started to shimmer then dissipate into gold mist in front of her, Eden licked her lips and did one more bit of magic.

It would be her last.

"I love you, Matt."

Faruq screamed while Matt faded away.

Chapter 47

Eight days later

MATT FINISHED THE LAST TURN ON THE FINIAL, brushed it off with a sheet of fine-grain sandpaper, and held it up. With some red paint and gold detail work, the spire-like point above a dome-shaped base would be a perfect replica of the fence posts he'd seen in Al-Jannah.

He tossed it toward the bin holding the others he'd turned over the week or so he'd been back, hours' worth of work destined for the furnace. He missed.

Nothing unusual there. Seemed like a theme lately.

God, he couldn't get her out of his mind. She was with that bastard. At Faruq's beck and call. At his mercy.

In his bed.

The pain socked Matt in the gut yet again. Why did he keep doing this to himself?

How could he not?

So much for the memories.

Sighing, Matt turned off the lathe, then grabbed one of the beers he kept in the workshop fridge. He popped the cap off on the workbench, leaned back, and took a long pull. Icy. Cold. The way he'd felt ever since he'd returned.

Matt gripped the edge of the workbench, utter frustration clawing at him. He'd been online into the early hours of the morning most nights, studying wind patterns of the Sahara, trying to find a way back.

She said she loved him. How could he let her go?

The moment his feet had touched ground in his living room, he'd looked for Obo, determined to take the amulet from him and go back. But the only feline in his home was the kitten Eden had conjured during dinner.

He'd toyed with the idea of booking a ticket to North Africa, but he had no idea what to do once he got there. The Sahara was huge. It'd be suicidal to set out on his own in search of a sandstorm. He needed the cat. He needed the amulet.

Hell, he needed Eden.

Matt took another swallow of the beer and looked around his workshop. Carving had always soothed him, helped him think, so he'd come out here at some ungodly hour one morning, grabbed a block of oak, and turned his first finial. Now he had a box of useless post toppers that only served as a reminder of what he couldn't have.

She'd given up her freedom for him.

She really did love him, and it was killing him, this inability to find her. To rescue her. To know what and who she was dealing with and would have to deal with forever.

The utter selflessness of her sacrifice humbled him and made him love her that much more—if that was even possible. Her sacrifice also put his refusal to swallow his pride and accept help in perspective. He'd fixed the structural supports on the Baker's pool house and had garnered a few referrals, but it'd be a while before they'd cover operating expenses. He had to do something else if he wanted to keep himself afloat and Jerry employed.

He didn't want to be the guy who'd ruined Jerry's family's life. Dad had said it was the memories you left behind, not the *business* you left behind. Matt's stubbornness had prevented him from admitting it, but there was no shame in his business not making it in today's economic climate. His services amounted to luxury items and people were cutting back.

So he'd do what he had to—which, compared to what Eden had done for him, was only a blip on the radar of sacrifice. If she could give up so much for him, he certainly could accept Paul and Hayden's offer and find a place for Jerry at Rogers and Son—Rogers and *Sons*.

He would put both Ewing Construction and Ewing Custom Millwork aside. Maybe someday he'd try again, but Dad's memory wouldn't go away just because his legacy to Matt did.

Someone knocked on the door to the workshop. Hayden peered in the window. Speak of the devil.

No. Savior.

Matt polished off the beer, tossed the bottle with the others in the recycle bin, and opened the door.

"You know that donkey's still in your yard, right?"

Matt nodded. "Francis."

"He doesn't talk, Matt."

If Hayden only knew.

"You have a permit for him yet?" His brother stepped inside and Matt shut the door behind him.

"Nope. Working on it."

Hayden kicked the finial, then bent down to pick it up. "You've been working on something, that's for sure." He poked around in the box where the rest of them were. "How many do you have in here, Matt?"

Matt shrugged. "Half a dozen? A dozen? More? I don't know." Didn't really care. What was he going to do with Middle Eastern architectural pieces around here except remember where he'd gotten the inspiration—hence the "destined for the furnace" designation.

"Any chance you could come up with a few dozen more?" Hayden pointed one at him. "It's why I'm here, actually."

"You're here to collect Arabic finials?"

"Believe it or not, yes. Among other things." Hayden stood and tossed the finial in his hand. "We need you, Matt. Dad and I."

Ah, well. No time like the present. "Hayden—"

"Hear me out." Hayden put the finial back in the box, then turned slowly. "We got the Riverwalk project."

This was news? With the economies of scale a large company like Rogers and Son could command—the reason they could weather the storm and Ewing Construction couldn't—he wasn't surprised. Yet another feather in their cap.

Feather. Feathers reminded him of hummingbirds and other things that flew. Butterflies. Gargoyles. Griffins. Dragons. A hundred other things he'd rather not think about or remember where he'd seen them. Or who he'd seen them with.

Yeah, right.

"Have you seen the plans for the project, Matt? The hotel, specifically?" Hayden raised the fiberboard tube he was carrying. "Those would be perfect for the Middle Eastern–themed rooms."

The last thing Matt wanted to do was make replicas of the place where he'd fallen in love with—and left—Eden.

The memories you leave behind.

He opened his mouth to say something to Hayden—
yes—when Hayden held up his hand.

"Look, Matt, yes, Dad and I know how you feel about
this, but we need you. No one else has the eye for detail you have. This project is getting all kinds of press.
We want luxury and we want authenticity. We need
someone we can trust to follow through with the vision.
You're that guy, Matt."

"I hear you—"

"Matt, listen. Dad and I, we respect your position.
We get that your father's dream is important to you, so
we're not asking you to give it up. We want to hire you."

That was a concession Matt hadn't seen coming.
Before, they'd always been after him to become part of
their company, make it a family business, but he wasn't
a Rogers. But this way—

"A subcontractor? You don't want to buy me out?"

"Yes, as a sub, and, no, we don't want to buy you
out. This way, you get to keep your company and we get
Ewing Construction as our in-house trim specialist. For
Riverwalk and all our projects." Hayden stuck out his
hand. "So, what do you say? Will you do it?"

A chance to help Jerry and Marybeth, keep his
business, his reputation, and his—and Dad's—dream.
"You've got a deal, Hayden. On one condition." A small
one on the surface. Inconsequential to everyone else, but
to him, it was everything.

"Name it, Matt."

"You hire Ewing *Custom Millwork* for the job."

Chapter 48

THEY'D SPENT THE BETTER PART OF THE NEXT HOUR
going over the plans, with Matt getting ideas of what he'd
do in each of the rooms—particularly the one that reminded him of Eden. The clarity with which the memories
returned should have amazed him since they were colored
by losing her, but, as Hayden said, he had an eye for detail.

Too bad every one of those details seared his heart.

When he returned to his office after Hayden left, it
turned out that he wasn't as detail-oriented as he thought.
Something was stuffed between his desk and the wall.

His jacket.

Matt set the site plans for Riverwalk on Dad's old
desk. He'd tossed the jacket there the night he'd returned.
Right after he lost the amulet and right before he'd tried
to forget everything with a six-pack or two. And maybe
some rum. The details were fuzzy, but he hadn't forgotten
the hour-long shower he'd taken later, ostensibly to rid
himself of the dirt and grime of the trip but really, to pour
his eyes out. He'd left the coat there because he hadn't
wanted to deal with the memories associated with it.

He ought to burn it.

Matt picked it up. Heard a soft *chink*.

Her bottle and the crystals. Those damn bracelets—
well, what was left of them after he'd ripped all the
jewels out. At least Faruq hadn't gotten them.

Matt laid the jacket on top of the Riverwalk plans.

What was he supposed to do with her jewels? He could hock them, but there'd surely be questions because of their size and rarity. Questions he couldn't—and didn't want to—answer.

And what about her bottle? What if he pawned it only for Faruq to find it?

No, he wasn't going to do anything with them. Especially since, aside from Francis and the kitten, they were the only reminders of her he had left.

Matt pulled the items out, bracing for the pain of seeing them again.

Yep, there it was. The pain. The mangled bracelets, her bottle with the blue obelisk, the yellow one, another yellow crystal—

How had the stopper gotten into his pocket?

"Meow." The kitten pranced through the doorway then sat, curling her tail around herself like a security blanket, little muddy paw prints all around her on the hardwood.

He'd feed her later. Poor thing hadn't exactly been getting all the love she'd been craving since Eden had conjured her. She didn't even have a name yet.

Matt fiddled with the stopper. When had this gotten into his pocket? The only thing he could come up with was Obo must have somehow slid it in when he'd been clinging to the jacket those last few minutes in the cave. But how had the cat gotten it?

"Meow."

"Not now, cat."

"Meow."

Matt sighed. "Okay, I'll feed you. And I guess I ought to come up with a better name than Cat, huh?" He scooped her up and headed toward the kitchen. "What about Midnight? Salem? Pagan?"

"Actually, it's Sheba. A bit more regal, you know."

Luckily Matt was passing the sofa when the cat opened her mouth. That way they both had something soft to land on.

"You speak?"

The kitten—Sheba—nodded. "Of course. Don't all cats?"

There was a question.

"So why haven't you talked before?" Matt asked, amazed that *that* was his question because, with Eden gone, magic no longer seemed possible.

The kitten shrugged. "I didn't have anything interesting to say."

And of course that made sense, too. "So you do now?"

She licked her front paw. "Yes."

"Well? What is it?"

Delicately, she put her paw on his leg. "There's something you might want to see. Out by the big tree in the back. Francis has been busy."

Which, in his world, made sense.

Matt followed the kitten out to the backyard.

Oh, yes, Francis had definitely been busy.

"Take a look," Sheba said, stopping in front of a hole Francis's muddy hooves had obviously dug.

Gold twinkled up at him amid the dirt.

Eden's original bracelets.

Matt looked at the kitten who'd chosen *now* to speak and who was, once again, cleaning the dirt from her paws. Then he looked at the bracelets. Then back at the window to his office.

Coincidence? Or something else?

Matt was so hoping it was something else.

He grabbed the bracelets and ran back to the house, tromping his own muddy footprints through the kitchen and living room and right back into his office.

He set the original bracelets next to the newer ones. Laid the corresponding crystals beside them. Placed the stopper next to the bottle.

He had no idea what he was doing, or if it'd even work, since he'd never conjured her—or any other genie—before. All he knew was that he had to try.

He took a deep breath. "I love you, Eden. Please come to me."

Twenty seconds later he exhaled.

No Eden.

He tried again. "I wish for Eden to appear."

Thirty seconds this time, but still, no Eden.

Matt looked at the treasure in front of him. Two crystal obelisks, four bracelets of mangled gold, two dozen perfectly faceted jewels, her bottle and its stopper—each item bewitched by Faruq to bind Eden to his bidding.

So how strong were these bonds? She'd said whoever owned the bottle owned her, and he owned her bottle— and every other item that defined her as a genie—yet she wasn't in her bottle.

Was there some way to *put* her inside it? Some magical saying or formula or item—

Or *items*.

Could it be possible?

He fingered the diamond obelisk. It was slim, the tip pointed.

He picked up her bottle.

What he was thinking was ludicrous, but it didn't

stop him from sliding the tip of the obelisk into the bottle opening.

The diamond obelisk *melted*, slipping through the neck until it disappeared inside.

Her original bracelets started to vibrate on his desk top.

Matt lifted one and the vibration sped up.

When he held it over the bottle opening, it, too, melted into the neck.

All of the items did: the serendibite obelisk, the other bracelets, and every single jewel. All but the stopper. That sealed the bottle closed.

Matt sat back. So now what? It wasn't just a sad co-incidence, was it?

Gnawing on the inside of his cheek, Matt fingered the stopper. Could it really work?

He'd never know until he tried.

Matt took a deep breath, wished with all his heart, and removed the stopper.

Nothing.

Shit. It *had* been too much to hope for.

He replaced the stopper and studied her bottle. What if he had seen it in Mr. Murphy's shop? He'd run by it every day. Would he have picked it up if he'd seen it? Realized its significance? Opened it?

Matt shook his head. No, he wouldn't have. He hadn't. He'd never been a big believer in magic.

Eden had changed that.

He set the bottle down. It was pointless to wonder anyway, because she would have been magically sealed inside in the shop. It wasn't as if he could have just said the magic words and she would have come flying out—

Matt stared at the bottle.

No.

It couldn't be that easy.

Could it?

Well, why not? It had worked on the cave and look what treasure that had held.

Eden was worth more to him than any piece in that cave.

Matt picked up her bottle again, hope rising once more. Stronger this time.

He took a deep breath, grasped the stopper, and pulled.

"Open Sesame."

Chapter 49

YELLOW MIST FLOWED FROM THE BOTTLE IN THE MOST beautiful plume of smoke Matt had ever seen.

And Eden materialized on the desk in front of him—the most beautiful sight he'd ever seen.

"Matt! You did it!"

He sure did—not that he got the chance to answer because she flung her arms around his neck and landed in his lap, and kissing her was the most natural thing in the world.

God, she felt so good. He could hardly believe she was here, in his home, in his arms.

Then she ran her fingers through his hair, tilted his head back, and swept her tongue inside his mouth, and Matt started believing really quickly.

His hands found her waist—the bastard had dressed her in yet another harem costume. Never again, Matt vowed. He'd keep her covered in sweat pants and parkas for the rest of her life before he'd subject her to this.

"Oh, Matt, I'm so happy you figured it out." She smiled against his ear. Then kissed it. Swirled her tongue around it.

Figured it out? More like wished her into being.

Then his fingers brushed the clasp at the back of her shirt, and Matt figured *that* out pretty quickly.

When her breasts were bared before him, Matt quit

figuring anything out. All he wanted—needed—was Eden. He'd deal with the *what*s and *why*s after.

"I need you," he whispered against her throat. Then again, on her collarbone. And yet again as he trailed his lips lower.

"And I need you," she half-groaned when he found her nipple. "Make love to me, Matt."

Inhaling the gardenia scent that would forever remind him of her, Matt stroked down her body again and drew her pebbled nipple into his mouth, swirling his tongue around it when she gasped.

Then he cupped her other breast and tweaked that nipple, and Eden squirmed against him. His cock jerked beneath his jeans, reminding him that his office chair wasn't the most romantic, nor optimal, place to make love to the woman he loved.

He slid his hands under her butt and stood, making his way around the desk, out the door, through the living room, and down the hall to his bedroom in record time and without breaking either the kiss or his legs.

Eden squealed when he all but dropped her onto the bed, his finesse sorely tested by his desire to be with her.

"Sorry," he muttered, trying to undo his shirt and his pants at the same time. That didn't work so well.

Fuck it. Matt ripped his shirt off in two seconds flat, then half-yanked his jeans off, all the while enjoying the show as Eden tried to wriggle out of the harem pants.

"Allow me." Matt slid his hands beneath the waistband and ripped. He should take this slow, savor every inch of her, every moment together, every breath, but he couldn't. All he could do was slide her back toward the middle of the bed, spread her legs, and slip inside.

Heaven. Paradise. Nirvana. *Eden*. She was so aptly named.

"I love you," he whispered against her throat.

"I love you back." She threaded her fingers through his hair.

"I know."

She tugged his head up. "You do? You heard me?"

"I heard you say the words, but *this*, Eden…" He sank into her a little more. "This says so much more than three little words."

"I know. And we have the rest of our lives to experience it." Her smile lit up the room and Matt waited for the butterflies.

He didn't have long to wait. Not for a lot of things: the blinding rush of their joining, the soft breeze of hundreds of butterfly wings, and the magic of a flying comforter—though, luckily, she kept them contained in his bedroom, rising and falling above the bed as shudders wracked their bodies while love flowed between them.

The comforter floated gently back onto the bed afterward, wrapping itself around them.

Matt played with her hair, running his fingers through the strands, then brushing the tips across his lips. God, how he loved her.

"Magical," he breathed against her temple, half afraid he was dreaming.

When a butterfly landed on his ear, he knew it wasn't.

Eden stiffened beside him.

"What's wrong?" Matt struggled to sit up, looking toward the door, expecting Faruq.

No one.

"Eden? Honey?" She had tears in her eyes. "What is it? Did I hurt you? Do you have to leave? What?" God couldn't be so cruel to give them this moment only to take her away.

Maybe God wouldn't, but Faruq sure as hell would.

Eden shook her head. "I don't know what it means, Matt, but none of this should be happening. Not the butterflies or the comforter. I'm not supposed to be able to do magic."

Relieved—sort of—Matt leaned on one elbow and laid his other arm across her waist. "You've lost me, Eden. You did magic before."

"I know, but that was before."

"Before?"

She blinked, but one tear escaped. "Before I told you I love you."

"Still lost here, sweetheart."

She picked up his hand and threaded her fingers through his, bringing their joined hands to her heart. "My father was a Roman soldier. A mortal."

He saw the parallel but still didn't understand the significance. "And?"

"My mother lost her powers and her immortality when she told him she loved him. It's part of The Code—a deterrent so we don't go around falling in love with mortals."

"So you lost your powers when you said you loved me?"

She nodded.

"But you didn't."

Her eyes flicked his way, then she went back to staring at their joined hands. "I did. But now they're back."

"Eden, what are you saying?"

Her fingers tapped his. "I don't know, Matt. I lost my powers that day when I said I loved you. I know I did. They were gone. Trust me, I tried every Way I could think of—Faruq made me try every Way *he* could think of, but nothing happened. Yet now, you've brought me here, back into my bottle, and I'm able to do magic again. And I don't know why." She bit her lip. "What if— What if I only *thought* I loved you?"

What if it's not real was what she meant. Matt smiled and tucked a strand of hair behind her ear. "Did you know what would happen when you told me you loved me in front of Faruq?"

She nodded.

"And what did Faruq do when you did? After I left?"

She smiled then, and it was wicked. "He cursed. Me, the High Master, every genie who'd come before him, and you, too, of course. Even Obo."

"So he knew what it meant for you to say that."

"Yes. It's why I said it when I did. Why I couldn't say it before. His vow on the Stone of Jabir was that he wouldn't interfere with your life once you returned home. Beforehand, however, you were fair game. I had to wait until you got away."

"So you told me you loved me, knowing it would remove your powers? Knowing you would be left to Faruq's mercy without any defenses?"

She nodded and Matt wanted to throttle her. She should never have put herself in such danger for him.

And she thought she might only *think* she loved him?

He had a thing or two to tell her. "So, could you have said you loved me without meaning it?"

Her gaze flew to his. "Well, of course I *could* have

said it even if I didn't mean it. Millions of people do it every day. But—"

"But what?" He knew it was there, just behind her words.

And then Eden smiled. "But my powers wouldn't have disappeared unless I meant it."

"And that's what had Faruq so pissed."

She nodded, her lip caught between her teeth.

"And did you do any magic when you were a pris— when you were with him for the past eight days?"

She sighed. "No. I told you, I couldn't."

"But how did you manage to fend off Faruq?" Matt's blood ran cold. He'd known the bastard would, but to hear it from her—God, if he could somehow have spared her that. "Eden, it doesn't matter what you had to do to survive. Whatever he made you do—"

She put a finger on his lips, her smile belying that awful image. "That's just it, Matt. He didn't make me do anything, because, although I couldn't use magic, I had something else on my side."

"I don't understand."

She leaned onto her elbow and kissed him. "His servants. Faruq isn't the most beloved of masters, and too many knew I was there. Remember the swordsmen? They got word to the High Master, and Faruq was summoned immediately. I actually haven't seen him since about two hours after you left. Most of which, he was trying to see if he could retrieve my magic. I don't know how or why you could summon me through my bottle, but I'm more than happy to be your genie."

Matt liked the sound of that, but not *quite* the way she meant it. He wanted her to be his, but not because of the bottle or code or any genie magic.

Well, maybe just a *little* genie magic. "Eden, remember when you offered me a wish and I turned it down?"

Her eyes narrowed. "Yes?"

"I want to use that wish now."

She went very still, her face solemn. Scared maybe. Disappointed even. "You... do?"

Hell. He couldn't do this to her. He smiled and kissed her softly. "Eden, I wish for you to be free. No more genie service for you. Live your life the way you want, beholden to no one."

"Oh, Matt!" she breathed and flung her arms around him. "But I want to be beholden—to you. And have you beholden to me. I love you, Matt. I do."

Matt smiled. "I know."

And he did.

Epilogue

HIGH ABOVE THE EARTH ON CLOUD THIRTEEN, THE High Master waved a hand over the crystal ball on the table beside his chair, watching the swirling blue sand cloud the last scene.

He'd miss Eden, he truly would. If not for that Roman soldier, she would have been his daughter, and Calliope *his* wife.

He'd mourned Calliope every day since she'd married her soldier, pleased she'd found true happiness but knowing there'd never be anyone else for him.

And then there'd been Eden. The daughter of his heart who should have been his in truth.

She was so like her mother it made him smile. Had for over two thousand years, though it was only in the last two hundred or so that he'd come up with the idea of shifting into baby dragons. He'd enjoyed the time he spent with her that way, but she couldn't exist for his pleasure. It wasn't fair to her or the love he'd held for Calliope. It's why he'd given Eden back her powers after she'd sacrificed them for Matt.

A love like theirs should always be touched by magic.

He smiled again, thinking how his change of her Way had made it easier for her to outwit Faruq. He'd enjoyed her successes against the vizier and had had great fun bringing her and Matt together in the kitchen. But when he'd seen how Matt had responded to Eden's natural

charms—after she'd freed him from magical influence—
he'd regretted interfering with the natural order. The
mortal loved her with no help from him.

That regret kept him from bestowing immortality
upon her. Losing Matt and their children would crush
Eden, and he couldn't face her sorrow.

Bad enough he'd had to condemn her for her master's
accidental death. The Code was antiquated; he'd seen it
then. But change took time—or so he'd thought.

The *Hadhayosh's* riddle was right; time swallowed
those who watched it pass, and it was time to make
those changes.

Right, Positivity, Oneness, and Happiness—his
catchphrases and how he wanted to rule his subjects. It
was time he applied that phrase to everyone.

And he'd already started. Obo's "Home Jeeves" had
returned Matt to his world and Obo to his: the Afterlife.

As a man, Obo, or rather, Titus, had been a thief, a
blackmailer, and an adulterer. As a cat, he wasn't much
better. But by helping Matt escape, Obo had moved up
in the ranks of Reincarnation and was, therefore, granted
the memory of his human life. A few more good lives like
that last one, and he'd move on to his Eternal Reward.

Checking the sundial and finding he had some time
before his meeting with Bastet, the High Master nudged
his Segway aside and sat back in the reclining massage
chair he'd imported the minute the microfiber version
had become available. Less sticky than leather—and in
the desert that meant something. He tugged his bunched
shudra out from behind him, then picked up the moving
photograph beside him, thanking J. K. Rowling for that
bit of inspiration.

He watched Eden as she'd been when she'd first arrived in Al-Jannah. Scared and alone, she'd had her mother's spirit. He'd seen it in her that first day, had known she would need someone special in her life.

It'd taken over two thousand years for that mortal to be born. Another thirty-four for Matt to become worthy of her and gain the experience needed to accept the implausible and outwit the *Hadhayosh*, but the High Master couldn't deny the child of his heart the man who would complete her—even if he was mortal.

He picked up Eden's original chipped bottle stopper from the mirrored tray next to the picture and his gold gypsy bracelets, remembering when he'd set the original plan in motion. Of course he'd known about the diamond bracelet connection; it was how and why Khaled had been permitted to discover it. Why he'd been brought to the same trial as Eden. Why he'd been placed next to her. And why he'd—

Ah, well. That was a story best left for later.

The High Master fingered the red brass lantern beside Mayat's—not Cleopatra's—amulet. Faruq had thought he could get away with betraying him. The vizier should have known better: nothing happened without the High Master's knowledge.

He shook his head as Faruq peered out from inside the lantern. The ex-vizier would have plenty of time to rue the folly of overstepping his bounds and threatening Eden.

Pushing a button on the console beside the chair started the massage wheels working the tight muscles in his shoulders. So many balls he had in the air, juggling them so they'd fall at just the right time. No wonder his predecessors had eventually gone into the Light. The responsibility was heavy, the work never-ending.

He picked up the crystal ball again and gazed a few years into the future, seeing the adorable boys Eden and Matt would create, and the soft swell of her stomach that he knew housed a daughter she'd name Callie. The High Master allowed himself a moment to close his eyes and savored all that he had wrought.

And then he heard Eden call one of her sons. "Adam, come here!"

Adham. No one ever called him that, not since he'd become High Master.

She would name her son after him.

Eden, like her butterflies, deserved to be free. He would always love her from afar, but it was Matt whom she would love intimately.

But naming a child after him?

That meant he would always live in her heart.

THE END

النـهـايـه

Author's Note

Djinn are religious figures in Islam, and while I tried to incorporate that history and culture into my world-building, this story is based more on U.S. pop culture references. No disrespect or insult to anyone's beliefs is intended.

I lived in Spain in college and was captivated by the beauty of the Moorish architecture, the history, and the longevity of sites such as the Alhambra, the Generalife, and the Mosque in Cordoba. Sevilla, too, is a beautiful city and I hope I've done them justice in this story.

The *Mandragora* plant has become familiar thanks to J. K. Rowling, but the fruit of the plant is really known as "djinn's eggs," so I *had* to incorporate the plants into the story. I did, however, fudge with their bloom time.

I also took celestial literary license with the appearance of the blue moon. The traditional idea of a blue moon—the second of two full moons in a month—puts blue moons on December 31, 2009 (the day this book was due to my editor) and August 31, 2012; neither worked for the story. But, according to the *Farmers' Almanac* definition, that a blue moon is the third full moon in a season of four full moons, November 21, 2010, fit better with the story and only needed to be moved ahead by three weeks.

Not only do I get to invent new characters, new worlds, and alter plant growth for my stories, but I also get to manipulate the moon.

This is the *best* job!

Acknowledgments

Keeping the pop culture genie perception separate from the religious and cultural mythology was a tricky wiggle for me, and I have to give a huge shout out of thanks to my Egyptian friend, Tarek Amer, for all of his help with the Arabic, the mythology, the customs, and the references, and for his time. Any mistakes are all mine.

Sincerest heartfelt thanks go to Beth Hill. Beth, there are no words (despite the 98,000 or so in the story, all of which you looked at in such great detail!). I am honored and grateful—and can't wait to return the favor!

The Martin siblings, Jim and Carolyn, and Kate Welsh for your divine assistance; my cousin, Kristen Tomasic, for always hopping online; Viv, #1 Fennell Fanatic; Sia McKye, again, for your wonderful promotion and other help; to Pat Shaw for that first read.

To Mr. Hank Miller and Ms. Jean Baker, who challenged me in their English classes, gave me an appreciation for Shakespeare, and let me believe that publication could be more than just a dream. Thanks, Mr. Miller, for coming to my book signing!

To my readers who embraced the Mers—I hope you enjoy the (flying carpet) ride here!

No acknowledgment would be complete without heartfelt thanks to my editor, Deb Werksman, for her enthusiasm, support, and incredible eye for storytelling.

Also, to my agent, Jennifer Schober, whose enthusiasm for my work keeps me going when the story doesn't want to.

And to Sue Grimshaw for so generously helping out an unknown.

May all of your wishes come true.

About the Author

Judi Fennell has had her nose in a book and her head in some celestial realm all her life, including those early years when her mom would exhort her to "get outside!" instead of watching *Bewitched* or *I Dream of Jeannie* on television. So she did—right into Dad's hammock with her Nancy Drew books.

Now she is a PRISM Award-winning author, a three-time finalist in online contests, and author of the Mer series: *In Over Her Head*, *Wild Blue Under*, and *Catch of a Lifetime*. Judi enjoys hearing from her readers—check out her website at www.JudiFennell.com for excerpts, deleted scenes, reviews, contests, and pictures from reader and writer conferences, as well as the chance to discover a whole new world!

Hex Appeal

BY LINDA WISDOM

"Kudos to Linda Wisdom for a series that's pure magic!"

—Vicki Lewis Thompson,
New York Times bestselling author of *Wild & Hexy*

JAZZ AND NICK'S DREAM ROMANCE HAS TURNED INTO A NIGHTMARE...

FEISTY witch JASMINE TREMAINE AND DROP-DEAD gorgeous vampire cop Nikolai Gregorivich have a hot thing going, but it's tough to keep it together when nightmare visions turn their passion into bickering.

With a little help from their friends, Nick and Jazz are in a race against time to uncover whoever it is that's poisoning their dreams, and their relationship...

978-1-4022-1400-4 • $6.99 U.S. / $7.99 CAN

Wicked by Any Other Name

BY LINDA WISDOM

STASI ROMANOV USES A LITTLE WITCH MAGIC IN HER lingerie shop, running a brisk side business in love charms. A disgruntled customer threatening to sue over a failed spell brings wizard attorney Trevor Barnes to town—and witches and wizards make a volatile combination. The sparks fly, almost everyone's getting singed, and the whole town seems on the verge of a witch hunt.

Can the feisty witch and the gorgeous wizard overcome their objections and settle out of court—and in the bedroom?

978-1-4022-1773-9 • $6.99 U.S. / $7.99 CAN

Hex in High Heels

BY LINDA WISDOM

Can a Witch and a Were find happiness?

Feisty witch Blair Fitzpatrick has had a crush on hunky carpenter Jake Harrison forever—he's one hot shape-shifter. But Jake's nasty mother and brother are after him to return to his pack, and Blair is trying hard not to unleash the ultimate revenge spell. When Jake's enemies try to force him away from her, Blair is pushed over the edge. No one messes with her boyfriend-to-be, even if he does shed on the furniture!

Praise for Linda Wisdom's Hex series:

"Fan-fave Wisdom... continues to delight."
—*Romantic Times*

"Highly entertaining, sexy, and imaginative."
—*Star Crossed Romance*

"It's a five star, feel-good ride!" —*Crave More Romance*

"Something fresh and new."
—*Paranormal Romance Review*

978-1-4022-1819-4 •$6.99 U.S. / $8.99 CAN

50 Ways to Hex Your Lover

BY LINDA WISDOM

"A magical page-turner...had me bewitched from the start!"

—Yasmine Galenorn,
USA Today bestselling author of *Witchling*

JAZZ CAN'T DECIDE WHETHER TO SCORCH HIM WITH A FIREBALL OR JUMP INTO BED WITH HIM

Jasmine Tremaine is a witch who can't stay out of trouble. Nikolai Gregorivich is a vampire cop on the trail of a serial killer. Their sizzling love affair has been on-again, off-again for about 300 years—mostly off, lately.

But now Nick needs Jazz's help to steer clear of a maniacal killer with supernatural powers, while they try to finally figure out their own hearts.

978-1-4022-1085-3 • $6.99 U.S. / $8.99 CAN